ALSO BY MARIE RUTKOSKI

The Cabinet of Wonders
The Celestial Globe

THE
JEWEL OF THE
KALDERASH

MARIE RUTKOSKI

The Jewel of the Kalderash

THE KRONOS CHRONICLES: BOOK III

FARRAR STRAUS GIROUX
NEW YORK

Copyright © 2011 by Marie Rutkoski
Distributed in Canada by D&M Publishers, Inc.
Printed in September 2011 in the United States of America
by RR Donnelley & Sons Company, Harrisonburg, Virginia
Designed by Jay Colvin
First edition, 2011
1   3   5   7   9   10   8   6   4   2

mackids.com

Library of Congress Cataloging-in-Publication Data
Rutkoski, Marie.
    The Jewel of the Kalderash / Marie Rutkoski. — 1st ed.
        p.   cm. — (The Kronos Chronicles ; bk. 3)
    ISBN: 978-0-374-33678-3
    [1. Magic—Fiction.   2. Kings, queens, rulers, etc.—Fiction.
3. Romanies—Fiction.   4. Fantasy.]   I. Title.

PZ7.R935Jew 2011
[Fic]—dc22

                                                    2010037716

This book is dedicated to Meredith Kaffel,
Janine O'Malley, and Charlotte Sheedy

Contents

THE
JEWEL OF THE
KALDERASH

1

Clouds

PETRA WAS LYING on the deck of the *Pacolet*, her face tilted up toward the sky. She was at the very end of the bow, where the ship's front narrowed into a triangle. The warm wind was strong and the waves were high. Pillowy clouds drifted overhead.

She watched them change shape. One cloud resembled the face of her older cousin, Dita, the closest thing to a mother Petra had ever had. Then the face stretched into an elm tree, like the one next to Petra's house in a far-off Bohemian village.

But her house had burned to the ground, and for all Petra knew, the tree had, too.

A sudden shadow loomed over her.

"Don't know if you realized, but this ship's got sailors," said Neel, standing at her side. His black hair was a snarled mess from many months at sea, and his bare feet were dry and frosted with salt. "You lie there long enough, you're gonna get stepped on."

Petra shrugged.

The sun was setting, and some of the clouds had dark gray bellies. One crawled. It reached out a bony, clawed hand.

Neel squinted at the sky, and didn't notice Petra's shudder. "Seeing things in the clouds, are you?" he said cheerfully. "Like to do that myself, sometimes. What do you see, Pet?"

"I see—" Petra swallowed. "I see someone who won't leave me alone."

Neel didn't move. He just stared harder at the sky. If Petra had been his sister, he would have nudged her ribs with his toe and called her a few inventive names.

But Petra wasn't his sister. She wasn't even one of his people. She was Bohemian, he was Roma. Her skin was a mix of gold and rose, his the color of strong tea. Petra and Neel were bound by friendship and shared dangers, but maybe, in the end, they were too different, and their bond might be the sort easily cracked by sharp words.

So Neel held his tongue, which was rare. But his shoulders hunched slightly and his stance, which had been relaxed and easy, went tight.

Still not looking at her, he walked away.

TOMIK CLIMBED DOWN the Jacob's ladder, having ended his shift working the sails. Neel was waiting for him at the bottom of the mast.

Tomik listened as Neel described his encounter with Petra. "It ain't like her," the Roma finished.

"Have you known Petra long enough to really be able to tell what she's like?"

"Then explain, know-it-all."

The wind rustled Tomik's fair hair, which he pushed out of his tanned face. Slowly he said, "She's been through a lot."

Neel spun his hand in the air, indicating that this was old news and Tomik should say something worthwhile. But Tomik watched the East African coast slip past. Finally, he observed, "We've been on this ship for a while."

"Yeah. It's been about six months now since we set sail from England. So?"

"So that makes this . . . what? November?"

"I guess."

"Oh," Tomik said wisely. "I see."

Neel threw up his hands and began to walk away.

Tomik grabbed his arm. "But which day is it, exactly?" He asked as if the answer was the most important thing in the world. "Which day?"

THAT NIGHT, in the sleeping quarters below deck, Petra tossed and turned in her hammock, thinking about the monstrous cloud. In London, she'd had screaming nightmares about the Gray Men. Eventually, they had stopped, but then she discovered that her father had been transformed into one of those deadly, scaled beasts. Now the nightmares were back.

There was a small, scratching sound as Astrophil poked his tin legs out of a knot in the wooden wall by Petra's head. The mechanical spider jumped to her shoulder.

I can't sleep, she thought to him, grateful that her magic allowed this kind of silent communication, unnoticed by the dozens of sailors sleeping in their swinging hammocks.

Hmm. Astrophil tapped one leg against the side of his face. *Whenever I had insomnia, I would study. Shall we study? Perhaps we could practice the Romany language.*

No.

Your accent is atrocious. And the errors you make are out of pure carelessness. Ah! I know what to do. Astrophil's green eyes glowed in the darkness. *We can conjugate verbs!*

NO.

Astrophil sagged in disappointment. Then he brightened. *I could tell you a story.*

Petra nodded. *One with a happy ending.*

Astrophil thought and thought, searching for the perfect tale for Petra. Then he glanced at her, and realized that in the minutes of silence she had fallen asleep.

As the ship gently rocked, Astrophil watched her breathe, noticing how her face had changed in little ways over the past several months. Petra was growing older. He almost wished she wouldn't.

The spider curled into a tiny ball. He supposed he should be considering what they would do when they reached the Vatra, the Romany homeland, where they hoped to find a cure for Petra's father. But all Astrophil could think about now was an event much closer on the horizon. He knew perfectly well what day tomorrow was. He wondered if he would have to remind Tomik.

Tomik found Treb in the captain's quarters the next morning. The Roma was smoking a pipe and bracing his salt-rimmed boots against a fine chair scavenged from a shipwreck.

The captain listened to Tomik's suggestion, sending puffs of foul smoke into the air. Then he stood and slung an affectionate but commanding arm over the boy's shoulders. "Tom, my ship is full of fine, fit sailors: the Maraki, best of the four Roma tribes. We're battle-tested, storm-ready, and on our way to present our queen with the most legendary prize in Roma history, the Mercator Globes. This is no party boat."

"It's thanks to Petra that you have those globes, and without them this voyage would have taken twice as long. The crew is grateful to her."

"Yeah. So what?"

"We'll celebrate her birthday whether you like it or not."

"That sounds like mutiny to me." The captain scowled and bit the stem of his pipe. "Fine," he said through his teeth. "Have your fun."

• • •

ASTROPHIL FOUND PETRA in the armory. Night had almost fallen. The light from the porthole was dim, and the room was illuminated by an oil lamp. Petra was playing with a dagger, flipping it in the air and catching it on its way down. A normal person (if, indeed, normal people play such games) would have been trying to catch the dagger by its hilt. Petra, however, pinched the flat of the blade between her fingers. Astrophil was not worried for the safety of her hands—he knew Petra's talents—but he did not like to see her so withdrawn, so sad. It might surprise you that someone who had had her life turned upside down in almost every imaginable way could be upset by the thought that everyone had forgotten her fourteenth birthday, but Astrophil knew better.

"Shall we go on deck?" he suggested.

She didn't look at him. She tossed the knife again. "The wind's too strong." Petra had forbidden Astrophil to go topside when the wind was high, afraid that he'd be blown into the water. He had replied that she had no right to order him around, and would not like it if he tried to do the same with her. She had then thrown a tantrum the likes of which he had not seen since she was eight years old.

"You have no idea what the wind is like." Astrophil sniffed. "You have been down here all day. It is already twilight, and I have it on good authority that the wind is kinder than you are to your poor spider."

Petra caught the knife and turned to him, an apology on her lips.

Astrophil hid a smile with one shiny leg.

When Petra climbed through the hatch that opened onto the deck, she nearly fell off the ladder. There was so much shouting. She blinked. Only her head and shoulders were poking out of the hatch, but that was enough to give her a good view. It took her a moment to realize that the entire crew was thronged on deck and cheering (really, truly) for her. She saw that someone had made colored lanterns and strung them between the two masts.

Her heart swelled, both glad and sore. She tried to forget the people who weren't here, and drank in the sight of those who were.

Treb stepped forward, grabbed her hands, and pulled her out of the hatch and onto the deck. For all his previous grumbling about the party, the captain had a theatrical flair and enjoyed being the master of ceremonies. In a booming voice, he announced, "I present Petra Kronos on the day of her Coming of Age: fourteen years old, and an adult in our eyes."

The gifts were simple, but Petra treasured them: a bar of soap, a dried apple saved from dinner, a pair of slightly used sandals. Most of the Maraki gave her promises. Nicolas, the best swordsman on the ship and Petra's trainer since they had left London, offered to introduce her to fencing masters in the Vatra.

"I'll steal you something nice once we get there," Neel added.

Tomik's voice was hesitant. "I made the lanterns."

She looked up again at the lanterns and saw that they were made of glass. "They're beautiful." She smiled. "And you gave me this party, didn't you? You and Astrophil."

Both Tomik and the spider were thinking how lovely Petra's smile was, and how much they had missed it, when someone thrust a violin at Neel. It was Nadia, one of the young Maraki. "Play," she commanded.

He shook his head. "I'm no good."

"You're good enough."

"That fiddle's waterlogged."

"You will be, too, if I toss you in the sea."

Neel gave her a disdainful look.

"Come on, Indraneel of the Lovari." She said his full name like a challenge. "Are you a true member of your tribe, or aren't you?"

Neel snatched the violin. He was the captain's cousin but, unlike the rest of the Roma on board, he had been raised by the Lovari, the tribe known for acrobatics, acting, and music. Neel tuned up and began to play. It was a sprightly but rough music, that of a player who could have been a master, but wasn't and never would be, because he couldn't care less about it.

The deck thumped with the feet of dancing sailors.

"Would you like to dance?" Tomik asked Petra.

Her smile slipped. She thought of Kit, the last boy she had danced with, someone who had betrayed her.

Tomik saw her reluctance. "Would you like to sit with me instead, and watch?"

"Yes." Petra looked at the rainbow lanterns and thought that happiness was something that must be protected, like the glass shielded the flames. "I would."

They settled onto a pile of coiled rope. Petra tucked her arm into the crook of his, and felt warm even when the sky darkened and the wind picked up.

The breeze strengthened like a muscle, and pushed them farther into the Arabian Sea—closer to India, and the Romany kingdom.

2

Danior of the Kalderash

———◆———

IONA, QUEEN OF THE ROMA, adjusted a silk scarf around her swollen neck. The entire Vatran court knew she was dying, of course, but that didn't mean they needed to be reminded of it.

"Let me help," murmured a lady-in-waiting. She tied the scarf into a clever knot, hiding the ugly lump on the queen's throat, and said, "Arun is waiting in the hall."

Iona nodded, indicating that her adviser could enter. She didn't like to speak unless she had to do so.

Arun, who knew that the queen's silent ways didn't mean that she was a patient person, was brief. "The *Pacolet* will arrive soon with the Mercator Globes. The crew was spotted in Ethiopia, restocking their supplies."

The queen cleared her throat. Her voice was a hideous whisper: "There is someone on board I need to see."

"Of course. The *Pacolet*'s captain will be brought to you directly."

Iona shook her head. When she spoke again, it felt as if a crab was lodged in her throat, attacking her with vicious claws. "No. He is not the one I mean."

PETRA JIGGLED the fishing line. There were so many impossible things she wanted to do—find a cure for her father, be with her family again—that it didn't seem fair that she couldn't even catch a measly fish. *Come on*, she ordered the iron hook sunk deep in the sunny water. *Catch a fish. Catch a fish.*

But she was not her father, who could tap a nail into a plank of wood just by thinking about it. Petra had a gift for metal, but it was weak. If she wanted to influence the hook magically, she'd have to be able to touch it.

"Bet you didn't bait it right," said Neel.

"Did you try using some of those dead little squids?" asked Tomik. "Or even meat. That works for catching yellowtail."

"Nah. That's for nabbing sharks."

Petra yanked on the line. It went taut. "I've got something!"

"You didn't use meat, did you, Pet?" Neel widened his eyes. "'Cause I don't want a shark."

"Don't be a baby," said Tomik.

"Baby? Just 'cause I don't fancy dragging up a gnashing, thrashing, biting—"

"Um, *help*?" said Petra.

Neel and Tomik rushed to her side, and the three of them hauled on the line. It was with relief and a little disappointment that they discovered that Petra had not caught a shark. It was a heavy net, dripping with seaweed and crusted with barnacles. A few shrimp wriggled from it and fell to the deck.

"Look." Petra reached into the net, pulled forth a corked bottle, and shook it. Something rattled. "What do you think is inside?"

Neel snatched the bottle from her and tossed it overboard.

"What'd you do that for?" she protested.

"We're in the Arabian Sea," he said. "Look to the east and you'll find India. But Persia's in the west, and folk there are always trapping nasty spirits in bottles and tossing them into the waves. You already managed to summon an air spirit back in England, and that was a mite too scary. You want to unleash a bottled-up fire spirit, too? Fine. But not around me."

Tomik rolled his eyes. "Don't tell me you believe those silly Persian fairy tales."

"Tales have got to have some truth, else why would people tell 'em?"

"What about the Vatra?" asked Petra. "Are there Romany stories about that?"

"Of course," said Neel with such a satisfied smile that Petra suspected he had only tossed the bottle in the sea to make her ask that very question. "Long ago, there were only three Roma tribes: the Lovari, Maraki, and Ursari. The Lovari danced and sang. The Maraki built swift ships and roved the waves. The Ursari had an uncanny way with animals: horses and hares, camels and cats, dogs and—"

"Elephants?" This was starting to sound familiar to Petra.

"Them, too," said Neel. "And there happened to be an Ursari named Danior, who was as keen-eyed and handsome as a hawk. He—"

"I know this story," Petra interrupted. On the first day she had met him, Neel had told her about Danior, who had the same magical talent as he.

"Well, don't you know everything," said Neel. "Guess I'd better not breathe another word."

But the story was new to Tomik, who pressed Neel to continue.

Petra listened as Danior was cast out by the Ursari and left to die in the desert. A cruel desert king sliced off every one of Danior's fingers and, even as the blood dried, Danior discovered that his dead fingers had become magic ghosts. They were longer, stronger, and quicker than any human fingers could be. Danior rode his loyal elephant into the king's city with vengeance on his mind.

Neel said, "Danior hatched a plan, and had something to do before he could take revenge on the king. He strode into a merchant's shop and offered to swap his one valuable possession, a jewel that shone like a star on his right ear."

"You never told me that," said Petra. "About the jewel."

"What's the fun in telling the same tale twice? Every story's got to change, or it dies." Neel frowned. "Interruptions aren't great for its health, either."

Petra stayed silent as Neel resumed his story. "Danior wanted a large wagon like a house on wheels. The merchant asked to inspect the jewel, so Danior suggested that the merchant's pretty daughter take it out of his ear. 'I can't rightly do it myself,' he said with a grin. The girl passed the earring to her da, who agreed to Danior's trade as soon as he clapped eyes on the jewel.

"That night, Danior used his ghost fingers to pick every lock in the wicked king's palace. He stole ten of the king's children and led them to the wagon he had hitched to his elephant. But Danior had a surprise waiting for him. For who was in the wagon but the merchant's daughter, with the jewel in her hand? A touch of Danior's ear and she was mad for him, and swore to go where he would go.

"With his new wife and children, Danior founded the fourth Roma tribe, the Kalderash. You might guess that a kidnapper wouldn't be kind or wise, but Danior was a good father, husband, and leader. He had the idea of binding all the Roma tribes together by creating a homeland. With the help of the other tribe leaders, he built the Vatra and became its first king."

"In London, you told us that the Romany queen is a Kalderash," said Tomik. "Why do the other tribes let the Kalderash rule all the time?"

"They don't," said Treb, who had appeared behind them. He picked up one of the shrimp squirming on the deck and popped it into his mouth, tail and all. "We rotate."

"The leader of each tribe gets to rule for four years," explained Neel. "Queen Iona's got about two years left."

"Unless she dies first," Treb said, chewing. "Which is likely, from what I've heard."

"Her husband's dead and she's got no kids," said Neel. "She refuses to name an heir, so if she croaks now there'll be no Kalderash to take over, and the next tribe will get two years plus the usual four."

"Which tribe is next in line?" asked Tomik.

"The Maraki," said Treb.

There was a glint in the captain's eye that made Petra gasp. "Not *you?*"

"King Treb!" Neel snickered. "Oh, I can't breathe, that's too funny."

"I'd make a fine king," Treb growled.

"Treb's older brother will take over," said Neel, still giggling.

"It's no laughing matter. The Maraki have been waiting years for this, and we've got plans."

"It's a shame, though." Neel caught Treb's furious glance. "Not that the Maraki will rule, but that no one knows who'll speak for the Kalderash after Queen Iona keels over."

"True," said Treb. "She *is* a direct descendant of Danior, and the line's been unbroken for hundreds of years."

"And you"—Neel wagged his finger at Tomik—"who's so sure there are no facts in fairy tales, just wait until you meet the queen."

"Which won't happen," said Treb. "Not one of you is important enough to rate an audience with the queen. I, on the other hand—"

Neel ignored his cousin. "I've never met the grand lady myself, but word has it that she wears Danior's earring. The very same one of the legend. They call it the Jewel of the Kalderash."

"How close are we to the Vatra?" Petra suddenly asked, staring straight off the ship's prow.

The others turned, and saw the green, scribbled outline of an island.

"Why, very close," said Treb. "Very close, indeed."

3

The Queen's Command

T**HE SETTING SUN** looked like a juicy orange, dripping color onto
the mountainous island as the *Pacolet* sailed toward the Vatra.
The shelves of limestone just beneath the waves created a natural
defense around the island that caused unfriendly ships to crash and
sink miles off the Vatra's shores. The *Pacolet's* captain, however, knew
the secret dance to reach the island safely. The ship swerved left,
bore right, and swooped around the cove.

"What if there is no place in the Vatra for me?" Astrophil murmured to Petra.

"What do you mean?" She gently lifted the spider from her ear
so that she could face him as he stood on her raised palm. "You will
always belong wherever I am."

"Yes, but . . . what will be my role? When Prince Rodolfo stole
your father's eyes and you decided to retrieve them, my purpose was
to keep you as safe as possible. When we were trapped in John Dee's
London house, I helped you analyze an air spirit's cryptic prophecies.
How can I aid you here? I cannot even do research for Master Kronos's cure." He added woefully, "The Roma do not like books. They
will have no libraries."

"They use writing for special occasions," Petra pointed out. Dangling from a leather cord around her neck was a miniature iron

horseshoe that Neel had had engraved in Romany. "Some of them can read and write, and maybe they do have books. They just don't trust the written word. The Roma believe that it makes things seem permanent, when they're not."

"I know," said the spider, but still looked glum.

"Astro, I'll always want your advice, whether there are books or not."

"Really? Even though you are now an adult? Perhaps you do not need me anymore."

Sternly, she said, "That is the only absolutely brainless thing you've ever said."

"Ah. Well. Very good." He relaxed on her palm, leaning his shiny back legs against her curled fingers.

They heard the rattle and splash of the ship's anchors being dropped and knew it was time to disembark with the crew, who began boarding small boats strapped to the *Pacolet's* sides. Petra and Astrophil climbed into a launch with Tomik, Neel, Treb, and the globes, and watched the island grow larger as they rowed to shore. Through the twilight, Petra saw a palace etched into the island's mountain. The cliffs were encrusted with man-made walls and terraces.

"Queen Iona is going to praise me to the pearly skies," Treb said gleefully, patting the two chests that each contained a globe.

"*Us*," said Neel. "Us to the skies."

The launch's hull scraped against the shore, and the passengers leaped into the shallow water. Dark, warm waves lapped against Petra's calves as she helped push and then drag the launch onto the beach.

"Of course, Neel. *Us*." Treb beckoned for another sailor to help him lift the trunks out of the bottom of the boat. They were heavy, for the globes were not made of merely wood and paper. Each globe had a large glass sphere hidden at its center. "Our gift's going to let the Roma wander the world wide with a speed like we've never known, now that the globes can show us how to get through Loopholes," he said, referring to hidden gaps in space that allowed someone to travel instantaneously between two places, even if they were thousands of miles apart. "The globes will go to the queen, but whatever she decides to do with them won't be worth more than a fish bone since the Maraki will soon inherit the throne, and then the game changes."

Petra glanced at Tomik. He didn't care about Roma politics or the globes, she could tell. His smile was like a lit candle behind a screen that showed his thoughts clearly: he was thrilled to be here, for his own sake as well as Petra's. In the Vatra he might be able to study his magical ability to manipulate glass, an opportunity he would never have in Bohemia. Their country boasted an excellent university for the practice of magical arts, but only students from high society were admitted to the Academy.

The crew plodded up the beach, some carrying the two chests, others holding Tomik's colored lanterns high so that they could see their way to the foot of the cliffs. Cut into the rock were winding stairs that would lead them through the stone city and up to the palace.

After what felt like an eternity of steep steps, sweat oozed down Petra's back and her feet ached. She was grateful when the rough stone stairs became smooth marble trimmed with coral tiles. She heard the sailors behind her lowering the two chests to the ground, and looked up to see the pillars of the Romany palace.

Someone was waiting for them: a man who stood like a thirsty flower, his body slender and his shoulders slightly stooped. He was framed by the palace entryway, which had no doors. Torches blazed inside the hall, transforming the entrance into a rectangle of red-gold light.

"I am Arun," the man said. "Queen Iona's chief adviser. You must be the *Pacolet's* sailors." His gaze flicked over them, pausing at Neel and then resting uncertainly on Petra and Tomik. "The Vatra has heard that two *gadje* sail with you. Bohemian, are they not? Prisoners, passengers, or crew?"

"Well, Tom's a bit of the first and last," said Treb. "For a while, we planned on selling him in Morocco, but then he became too valuable to part with. As for Petra . . ." He studied her. "She's a passenger," he concluded, but Petra had seen his features soften for a second, and suspected that he didn't want to hurt her by telling the truth: she was a refugee.

Arun pointed to Astrophil, who clung to Petra's shoulder. "And what, precisely, is that?"

"I am a spider," Astrophil gravely replied.

Arun lifted one brow. "If you say so." He turned again to Treb. "You are the *Pacolet*'s captain, I assume?"

"Well spotted," said Treb. "Guess you couldn't miss my air of authority. I'm a natural leader, like my brother. You know him, I'm sure: Tarn of the Maraki, heir to the Roma crown."

An emotion flashed across Arun's face, too quick for Petra to identify. "Tarn happens to be here in the Vatra, and"—Arun spoke over Treb's noise of delighted surprise—"we are also well aware of the gifts you bring for your people."

"That's right," Treb said proudly. "I suppose the queen would like to feast her eyes on the Mercator Globes."

"All in good time. She has more important matters to attend to first. There is someone among you she needs to see right away. A youth. Perhaps you've left him on the ship, or down by the shore, but I think he's here with you now."

"Him? What? Who?" Treb spluttered. "What could be more important than the Mercator Globes?"

"Indraneel of the Lovari," Arun said.

4

Before the Blue Wall

———◆———

"ME?" NEEL WAS AGHAST. "What'd I do?"

"The queen will explain," said Arun. "If you'll just follow me—"

"Yeah, follow you like a lamb to the slaughter. And that's what I am, got it? An innocent, sweet little lamb who's done nothing wrong. *Baa*."

"You have nothing to fear, Indraneel."

"Neel. And like I said: *baa*."

"If you don't trust me, perhaps you'll trust your mother, who is waiting for you inside the palace. Damara was summoned—"

"You summoned my *ma*?" Neel shrilled the last word, then whipped around to face Tomik and Petra. He seized them. "I'm in trouble."

"You can't be sure of that," Tomik said.

"Trouble," Neel insisted. "Ghastly, boil-you-in-oil trouble. You two are coming with me. Astro, too."

"Of course we will," said Petra. "But—"

"Good." Neel sucked in his breath and marched toward the entrance, dragging Petra and Tomik after him, ignoring their protests that they could walk on their own, that they wouldn't abandon him, and would he please let go? Arun and Treb followed on their heels,

Arun arguing that it wasn't Treb's place to intrude uninvited on a queen's audience. Treb fired back that he was going to intrude on Arun's face if the man didn't get out of his way.

Inside, the palace echoed with the sound of trickling water. Petra saw that while some of the walls were glossy marble dotted with mosaics of wriggling octopi, at least one side of every hallway showed the untouched surface of the mountain on which the palace was built.

Neel blindly turned a corner, and the others followed him down a wide chamber. On their left, a natural fountain poured from a jagged rock wall. Water spilled down and rushed across their path in a stream that cut through the floor. Neel forged ahead, pulling Petra and Tomik after him into the water.

"Stop!" Arun moaned from where he and Treb stood at the stream's edge. "That's drinking water, and you're absolutely filthy! Besides, there's a bridge, if you'd only let me show you . . ."

Petra tugged her arm free of Neel's grasp, and Astrophil squeaked as her foot slipped against the stream's tiled bottom, plunging her and the spider beneath the water's surface. But the river was shallow, and when Petra scrambled to her feet, the water only came up to her waist.

Neel had finally stopped his mad dash through the stream. He looked at Petra and Astrophil. "Are you all right?"

Fury mounted in Petra's bones and spread through her blood. This evening wasn't supposed to be about Neel. Meeting the Roma queen was supposed to have nothing to do with him. Petra had imagined what would happen when they reached the Vatra. This is what she had seen in her mind, so many times: that the queen would be grateful for the globes, and to Petra for her role in obtaining them. As a reward, Queen Iona would offer any resources her country had to help find a cure for Petra's father.

Neel wasn't part of this picture, and he certainly had no business tearing around the palace in a panic over nothing. He wasn't the one with problems. *She* was. "No, I'm not all right!" She shoved wet locks of hair out of her face so she could glare at Neel better. "And you're behaving like an idiot!"

"Really?" Neel grew calm, thoughtful. "I'm an idiot?"

"Yes!" cried Petra, Tomik, and the spider.

"But it's strange." Neel's voice dropped. "The queen wanting to see me. Maybe I stole something of hers without realizing it, or . . . I don't know . . . this is a surprise, and an odd one, odd as a two-headed dog, and that kind of beast bites twice as fierce."

"Surprises are not always bad," Astrophil said hopefully, but in Petra's experience they often were.

She looked at Neel's dripping face and remembered when he had helped her steal her father's eyes from Prince Rodolfo's Cabinet of Wonders almost a year and a half ago. A sudden flood had swept Petra, Astrophil, and Neel through the prince's castle, and they were as wet then as they were now. Neel hadn't been afraid that time—or, if he had been, he had hidden it well. But here in the Vatra, anxiety lurked in his yellowy eyes. Petra realized that fear doesn't strike everyone in the same way. With a sense of shame, it also occurred to her that her anger had a selfish edge, a belief that her worries were more important than his.

Tomik sighed. "Can we please walk through the palace like normal human beings and not members of an underwater circus?"

"Indeed," said Astrophil, shaking water from his legs one by one.

They turned and waded back to Arun and Treb.

Every step Arun took seemed louder than necessary as he led them over the bridge. His feet stamped against the planks. "No respect"—*stamp*—"the glory of our homeland"—*stamp*—"a pair of outsiders"—*stamp*—"dirty children"—*stampstampSTAMP.*

"We're not children," Tomik objected. "We're all of age," he added, though none of them knew if his statement truly applied to Neel, whose exact birthday was a mystery. He had been abandoned by a Lovari campsite as an infant.

Arun stepped onto the stone floor on the other side of the river and swept ahead to a broad staircase that led into a deep-bellied cave. A torch-lit tunnel glowed at the back of the cave, one so narrow that all of them had to enter singly, and the space inside was so tight that smoke from the torches stung Petra's eyes. She heard Neel shuffle behind her and glanced back to see whether his fear had returned. He moved ahead silently, his face grim.

Tomik, walking behind Neel, looked past him to catch Petra's look of concern. Tomik reached forward to lay a steady hand on Neel's shoulder, and the other boy seemed to breathe more easily.

Why is Neel acting like a trapped animal? Petra asked Astrophil after she had turned to continue down the tunnel.

We know very little of the Roma queen, the spider replied. *She may be . . . cruel.*

Petra thought of Bohemia's prince: a twenty-year-old with a brilliant smile and an ambition as cold as winter. What would happen if she were brought before her country's ruler? Death, or maybe something worse. *I am not going to kill you,* he had told her when they last stood face-to-face. *I am going to keep you.*

Petra wrapped her fingers around the hilt of her invisible rapier. She knew what it was like to be at the mercy of a ruler's whim. But would she defend Neel, if it meant shattering her hopes that the Vatra could offer a cure for her father? Would she and Tomik share Neel's fate, whatever fate it was that waited for him in the queen's reception hall?

Before she could begin to answer these questions, the tunnel opened into a vast chamber. Arcades of windows were cut into the walls, and the night breeze poured in, guttering the torches. Petra could see that each of the room's four walls was painted a different color.

"Every wall represents a Roma tribe," Treb explained. "Green for the Maraki, red for the Ursari, yellow for the Lovari, and blue—"

"For the Kalderash," Neel muttered as they walked slowly, now side by side, toward the three people seated in front of the blue wall.

Petra had never seen someone who had only weeks, maybe days, to live. But even the quickest glance was enough to tell that Queen Iona was fighting death tooth and nail. The enthroned woman's hair was thin and lank, her nose a sharp beak in a sunken face. Iona had four things that glittered: she gripped a golden scepter in her bony hand, a sapphire earring shone on her right ear, and her eyes, too, were as bright as jewels.

"Ma!" Neel shouted, and rushed toward the woman seated to the queen's left. For a moment, it seemed like Damara would pull him onto her lap as if he were still a small boy, but then she stood and simply rested a hand on his shoulder.

Treb stepped forward to greet the man to the queen's right. Though shorter than the captain, the man resembled Treb so much that Petra knew this was Tarn, whose face was not as merry as his younger brother's.

"Something really *is* wrong," Tomik whispered.

"Yes," Arun said shortly, and left them to stand by his queen.

Astrophil urged Petra to approach the throne. *There is something unusual about Queen Iona's eyes*, he said.

Petra had seen many Roma, and they all had eyes whose color was somewhere between brown and black—except for Neel. His irises were yellow flecked with green, like autumn leaves with only a few drops of summer left.

Queen Iona looked at Petra with those very same eyes. The scepter dropped from the queen's weak hand, and an unseen force caught it before it could clatter against the floor. The queen had not moved, yet there was the scepter, secure again in her grasp.

She has the gift of Danior's Fingers, said Astrophil.

Petra's brain felt like a machine. Pieces clicked into place and her thoughts were spinning, whirring, driving toward a realization. She gazed at the jewel on Queen Iona's ear and remembered Neel's older sister telling her, in the dark dormitory of Salamander Castle, that Neel's full name meant "sapphire." Sadie's voice drifted through Petra's memory, explaining how her brother had been adopted as a baby:

Nobody wanted to take him at first, especially because he had no token around his neck.

Token? Petra had asked.

A string. Or a bit of leather with a ring or a stone on it. Anything, really, that means that a father has acknowledged a child as his. Neel was just wrapped up in a blue blanket, with no clothes or anything else.

The color blue had trailed after Neel all his life, and now it was staring him in the face. The blue wall framed the queen whose magical gift matched his. Although Neel had told Petra on the very first day they met that Danior's Fingers was a talent found in every tribe, no Roma doubted that it was first and foremost a Kalderash trait.

Could Petra's suspicion be true? She glanced at Neel and saw anxiety flare again across his taut features.

"Ma, what's going on?" he asked Damara. "Why're you here?"

Before she had a chance to reply, the queen opened her thin mouth. "She's here because she is not your mother," she rasped. "I am."

5

The Heir

———◆———

WRONG!" SAID NEEL. "You're dead wrong!"

"I wish I were," said Iona. "It does seem unfitting that a dirty guttersnipe should be the Kalderash heir, but"—she studied him from top to toe, then continued in a croaking, amused voice— "at least someone tried to give you a bath."

Damara's eyes flashed. "Don't insult my son."

"I am dying," said Iona, "and I am your queen. I will do whatever I like. Moreover, old friend, we both know full well that Indraneel is not your son."

Petra recognized the emotion blazing across Neel's face, because it was one that she had felt before, when she learned that her father had been transformed into a monster. It was the feeling that the known world is crumbling apart.

Damara gathered Neel into her arms, sighing. The resigned sound of that one low breath said everything. It was true.

"Neel," she began, "this is no more than what you've always known: that I didn't give birth to you."

"It is more!" He twisted out of her embrace. "It's a whole lot more. It's years of mocking. 'Neel, left by the fire, the trash baby no one wanted—'"

"I wanted you."

"Insults and jibes like little, salty cuts. 'Neel, the by-blow, the blackguard foundling, bastard boy—'"

"'That is correct," said the queen. "You are entirely illegitimate. Your father was no husband of mine. He died, thrown by a wild horse. You were a mistake, and had to be hidden."

Tarn spoke for the first time. "This is a trick."

"Kalderash sneakery," Treb added. "A plot to steal the throne from the Maraki. When you die, dear queen, it's rightfully ours."

"Yes, I do wish to keep the throne for the Kalderash," Iona acknowledged in her ruined voice. "But I am not lying. Damara will testify that this boy is my child, and few will doubt it." She lifted her left palm, and Neel strained against unseen fingers that reached across the room to grasp his chin and turn his face from side to side, so that everyone in the room could observe the uncanny resemblance between him and the queen.

"Stop that!" Neel's hand twitched, and Petra imagined what she could not see: his ghostly fingers swatting away the queen's.

"Even his magical talent is proof," said Iona. "He has the Gift of Danior's Fingers, and of course he would. However illegitimate he may be, he is still a direct descendant of Danior."

Petra recalled the anger that had ripped through her when she had stood in the palace river. She felt it again, this time for a different reason. "Why are you doing this to him?" she challenged the queen.

"Why, I thought it was clear, little *gadje*. There is no one else left to be the Kalderash heir, no one else whose veins flow with Danior's blood. My tribe has plans that need to be carried out over the rest of our reign. No doubt the news about my son will be shocking to some, but I am too tired to care, and too sick to feel any shame. It is my right to name an heir, and I name him."

Tarn stepped forward, and Petra could see that he and Treb shared the same oil-black eyes and a physical strength that could be brutal.

Tarn looked at Neel with resentment. "If you knew what was good for you, cousin, you'd deny any claim to the throne."

"I do." Neel's voice was low. "I do deny it."

But Tarn had already left the room. Treb was not far behind him, and shook his head at Neel on the way out. "There's something about you, lad, that attracts trouble. It follows you like a bad storm."

"Neel," Damara said quietly. "I'm sorry that you discovered the truth like this, but don't let a golden opportunity slip by denying it. You are the rightful Kalderash heir."

"You've known all my life about this?" said Neel.

"Yes."

"How come you kept it a secret? Didn't I deserve the truth?"

"You deserved not to be broken by disappointment. Iona and I have been friends since we were little girls. Fifteen years ago, she came to me, pregnant and unmarried. She was the Kalderash heir to the throne then, and feared what would happen if her secret became known. She begged me to adopt her child. I agreed."

"Don't sugar the story," said Iona. "You said yes because I threatened to abandon the baby to the wolves."

Damara shot a warning look at her. "Iona planned to marry another man," she continued, "and to have legitimate children by him. One of them would inherit the throne after her."

"They were never born." The queen shrugged. "And my husband is dead, so that leaves you, Indraneel."

"What point was there in telling you until now?" Damara brushed the damp hair off Neel's face. "You would have grown up feeling cheated of a destiny that could have been yours. But now it will be. You'll become king of the Roma."

"Well, I don't want to! Who'd want to be that bony hag's son? Not me. And I guess I'm not your son, either. Never was." Neel turned away from her and fled down the narrow tunnel.

Petra and Tomik ran after him, with Astrophil helping track

Neel as he burst from the tunnel and zipped down palace passage-ways.

He wasn't easy to follow, and soon Tomik said, "We should let him go. He's hunting for a place to be alone."

They stopped, hearts beating, breath quick, then slower, then calm.

They stood on a balcony that stretched into the night air, the stars above shining sharp and brilliant. There was no moon, so they couldn't see the waves below, but they could hear them rushing against the rocks. Petra stepped to the balcony's edge and felt like she was floating in darkness.

Tomik joined her at the railing, leaning his back against it. Settling onto his propped elbows, he said, "A king. Neel's going to be a king. Where does that leave us?"

"I believe that leaves us approximately three thousand, four hundred miles from Prague, Bohemia," replied Astrophil. "It leaves us, as Neel would say, in something of a fix."

They smelled Treb's burning tobacco before they heard him speak. "Yes, you're in a fix, but I haven't forgotten about you."

They whirled to face him.

"Your honorable pal Captain Treb has arranged for you to meet the Metis tomorrow," he said.

"The Metis?" said Petra.

"They're the Vatra's experts on magic, and if anyone can help you find a cure for your father, it's them. They're a bit dangerous, though. Snappy. Quick to take offense. Powerful, too. So don't get them angry, or they'll turn you into worms for baiting hooks."

6

The Metis

"Petra, wake up!" Astrophil cried.

She bolted upright in bed. "What's wrong?" She ripped away a frothy mosquito net. "Where are you?"

"Here!" he called from a corner of the white stone room. "Help me!"

Petra swung her bare feet to the floor and was about to race to save Astrophil. Then she saw the cause of his distress and laughed.

A furry brown spider had cornered Astrophil and was trying to touch him with one curious, hairy leg.

"Who's that?" asked Petra. "Your sweetheart?"

"Ha. Ha. Ha." Astrophil folded his front four legs. "Very amusing. Now get rid of it."

Petra reached for one of her sandals.

"Don't kill it!" he cried. "Just . . . make it go away."

Petra crossed the room, nudged the brown spider aside, and scooped up Astrophil. "It'll go away on its own."

As Astrophil crept up her arm to her shoulder, Petra looked around the sun-bright, simple room. It contained one luxury: a sunken bath filled by a mountain spring. Petra dipped in a dirty foot. The water was a chilly but refreshing contrast to the tropical heat of the morning. She pulled off her shift and slipped into the small pool, leaving Astrophil on its edge. He kept a wary eye on the brown spider.

Aside from standing fully clothed on the deck of the *Pacolet* during the occasional rain shower, Petra hadn't been clean in ages. She discovered a bar of coconut-scented soap in a nook carved into the stone wall, and as she scrubbed away, her body seemed like it belonged to someone else. It had been so long since she had seen her skin uncovered by salt-encrusted clothes, and her dark brown hair felt like knotted yarn. Once, she would have hacked it off with her dagger, but now she discovered that there was something calming in trying to untangle it. Doing this helped her think, as if working out the knots in her hair somehow made it easier to untangle her emotions.

Petra was anxious to meet the Metis, but what kind of help could they offer her father? She doubted his cure would be simple, and even if it was, returning to Bohemia and finding him wouldn't be. Would her friends go with her? Astrophil would, of course, but what about Tomik? Petra admired him—and envied him. He seemed to succeed at everything he tried, like becoming so skilled at sailing that Treb had once called him Tom of the Maraki. Tomik fit so easily into Roma life. Maybe he would want to stay in the Vatra and study magic.

As for Neel . . . Neel had his own problems.

She ducked her head under the water and rinsed the soap from her hair. When she surfaced, she turned to Astrophil. "Why do you think Neel was so nervous last night, even *before* he entered the palace and the queen spilled her secret? I know he thought he was in trouble, but he's been in trouble lots of times. Usually, he pretends like nothing's wrong."

Astrophil considered this. "Some people in this world have unusual origins. Like somebody abandoned at birth and raised with no knowledge of his true parents. Or a creature with sparkling legs and an equally sparkling wit who was built out of tin to look like a spider. Now, in these cases, one might imagine many things about one's own existence. A boy, tired of being mocked, might pretend that he is in fact a lost prince. I used to wish sometimes that I was a real spider, but"—he glanced at the brown spider in its corner and shuddered—"I have changed my mind. It is easy to dream dreams—even if, in our secret hearts, we do not really want them to come true, and we might be in danger if they did."

Danger. The word echoed in Petra's mind when she stepped outside the palace entrance to meet Tomik and Treb, as they had agreed last night. Like her, they were so clean they looked like strangers, and wore cotton clothes as bright as the orange dress someone had left folded at the foot of Petra's bed. The skirts swished against her ankles, thin and airy. Astrophil perched on her shoulder.

"Where's Neel?" she asked. "Is he coming with us to see the Metis?"

"He's missing," Treb said.

"Missing?" Petra turned to the captain. "'Missing' as in your older brother tossed him off a cliff because he's competition for the Roma crown?"

Tomik rolled his eyes. "'Missing' as in he's sulking somewhere." He caught Petra's reproachful glance. "What? Do you expect me to feel bad for him because he's going to become king?"

"I expect you to try to understand what it's like to have your life change so suddenly you can't recognize it anymore!"

"Quit your yammering," Treb told them, "or I'm not taking you anywhere. If Neel doesn't want to be found, he won't be."

Petra fell silent, and the friends remained quiet as they followed Treb down through the city.

Every house and shop in the Vatra seemed as if it had sprouted from the mountain. As they walked past a cliff, shuttered windows in the rock wall sprang open like clam shells, the people inside cranking out long, wooden rods clipped with laundry. Petra had become familiar with the way the Roma here liked to mix nature with the man-made, but she was still surprised when Treb led them to the mouth of a cave. She had been expecting . . . well, she wasn't sure what she had expected. Something like a schoolhouse, perhaps, or a temple.

"Go on in," he said. "The Metis are expecting you."

"Aren't you coming with us?" Petra asked.

"I've got a political crisis to attend to," said the captain. "Plus a grouchy brother and a missing cousin. My poor aunt Damara constantly looks like she might burst into tears. So I've got enough on my hands and, anyway, the Metis make my skin creep and crawl. See you back at the palace." With a flip of his hand, Treb turned around and walked back up the steep street.

Tomik looked at the cave. "Treb did say that the Metis are human, right? Not bears or mountain lions or dragons?"

"Hmm," said Astrophil, "I think he neglected to say exactly what they were. He only warned us not to anger them."

The three of them looked at each other. "Well, let's not waste any more time," said Petra. "We'll find out soon enough what they are." She reached into a pocket and pulled out a small oval crystal. Tomik did the same, and they stepped into the cave.

They squeezed their Glowstones, which flared with pale blue light. For a moment, all Petra heard was the sound of her heartbeat and their footsteps on the rocky floor. Then she seemed to hear a soft whispering, and saw a tricky sort of light, white and flickering.

They stood at the mouth of a tunnel. As they ventured down it, the light became clearer, and they soon saw four sunken pools. Floating in each one was a body.

"Are they dead?" Petra asked uncertainly. The submerged bodies were ancient—so old and shriveled that they were as small as children. Although they were naked, the vast number of wrinkles made it impossible to tell which bodies were male and which were female.

Petra stepped closer to the edge of a pool, and noticed the ball of white light in the body's open mouth. Suddenly, the eyes jolted open, the mouth coughed, and the light rocketed to the surface, bursting through the water to bob up and down in front of Petra's face.

"Dead? Of course we are not dead!" exclaimed the light, which stretched into a shape like steam from a kettle.

Three lights exploded from the other pools.

"The dead learn nothing," said one of the four. "And so they are not very wise."

"And we," said another, "are the Metis, and most knowledgeable indeed."

"Indeed!" chorused a third.

"Although," one said in a soft tone, "death must be a fascinating experience, else why would everyone do it?"

"Not everyone!"

"Not us!"

"Sister, why must you always doubt our choice?" a Meti said. "For a hundred years now, it's been nothing but 'death might be nice after all.'"

"One hundred and twelve years," corrected another.

"I am simply curious," said the soft voice. "It is our calling to be curious."

"Not about that!"

"Never that!"

"We are neither here nor there, you understand," a Meti said to Petra.

"Not quite dead, yet not quite alive," another agreed.

"You're ghosts," Petra stated. The cavern echoed with her words.

"Oh, I suppose."

One giggled. "If that's how you want to put it."

Tomik said, "We thought this cave was a school for magic. Are you the teachers?"

"Just as you are students," a Meti replied.

"People come, they inquire, we answer."

"We have many answers, do we not, brother?"

"Indeed. Almost a thousand years' worth."

"And what sort of students have we here?"

A shining vapor approached Tomik. "A handsome young man!"

"Like in a fairy tale!"

"With sighs and swoons!"

"But, you know, my dear boy," one said in a serious, wispy voice. "Beauty is a burden. Not every tale ends happily. We know the dark stories, and heroes like you sometimes suffer."

"We could help him, sister."

"He doesn't have to be so smooth and bright."

"Indeed! Shall we cut him, brother?"

"Or stretch him?"

"Burn him, I think. That will make him better."

"Stop that!" said Petra.

The four lights flew to her shoulder and clustered around Astrophil, who shrank into the hollow of her neck.

"A cunning machine!"

"Built with gears. Built to last. Built to live forever."

"Like us!"

"But how will the spider feel, my brother, when he outlives his mistress?"

"Petra," Astrophil said in a shaky voice, "may we leave, please?"

"And what kind of person is this mistress?" The Metis ignored Astrophil and flew close to Petra's face.

"Ah," said one knowingly, "she is the one with the questions."

"I've come to ask you about my father," Petra said.

"Well, where is he?"

It was difficult for Petra to bring herself to explain. "He was seized by the Bohemian prince."

"I see."

"He was taken from you."

"Or perhaps she lost him, brother," suggested a Meti. "It is careless to lose your family, and we don't teach careless girls."

"I didn't lose him," said Petra. "Either I would have gone to prison with him, or would have tried to find some way to free him. Except . . ." Her fingers lifted to touch the scar that ran from her jaw to the base of her neck. "I was attacked by the prince's monsters, creatures called the Gray Men. Someone rescued me by pulling me through a Loophole to London. He saved my life, but trapped me for months in England."

"And who was he?"

"His name is John Dee," Petra said. "He's a spy for the English queen."

"Well, why would he want to keep you? What are you, that you were special to him?"

"I think . . ." Petra searched for a response, and slowly spoke what she thought was the truth. "He was intrigued by my magical talents. He tried to teach me . . . maybe because he thought I'd be a useful tool for him. Or maybe because he genuinely wanted to protect me. I'm not sure."

For a moment, the Metis were silent. Then one whispered, "Did she say *talents*, brother?"

"She did! But almost no one in the world has more than one magical gift."

"If, indeed, they have *any* gift."

"Which must make her . . ."

"I'm a chimera," Petra said. Her gaze lowered to study her feet. "I have two gifts"—she shrugged—"but they're weak. I have mind-magic, and power over metal."

"A chimera!"

"How rare!"

"Would you like to join us someday?"

"What a nice addition she'd make!"

"Of course," said Petra. "Because I want to be a blobby ghost whose body is a dried-up prune."

"Is that sarcasm, brother?" One Meti turned to another.

"I do not know, sister. I do not remember sarcasm very well."

"We have used it before, two hundred and fifty-six years ago," reminded the third ghost.

"Very true!" said the fourth.

"But, now that I think of it, my sister, I recall that sarcasm is not very polite."

The four ghosts fell silent, and Petra uneasily remembered what Treb had said about the Metis changing people into worms. "I—uh—meant what I said," she stammered. "No sarcasm here. Who wouldn't want to be a Meti? Look how, um, pretty you are. You're so . . . see-through."

"Indeed," one said with satisfaction. "Remember that, young lady, when you think about our offer. Not everyone is worthy of becoming one of us."

"She has time to decide," said the hushed voice of the ghost who was curious about death. "And things to do beforehand."

"She wants to find her lost father," one guessed.

"Yes," said Petra, "but it's complicated. He's no longer human, exactly."

"Oh?"

Petra couldn't speak, so Astrophil explained. "He was transformed into one of the Gray Men."

"Tell us about these Gray Men." One of the lights bounced in front of the spider. "We do not know about them."

"They are also known as Gristleki," Astrophil said. "They are experiments. Prince Rodolfo collects many things, and he enjoys collecting people, too. There is a woman who works for him named Fiala Broshek, and she has a magical power over the flesh. She found a way to transform people into monsters by emptying them of human blood and giving them a transfusion of blood from a shadow dragon."

"How clever."

"It's not clever!" said Petra. "She changed ordinary people into clawed beasts that run on all fours and suck blood. That's *vile*."

"Ah," said a Meti, "yet it is clever, too."

"I don't care what it is," said Petra. "I just want to know how to change my father back. Please tell me how."

The four vapors floated close to one another and conferred in whispers. Then they separated.

"We do not know," one of them admitted.

"This woman's experiment is something new," said another.

"We are experts in what is old."

"Then what good are you?" Petra clenched her fists. "Why did I travel thousands of miles if you have no answers for me?"

"Perhaps," said the quietest Meti, "we could offer a suggestion."

"Oh, you and your suggestions!" laughed a ghost.

"Sister, suggestions are merely ideas. They are of questionable worth."

"What is it?" Petra stepped forward. "What is your suggestion?"

The Meti's voice fell to a whisper. "If you have questions about creation, it is always best to ask the creator."

"That's my answer?" Petra said incredulously.

"Yes."

"That makes no sense!" Then Petra's mouth slammed shut as she realized that, yes, it did. She turned toward Tomik. Her silver eyes glinted with the fire of a dangerous idea.

"I know exactly what we're going to do," Petra said. "We're returning to Bohemia, and we're going to kidnap Fiala Broshek."

7

The Waterfall

FOR DAYS, Tomik tried to reason with Petra, but she only grew more impatient that they weren't already on their way back to Bohemia to carry out her insane plan.

"Kidnapping one of the prince's inventors?" he said. "Really, Petra."

"Fiala Broshek isn't going to cure my father willingly," she said. "All she cares about is cutting people up, creating monsters, and pleasing the prince. So some force will have to be involved. And that's what I learned during those months in England: how to use force." She flexed her fingers on the hilt of her invisible sword.

"I thought you were learning how to control and improve your two magical gifts," said Astrophil, "and the ways of being sly. Not how to trample and storm your way into sure captivity."

"You sound like John Dee."

"You might want to take a page from his book," said Astrophil.

"What's that supposed to mean?"

"It means that you might want to try being like him, for Dee is far too clever to plunge headlong into danger without a well-considered plan."

"That's what I'm trying to do," she said. "Come up with a plan. But neither of you is helping."

"Only because you want to do the impossible," said Tomik. "The instant you set foot in Bohemia you become a prime target for the prince. He wants to keep you in his court like some kind of prize pet—*if* he doesn't change his mind and have your head chopped off in a public square. Plus, we are thousands of miles from Prague. How would we even get there?"

"We'll steal a ship."

He gaped at her. "And sail it *how*?"

"You could sail it."

Though secretly flattered at her confidence in him, Tomik said, "You know full well it takes *at least* half a dozen people to sail a ship big enough to brave the ocean. Are you ignoring facts because they get in the way of what you want?"

"Yes," said Astrophil.

Tomik exchanged a look with him. He suspected that the spider had already had many private arguments with Petra.

"You're not taking me seriously!" she accused. "Neither of you."

"I am, Petra," said Tomik. "That's the problem."

"I'll go to Prague," she said through gritted teeth, "if I have to walk there."

"How?" he said to her turned back. "On the waves? We're on an island!"

She stalked away, her shoulders high and stiff.

Soon it became clear to Tomik that they had another problem, and it involved Neel. He was nowhere to be seen, but Tomik knew Neel well enough to guess at his feelings. Neel wouldn't relish the thought of being kept like a high card up someone's sleeve—even if it was a queen's sleeve—and then slapped down on the table of Roma politics to beat all the other players. Neel was himself an incorrigible cheater at cards, but the last thing a trickster likes is to see his own tricks played on him.

When Tomik and Petra tired of arguing about whether to return to Prague, they would argue about hunting for Neel. Petra insisted on finding him.

"He wants to be alone," Tomik said. "We should respect that."

Petra fell silent for a moment, and Tomik entertained the astonishing thought that he had persuaded her—stubborn, fiery Petra—of something. Then, in a low voice, she said, "It's not always easy to understand what someone wants. What's important is for us to show Neel that we are there for him. We are his friends, whether he's the Romany king or just Neel. How will he know that, if we don't tell him?"

Tomik glanced at Astrophil. The spider slightly lifted two legs, like someone might raise his brows in surprise.

"Let's look for him on the beach," Tomik said.

But Neel was not on the beach, nor by the tide pools in the heart of the island's jungle, nor on the city streets that spiraled up the mountain.

They found him high on a palace wall, tossing small, puffy animals down the waterfall that poured from the cliff on which the palace stood. The creatures squealed as they fell.

"Neel!" Tomik shouted. "What are you doing?"

They ran to him, and Petra snatched a furry animal out of Neel's hands. "I know you're upset," she said, "but—"

"The scoots like it," said Neel, startled. The fuzzball squirmed out of Petra's hands, bounced onto the stone railing, and leaped off into thin air. "It's how they learn to fly."

Tomik and Petra saw the falling scoot puff out, then puff further, then puff into a balloon shape that caught the wind and sailed toward the trees.

"A scoot." Astrophil peered at one clambering up Neel's leg. "I have never heard of a scoot. And I have read many books on zoology."

"Yeah, but your *gadje* books say zero about the Vatra." One of the scoots clung to Neel's shoulder. "This fellow ain't keen to jump. Guess he's not ready yet." The scoot nuzzled his ear.

"Maybe he just likes you," said Petra. "Like we do, Neel."

He looked at her. "Oh." He smiled slowly. "Well, course you do."

Tomik knew that cocky attitude came when Neel was at his most vulnerable, so he kept his patience and said only, "Will you stop hiding from us now?"

"I'm not hiding from you. I'm hiding from everybody."

"We know that you need to make a decision—"

"To accept the queen's offer to be her heir," said Petra, "or turn it down. But she can't *make* you be king, can she?"

Neel frowned. "Nope. And believe me, Tarn and Treb would be a whole lot happier if I told the queen to stuff it. I'd be better off, too. Being king . . . it seems like an awful lot of work."

"Have you discussed it with your mother?" asked Astrophil.

"You mean Damara? My ma who ain't my ma? See, when I said I was hiding from everybody, I really meant I was hiding from *her*." The scoot on Neel's shoulder chittered and put a three-toed paw on the boy's head. Neel leaned his elbows on the stone railing and looked out over the jungle, which made the scoot nervously clutch him with all four stubby legs. "Shh, there, little fuzz." Neel backed away from the railing. "I get it. No jumping for you yet." He turned and looked again at his friends, then more closely at Petra. "You seem happier." His troubled face lit up. "You've got good news, don't you? A cure for your da! I knew you'd find the secret here in the Vatra."

"No." Astrophil sighed.

"Then . . ." Neel paused. "Oh. I know that look on your face, Pet. You've got a *plan*."

Tomik's heart tightened. He wished that Neel weren't so skilled at reading Petra's emotions. "Help me talk her out of it, Neel. It's too risky."

"Risky?" Neel's laugh had an edge. "What isn't? You can play life's game and think you're being oh so smart, and then it'll flip you on your head, and everything's upside down, and you didn't do anything, nothing at all." He looked at Petra. "Tell me. Tell me everything."

"Neel—" Tomik protested, but Petra was already eagerly spilling forth her plan.

"Impossible," Neel said when he'd heard everything.

"Thank you," said Tomik.

"Well, it's *possible*," Neel amended, "but it ain't gonna be easy. It'd take forever just to get back to Prague. The globes belong to the queen now, and traveling there without them . . . I'd say that's a year's worth of sailing and hoofing it, no less."

A silence fell, and Petra's eyes were suddenly too shiny. Her body went rigid, and Tomik could almost feel her holding her breath against the tears. "Petra—"

"If I were king," Neel said thoughtfully, "I'd have gobs of power. Oodles." He dropped his hunched shoulders and one hand twitched oddly in front of him, as if he were tapping his chin with his invisible fingers. Then he spread his arms wide. "I could do anything!" He gave Petra a smile. "I could help you."

Petra exhaled, and looked as if she didn't dare speak. Then one tear *did* fall, slipping down her cheek. She hugged Neel fiercely, scoot and all, and the Roma laughed as the scoot jumped from his head to hers.

"Excuse me." Astrophil bristled, pointing one leg at the creature. "This is *my* mistress, and only *I* have the honor of sitting on Petra's head, or ear, or shoulder, as the case may be."

Tomik looked at them, at the tangle of boy and girl and scoot and spider, and told himself that the hug Petra had given Neel was no different from the countless times she had embraced *him* over the years.

This only made him feel worse.

Neel lifted his chin from Petra's shoulder. "Good." He nodded hesitantly, as if to encourage himself. "Good," he said again, more firmly. "A king. Why not? I've always wanted to be the boss."

8

The Coronation

A BASTARD KING," the people muttered when Neel announced his decision to the court. "A king of rags and tatters."

"You're on your own," Treb told Neel before turning to walk out of the royal chamber with his brother.

Damara said nothing as she tried to catch her son's eye, but Neel avoided her, glancing at Petra and Tomik as if for help. Finally, he looked at the queen.

Iona's laugh was horrible, scraping: the sound of seashells breaking under someone's boot. Thankfully, it did not last long, and when it stopped, she threw everyone but Neel out of the room. She grabbed his ghostly fingers with her own and tugged him close.

"You cannot trust them," she said.

"I know," he muttered. "The Maraki're gonna get feisty over this."

"Of course. However, I did not mean *them*. The *gadje* boy and girl. They don't belong here. They will use you."

Neel arched one black brow. "Guess you're right," he said coolly. He nodded as the queen listed the Kalderash goals for the future, and smirked in agreement as she hissed the flaws of the Lovari, Maraki, and Ursari tribes. Anyone who knew Neel well knew he was a smooth liar. But the queen did not know her son well. So she talked until her eyes grew feverish and her voice hoarse, and when she eventually slumped in her throne with exhaustion, she was satisfied with her heir. "Hold it." She thrust the golden scepter at him, and for the first time since he'd made his choice clear, a crack showed in his proud façade. Ever so slightly, he shrank away. Then he took the scepter with his invisible fingers. He couldn't quite bring himself to let it touch his skin.

"It's a curse," Iona whispered. "Yet it is a gift, too."

"It's still yours." He gave it back to her.

"Not for long." She chuckled and waved him away.

The tension drained from Neel's body. He felt wobbly, as if the stress of the moment had been his skeleton, and now it was gone, leaving only soft, vulnerable flesh.

He left the royal chamber and found Damara waiting for him outside its doors.

The sight of her made his spine stiffen once more, and that was what gave him the strength to keep walking, to walk away, to walk down the hall without a word, without one backward glance at the woman who had raised him.

THE CHANGES WERE RAPID, and Neel hated them. The royal adviser, Arun, was to blame.

Arun had several guards ambush Neel, hold him down, and cut his hair.

He thrust a pile of richly dyed silks at Neel, saying he wasn't leaving his room until the boy looked the part of the heir to the throne. Neel's heart leaped with glee when he saw the clothes—he loved finery—but he hid his pleasure with a scowl that plainly said he wouldn't be told what to do.

Arun told him anyway. He appointed a thin, eager man named Karim to give Neel manners lessons and advise him on courtly procedure. Another adviser, Gita, was an elderly woman who would instruct him in international politics. Both advisers were Kalderash, like Arun, who lectured Neel for hours on end about the very different skills and needs of each tribe—as if Neel didn't know that the Roma were a fractured people. Even if they shared an "it's us against the world" attitude, they didn't always have a lot in common. This was obvious.

The worst, the very worst thing Arun did to Neel was insist that guards be stationed outside his door at all times, and follow him everywhere. They were a shell of armor around him, and no one Neel cared about could get inside. He had never felt so alone.

One night in December, almost a month after the *Pacolet* had reached the Vatran shore, Neel lay in his new, unnervingly large bed. He heard a dim ruckus outside his door, and raised voices. He sat up, and had almost snatched a dagger from under the sheets, when moonlight from an open window caught a silvery twinkle by the crack below the bedroom door.

It was Astrophil, glittering his way across the floor. Neel jumped from the bed and met the spider halfway, crouching to lift the tin creature up to eye level. "What's going on, Astro? Who's getting rowsy out there? Petra?"

Astrophil shook his head. "She is asleep. Tomik is outside your door. He wishes to see you, because—"

Neel had heard enough. He stalked to the door and flung it open to see Tomik bucking against the guards' grasp. "Let him in," Neel told the guards.

"Arun said no visitors," one of them replied.

"Well, *I* say let him in."

The guards did not let Tomik go.

"Who's in charge here?" Neel demanded.

"Queen Iona," the guards chorused.

"Yeah, and how long is she gonna last? She seems awful sickly to me."

Silence.

"When she snuffs it," Neel said, "*then* who's in charge?"

One of them muttered, "You."

"That's right. *Me.* And I've got my likes and dislikes, and right now I don't like *you.* I'm going to remember this, when I'm king. So if I were in your smelly shoes, I'd be working hard to get into the heir's good graces. That is, if I were smart. Are you smart?"

Silence.

"Now," said Neel, "who's in charge?"

"You," the guards said sullenly.

"Then let. My friend. *In.*"

They obeyed, but one of the guards couldn't resist giving Tomik a good shove over the threshold, and another slammed the door shut. Neel bit his lip.

He might have to pay for this.

"Thanks," said Tomik.

"What're you two doing creeping around at this time of night?"

"No one will let us near you," said Astrophil. "Petra has been trying to see you for more than a week—"

"How come you're here without her?" Neel peered at the spider on his palm. "It's weird. Seeing you right now, away from her . . . it's like seeing a part of her that's come loose."

Astrophil stood as tall as he could. "I am helping Tomik. He has an idea. He would like you to—"

"Talk Petra out of her loony plan. Well, Tom, I know how you feel, but it's not going to happen. Don't you see that her plan is all she's got, and that the guilt of doing nothing to help her da would be worse, to her, than anything she might face in Bohemia? She won't change her mind."

"Yes," Tomik said heavily, "I know. That's why I'm going with her."

"We will protect her," Astrophil squeaked.

"Oh. Well, I'm going, too, of course," said Neel. "This whole gimcracky king thing's just a way for us to get a boat, some fleet horses, and—"

Tomik shook his head. "Listen," he said, and explained his idea.

"Oooh," said Neel. "That'd make the Vatra crazy. They'd *hate* me."

Astrophil's tin legs sagged with disappointment. Tomik's face fell.

"I'll do it," said Neel.

QUEEN IONA DIED in her sleep several days later. Some people muttered that this was far too easy and peaceful an end for someone who had used her last breath of life to stir up as much trouble as she could. Others said she had suffered her painful disease long enough, and no one could guess what she might have suffered inside to live her life as she had. But few shed any tears for her. Certainly not Neel.

He was crowned with a fanfare that he found surprisingly boring. As he walked in a procession through the Vatran streets and finally returned to the palace to sit in his throne as courtiers played music and threw flower petals, it occurred to Neel that, not so long ago, he would have craved to be the center of attention.

Neel scanned the crowd. There were Petra and Tomik, on the fringes. Astrophil was a bright star in Petra's hair. Damara was there, too, farther back, her cheeks shining with tears.

Neel looked away.

Arun—*his* adviser now—opened the gold hoop in Neel's ear, and Neel felt a pang as he saw the small circle disappear into the man's pocket. It was just a trinket, he told himself, something he'd nicked long ago from a Moroccan market. It was nothing. Nothing compared to the Jewel of the Kalderash.

Arun slipped the sapphire earring through the pierced hole the hoop had left behind. He fastened it with a sharp pinch that made Neel wince.

Everyone cheered.

"Hey!" Neel stood. "Pipe down! I've got something to say."

The crowd quieted.

"This is . . . uh, an important day." Neel felt a snaky kind of nervousness. Had he really once liked to have everyone's eyes on him? He reached with his invisible fingers—Danior's Fingers—to touch the jewel that had belonged to Danior. His ancestor. The sapphire was cool beneath his ghostly fingertip. "And I want to do something to com—commemorate it. I want to give a gift."

Startled, the crowd began to whisper.

"Tomas Stakan," Neel called. "Come here."

Tomik pushed his way through the crowd, his tanned skin glaringly different from the darker tones of the Roma. Everyone stared.

When Tomik stood before him, Neel said, "I give you the Terrestrial and Celestial Globes."

The gasps of the crowd rang in Neel's ears.

"You're mad!"

That was Treb, storming right up to the throne, shoving guards out of his way. "Neel, why would you give them to *Tom*? Why would you do such a stupid, *gadje*-loving thing?"

"So that he can destroy them," said Neel.

9

Tomik's Idea

PETRA BURST THROUGH Tomik's bedroom door and caught him with the globes on a large worktable, and a small saw in his hand. "What is going on?" she demanded. "Did you know Neel would do that?" After Neel's announcement, the crowd had roiled with shocked anger, and Petra had watched, helplessly straining against the current of people, as Neel and Tomik left the throne room under heavy guard.

Tomik dropped the saw to the table and rubbed tiredly at his brow. "No. Yes. I mean, I asked him, and he said he'd give me the globes, but I didn't expect him to do it *then*, or like *that*." He shook his head. "He's such a show-off."

"It will make him very unpopular," said Astrophil.

"You asked him if you could destroy the globes, and . . . he agreed?" Petra's hand strayed across the red fabric of her sleeveless dress to touch her shoulder, where a fencing scar stood out like a brand. She had earned that scar fighting for a globe.

"I'm not going to *destroy* them." Tomik glanced at the handsaw. "Well, fine. Yes, I am. But I have an idea. I couldn't tell you before—in fact, I wish we weren't talking about this *now*—because I didn't—I *don't* want to get your hopes up. I wanted to wait until I was done, but . . ."

"Tomik."

"I want to replicate the globes."

Petra stared.

"Oh," Tomik said in a low voice. "You don't think I can do it."

"Do you know—" Petra's voice cracked. "Do you know what this looks like? It looks like you're trying to ruin the one thing that might help me get home."

"Petra, don't you trust me?"

Have some faith in me, Kit had told her, sometime soon after he had kissed her, and soon before he had stabbed her deep in the shoulder.

"I'm not sure I can," she whispered, and left.

She stood for some time outside Tomik's closed door. Then she heard it: the rhythmic, dry whine of a saw cutting through wood and paper.

She forced herself to walk away slowly, but as the sound grew fainter it cut more deeply at her heart, tearing at a hope she would never have dared admit, would never have let see the light of day, because she would never have asked Neel for his kingdom's greatest treasure.

Petra, Astrophil murmured in her mind. *Tomik would never betray you.*

She didn't know. She just didn't know, and there was so much she didn't know. An overwhelming awareness of her ignorance crashed over her in a great wave. Who was Petra Kronos, to think of slipping close to the Bohemian prince and kidnapping his most valued magician?

She had gifts—she knew this. She could fence like a sword was part of her body. And she had magic. A feel for metal. Glimpses, sometimes, of the future or someone else's thoughts.

Yet she was no master. None of her gifts was strong enough. None of them showed her whether Tomik was telling the truth. None of them promised she could save her father.

Her feet picked up pace, and Petra followed them out of the palace, down, down, down the city streets, and deep into the darkest dark she had ever seen.

In the depths of the cave, four lights sprang to life around her head.

"She has returned!" a Meti squealed.

"Why?" said another.

"Indeed, brother, why? I thought she did not like us."

"Please—" Petra said. She tried again. "Please—"

The Meti with the softest voice said, "Little woman, young braveling, why are you here?"

"Teach me," Petra said.

10

Gifts

NEEL WAS SLINKING DOWN a palace passageway, eager to escape the hordes of angry courtiers, when a hand reached out and touched his arm.

It was his mother.

No, he told himself, *it's Damara*. He instantly regretted he had succeeded in commanding his guards not to follow him everywhere. This wasn't a conversation he wanted to have. Not alone. He didn't want to stand in front of this woman and realize that somehow he had grown taller than her. He didn't want the emotions that realization unleashed inside him.

"Neel," she said. "You can't do this. You can't give away the globes."

"Can't I?" His voice was taunting. "I'm the king!"

Her black eyes narrowed. Neel recognized that look. It was the one she usually gave before smacking the back of his head for doing something dumb.

"Anyway," he said, "it's done. Tom's a quick one. I bet he's already sliced 'em open by now."

Damara briefly covered her face. "As it is, people don't want you to be king. After this . . . Neel, you can't afford to be seen as a boy being used by a pair of *gadje*."

"I am not a *boy.*"

"This is about how you are *seen.* You—"

"It was my choice to give Tom the globes. Mine. I deserve my choices. Especially after you tried to take them all away."

"I didn't—"

"You kept the greatest secret of my life from me," Neel said, yet he didn't voice the fear that simmered below his hurt, the fear that there was something else Damara wasn't telling him. He didn't ask, *If you kept that secret so long, why did you let it come out? Was it because you have something at stake? What do you want, Ma, now that I'm king? People will try to use me, sure as sure.*

Will you?

Damara looked as if the wind had been knocked out of her.

Quietly, Neel said, "I wish Sadie were here." He missed his older sister, who was sweet, and kind, and would so easily mend things between him and his mother.

"I do, too. But—"

"Don't say it. Don't say what everybody says, that it's good she's stuck in Prague. That spying on the Bohemian prince is the best thing she could do for her people. Don't."

"I was going to say something you'd like even less."

"Oh, yeah? Out with it, then."

"I'm sure you *did* want to give the globes away. I know you." She gave him a small smile. "It's not easy to make you do something against your will. But if you love Sadie, you have to stop thinking about what you want."

For a moment he couldn't speak. "*If* I?" he choked out. "*If* I love her?"

"Neel, we live in dangerous times. Thousands of our people are locked inside Prince Rodolfo's prison. The choices you make as king will affect Sadie, and every Roma. They need you. They need you to stop thinking only about yourself and what you want."

Neel stared. "You don't know me at all," he said coldly.

He walked away.

A WEEK WENT BY, then two. Neel avoided Tomik, because he couldn't bear the thought that he had made a terrible mistake in giving his friend the globes. Tomik was gifted, but would he really be able to do what he planned with the glass spheres inside the globes?

As for Petra . . . Neel didn't avoid her. But she was elusive. Sometimes he saw her shadow slip around a corner of the palace. Sometimes he'd meet her silver eyes across a distance and be surprised, as he always was, by their unusual color. He'd think that they looked like something precious, like moonlight, maybe, and by the time he'd finished that thought she'd glance away again. Then she was gone.

Petra unsettled him. He wasn't sure why. He supposed it was because everything unsettled him these days.

One day, he caught a glimpse of her dark brown braid as she crossed the wooden bridge over the river Neel had plunged into the very first time they'd entered the palace. Her figure dwindled as she headed toward the doors that would take her down to the city.

Neel bunched the hem of his blue silk jacket into a fist, then let it go. He stopped a servant and demanded they exchange shirts.

He had to wear something a lot less flashy if he was going to follow her.

WHEN NEEL SAW HER disappear into the Metis' cave, he ducked behind a natural pillar of rock that served to hitch several hardy beach ponies. Neel waited for hours as the horses whickered and nudged at him with their velvety noses.

Petra emerged from the cave as the sun was setting, her face distant and thoughtful. Astrophil bounced on her shoulder, trying to get her attention.

Well, Neel thought. *He* would get her attention.

His ghostly fingers unfurled and stretched, reaching their very limit. The tips of his flesh and blood fingers ached a little, feeling the tug of the ghosts. Just as the pain began to sear him, and it felt like the ghosts might rip away, Neel touched the tip of Petra's nose with one invisible finger.

She whirled around, and he chuckled. "Neel!" she cried.

"Who, me?" He stepped out from behind the pillar.

She smirked as he walked toward her. "Good thing you didn't try staying hidden. I would have found you."

"Nah. Don't think so."

"Truly." Astrophil pointed one leg at him. "She would have. Had she tried."

The smug looks on their faces made Neel realize that there would have been something special in the way Petra might have ferreted out his hiding place. He glanced back at the mouth of the Metis' cave. "Petali," he said slowly, "what have you been up to?"

Her smile grew wider.

Neel slipped his hand into hers—his real hand. He felt her skin with his skin and thought about how different that felt. He could touch things with the Gift of Danior's Fingers, of course, but this . . . felt different. "Come on," he said. "Let's talk."

THEY CLIMBED A TREE that grew out of a cliff and sat in its branches, looking at the wide green sea.

"You go there every day, all day, don't you, Pet?" Neel said.

She nodded. The wind pulled a dark lock of her hair from its braid and danced it on a breeze.

Neel caught it, then let it fly again. "Tell me your secret."

"It's not a secret. It's just . . . Fiala Broshek must have the answer to my father's cure. I need to talk with her. And I can't stand waiting."

"Petra, we have been over this before," said Astrophil. "Which is better? To leave right away with a boat and make our way slowly to Bohemia, or to give Tomik some time to work on the globes? If he succeeds, we can travel home almost instantly. Be reasonable."

"Maybe Tomik won't succeed," Petra said in a dark voice. "Maybe he doesn't really *want* to."

"That's silly." Neel was startled. "Why would he . . . ? Oh. To keep you here." He shook his head, trying to dislodge an instant doubt. "No. Tom wouldn't do that."

Petra was silent.

"Well, then *we'd* go," Neel said. "You and me."

"And *me*," Astrophil squeaked indignantly. "Do not forget *me*."

"Course. Astro, too. We'll sail the choppy seas. You want a ship, Pet? I'll give you one."

"You'd really come with me?"

"A swashbuckling adventurer like myself? You couldn't stop me. But . . . what's all this got to do with the Metis? Why're you lurking around them? They're kind of creepy."

Astrophil shuddered. He agreed.

"I used to be . . . afraid of what I am," Petra said. "A chimera. Someone with *two* magical gifts. I'm strange. An oddity. A . . ."

"An anomaly," Astrophil said helpfully. "An aberration."

"Yes." Petra rolled her eyes. "Thank you for the vocabulary lesson. Now I have several ways to describe my weirdness."

"It's not weird," Neel said. "It's nifty. Two gifts are better than one, right?"

She shrugged, her shoulder brushing against the bark of the tree. "Not if I don't make the most of them. Before I came to the Vatra, I'd practiced my first gift—I mean, the one I think of as my first gift. My magic over metal. I like that one, because it's my father's. It makes me feel close to him. But I hadn't done anything with my mind-magic, aside from when Dee gave me lessons in London. I didn't pay a lot of attention to those lessons, because I didn't *want* my second gift to get stronger. I don't want to see what my mother saw . . ."

"The future," said Neel.

"The future scares me. What if the people I love aren't in it?"

Astrophil looked solemn. Neel slowly nodded.

"But I can't help my father unless I'm the strongest person I can be," Petra said. "So I'm practicing my gifts. Both of them. And mind-magic isn't as bad as I thought. The Metis say mind-magic is like a cloud. You know how clouds take shape? When someone's born with mind-magic and it's strong, it takes shape. It becomes the ability to see the future, or read someone's thoughts, or sense hidden things. But me . . . the weakness of my gift means that it's a cloud with no form. So I can do a little bit of all kinds of mind-magic."

Neel's eyes widened. He instantly recognized the power of Petra's so-called weakness. "So you really *could* have sussed out my hiding place."

"Of course," said Astrophil.

"Is that why"—Neel touched Petra's nose again with one ghostly finger—"you can feel that? Because you can sense hidden things?"

"Yes."

Neel drew his hand away and wrapped it around a limb of the tree. The rough bark felt comforting under his suddenly nervous fingers. Why should he feel nervous? Because of what Petra had told him? Surely not because he had touched her. He had done the same exact thing only a half an hour ago and it had made him laugh.

That time, though, it had been a joke. This time it wasn't.

Neel cleared his throat. "I've always wondered. You shouldn't feel the ghosts, you know. No one else does."

"Petra is special," Astrophil said proudly.

"Sure," said Neel. "Sure she is." His voice sounded too cheery to his ears. Brassy, like he had polished it up to shine. "Me, too. And special Neel had better get his special self back to the palace, else the court's going to get pleased at the thought that I've drowned in the sea or run off. Well." Neel squared his shoulders. "Time to be kingly."

NEEL WAS ALONE in his bedroom when Tomik barged in, his eyes blazing with fear.

"The globes?" Neel asked. "Did you—?"

"You'd better call the court. You need to tell them what I've done."

THE COURTIERS SHIFTED RESENTFULLY. They'd already gotten a taste of their king's love of theatrical announcements. They eyed his pet Bohemians, standing close to his side, and wished he were a great deal less attached to these outsiders. They also wished he were less whimsical. And dangerous. And completely disrespectful of them and his own office.

In fact, they wished he didn't exist at all.

"Tribe leaders, step forward." The king rapped his golden scepter against the marble floor. "Ursari, Lovari, and Maraki—oh, yes, you, too, Tarn. Don't you ignore me. Get on up here." He crooked his finger, and the three leaders dragged their sullen feet to the dais on which the throne stood. "I've got presents for you." He waved his hand in a flourish, and Tomik stepped forward, a large wooden box in his hands. Tomik opened it, and inside were several smaller boxes. He gave one to each of the leaders, then passed the large box to Neel.

Tarn cracked open his box, and the barely contained anger on his face changed to puzzlement.

"Well," said the king, "don't you like your prezzies?"

"I don't understand." Tarn tipped the box and spilled two small glass spheres into the palm of his hand. "What are *these*?"

"Globes." Neel's grin was proud and wicked. "Happy now, aren't you?"

"The globes are *dead*. He"—Tarn gestured at Tomik—"destroyed them."

"Only in order to find out how they work," said Tomik, "and to reproduce them. The globes had glass centers that marked the exact location of a Loophole and could guide someone through it. I melted the centers, and molded five pairs of smaller spheres from them. I've got a magic gift for glass."

"He's also smarter than a pack of foxes," said Neel.

"The globes were big, and there was only one set," Tomik continued. "They weren't exactly easy to share, or easily transportable. What if you wanted to travel somewhere by horse, or on foot? Can you imagine lugging those two huge spheres everywhere? Now you don't have to. Each box contains a map that shows—just like the Terrestrial Globe used to show—the general location of all the Loopholes in the world. Go to one of the places marked by a dot on the map, touch it, and another dot will light up. That'll show you where the Loophole will take you. Then the spheres will float, and position themselves by the exact opening of the Loophole. You can travel from here to China, from there to the North Sea . . . anywhere a Loophole goes, in the blink of an eye."

"Every tribe gets a set." The king plucked a small box out of the larger one. "Me, too, since I'm the Kalderash leader, and your wise and canny king. And Tom, of course. That's the price for his work." Neel passed the last small box to Tomik, who gave it to Petra.

She curled her hands around it, and the face she turned to Tomik was so raw with feeling that many people looked away—including, oddly enough, the king.

Neel's chief adviser leaned forward to whisper in his ear. "Couldn't you have explained your plan earlier," Arun said, "during your ridiculous, politically disastrous gift of the globes to Tomik at your coronation?"

"I could've," Neel hissed back, "but that wouldn't have been smart. See, now when I make a mistake—and I'm bound to, it can happen to anyone, and what do I know about being king?—people will think I've got something up my sleeve, just like this time. That'll give me time to fix whatever mess I've got on my hands. Smart, huh?" Neel tapped his temple.

Arun raised a skeptical brow, then turned his sharp gaze toward the Bohemians. "Why does that young lad look so frightened?"

Neel glanced at Tomik and bit his lip. "I suppose because he knows it's time to leave."

NEEL WAS SINGING as he strolled along the palace wall through the darkness. He knew lots of drinking songs in several languages, and even though he hadn't touched a drop of the sweet island wine, he sang them all, feeling drunk with success.

And a little anxious, though he tried to ignore this. Now that the miniature globes were ready, Petra and Tomik would leave the Vatra.

Which meant that it was time for Neel to leave, too.

He sang more loudly and swaggered through the warm night. His sandals made a slight rasp over the stones, and Neel guessed that the palace wall was sprinkled with reddish brown dust he couldn't see. The wind carried it sometimes. Depending on which way it blew, a breeze would dust different parts of the palace. The palace servants were quick to clean, though, and they hated this dust, especially because it stained clothes. Come morning there wouldn't be a speck of dust on this wall. Nothing to see—not that Neel could see much now, in these shadows.

His foot connected with something. He heard a squeak and glanced down. There was a fuzzy ball scampering by his foot. It was a scoot.

"Sorry, little fellow." Neel scooped the creature up. He peered at it and recognized the white markings on its chest. "Oh, it's you. The one who doesn't want to fly." He set the scoot carefully on the ground. "I don't blame you." Neel looked over the edge. He could see nothing in the black distance below the palace wall, but he knew it was a long way down. "You and me, we'll just keep our feet on the ground, yeah?"

The scoot chirped, and Neel might have whistled in reply if someone hadn't rammed into his back. Before Neel could react, unseen hands shoved him over the palace wall.

11

Sadie's News

———◆◆◆———

NEEL FORGOT TO SCREAM. He tumbled through the night, the wind pummeling his body as he sped down toward the trees and rocks. *I'm dead.* The thought paralyzed his brain, and for a moment he was grateful, because if his mind didn't work he couldn't think about how much it would hurt to smash against the bottom of the cliff.

He wouldn't think about how, whatever choices Damara had made, she loved him.

Neel skimmed past the palace wall.

Yes, she loved him, and she was his mother. That was what mattered. This realization struck him with the full force of grief, and he choked on the rushing air that filled his mouth. It was unfair to understand this now, seconds before his death.

But Neel remembered something Petra had said a long time ago, about how people make their own luck. He remembered he wasn't helpless. He flung out his ghost fingers as high as they would stretch, and slapped them against the palace wall.

Neel's invisible nails raked over the stones, dragged down by his weight as he scrabbled for a grip. He tried to dig Danior's Fingers into the wall, fumbling for a nook or cranny, but they skidded uselessly. Then he felt it: two fingers caught at something.

His body stopped falling. He swung, and smacked into the wall.

The pain was so intense Neel almost let go. He gritted his teeth and jammed as many invisible fingers as he could into the hole his right hand had found in the wall. His toes scraped against stone, but the wall beneath them was too smooth. His feet slipped, and slipped again.

Neel tipped back his head and stared up toward the spot he'd fallen from. *So far away,* he thought. Panicky sweat trickled past his temples as he realized he was going to have to pull himself up, hand over invisible hand, hundreds of feet to safety.

Safety, huh? a snide voice said inside him. *What if whoever chucked you down the cliff's still up there, waiting?*

Neel swallowed. His heart hammered, and the tips of his real fingers burned as the ghosts stretched. Could the ghosts rip off? He had never demanded so much from his gift. How long would his magic bear his weight?

Neel had no choice. He braced his feet against the wall and pulled at his ghosts as if they were a rope. Carefully, he began to climb.

His arms were screaming hot hatred at him when he finally reached the hole his right hand had clawed into. With shuddering relief, he saw that not far below this hole was a small ledge. Neel wedged his feet onto it and rested. He pressed his face into a small, aromatic plant growing out of the jagged hole his hand gripped. He gasped for breath.

A ledge? Why was there a *ledge* in the palace wall?

Because, his slow, terrified brain said, *the wall is just like the rest of the palace. It's part man-made, and part natural. You're on real rock now. You're gripping the side of the mountain.*

And the mountain, he realized, was bumpy and pocked with holes. He could climb this. He could find cracks for his hands and feet. He'd have to stay away from the smooth stones the Roma had built into a wall hundreds of years ago. He'd fall for sure if he tried to make his way up the slick, man-made surface.

But he couldn't see much through the dark. He couldn't see, beyond a few feet in front of him, which part of the wall was mountain and which part man-made.

He took a steadying breath and felt the prickle of the plant against his cheek. He inhaled its scent. What was that? Rosemary. He almost laughed. Too bad he didn't have a pot to cook with. Rosemary was growing right out of holes in the wall.

Neel blinked sweat from his eyes. He stared at the shallow dirt in the pocket his fingers clutched. Of course. Plants grew where seeds had blown, and where there was enough dirt to take root. If there was enough dirt to take root . . .

There were holes in the rock to hold it, just like this one.

Right, then. He'd sniff his way to the top.

Neel began to climb again, following the scent of rosemary to find the next little bush growing out of a hole, and then the next one.

He was about fifteen feet from the balcony from which he'd fallen when he stopped. The rocky surface was gone. There was nothing between him and the top but perfectly smooth stones.

He bit his lip so hard he tasted blood. Then, one ghostly hand clinging to the rock, Neel threw his other fingers high into the air. They snagged the top of the wall.

Neel hauled himself up.

When he tumbled over the lip of the wall to rest on the dusty floor of a terrace, he lay there, sweating and shaking. Safe. He was safe.

Was he?

He couldn't bring himself to look, to see if his would-be assassin had stuck around long enough to watch him fall, and then climb.

Something small and cold and wet nudged his cheek. Neel opened his eyes.

It was the nose of the scoot, chittering worriedly. It held something in its mouth, which it dropped in front of Neel's face.

It was a small, clear crystal bead.

Neel shoved himself up. His dazed eyes took in the furry animal and the bead lying on his palm, then swept across the terrace.

He was alone.

PETRA AND TOMIK studied a map spread across a table in Petra's room as Astrophil strutted over the drawn continents and oceans. The spider pointed to various Loopholes, listing the advantages and disadvantages of each possible path they could take to Prague.

"What about this one?" Tomik tapped a Loophole not far off the Vatran coast.

Another Loophole glowed near the border between Bohemia and Austria.

"Austria . . ." Petra said thoughtfully.

"Oh, no," said Astrophil. "That Loophole is in the *mountains*. Do you realize that it is January? It is *winter* in Europe. I do not mind the cold, but you two would turn into human-shaped icicles."

Petra studied the map more closely. "The mountains aren't far from Krumlov."

"Ah." The spider stood over Austria. One leg arched up to rub his tin head. "I see."

"Well, I don't," said Tomik. "Krumlov's a nice part of Bohemia, sure, but unless you plan on sightseeing, I really don't understand your sudden interest in it."

"A friend of mine lives there," said Petra.

"Iris December, the Sixth Countess of Krumlov, is not exactly your *friend*," said Astrophil.

"She helped me once."

"And very likely regretted it."

"I trust her."

"Be that as it may, the countess's home is in Krumlov, but she *lives* in Prince Rodolfo's palace."

Petra frowned. "Maybe not anymore."

Tomik looked at her. "Is this something your mind-magic is telling you?"

Petra smoothed a finger over the sketched triangles that represented the Novohrad Mountains. "I'm not sure," she admitted. "It's hard to know what's magic, and what's just hope. Sometimes they feel exactly the same."

Tomik studied her, then the map. "So, Iris is an aristocrat."

"A powerful one," said Astrophil. "Her nephew is the prince's cousin, and if Bohemia were not part of the Hapsburg Empire, Lucas December would be its king."

"All right." Tomik rolled up the map. "We'll dress warmly."

"But—"

"Petra's right, Astro."

"She most certainly is not."

"We need information before we get even close to Prague. Iris can help us."

"*If* she is there!" Astrophil wrung four legs. "This is a terrible idea. You will freeze! And the mountains are dangerous, very dangerous. I have read all about it."

"Good," said Petra. "Then you can help us prepare. We'll leave tomorrow."

NEEL STAGGERED into his bedchamber. He found Arun standing near a window, looking out into the night, his hands folded behind his back.

"Nice view, ain't it?" Neel said. "That is, when there's light to see it."

Arun spun around, and his eyes went wide. "Your Majesty, what *happened* to you?"

Neel didn't want to think about what he looked like. He had bruises and scrapes everywhere. Reddish dust was smeared across his shirt, and his gold-threaded trousers were in shreds. He sighed. "I wrestled a bear."

His adviser choked.

"Don't worry," said Neel. "I won."

"King Indraneel—"

"*Neel.*" He stamped his foot.

"—you must see a doctor. You are bleeding, and you need—"

"No. *You* need to tell me what you are doing in my room in the middle of the night."

"A message came, an urgent one, from the Riven silk merchants."

The Riven brothers were part of a chain of *gadje* merchants the Roma trusted to pass information along, and the Rivens traded with Bohemia. Any news from that country that could make its way to the Vatra had to come from one source, the only free Roma left in Bohemia: Neel's sister. Sadie, who was half *gadje*, and whose skin was light enough that she could pass for white. Sadie, who was a chambermaid in Prince Rodolfo's castle.

"My sis," Neel whispered. "She sent a message for me?"

Arun shook his head. "News travels slowly. She can't possibly know you're here, or that Queen Iona is dead, or that you're now king of the Roma. Her message was for the queen."

"Well, you're going to send a message back. You're going to tell Sadie of the Lovari to get out of that cursed country now, right now."

"Your Majesty—"

"I'm summoning her to the Vatra. Got that? By order of the king."

"Your Majesty, you are not listening to me. Surely you want to know the information she risked her life to discover."

Neel fell silent.

"The numbers of Gray Men are growing," Arun said. "Prince Rodolfo seems to be building an army of them."

Neel stared. He'd never seen a Gray Man, but Petra had described their horror: their scaled skin, their speed, their poisonous tongues, and the eyes that were the only trace of what they had once been—humans.

"That's not all," Arun said. "Until recently, the prince's prisons were full—packed, because of his decision to jail every Roma in his country. Sadie says that now there are rows of empty cells. The imprisoned Roma are disappearing."

It took Neel a moment to find his voice. "Are you saying that Prince Rodolfo is turning Roma into monsters?"

ASTROPHIL TRIPPED and fell off the table when Neel slammed open the door to Petra's room. "Manners!" the spider scolded the king, scrambling onto the tips of his legs.

"*Neel.*" Petra gasped.

"What happened to you?" said Tomik.

Neel rubbed at his dirty forehead, his expression wild. Then he paused and noticed the half-packed bags on the floor.

"We've decided to leave tomorrow," Petra said. She started to explain their plan.

Neel shook his head. "Sorry, Pet. I can't come with you."

12

A Nighttime Visit

NEEL TOLD THEM Sadie's news. "I know I said I'd go, and I may be a snaky liar sometimes, but I hate not keeping my *word*. I'm not the type of fellow to break a promise. Not to you. But I guess . . . I guess I have to. 'Cause my ma's right. What I do—or *don't* do—as king will affect all the Roma. It'll affect Sadie, too. I can't run away from that. If I leave with you now, part of me will be running away from *this*." He spread his arms wide, as if they could hold the entire island. "This . . . responsibility."

"Neel—" Petra began.

He cut her off. "I'm sorry. I'll do anything to make you see that, d'you hear? I'll—"

"I understand," she said.

Neel was silent. Tomik was, too, because he wasn't sure he *did* understand. If he made a promise to Petra, he would keep it, no matter what.

"The Roma are your family," Petra said. "They have to come first."

"But you're my family, too. I said so."

The tiny iron horseshoe of Petra's necklace swung slightly, flicked by an invisible finger.

"It's not the same," Petra said. "I know that. This"—she touched the horseshoe he had given her long ago—"it's . . ."

"Symbolic," Astrophil supplied.

"Yes. It doesn't mean that I *am* your sister. Only that you wish I were."

"But I don't—" Confusion crossed Neel's face.

"We'll be all right, Neel," Tomik said firmly.

"Yes." Petra attempted a smile.

"What can I give you?" Neel said. "I'm the king. I can get you anything. Gold? Oh! I know. Horses. You'll need 'em, and I've got some beauties in the royal stable—"

"No," said Astrophil. "We need furs. Dried food." The spider raised one leg each time he listed something, like someone might tick off items on his fingers. "Snowshoes. Brassica oil for me to drink." Two more legs waved. "Rope. Matches. Kindling." Astrophil was now standing on one leg as seven others flickered in the air. "And a rowboat." He hopped on his remaining leg.

The three friends couldn't help it. They laughed.

"Psst."

Petra opened her eyes and glanced at Astrophil, curled into a tin ball on her pillow. He snored gently.

"Psst." She heard it again. She scanned her dark bedroom. Her heart beating, she reached for her Glowstone with one hand and her invisible sword with the other. She slipped from the bed, her nightgown whispering against her legs.

"It's me," Neel said, just as the Glowstone came alive in Petra's hand, and she gasped.

Neel was hanging outside her open window, miles above the sea.

"Neel! How did you—"

He swung into her bedroom. "I climbed."

"You climbed." Petra gave a breathy chuckle. "Astrophil would be impressed."

"Don't wake him. See, I've got an idea, and I don't think he'll approve."

Petra raised one brow. "A secret idea, it seems. One so secret you had to climb through my window instead of taking the hallway and stairs. Or are you simply showing off?"

"Maybe. Listen. I hate to send you off to Bohemia like this. At least let me give you something."

"You already—"

"*Pfft.*" He waved a hand. "The supplies Astro asked for? That's nothing. How about I give you a little bit of me to take along for the ride?"

She frowned. "What are you talking about?"

"A mental link."

Understanding dawned on her face, then fear, then anger. "No."

"Like the one you had with John Dee. It let you chat with each other, in your minds, even when you were far apart, until you broke it."

"No."

"You can make one, for me and you."

She raised her voice. "*Neel—*"

"I'm Roma. All Roma know enough about mind-magic to know that *that's* what it takes to forge a link. You've got the gift. You should *use* it—"

"Neel, stop!"

Astrophil squeaked in his sleep. Petra and Neel held their breath as the spider rolled onto his side and then onto his pointy face, his eight legs fanning wide around him.

"Why not?" Neel whispered. He looked hurt. "A mental link wouldn't let me poke around inside your personal thoughts and inklings. We'd just be able to talk without speaking, like you do sometimes with Astro. It's sure as fire a faster way to swap news than sending letters. So unless . . . unless you don't fancy us being hooked together like that, I don't see what the fuss is about."

Her silver eyes were fierce. "I could hurt you."

"Nah."

"So you know everything, don't you, King Neel?" She stabbed him in the chest with one finger. "Then you must know that forging a mental link is like *scrying*, and that scrying opens the mind in dangerous ways. You could go *mad*."

"I trust you."

"You shouldn't! I don't have the skill. Practicing with the Metis for a few weeks doesn't mean I can bumble around inside your brain."

"But I bet you know how. I bet you asked them, because you were so groused at Dee for having done it to you way back when that you'd want to know exactly *how* he did it."

Her eyes glimmered with anger.

"Ha!" he said. "I knew it. Pet, don't you see how useful a link would be? What if you need help? What if *I* do? Please, Petra. Please. If you did this, you'd be giving something to me, too."

She sighed. She knew this was wrong, but it's hard to deny someone who's pleading for the very thing you want. She felt suddenly, and sharply, how difficult it would be to say goodbye to her friend.

Neel's bruised face was eager in the light of the Glowstone.

Slowly, Petra said, "We'll need something that shines."

Neel clapped his hands. "There's a humongous mirror in the ballroom that'll do fine. It's very flash."

Petra had already turned to her nightstand for a small golden coin that had been hidden in its drawer. "No," she said. "This." She drew Neel into the center of the room and they sat on the floor with the coin on the cool, marble tiles between them, lit by the radiant blue of the Glowstone.

"Look at the coin," Petra said. "Breathe deep, and calm. Try to . . . try to loosen the knots that tie you together into who you are. And . . ." her voice wavered. "Trust me."

"Course I do."

"Shh. Don't talk. When your mind is opened like this, you might say something private. Something you'd never normally tell me. I don't want to steal your secrets."

Neel's hand twitched, then lay still, and Petra knew in that uncanny way she had that he'd been ready to trace one of the long scrapes on his arm. She took it all in again—his ripped tunic, his dirty hands, the dark bruises. Again she wanted to ask what had happened to him, and again she told herself that he clearly didn't want to say. "Promise me," she said. "No talking."

He nodded.

"Now," Petra said. "*Look.*"

He dropped his gaze to the gleaming coin. Time unwound like a ball of yarn, the minutes spinning away into the shadows. Neel's shoulders slumped. His eyes widened eerily and did not blink.

It troubled Petra to see Neel so vulnerable.

She lifted his chin and stared straight into his face.

"I'm afraid," he said, his voice toneless and empty.

"Shh." Petra felt a stab of panic, and would have broken the intense gaze between them if it wasn't too late. The spell had already begun.

"I'm afraid for my sis. I'm afraid for you. I'm afraid for me."

She would have to do this quickly. Her mind seemed to shiver, and she felt like she was slipping inside of herself. She searched for some loose part of her mind—it didn't matter which part, any part would do—and tugged. Holding Neel's yellow-green stare, Petra stitched a mental thread between her and her friend, and pulled tight.

Neel blinked.

"Neel? Are you all right?"

He rubbed his temples. "Yeah." The word was slurred. "A little swoony. Did it work?"

You tell me, she murmured in his mind.

He jumped a little. "Boxers and jugglers, that's weird." *I mean—* his words formed silently, tentatively—*nice. Good. That's good.*

An awkwardness rose between them, and Neel glanced again at the coin. "Shouldn't keep gold in your nightstand drawer, Pet. Too easy to steal. You ought to keep it in your shoes. Nigh impossible to nick it that way."

She smiled. He'd said something like this to her before. "It's hot, and I like to go barefoot. Besides, this is your palace. I doubt it's crawling with criminals."

"Oh, you'd be surprised," he said darkly, and this time he *did* touch one of his bruises. He caught Petra's startled glance, then added in a lighter tone, "After all, *I* live here, don't I?" He picked up the coin and peered at it. When he saw that it was stamped with a bird and ringed with Romany letters he recognized but could not read, surprise showed on his face. "This is Roma," he said. "And *old*. Is that . . . ?" he touched the bird. "That's the sign of Danior."

"Yes. It was minted during his reign, hundreds of years ago."

He stared at her.

"I found it in England," she said. "Keep it." She folded his fingers around the coin. "To remember me by."

Don't need that. He grinned.

"Keep it anyway. And go back to bed. You've got to be tired."

"Nah." But when he stood, Neel wobbled on his feet.

"And *walk* back to your rooms. You're in no shape to clamber around the palace walls." She stood, too, and pushed him toward the door. "Will you . . . be there tomorrow, at dawn, to see us off to the Loophole?"

"Course." He turned to leave, but Petra stopped him.

"You spoke to me," she said reluctantly. She knew he wouldn't remember what he'd said under the spell, but she didn't want to keep the fact of it from him.

He shifted uneasily. "What'd I say?"

"I *told* you not to talk."

"Petra. What did I say?"

She told him.

"Well, then." His gaze was steady. "I said nothing I'm ashamed of."

13

Into the Mountains

NEEL WAS THE ONLY ONE on the beach the next morning to see his friends off. Astrophil, with a keen glance at Neel, had suggested he come alone and pass along the travelers' goodbyes to the others. While it would have been nice to see the sailors of the *Pacolet* one last time before leaving, none of the friends wanted to mar the moment by ignoring the black stares many of the *Pacolet's* crew would surely send Neel's way. The Maraki had not forgiven him for accepting the crown.

Neel kicked the rowboat. "I'm not so sure this is seaworthy."

"It'll be fine," said Tomik.

"Wait another day. I'll get you something better. A crack little vessel with a sleek hull—"

Petra shook her head. "Time to go home. It's been too long already."

Neel tugged at the high collar of his silken sleeveless tunic. "Watch out for riptides. The current's got a wicked pull, and—"

"Neel." Tomik dumped their bags in the boat. "We know how to row."

Neel looked at him—at his sea-blue eyes, and shoulders strong from months of sailing. Standing next to Tomik, Petra was slighter than her friend, but Neel had seen her wield both knife and sword with lethal skill. They made a good team. They would be all right, he told himself.

Petra turned to him, her features softer than usual. There was a farewell on her lips. Neel could see it forming, but found that he couldn't bear to hear it. He raised a hand to her shoulder and held out one finger for Astrophil, perched near her collarbone, to shake. The spider gripped it with a few legs.

"Stay safe," Neel told the spider. "No heroics, you hear?"

"From me?" Astrophil said. "Hardly. As for you, Your Majesty, may I recommend that you behave yourself? Also: learn how to read."

Neel let go of the spider's legs. He stared.

"Unless, of course," the spider continued, "you wish to trust other people to do it for you. Personally, if I were king, I would not like to be so much at the mercy of people with better access to information."

The Roma king sputtered.

"Agree with him," Petra suggested. "It's easier that way."

Astrophil rolled his tiny green eyes. "Yes, as Petra knows, since she *always* listens to what I say."

Petra smiled down at him, but when her gaze turned back to Neel her smile faded. Neel rummaged around inside himself for something to say, yet could think of nothing other than the fact that he was exactly the same height as Petra, her eyes were level with his, and she was leaving, and there was no promise that they would ever see each other again.

Take care of yourself, she said, and he marveled for a moment at the sensation of her words inside his mind.

Then she turned, quickly, and her braid struck his bare shoulder like a soft whip.

Startled, he still said nothing as she climbed inside of the boat, and nothing as Tomik raised a hand to wave at him, and nothing as Astrophil sniffed and rubbed at his eyes, smearing a greenish speck of oil that looked suspiciously like a tear.

The skin of Neel's shoulder tingled as his friends pushed the boat from the shore. He felt it, and felt the pressure of the link between him and Petra. His mind touched it, resting on that little stitch, long after the boat had rowed away.

PETRA FELT STRANGE as she pulled at the oars. Waves slapped against their boat, and different emotions pushed and tugged at her, as if the ocean were inside of her—deep, and too murky for her to see clearly to the bottom of things.

She knew she felt eager. It had been agonizing to see each day slip past, with her no closer to the only hope she had to save her father. She seemed to betray him with every sunset.

And now . . .

I'm afraid for you, Neel had said. *I'm afraid for me.*

Fear. She supposed that's what it was, coiling inside her alongside her eagerness to return home. But Petra felt Astrophil scramble to the top of her head, his tin legs pricking against her scalp. She looked at Tomik seated in front of her, his back turned, his golden hair windblown and wild, his arms rising and falling as he hauled at the oars. Petra took heart.

When they'd rounded a crag jutting out from the island's shore and the dwindling figure of Neel disappeared behind the rock, Tomik called for them to shift directions and head into the open sea.

Finally, they paused, the oars thunking against their locks, the boat bobbing on the rough waves.

"Oooh," Astrophil said. "I feel seasick."

Something wet seeped down Petra's head. "Astrophil. Did you throw up in my hair?"

"No," he said, then added weakly, "Well. Maybe a little bit of oil."

"We'll soon be on dry land." Tomik unfolded the Loophole map and consulted it. "Here's as good a spot as any to set the globes free." He opened the wooden box, and the small spheres vibrated as they sensed the nearness of a Loophole. They burst from the velvet-lined box, whizzing across the waves until they paused, humming and hovering as they marked the Loophole's invisible entrance.

"You know, Tomik," Petra said, eyeing the globes, one red and one white, "we've never had an adventure together. Just you and me."

"I beg your pardon?" Astrophil rapped her skull. "And what about me? I suppose I do not count. I might as well not even exist. You probably have forgotten I am even here."

A large wave rocked the rowboat. Astrophil made a burping sound, and Petra felt another dollop of oil dampen her hair. "Don't worry," said Petra. "I know you're there."

Tomik laughed. He tucked the map into a pocket and reached across the boat to take Petra's hand. "To our adventure. Let's not get killed, all right?"

"Deal." Petra shook his hand, then tightened the belt that bound her sword to her side. She and Tomik shrugged into their furs and sweltered under the Indian sun as they rowed toward the globes, Astrophil standing tiptoe on Petra's hooded head as if it were the crow's nest of a boat. He had the best view, even if it was making him ill.

"Perhaps you should not row so fast," he said.

"Why not?" Petra pulled at the oars that would bring her home.

"We do not know where the Loophole will take us."

"Sure, we do," said Tomik. "The Novohrad Mountains."

"Yes, but we do not know *exactly* where . . ." The words died in the spider's throat as the boat passed between the spheres. The hull scraped against rocky ground. There was a gentle thud as the globes dropped into their velvet-lined box. Freezing air punched Petra's face, and for a moment she was blinded by the sheer whiteness of snow.

She leaned against the side of the boat, squinting her eyes against the bright light, trying to see where they had landed.

"Stop!" cried the spider, who saw the icy valley yawning beneath them. The boat teetered on the edge of a cliff.

Petra froze. Tomik dropped the oars in their locks and reached for Petra. The wooden rattle of the oars echoed across the valley, and the boat rocked as if still on waves. With one final wobble, the rowboat plunged off the cliff.

14

Snowdrifts

THE ROWBOAT WHIPPED DOWN the mountain, hissing and slamming over stones and snow.

Petra gripped the sides of the hull, aware of little else than Astrophil's screams and Tomik's arm around her waist. The boat thumped over a pile of rocks, and several boards broke beneath Petra's feet. She saw a chunk of wood wing away into the crystal sky.

"The boat's coming apart!" Tomik shouted.

"ACK!" Astrophil cried. "RORR! OCK! SSS!"

What? Petra's brain rattled in her head. She sucked in lungfuls of icy air and tried to focus on the panicked spider's shouts. What was he trying to say?

Then she saw it, looming ahead of them.

Oh.

They were heading right toward a giant pillar of stone.

"ROCKS!" she yelled.

Tomik's arm tightened around her. He yanked her to one side of the boat. With a wooden creak, the rowboat veered left, shooting up a spray of powdery snow behind them. Tomik and Petra leaned as hard as they could against the boat's side, but they were still careening toward the rocks.

They bumped over a small hill of snow, and one of the five bags whirled out of the boat.

"No!" cried Tomik.

"Yes!" Petra kicked another bag out of the boat. The weight of the boat shifted. They leaned left again, and whizzed past the stone pillar.

And straight over a ledge.

The boat launched into the air, soaring over the snow. Then it hit the slope again and burst into pieces.

Petra spun down the hill. A stray board smacked into her. She kept tumbling, headfirst. No magic she had could save her from this.

Pressing her face against the snow, she jammed her fists deep into the freezing white powder and swung her legs so that her feet were pointing down the mountain's slope. Her fists created friction, and her body slowed, but didn't stop. Petra dug in her toes, and she sank into the snow, buried almost entirely. She dragged to a halt.

For a moment, she simply lay there, panting into the snow, her face blazing with cold. Then she shoved herself up. "Astrophil?" *Astrophil!*

"Here," he said faintly. He was hanging onto her braid.

Petra's relief was short-lived. "Tomik!" She scanned the mountainside for him, but saw only the ruins of the boat.

She was plunging through the snow, terrified, when one of the boards shifted. A dark shape lifted it aside, pushing through the snow's surface.

Petra waded toward Tomik and flung herself into his snowy arms. They huddled together, warm cheeks and freezing noses. They breathed, and breathed, and were grateful.

"No bones broken?" Tomik murmured in her ear.

"No. You?"

He shook his head. "We were lucky. The snow softened our fall."

A gasp from Astrophil broke them apart. "The supplies!" wailed the spider, pointing at the ruins of the boat. "They are gone!"

The blood drained from Tomik's face. Petra stared at him, then at their surroundings: the mirror-bright snow, the frozen sun, the sharp peaks that caged them in at all sides except the only way down. A dark smudge marked a ridge of trees far below.

Petra attacked the jumble of wooden boards at Tomik's feet. He joined her, and they flung parts of the boat away, searching for the bags that contained everything they needed to survive in the mountains. They had vanished.

Tomik suddenly sank to his knees. His silence changed. It hardened, and struck Petra with its force. Tomik had seen something. She followed his gaze.

Peeking out from under the paddle of a broken oar was a brown box. It was flung open, and the blue velvet interior held nothing but glass shards.

"The globes," Petra whispered.

Tomik stared at the broken glass. "We'd never find the Loophole again on our own," he said. "There's no going back."

Petra glanced up the slope. "We need to find the bags."

"That is suicide!" said Astrophil. He scrambled up Petra's braid and tugged at her fallen hood, trying to drag it up over her head. He struggled under its weight. "We flew down hundreds of feet. The bags could be anywhere, and you will waste precious time searching for them, climbing *up*, when you should be moving as quickly as you can *down*, to the forest. There you will be sheltered from the cold. You will find food."

"Not for you, Astro." Frowning, Petra plucked the hood from his legs and pulled it over her head. Astrophil climbed inside. "The brassica oil is gone."

"Oh, me. I am fine. I can go days without eating. I am a machine."

Petra said nothing to this. While it was true that Astrophil had once gone almost a week without his usual daily dose of brassica oil, no one had any idea of how long he could run without it, or what would happen if he stopped working. Would his gears start whirring again the instant they poured brassica down his mouth? Or, if he stopped, would he never start again?

Petra did not want to find out. Yet she gazed at the sparkling slope and knew that it would be risky to flounder up the mountainside in search of the missing supplies. Perhaps Astrophil was right. He usually was. This kind of cold was dangerous, and the sooner they reached the forest, the sooner they'd reach Krumlov and the brassica oil Iris surely kept in her castle. The rich always had some oil on hand, for lighting lamps if for nothing else.

"All right," she said. "Let's go."

"Do you have your sword?" Tomik asked Petra, his breath fogging the air.

"Yes," she said, and was grateful, at least, for that.

"Maybe you can hunt in the forest."

"And what, fence a rabbit?" She shook her head. "Swords aren't made for hunting. They're made for killing people." She had never spoken so bluntly about her father's gift, and her own words shocked her.

Petra had the power to kill someone.

The thought was colder than the snow at her feet. A memory hissed in Petra's mind. *Assassin*, an air spirit had called her with a sly smile. *Assassin.*

Tomik must not have liked what he saw on Petra's face. He turned away and began picking up pieces of wood and stuffing them into his coat. "We're wasting time. Come on. Take some wood, too. We can use it for a fire."

"We've nothing to start a fire with," Petra said grimly. "No matches."

"That is not what I would call a positive attitude," Astrophil said directly in her ear.

Petra sighed and packed the inside of her coat with fragments of the rowboat.

They started down the slope.

THEY STUMBLED THROUGH THE DARK, their Glowstones lighting the way as they slogged down the mountain. They could no longer see the distant trees—only the snow surrounding their feet in a circle of blue light. They had no idea if they were still heading for the forest, or if the forest would really be any better than this.

It has to be, Petra thought numbly. A cold wind scraped at her cheeks. She couldn't feel her toes anymore, and the only thing that kept her moving was the thought of her father—and the certainty that if she stopped, the sweat slicking her skin would ice over.

Astrophil jabbered in her ear, reciting reams of crazy poetry about a man who flew a winged horse to the moon to find his bottled-up soul. *He's trying to distract me.* The thought was fuzzy. *That's nice.*

The spider poked her cheek. "Don't ignore me!"

Or not so nice.

Tomik grabbed her hand and tugged her through a snowdrift. "We have to go faster!"

Everyone was yelling at her. Even Neel, she thought, seemed to be trying to get her attention. She could feel a pressure on the mental link. An insistence. But she didn't have the energy to listen.

I could freeze to death, she realized. It was hard to care. Everything was so cold.

Her foot hit a jumble of pebbles and skidded. She slipped, realizing that they weren't walking on snow anymore, but on a scree. Tomik caught her, and they slipped together, tumbling down the slope in a shower of small rocks.

When they stopped, Petra lay on the ground, faceup. Astrophil was standing on the tip of her nose. "Petra! Speak to me!"

She focused and saw a fringe of pine branches above him, oddly blue in the light of the Glowstone that seemed to still be in her hand, even if she couldn't feel it. She heard a muffled chopping sound and turned her head to see Tomik using a board to dig into a large, hardened snowdrift at the base of a tree. "The forest," she said. "We made it."

"Are you all right?" he asked.

"Of course. I'm very warm."

Tomik stopped digging. "Astro." His voice was tight. "Keep her awake."

Oh. The thought prickled at the back of her mind. *That's right. People feel warm, just before they sleep and freeze and die.*

She tried to worry about this, but the cozy warmth spread through her like liquid. Even with Astrophil jabbing her face and shouting in her ear and mind, Petra's eyes slipped shut. The spider pried one lid open, and she could see Tomik hollowing out the snowdrift, working quickly with his broken board.

He tossed it aside, yanked open his coat so that the wood inside fell to the ground, and crunched over the snow to Petra.

She couldn't really understand words anymore, just heard the anxious tones of Astrophil as Tomik fumbled with her coat and dragged out pieces of wood. She was vaguely aware that she should feel colder with her furs open to the air, but she didn't.

Tomik grabbed Petra under her arms, dragged her to the snowdrift, and pushed her into the hole he had made. Then he slipped inside, squeezing next to her in the coffin-shaped hollow in the snow.

"Petra." He was murmuring in her ear, reminding her of stupid pranks they'd pulled on the village schoolmaster back home, telling her that they *were* home, or almost, that they were so close to the Bohemian border, and didn't she remember her plan? "This is our adventure. Ours. And I will help you, I'll do anything. Just tell me you're all right."

She blinked in the blue Glowstone light, and realized her head was pillowed against his chest, and that Tomik had pulled his open coat over her furs and the invisible rapier at her hip. She saw the green Vatran shirt he had worn at the beach, felt its soft cotton on her cheek as Tomik's heat radiated from his body to hers. It was a healthy heat, so different from the otherworldly one that had almost sent her to sleep outside. This warmth smelled like him and her and spices from the delicious island food they'd eaten for weeks. She sighed. It was a gorgeous heat.

No, she thought a moment later. *A painful one.*

It started in her hands and toes: a cramping, searing ache as warmth ate into her cold skin. She cried out. Her body trembled, then shook violently. Tomik was trembling too, and she realized how cold he must have been, how hard it must have been for him not to give in to the same winter she had let creep inside her.

Then the pain became too great for her to think such thoughts.

When her shivering eased, and his, she whispered, "Thank you."

He said, "You're safe. You can sleep now."

"Astrophil?"

"He's outside. He won't get cold, and he said he wanted to keep watch."

"Yes. He should," Petra said. "They might come here."

She wondered what she'd meant by that. They? They who?

But if her mind-magic knew the answer to that question, it wouldn't say.

She fell asleep.

Tomik felt Petra startle against him. He opened his eyes, and his first thought was not really a thought, but an unformed feeling of great happiness to be this close to someone he had loved since she was a skinny-limbed little girl who had given him a fistful of grass.

Then he saw Petra's face and his heart stopped.

Her eyes were stretched wide. Her voice came in a halting, terrified whisper. "Turn off the light."

He fumbled for the two Glowstones that had fallen between their bodies. He squeezed them, and the blue light died.

"Petra? What is it?"

Her answer was a whimper. "I hear them. They . . . they can smell us. They're coming."

"Who?"

The darkness between them was alive with Petra's silent fear.

"Petra. *Who?*"

"The Gray Men."

15

Death in the Forest

———◆—◆◆—◆———

G ET OUT GET OUT GET OUT!" Petra shoved at Tomik.
He tried to stop her beating hands. "We can hide in here."

"We will *die* in here. They smell us already. We smell like sacks of skin filled with hot blood, and they are hungry. So *get out*."

Tomik pushed through the hole as a screech split the air. It was the sound teeth would make if dragged over stone.

Petra joined Tomik and pulled the rapier from its scabbard. Astrophil jumped from a pine branch to her shoulder. "How many?" the spider asked.

"Four." Exactly like when she had been attacked by the Gristleki a year ago. She had panicked then. She had fainted.

She could not do that now.

Petra looked at Tomik, lit by the full moon, and wanted to tell him to run. But she'd seen the speed of a Gristleki loping on all fours. She knew it was hopeless to run.

She tightened her hand around the sword's invisible hilt. *Four of them.* What was she thinking? Fighting them was hopeless, too.

A branch snapped in the distance. Petra's heart jumped. Fear burned through her like acid.

"Don't let them touch you," she told Tomik. "They'll scrape you raw. Their skin is poisonous, and their tongues . . ."

Tomik nodded. He looked so brave. If Petra had been capable of anything other than terror, she might have wept at the thought that he was here because of her.

"I will help you, Petra," Astrophil said in her ear.

Another branch cracked the silence. Then another, closer.

The monsters burst through the trees.

A Gray Man leered at Petra, stretching its ashen human form. It leaped across the clearing and rammed into her.

Petra's blade fell from her hand as the creature straddled her, scrabbling at her coat, enraged at the fur that covered her skin. She flung her arms over her face. The Gray Man pried them back, gave her a great, toothless smile, and pushed its face toward hers.

Astrophil jumped from Petra's shoulder onto the Gray Man's cheek. The spider stabbed his legs into one dark eye.

With a howl, the beast reared its bald head and swatted the spider off its face. Petra swung onto her side, grabbed the hilt of her rapier, and stabbed at the Gray Man's chest.

The point of her sword glanced off its scaled skin.

The Gristleki giggled. "Sssilly girl," it hissed. Black blood trickled from its eye.

She scrambled to her feet and stabbed again, straight at its heart.

This time, when the blade skittered harmlessly off its chest, three Gray Men laughed. Petra saw two of them sitting on their haunches below the trees, eyes eager, enjoying her pathetic attempts to retaliate.

And the fourth? she thought with a fresh burst of panic. *Where is the fourth?*

Where is Tomik?

Astrophil jumped to Petra's knee and raced up her body. *He is in trouble*, the spider said.

Petra heard scuffling behind her, and a strange, whacking sound.

She turned, and saw Tomik beating the monster away with the wooden board he had used to dig the snow cave.

The sight filled her with desperation. She had been saved from the Gristleki once by John Dee, but there was no one to save them now.

No one except her.

A clawed hand reached for her. She ducked and executed a move Nicolas had taught her months ago at sea. She planted a boot in the Gray Man's face, jerked away, and curled her sword arm back for a double-handed swipe at the beast's neck.

The rapier chopped off its head.

Black blood spurted, and the headless trunk of the monster collapsed to the ground. It was only then that Petra remembered what John Dee had told her: that while she was unconscious, he had cut off the heads of the Gristleki that had attacked her.

Petra whirled. She snatched Tomik's shoulder, knocked him to the ground, and thrust her rapier into the second Gray Man's throat. Blood bubbled down its neck as it clawed at the sword it couldn't see. Petra dragged her blade, and the monster fell.

The remaining two Gristleki sprang at her.

They came too close, too fast for Petra to swing her long rapier, but she had seen what Astrophil had done to the first Gristleki, and knew their eyes were also vulnerable. She jerked up the hilt of her sword to smash it against a face. The creature stumbled back, hissing, but the second Gray Man tore off Petra's hood, exposing the flesh of her neck. She jumped back.

Forward! Astrophil silently shouted.

Petra immediately understood. The Gristleki were used to people backing away from them. Humans always did.

She rushed at the two monsters and slipped between them as they flinched in surprise. She delivered a backhanded coup with her sword, digging her blade halfway through a neck. The body toppled against the last Gristleki. She tugged the sword free.

The Gristleki shoved aside the gray corpse. Its face was fixed on Petra's, and filled with insane delight. Here, at last, was a challenge.

Petra remembered her lessons with John Dee, and with the Metis, who had told her to crave her mind-magic like a drug. Call it forth and let it rule you, they had said. Let it use you.

It was almost the hardest lesson they had taught her.

She let the magic fill her stomach and lungs until it seemed to suffocate her. The idea of who she was—that she was Petra Kronos, and had a history and hopes—receded.

She looked at the monster and thought of only one thing: which way it would move.

It clawed left, she swerved right. It kicked at her feet, she jumped. She let it make its moves, and with every move she dodged, letting it advance, letting it herd her back into the trees, yet never allowing it to touch her, always dancing away until she saw it cock its head with surprise.

She stabbed her sword into the side of its exposed neck and pushed.

Blood spat forth. The body crumpled.

Petra stood, her rapier visible now, slick with inky blood. Her stunned senses registered one thought: she was the only thing left standing.

The only one, she thought again, and realized what this meant just as Astrophil shouted, "Tomik!"

Petra rushed to his fallen body and dropped to her knees. He must have been touched. He must have been poisoned. She illuminated a Glowstone, turned him over, and searched for a scrape or suction mark, wondering how she could possibly ever cure him. Astrophil dragged a lock of blond hair aside and Petra saw the red blood oozing from his temple. She saw the bloody rock on the ground. He had hit his head when he'd fallen.

"Tomik." She shook him. "Tomik!"

He opened his eyes and stared blearily at her. Then he turned his head and vomited.

Petra wiped his mouth with the sleeve of her coat. Fur fell in tufts, drifting onto Tomik's cheek, and she saw that patches of her coat had disintegrated, burned away by the touch of the Gristleki's poisonous skin. Tomik's coat was also ragged and splashed with black blood. Gristleki blood was flecked on his skin.

And on hers. In fact, she was covered with it. If their skin and tongues were poisonous, what could the blood of a Gristleki do?

She clamped down hard on that question and shoved it into the back of her mind. It was useless to try to answer it. Time would tell. In the meantime, she had to take care of Tomik.

The monsters seemed not to have touched his skin, but she was worried about his head. He mumbled incoherently as Astrophil peered into his eyes.

"My extensive medical research leads me to conclude that Tomik is concussed," said the spider.

"What does that mean?" said Petra.

"He hit his head."

"I can see that. What does it *mean*?"

"He should lie still. If he did not fracture his skull, he should be fine in a few hours. If he did . . ."

Petra did not want to consider the end to Astrophil's sentence. "How many hours?"

The spider wrung four legs. "It is difficult to say. Sometimes these illnesses pass quickly. Sometimes they do not. But if we do not move him and he is to remain here on the ground, we will need a fire."

Petra burst to her feet, eager for something to do, and gathered the scattered wood from the rowboat. Yet even as she heaped the scraps into a pile near Tomik, she knew she had nothing to light them with. There were no matches. There was nothing. Nothing except . . .

She wiped her sword on the snow and considered it. She knew, from having watched her father forge horseshoes and other metallic things in his smithy, that metal could produce sparks. But that required a lot of force, and usually heat.

Her magic would have to do. She grabbed a small rock and struck it against the sword's hilt.

It took several attempts before she managed to draw a spark from the sword, and then it fell on a board and immediately died. The second spark burned a little longer. Petra was blowing at it frantically, certain it would fade like the first, when Astrophil stepped onto the wooden board, hawked, and spat a drop of brassica oil onto the smoldering spark.

A small flame licked the wood.

"It worked!" Astrophil jumped up and down, and the burning board trembled beneath his small weight.

"Astrophil! Don't—you—dare—" Petra scolded him as she puffed at the flame. "Do—that—again!"

"But am I not a clever spider? I thought, 'Now if only we had some oil. Oil is so flammable.' And then it occurred to me that *I* had oil. I admit that was a rather disgusting and ill-mannered way to use it. Normally, I would never approve of spitting, but—"

"You need that oil. It's all you have."

"Oh, but I am a machine. I can run for days on very little."

Petra narrowed her eyes. "How *many* days?"

"Many, many!"

"Astrophil. Promise me. Never again."

The flame ran along the board, and Astrophil jumped from it to the snow. "Oh, very well. I promise."

Once the fire was burning steadily, Petra gathered fallen branches and stripped bark from the trees to add to the flames. She used one large, curled piece of bark to scoop some clean snow, then held the makeshift bowl close to the fire until the snow melted. She trickled the water into Tomik's mouth.

He seemed to be doing better, and when he said her name, Petra relaxed, thinking that the worst was over. As her tension eased, a sense of pride grew inside of her, dancing like one of the small orange flames. She had fought the monsters. She had fought them, and had won. They were all dead.

Then she remembered the eyes of the first Gray Man she had killed, and her pride vanished.

They were all dead. And they had once been human. She had killed four people. Four people like her father.

Petra choked. She turned away from Tomik and hid her face in her hands, yet couldn't block out the knowledge of what she had done. Maybe she couldn't see the bleeding gray carcasses, but she could smell them. She knew they were there.

Dark eyes. The first one had had dark eyes. And the others? What color were theirs? Everything had happened so quickly. She had not noticed. She didn't know.

Petra pressed her fingers against the tears sliding down her cheeks.

Had one of the monsters had silver eyes?

What if . . . ?

She couldn't finish the thought.

Astrophil climbed up her wrist and pulled away one finger. "Petra, what is wrong? Tell me."

"What if . . ." she whispered. "What if one of the Gray Men was my father?"

Astrophil fell to her lap. Horror filled his tiny face. "No."

Petra let her hands drop away, and her wet cheeks shone in the firelight.

When Astrophil spoke again, his voice was heavy. "Stay here," he said. "I will look."

Petra stared at the fire as the spider noiselessly crept away. She tried not to imagine him peering into each monstrous face, searching for silver eyes that would be strangely hard, because they had been enspelled at Prince Rodolfo's command.

A lifetime seemed to pass before the spider crawled onto her knee. "Master Kronos was not one of them," he said.

"Are you lying to me?"

"Petra. I have never lied to you."

"You might. You might, to protect me."

"I have looked. I inspected very carefully. I swear to you that I did not see your father's eyes, and I would know them if I saw them."

Petra nodded shakily and pushed a handful of snow down her mouth. She wanted it cold. She wanted the freezing lump traveling down her throat to scour clean everything she felt inside her.

"Petra?" Tomik muttered.

She wiped the tears from her face and turned to him.

"I thought of something," he said.

"What?" The look on his face gave birth to a new dread within her.

"What were the Gray Men doing here, in the Novohrad Mountains?"

Petra hesitated. Then she said, "It was a random attack. They were here and caught our scent. That's all." But she was not so sure.

"Maybe they knew we were here," Tomik said. "What if they were searching for *us*?"

16

The Beach

———◆◆◆———

I T WAS DAWN when they decided to leave the clearing, and then only because Tomik stalked away from the campsite.

"You need to rest!" Petra dragged at his elbow.

"And if I'm right?"

"You're not. You can't be right."

He shook off her hand and kept walking. "If the Gray Men were here to find us, we need to move."

"No. *You* need to listen to *me*."

Tomik stopped. "Is my opinion that unimportant to you? Am I your slave, for you to tell what to do?"

She was struck silent.

Astrophil raised a timid leg. "May I say something?"

"Of course not," Petra told Tomik. "Of all the stupid things to say!"

He looked at her. "Do you know why you're angry?"

"I am not!"

"I wish to say something," said Astrophil.

"You're angry," Tomik told Petra, "because you know I'm right. We might not survive another attack. If the Gristleki are hunting in the mountains, we must get out of them, fast. That frightens you, and makes you feel powerless, and guilty because even though you're telling me to rest, part of you wants to push me to run as fast as I can."

"Aren't you clever. Don't you know everything. Well, let me tell you—"

Astrophil put the tips of two legs in his mouth and blew a shrill, tinny whistle. When Tomik and Petra fell silent, the spider said, "I, as a scholar of many subjects, including medicine, believe that Tomik is perfectly fine."

"He is?" Petra whispered.

"He is rushing about, arguing with you, is he not? His pupils are a reasonable size, and he is not wavering on his feet. I would say—if anyone cared for my opinion—that you are arguing over nothing."

Nothing, Petra thought, except that everything Tomik had said— everything he had accused her of—was true. "So we should leave."

"Quickly," said Tomik. "While there's sunlight, we should look for food and shelter."

"Let us find some rabbits for you to fence," Astrophil told Petra.

IN THE END, Petra used her sword to bring down a fox—a winter-starved, stringy fox who had snaked past her as she had crouched, perfectly still, in the shadow of a tree. She had been waiting for more than an hour when she sensed its approach and sliced the invisible rapier through the air. The fox didn't even pause in the moment before the blade cut its body in half.

Tomik lifted his brows when Petra brought back the bloody halves of the fox, but he knew better than to say anything. He skinned the split carcass while Petra started a fire, her eyes narrowed at Astrophil the entire time. "Don't you spit on it," she told him.

"I do not spit," he said. "I expectorate."

ON THEIR SECOND DAY traveling through the forest, after Petra had returned from hunting with a weasel neatly pierced through the heart, Tomik said, "You're getting better at this."

Petra struck a rock against the pommel of her sword, and blew at the spark that jumped onto a curl of bark.

"You're getting better at that, too," Tomik said.

Petra shrugged. "Practice."

"Two days' worth? You're not just drawing on your magics, Petra. You're adapting so quickly to them. If I learn a new technique, it takes me a long time to perfect it. Weeks, even. What exactly did the Metis teach you?"

She glanced at Astrophil, who slept near a tree in a nest of snow. He had been with her for every lesson with the Metis, even the most troubling one. "I'd rather not talk about it."

"Oh, come on."

"Tomik, you were thrilled at the thought that you could study magic in the Vatra, but you didn't go back to the Metis, like I did. You didn't ask them to teach you. Why not?"

Tomik pushed a twig near the growing flame. "They seemed heartless."

"Exactly."

He looked at her differently. "In fact, I thought I'd pay a high price for any lesson I might learn."

She blew at the flame.

"Petra, you didn't. You didn't agree to become one of them."

"No." She sat back on her heels. "They . . . explained that magic comes at a price. It needs energy, just like a fire needs kindling or brassica oil to burn. Magic usually borrows it from your body—from your breath, your energy, the food you eat. The hours you sleep. It's not always noticeable that it takes something from you. But if you *do* notice, you can feed your magic what it needs, and that makes it stronger. You pay for it later. I'll be tired in a few hours."

Tomik peered at her face. He knew it well, and knew she was hiding something. "There's more. What else did they teach you?"

Reluctantly, Petra said, "I have a Choice."

"What do you mean, *Choice*? About what?"

"I'm a special case. Because I'm a chimera. Because I have two magical abilities, I can choose between them. I can feed one to the other."

"I don't understand."

Petra wished Astrophil were awake to explain, though he didn't like discussing the subject any more than she did. "I could only do it once. I could choose to pour my mind-magic into my skill over metal—or the reverse. If I did, my one remaining talent would become very powerful. But only for a short time, as long as it takes for one magic to consume the other. Entirely. Once that short burst of power fades away, the magic that is left will start to eat itself until it disappears, too. My magic will be gone."

Tomik's hands fell to his sides. "You'd be helpless. Ordinary, for the rest of your life. It wouldn't be worth it, Petra. How long would this 'short burst of power' last? Ten minutes? Twenty?"

"I don't know."

"What if you had made this . . . *Choice* when the Gristleki attacked, and your power ran out in the middle of the fight? We'd be dead."

"That's why I didn't choose," she said softly.

"And you didn't need to. You defeated them anyway."

"But if I was desperate—"

He shook his head. "Say that you were, and made your Choice, and succeeded. Say that you felt your magic burn out, and didn't care because you thought it was a fair price to pay. What if, the next day, something worse came along? You'd have nothing left to fight it."

"I know the risks, Tomik. I know the cost."

"Then promise me you won't do it."

This was exactly what Astrophil had said, once they had left the Metis' cave.

"I wouldn't be able to control the surge of power anyway." Petra glanced away from Tomik. "The Metis told me so." She stoked the fire. "Please, let's not talk about this. The Gray Men might track us, and . . ." She looked at the rash on her fingers, from where black blood had splashed. She tugged on a mitten. "Things are hard enough."

As DAYS PASSED and Petra and Tomik didn't sicken, they gave up worrying that the Gristleki blood might have poisoned them.

She grew deft at hunting, but the forest didn't have much to offer. It was better here than in the bone-freezing mountains. It was warmer. The pine trees were like giant fur coats that blocked the wind, and heat always flushed through Petra's body during the end-less hours of walking. But her breath fogged the air, and it was too cold for there to be many animals for food. They were hibernating or had migrated months ago.

Petra killed what she could. Once, she let her mind-magic un-furl and slipped over a stretch of snow. She was looking for a hidden thing, and when her hand plunged through the snow and into a hole in the earth, she found it. She hauled up a sleeping rabbit by its ears and cut its throat with the base of her blade just as it began to twitch itself awake.

Holding the warm, bloody rabbit in her arms made her feel like crying again. It had the weight of a baby. With its dark, liquid eyes, the rabbit looked like a human enchanted into an animal shape.

Petra told herself that she was being foolish. They needed to eat. And she had grown up in a village. She knew that cows in the field would die, and had helped her cousin Dita kill chickens. It wasn't pretty, but it was food. It had never bothered her—before.

Petra went alone to hunt, insisting that Astrophil stay with Tomik. The spider didn't like it, but Petra said he distracted her. The truth was that she couldn't bear the thought of Tomik stranded in the trees by himself. If the Gristleki attacked, at least he and Astrophil would have each other.

They wouldn't stand a chance. Petra knew this. Still, every day she plucked the spider from her shoulder and set him on Tomik's.

The three would meet again later, eat whatever Petra had caught, and trudge on through the snow-filled forest, forcing their way through pine branches when there was no clear path. Tomik checked the maps he had tucked inside his coat before passing through the Loophole, and seemed to know where they were going. If he sometimes looked a little anxious around the eyes when he suggested they head south, or west, Petra didn't question him.

Astrophil chattered at first, saying he was going to cheer them up by teaching them a new subject every day. But eventually Petra and Tomik's silence, and the silence of the forest, began to affect the spider, too, and he crouched quietly on Petra's ear or slept in the crook of her neck, one leg wrapped around a lock of her dirty hair. He insisted on keeping watch at night.

Petra had trouble sleeping, curled together with Tomik in a new snow cave he built each night. When she closed her eyes she saw gray, scaled claws.

She should have been able to take comfort in Tomik. She should have felt safe next to his solid, slumbering warmth. But it made her uneasy. Tomik was the brother she never had. There should have been nothing wrong, then, with sleeping next to him. Yet as much as she tightened her mind-magic when she was around him and screwed it down into a tiny knot she refused to untie, her heart didn't need magic to sense that this—being together, being so close, so warm, so secreted from the world—meant something more to him than it did to her.

Terror waited when she closed her eyes. When she opened them and saw Tomik, she worried.

Sometimes, Neel tried to speak with her. She could sense him, could feel a tendril of his thought unfolding like a tiny pea shoot in the earth of her mind. She stopped it every time. *We're fine,* she told him once, then closed herself against his eager response. She didn't want to tell him what had happened after they'd rowed away from the Vatran shore. That would make everything more real.

Neel didn't know what he was doing. He might try to touch the edges of Petra's mind, but he was far away in India, and as Petra had learned long ago from John Dee, distance made it harder to send thoughts through a mental link. Neel didn't have the mind-magic to force the issue, and it was easy to keep him at bay. Usually.

It was harder at night. When she was tired, it was difficult to find the energy to strengthen her defenses against him, and sleep meant surrendering all control. If Neel wanted to reach her while she slept, she wouldn't be able to ignore him. Petra and Tomik had finally crossed—or at least they thought so—into Bohemia, and the sun set a few hours later in the Vatra than it did here. Each night, Petra waited to close her eyes. She waited until the trembling sensation of Neel wandering at the outskirts of her mind faded. There was a physical kind of silence. It stretched, and Petra knew that Neel was asleep. Only then would she let herself relax and fall into a fitful sleep of her own.

Yet the days were long and exhausting, and one night an aching weariness consumed her. She fell asleep next to Tomik even before he closed his eyes.

She dreamed a beach. The pinkish sand was hot under her skin, and as she lay there, green waves foamed at her toes. The sun had set, but a violet light lingered in the air. Petra smelled the brine of the sea, and something else, too: sandalwood soap. She recognized it, and didn't realize until she caught its scent how much she had missed it.

She sat up and turned, and there was Neel.

"Hello," she whispered.

She expected him to be angry. They had yelled at each other before, voices full of fury. This wouldn't be the first time, and she knew that she deserved whatever he might say.

But he was silent, and his eyes were narrow with hurt.

Petra stood. Her feet sank and burned into the sand as she crossed the few steps between them. "Can you see me?"

The question startled him into speaking. "See you? Why in the name of the four tribes would I *see* you?"

"Oh." She understood. She remembered how, when John Dee had used their mental link to tap into her sleep, her dreams had painted themselves around the words he'd said. Neel must still be awake. He would be in his palace, in his black marble-tiled bedroom, perhaps, with the mahogany bed hung with blue silks and a cloud of tulle to keep the mosquitoes out. He could hear Petra's words, but that was it.

Neel's gaze shifted to stare at the sea, and the Jewel of the Kalderash glinted on his ear. "Oh," he mimicked her tone. "That's all you got to say to me, after more than a week of stark nothing. *Oh.*"

His voice pierced her. Petra did something then that she never would have dared do if awake. She rested her palm on his cheek and turned his face to look into hers. His eyes were golden in the dim light. "I'm sorry," she said.

She knew he wouldn't be able to feel her fingers against his skin. This was *her* dream, not Neel's.

"Don't do that," he said, and she snatched her hand away. But he went on: "Don't hide away from me like that."

"I didn't mean to. All right"—she spoke over his angry sputter—"I did. But . . . there's . . . there's a blackness inside me, Neel. Like I swallowed the blood of a Gristleki. Sometimes, it bubbles. It fountains up. It's so hard to ignore it. I had to seal myself shut. If I let you inside, I didn't know what might slip out."

His face softened. He said, "Tell me."

So she did.

Neel laughed when she described the rowboat slinging down the mountainside, and she realized it *was* funny, a little, now that they had survived. He fell silent when she told him about the Gristleki attack, and grew grim at the thought of Astrophil picking his way from corpse to corpse, searching for evidence that Petra had killed her own father.

"But you didn't," he said. "You're safe."

"For now."

"And right now you're sleeping."

"Yes."

"With Tomik, tucked in the snow. Snug as cats."

She felt awkward. "I guess."

"Well, good."

"Yes," she said. "Good."

"I, uh, ought to say something." He shuffled a bare foot in the sand. "All this truth-telling you're doing makes a fellow feel sort of small. 'Cause I've been hiding from you, too, Pet, in a way."

She waited, and wouldn't let herself guess what he would say. Her heart rattled within her.

He said, "That last night on the island, before I snuck in your room and you forged the link, someone tried to snuff me."

She stared.

"I mean, someone tried to kill me. Pushed me off the palace wall."

Petra demanded an explanation, and when she got one, shook her head. "You never should have pulled that stunt with the globes. Giving them to Tomik, announcing they'd be destroyed. You made people mad."

"Only for a bit!"

"You toyed with them."

He made a dismissive noise.

"Anybody could have tried to assassinate you, Neel."

"Assassinate." He tugged thoughtfully at the hem of his white tunic. The cloth was far too simple for a king, but Petra didn't want to see him as one.

"That's the word you use when you murder royalty," she said. "This is political."

He rubbed a hand through his longish black hair and sighed. "Personal, too, maybe."

"You have to figure out who pushed you. If you don't, you won't be safe."

"It's a Maraki, I bet." Neel's voice was glum. "They were itching to get the crown."

"I don't know. They'll get it in less than two years, anyway. That's not so long to wait."

"Yeah, but it's a dicey time for the Roma. Some of us want to stop being so secret in our ways. To step forward, declare our kingdom, and play that lousy chess game of international politics. But plenty of Roma want things the way they've always been. The Maraki do, most of 'em. And the Kalderash, too. Queen Iona made that clear to me. Maybe for some Roma, less than two years is too long."

"If that's the reason someone tried to kill you, it can't be a Maraki, then. Not if they and the Kalderash want the same things. After all, you're Kalderash now, and . . ." She trailed off when she saw something bitter twitch across Neel's face.

"Nope," he said. "Not me. I'm Lovari, through and through. The trickster tribe."

Petra bit her lip. She should have known better than to say something that would rub right into Neel's fresh wound. Hesitantly she asked, "Do you have any ideas about who might have done this? Some clue?"

He described the clear, sparkling bead he'd found on the palace wall. "Could have been from a necklace, hung 'round a girl mad with love of me."

"It could have fallen off a man's clothes," Petra said. "Roma men wear fancy outfits. Flashy colors. Beaded shirts and shoes, too."

"I like my theory better."

"The theory where you nearly got murdered by someone in love with you."

"Sure. Makes me seem dashing, don't you think?"

She rolled her eyes.

"You know," he said, "I think I can hear you rolling your eyes."

She laughed, and it felt foreign—but good—in her throat. "No, you can't."

Neel didn't move, but seemed suddenly closer. An emerald wave brushed over their bare feet. The sky was darker now. "It's hard," he said, "to just hear your voice. Wish I could see you."

Petra hadn't meant to say it, yet she did: "I can see you." She hastened to add, "But it's not real."

"You can? How? What d'you mean, 'not real'?"

"It's because I'm asleep," Petra said. "My mind is . . . painting a picture to match your words. I'm dreaming while we speak." Neel's expression was fascinated, like it might have really been. But now a gold hoop, not a sapphire, gleamed in his ear. "That's why it's not real. You can't trust dreams."

Neel grinned. "How do I look, then? Handsome as sin, I'm sure."

Petra saw the familiar planes of his face, the little scar nicked across his cheek. Nail-bitten fingers. Bright eyes. "You look like you," she said.

"What else do you see?"

"A beach. Stars. Constellations that don't exist."

"Describe it to me. Tell me everything you see."

"Why?"

"So I can dream, too, next time, and be there with you."

Petra said nothing.

Defensively, Neel asked, "Something wrong with that?"

"It wouldn't work. Even if we were both asleep, right now, we wouldn't see the same things. I would dream my dream, and you would dream yours."

"Tell me anyway."

Darkness fell swiftly as Petra described the beach that she could, in fact, no longer see. Neel shifted into a slightly lighter shade than night, then disappeared into the black. Yet Petra could sense that he was still listening, so she told him about the pink sand and the shaggy bark of the palm trees. Her mind began to feel fuzzy, so she sat down.

She felt Neel settle onto the sand next to her. She turned to him.

And opened her eyes. Dawn was shining through the shell of snow that cocooned Petra and Tomik. Their cave was transformed into a halo of light.

Petra's hand held Tomik's, her fingers intertwined with his in a way that felt new, and strange.

And he was wide awake.

Petra pulled her hand away.

Tomik looked down at her and smiled.

17

Astrophil's Decision

PETRA SCRAMBLED out of the cave. When she emerged, the light hurt her eyes, and somehow her heart, too.

She heard Tomik's boots scraping against the inside of the cave but kept her back turned. She didn't want to see him push his way out. She couldn't bear the thought of looking him in the face. *I didn't mean it*, she wanted to say.

What *had* she meant, then?

Petra's dream had been so vivid. She had felt Neel's hand in the darkness—*his*, with its rough palm and the watery sensation of his ghost fingers spilling past the tips of his real ones, reaching to slip down her arm and across her wrist as they sat on the beach. And she had reached back.

Heavy boots crushed the snow behind her. Tomik. "Petra—"

"Good morning." Astrophil dropped from a tree branch onto Petra's head. "I trust everyone slept well?"

Tomik chuckled, and Petra wheeled at the sound and faced him. "No," she said. "I didn't."

"If you say so," Tomik replied, but the confident grin didn't leave his face.

She should tell him the truth.

Petra flushed. How could she tell him the truth?

What *was* the truth? It had been a dream. Petra had seen what she'd wanted to see. What she hadn't even known she wanted. It was a revelation, but one that made her heart feel stupid and sore. It had nothing to do with what would happen if Neel were there, right now.

It had nothing to do with the terror that might be stalking them.

She looked at Tomik, and saw him misinterpret her blush—misinterpret everything.

Petra briefly closed her eyes. When she opened them, she meant to say something to Tomik—what, she wasn't quite sure—but then she squinted against the light. Something was different. It hadn't been so sunlit before, in the forest. They had always been shadowed under a canopy of fir trees. Now Petra could see patches of blue sky.

The forest was thinning. They hadn't noticed it in the darkness last night, but the trees here were fewer and not so thickly clustered together.

Then Petra saw it: a tree stump. Where there were tree stumps, there were people.

"Give me the map," she told Tomik, and he handed it over. She unfolded it. "We're close to Krumlov." Her voice was bright with hope.

"Not that close," said Tomik.

"We can make it by nightfall, if we push the pace."

"A *breakneck* pace. A fool's pace. We'd have to practically run."

"Let's get moving, then."

"We can make it to Krumlov Castle tomorrow, easily. What's the harm in spending one more night in the forest?"

One more night of not knowing how she would find Fiala Broshek and transform her father back into a human. One more night of sleeping next to Tomik.

"No," she said. "We reach Krumlov by nightfall."

Tomik crossed his arms and studied her. "Let's put it to a vote. There are three of us, after all. Right, Astrophil?"

After the briefest of pauses, the spider said. "Yes."

"Then Astro's vote will break the tie."

"Wait a minute," said Petra.

"You wouldn't deny Astro his say in the matter, would you, Petra?"

"No, but—"

"Then I'm sure that we'll come to a fair, sensible, and *safe* solution." There was that confident smile again.

Astrophil trickled down Petra's hair and crept onto her ear. He held on loosely. There was an odd delicacy in his grip that reminded Petra of something, though she couldn't decide what. *Astrophil*, she thought to him silently. *I—*

"It would be wise to reach the castle as soon as possible," the spider said in a quiet voice.

Tomik's smile vanished.

Thank you, Astrophil, Petra told the spider.

"Let us go," he said, and fell asleep.

The frustration was plain on Tomik's face. Petra turned from it and strode quickly over the snow.

She thought she knew what Tomik would say if he dared, because underneath his frustration she sensed confusion, but also a barely suppressed joy. *Don't be embarrassed,* he wanted to tell her.

I'm not, she wanted to reply.

Yet she was. Petra was ashamed to be thinking what she was thinking when her father was a monster. The only thing she should want was for him to be returned to her, and for her and her friends to be safe. She should focus on what mattered.

It had been only a dream.

She would not think of it.

She would not.

IT WAS LATE AFTERNOON, and the trees were casting long spears of shadow across the snow, when Petra felt a light pressure on that mental stitch that linked her to Neel. *You've gotta help me, Pet,* he said.

What's wrong? she answered, alarmed.

I am SO BORED.

She couldn't help it. She laughed. Tomik gave her a quizzical sidelong look, which made her bite back her smile and shrug. Astrophil slumbered on.

Poor you, she told Neel. *How many tears should I shed for your pitiful fate?*

A whole ocean's worth. I'm learning how to read.

I thought you didn't believe in that. You said that anything written was dead. That books box stories up, and leave them no room to breathe.

Yeah, but a fellow could get buried in the papers that get shoved under a king's nose. He sighed. *I guess I ought to know what they say. If someone thought it'd be a lark to kill me, people here probably wouldn't think twice about telling me a little old lie.*

You have advisers. Arun, Gita, Karim—

It'd be too easy for someone to read one thing, and tell me another.

Talking with Neel—now, after last night—was going more smoothly than Petra had imagined. As long as she pretended that everything was normal, it was. *Who's teaching you?* she asked.

Nadia.

Petra remembered the Maraki girl who was a couple of years older than them, and had black, flashing eyes. *Oh.*

*She's pretty good at it. And she's honest as a tiger with a hunk of bloody meat. Nadia will do exactly what she wants. Say what she wants. And heaven help you if you disagree. So I knew that if I asked her to teach me and keep it a secret, and she thought that was a sea-weedy shipwreck of an idea, she'd tell me to go chop off my toes and juggle 'em. But—*he sounded amazed—*she agreed.* He groaned. *Wish she hadn't. My head HURTS. And she keeps shooting me these*

*evil looks, like she knows I'm dazing off instead of studying—what is
this thing, anyway? A chart of the price of coir over the last ten years?*
Petra imagined Neel hiding his face in his hands. *She hates me.*

She's there with you? Right now? Petra tripped over a fallen
branch. She wobbled, then caught her balance.

"I told you," Tomik said under his breath. "We have to slow our
pace. One of us is going to break a leg."

Petra glared and walked faster.

Yeah, Neel was saying. *We're in the library.*

*I didn't even know the palace had a library. I mean, most Roma
don't believe in reading.*

*Sure, but I'm starting to get the idea that being king means doing
and having lots of things you don't believe in.* Neel paused. *Wish I was
there with you. Astro could teach me how to read. This was his blasted
idea, anyway. How'd he learn?*

He taught himself.

*Huh. Weird to think that something that looks like a mash-up of
tiny forks and knives could such be a genius. How's Astro doing?*

Petra became conscious of the faint whirring of Astrophil's inter-
nal gears. They hummed against her ear. She thought about Neel's
question, and realized that Astrophil had been unusually quiet lately.
Of course, he spent most of the day sleeping, to make up for nights
keeping watch. Still . . .

A fear that Petra had shoved deep down inside her floated to the
surface of her mind.

How much brassica oil was pumping through Astrophil's tiny
body? How long, really, could it last?

Was Astrophil just tired during the day, or was he winding down?

OW! Neel howled. *Nadia slapped me! I can't believe she slapped
me! I'm the king! Oh, you're going to regret that, you are, you—*

Petra closed her mind like a fist around Neel's voice. She couldn't
listen to it. Not now. She felt Astrophil clinging to her ear and realized

what his light touch had reminded her of: the day the spider had fallen asleep for the first time. They had been in Prague, and the spider's hold on her ear slackened. Then he had fallen.

Astrophil's grip wasn't delicate. It was feeble.

Petra stopped in her tracks and tugged off her mittens. Tomik, surprised, stopped too, and watched as Petra gently lifted the spider from her ear and cradled him in her palm.

"Astrophil?" Petra touched a tin leg. *Astrophil? Wake up!*

The spider slept.

He had never slept like this.

"What's wrong?" Tomik asked.

"He—he—" Petra stuttered in panic. "He hasn't eaten in almost two weeks."

"He said he was fine. That he could run on very little."

Petra stared at Tomik. "Maybe . . . he was being brave. He was trying to be strong and make it to Krumlov. But he knows we're close now, close to safety. I think he's given up." Petra's voice dropped to a whisper. "I think he's dying."

Tomik reached for Petra's free hand and pulled her into a run. "Hurry," he said.

IT WAS TWILIGHT when they pushed their way out of the forest. The pale moon loomed low over a hilltop castle.

Krumlov. They had made it.

But Tomik and Petra didn't slow their pace. Not when they floundered up the hill, slipping on its light coat of snow. Not when night fell, and they saw faraway torches blaze near the castle's entrance. Not when those fires grew bigger in their sight, their feet crunched over the small rocks strewn across the courtyard, and they saw that one of the castle towers was a black ruin, and the walls were splashed in a crazy quilt of color.

Not until Petra felt something change in the palm of her hand.

She halted. Castle guards were shouting at them, but she couldn't hear them. She couldn't hear anything at all. Petra stared at the tin spider crumpled in her hand and remembered the mechanical sound she had always heard, so steady, like her own breath or heartbeat. She couldn't hear it now.

Astrophil's gears had stopped.

18

The *Tarantella*

——◆——

IRIS!" Petra screamed when the guards seized her and Tomik. "Iris!"

"What's this?" As one guard held her, another forced back the fingers Petra had curled protectively over Astrophil. He peered at the spider with light eyes. "Give that here."

Petra let her mind-magic crackle through her, and sensed that the ribs of the light-eyed guard were sore, newly healed from a brawl last month. The other, leaner guard still had his hands locked on her upper arms. Petra leaned back into his grip and hitched up her legs to smash her feet into the light-eyed man's torso. He dropped to the stones, wheezing for breath.

The guard holding Petra slackened his grip in surprise. She wrenched free. She ran for the entrance, shouting Iris's name, leaving Tomik behind.

"Silence!" someone bellowed.

In the shadow of the castle entrance, beyond the gate of its portcullis, was a short, elderly woman. Her hands were planted on her hips. "You caterwauling ninny! I am Irenka Grisetta December, Sixth Countess of Krumlov, and I'm not about to let a ragamuffin nobody take the liberty to call me *Iris*. Who are you? I'll 'Iris' *you*, young lady, you upstart mushroom, you—"

"Iris." Petra grabbed the iron gate. She heard the scatter of stones behind her as the guards rushed toward her back. "Please let me in."

The torchlight glowed on Petra's face. Iris paused, peered at Petra over the tops of her spectacles, and sucked in her breath. "*You,*" Iris hissed.

The guards descended on Petra and dragged her back from the portcullis. Petra felt like they were dragging her away from all hope.

Her hand was already reaching for the hilt of her invisible sword when Iris said, "Raise the gate!"

The gate rattled up, and Iris stormed into the courtyard. "Oh, let them go!" she told the guards.

The men didn't loosen their grasp on Tomik and Petra, but looked uncertainly at the white-haired woman.

"Isn't that sweet," Iris sneered at the guards. "Are you worried for your poor old mistress? Don't be fools! They couldn't possibly hurt *me.*" She extended a thin, papery hand, palm up. She smiled wickedly, as if her hand itself was a weapon.

The men set Tomik and Petra free.

"Well well well." Iris tapped a foot against the stones. "I'd say some explanations are in order." She shoved her heavy spectacles up the bridge of her nose and glared at Petra.

"I need your laboratory," Petra said. "You must have one here."

"*Need,* eh? Everyone needs something. I need a new hat, since mine blistered off my head a few minutes ago. I need to stop having acid attacks, because every time something upsetting happens, like *you* screaming for me at the top of your lungs, my skin leaks acid and *ruins* things."

"You don't seem acidic now," Tomik said.

"Shut up! I *liked* that hat!"

"Iris," Petra said. "Your laboratory—"

"Oh, no. Do you honestly think I'm letting you inside? I'll have your story first, you little troublemaker. What are you doing here?

You look like you've been tramping around the wilderness. On a *diet*. Your face is positively skinny! And who is this handsome—and *grimy*—young man?

"There's no time to tell stories!" said Petra, and ran into the castle. She heard Iris shout, "I can run, too, you know! Oh, yes I can! I may be old, but I'm no invalid!"

Petra barreled down the hallway, with Iris calling her names and Tomik yelling that he was right behind her. She ran without knowing where she was going, but as her feet pounded against the uneven marble tiles, Petra noticed that parts of the stone floor were burned away, and that the walls were splashed with color. Petra imagined Iris flinging pots of dye at the walls, and destroying the floor under her feet when frustration made her skin flare with acid. Dye was everywhere.

But, Petra realized, there would be *more* closer to a laboratory. That's where the heart of Iris's experimentation on color would take place. That's where Petra would find the greatest scenes of disaster.

So Petra ran after the color. An ugly purple smeared across a windowpane. Chartreuse paint oozing down a mirror. Glittering black handprints on a wall.

Petra saw a ruined archway and ducked under it, racing through a dusty ballroom whose wooden floor was caked with multicolored layers of paint.

Then she noticed what seemed to be an alcove, shrouded by a black velvet curtain. Petra had seen one just like it before, almost two years ago in the prince's castle. Iris used curtains to protect her most light-sensitive experiments.

Petra tore aside the curtain.

The alcove wasn't an alcove, but an enormous room latticed with shelves, and on those shelves were hundreds of glass and ceramic bottles filled with snakeskin and powders and things Petra couldn't even begin to name.

"Get out!" Iris shoved past Petra, and Tomik shoved past Iris. A distant clatter and jangle of metal told Petra that the armored guards weren't far behind.

"Where's your brassica oil?" Clutching Astrophil with one hand, Petra riffled through bottles with the other. "I know you have some. You need it for really hot fires."

The first guards burst into the laboratory, gasping for breath.

"*Get out!*" Iris screamed at them. She advanced toward one of the guards, and when she held out her hands as if to shove him, a look of terror crossed his face and he turned and ran. The other men followed suit.

Iris cackled.

"Here!" Tomik shoved a clear glass bottle filled with green liquid into Petra's hands.

"Just a moment!" Iris said. "Exactly *what* do you think you're doing with my only supply of *very expensive* brassica oil? You listen here, Petra Kronos—"

Petra ignored her. She gently set Astrophil on a worktable littered with burners and bowls.

"What is *that*?" said Iris.

Petra uncorked the bottle.

"That looks like a spider," said Iris. "I don't like spiders."

Petra pried open Astrophil's mouth with one ragged fingernail and tipped the bottle carefully, so that a green drop hung and then fell.

Petra's aim was perfect. The oily drop splashed into Astrophil's open mouth. But then it pooled and dribbled down the spider's face as if his throat was blocked, perhaps by a stuck gear.

Petra's brain seemed to cramp and shake and bleed out any rational thoughts except a clear certainty that if her father were here, he would be able to save Astrophil.

But her father wasn't here. There was only her.

She would have to do.

Petra yanked open one of the worktable drawers and rummaged through it until she found a narrow metal file and a long, thin pipe she recognized from her days working as Iris's assistant in Salamander Castle. "It's an aspirator," Iris had told her when Petra had first seen the pipe. "I use it to aerate certain dyes."

That means she uses it to blow air into the dye, Astrophil had silently explained.

I know! Petra had told him, but she had lied. Tears welled in Petra's eyes at the thought that he might never explain something to her again. A tear fell into Astrophil's mouth. Like the oil, it ran right back out.

Petra rubbed her eyes clear. Then she inserted the file in the spider's mouth and probed.

It was like picking a lock, which Neel had taught her how to do during the long months at sea. Petra delicately pushed against the gears in Astrophil's throat, looking for one with a springy tension. She couldn't see down into the tiny opening of Astrophil's mouth, so she would have to feel for the right gear.

She found it. The tip of her file touched a gear that moved in place. With a quick, nervous breath, Petra jabbed at it. It sank, pushed back, and released.

Astrophil did not move.

But his throat was clear. This time, when Petra trickled oil into Astrophil's mouth, it stayed inside, dripping down, mingling with a trace of Petra's tear.

Astrophil still did not move.

Petra set the pipe in his mouth and blew. She imagined the oil forcing its way through a network of pin-thin pipes and metal joints the size of poppy seeds. Yet even when Petra was sure that Astrophil's body was flush with oil and she set the pipe aside, the spider lay motionless on the table, legs limp.

"It's not working," Tomik said in a low voice.

Iris looked at him, then at Petra. "What is all this fuss about?" she said. "It's a machine. A peculiar one, I'll give you that, but if it won't start, toss it out and get a new one."

Petra stared at Iris, stunned at her suggestion, though Iris had no way of knowing what and who Astrophil was, since he had hidden in Petra's hair the entire time she worked as Iris's assistant.

"Well, really, Petra." Iris shrugged. "If it doesn't work, what can you do?"

Petra's gaze dropped to the spider, and she rested one finger on his cool, silvery head. *That is not my "head,"* she remembered him saying crossly. *Spiders do not have "heads." That is my cephalothorax.*

It seemed to Petra that Astrophil's silence was expectant. That he was waiting, like when he would wait for her to figure something out on her own. She considered making her Choice, as the Metis had taught her. She could increase her magic over metal.

But the Metis had warned that the sudden shock of power would confuse her. She might not even remember her own name, or who Astrophil was.

Then what could Petra do?

"I will *make* him work," she said.

Petra's own, familiar brand of magic pulsed through her fingertip. Her skin tingled as she imagined Astrophil's central mechanism, a heart of cogs and gears. *Start,* she commanded the metal parts. *Spin.*

Astrophil's body made a tiny wheeze, then a crank, then a buzz. His eight legs sprang straight. He popped up in the air, fell down flat on his abdomen, and zigzagged across the table, his legs wild. "Stop!" he shouted at his legs. "Cease! Desist! Please?"

"Astrophil!" Petra laughed.

"I see no humor in this situation!" The spider careened off the table and crashed onto the floor.

"Astro? Are you all right?" She scooped him up.

"Of course I am all right." His legs still waved crazily, but he didn't move from Petra's palm. "Why would you think otherwise?"

"Um, you died," Tomik pointed out.

"Surely not."

A smile quirked at the corner of Iris's mouth. "And then you seemed to have some sort of seizure," she added.

"Seizure? Just now? Oh, no. I was dancing. In fact, that dance is called the *tarantella*, a lovely Italian step inspired by a cousin of mine, the tarantula. Of course, the tarantula is from the rather unattractive side of the spider family. It is so *hairy*. But—"

"You really are all right." Petra raised her hand so that she and the spider could see eye to eye. Astrophil's legs jerked a few more times, then calmed.

"I feel very well rested," he said. "And full. Mmmm." He smacked his tiny mouth. "I have clearly been drinking very high quality brassica oil. A fine vintage. Delicious. Although . . . there is a salty aftertaste. How strange."

"Very." Petra smiled.

Astrophil considered her face, then stretched out one leg to brush a tear from her lashes. "Perhaps it is not so strange after all," he said.

19

The Peasants' Darling

———◆———

THEY MET AGAIN in Iris's sitting room, after Petra had taken a bath in a sunken marble tub so large she could swim in it. It had three golden faucets, each topped with the curved shape of a sleeping ermine, the symbol of the Krumlov family. Petra was less amazed by this, however, than by what the faucets could *do*. Two of them spouted hot and cold water, and the third gushed bubbles. Then Petra spotted a fourth faucet that didn't point into the bath, but curved over the marble edge of the pool, right above a porcelain cup that rested on the stone floor of the bathing room. Petra fiddled with the faucet, and hot chocolate poured into the cup. She swam in the bath's rainbow froth. Then she floated, drinking the rich, melty brown liquid in her cup. After days of weasel meat, the hot chocolate was a delight.

When Petra entered the sitting room, wearing a velvet nightgown with Astrophil clinging to the midnight purple of its fabric, she saw Tomik seated at a table before a fire. His hair was clean and damp, and he was wolfing down roasted chicken, buttery vegetables dusted with spices, and fizzy cider.

"And bread!" Petra gasped. "And apples!" She snatched a fork to help Tomik demolish the food.

"Hello to you, too," Iris said dryly from her plush chair. It was drawn up to a desk on which lay a sheet of paper half-filled with swirly lines of cursive writing. Iris set her quill into its inkpot, drew a clean page to cover the written one, and pushed her chair back to face the three of them.

"Fohrry. Umbello, Girish," Petra said, her mouth full.

Iris scowled at her, then focused on Astrophil, who was busy scolding Petra in tones of dismay. "You are using the wrong fork," he moaned. "Would you *please* remember your table manners?"

"You." Iris pointed at him. "Tell me what you're doing here, and what has happened since I last saw Petra blasting and flooding her way out of Salamander Castle."

It was a long story that began with Petra's first encounter with the Gray Men, and how John Dee had saved her only to imprison her in his London house. Bargaining for her freedom in exchange for solving a murder, Petra had gotten tangled up in English politics that led to her facing Prince Rodolfo in a deadly, destructive encounter.

"None of that explains why you are *here*, in my home," Iris said.

Astrophil searched for the most diplomatic way to phrase his next words. "Countess, your generosity toward us already has been deeply moving," he began. "And we honor you for it. Yet—"

"Oh, stuff it. Do you think I'm an idiot? I know exactly what you want."

"Really?" said Petra. Astrophil hadn't even explained yet what had happened to her father. "How?"

"Well, maybe I don't know exactly what made you turn up on my doorstep in such a hysterical, bossy manner, but one thing is clear: you want my help." Iris folded her arms, settled back in her chair, and propped her slippered feet on a lurid green footstool. "And whatever you want my help *for*, it'll be directly in defiance of our Bohemian prince. You're an outlaw, Petra, do you know that? If I turned you over to the authorities, I'd receive a very nice reward. Of course, I don't really need that. I am rich enough. But delivering you to the prince *would* put me back in his good graces."

"You're not in his good graces?" said Petra. "What did you do?"

"Do? I helped *you*, that's what I did. I helped you and that Gypsy escape from Salamander Castle by the skin of your pretty white teeth."

"He knows? How did he find out?"

"Oh, Rodolfo doesn't know anything for sure. He certainly suspects me, though. The Krumlov family is too powerful for him to accuse me without proof, but I've been banished from court. All because of you—Petra Kronos, the peasants' darling."

"But you didn't *like* being at court," Petra said.

The grouchiness of Iris's expression didn't change. However, one brow arched above the rim of her spectacles. "Oh?"

"You hated it. People were always pestering you for hair dye. It was a waste of your talent."

Iris showed the faintest hint of a smirk.

"And you didn't like what was going on in some of the prince's other laboratories," Petra continued. "What he was having done to people. You thought it was wrong. And it is." Her voice dropped to a whisper. "It *is* wrong."

"Be that as it may, what am I to do about it?"

"Help us."

"You see? I am supposed to help you. *Again.* Help you do *what*, precisely?" Iris's sour expression returned. "Kill the prince, I suppose."

The words were like a blow. "No." Petra tried to block the memory of black blood seeping into snow. "Not that. I don't want to kill anyone."

"Then what *do* you want?"

"To talk to Fiala Broshek," Petra said, and explained her hope that the woman who had turned her father into a monster would have a way to change him back.

As Iris listened, the fire lowered and crackled, casting a garnet-colored glow about the room. Iris leaned forward and propped her pointy chin on one small fist. Finally, she said, "Fiala Broshek has left the court as well. She's taken up a post as a professor of the Academy. Prince Rodolfo hopes that she will make some necessary changes to the Hapsburg Empire's premier school for magic."

"The Academy?" Tomik's eyes went wide. "So that's where we'll have to go, right, Petra? I can't believe it. I can't believe I'll get to see the Academy." Then his face fell. "But we'd never get through the door. They'd never let us in."

"They will," said Iris, "if you are students there."

Petra and Tomik stared.

"Oh, yes," said Astrophil. "A splendid idea!"

"No, it isn't," Petra said. "We can't be students at the *Academy*. The Academy is for rich people. For aristocrats and the gentry and people with high connections. Not *villagers*. Besides, we'd have to take a magical exam, and—"

"What," said Iris. "Don't you think you'd pass?"

Petra shut her mouth.

"As for connections," Iris continued, "I believe I could pull a few strings."

Petra couldn't look at Tomik, his face was so vivid with hope.

"Ahem," said Astrophil. "As much as I admire your proposal, Countess, I must point out a flaw. It sorrows me to say it. I was so overcome with rapture at the thought that Petra might actually sit at an Academy desk, might learn from the wise words of an Academy professor—"

Petra rolled her eyes.

"—that the idea's flaw did not even occur to me. Yet it is obvious. Petra, as you say, is an outlaw. Prince Rodolfo must have spread word that she is to be arrested on sight, and she has very unique features. I do not know if the prince is searching for Tomik as well, but Tomik has been seen by him. The prince, and several of his guards, know exactly what Petra and Tomik look like."

"Leave the disguises to me," said Iris.

Astrophil looked as if he might weep for joy. He clapped six legs in a flurry of fierce applause. "Hurray!"

"Thank you, Iris," said Petra. "But . . . why are you helping us?" It wasn't until this moment that Petra realized that she had never really trusted that Iris *would* help them, or that she would even be here, in her castle. Petra had simply clung to that hope, since some plan was better than none. And now, it seemed, her plan had worked.

"Because what you said is true," Iris answered. "What Fiala Broshek is doing—what the *prince* is doing—is wrong. Because the number of Gristleki is growing, and there have been rumors of strange deaths all over Bohemia. Because, a little more than two weeks ago, on the night of the day you say you entered the Novohrad Mountains, one of the prince's older brothers died."

"He did? But that means—"

"That only one man—the prince's remaining brother, Frederic— stands in the way of Prince Rodolfo inheriting the empire. The emperor chooses who will claim his crown, but if Emperor Karl has only two sons, instead of three, the choice narrows."

"How, precisely, did Prince Maximilian die?" Astrophil asked.

"Quietly," said Iris. "In his sleep. There was no obvious sign of any foul play. As a countess, I have access to information that few do, and I can tell you that the only trace of anything remotely odd was a tiny welt the size of a mosquito bite on Prince Maximilian's wrist."

"A mosquito bite?" said Tomik. "In winter?"

"Indeed," said Iris. "The death's shady, I'd say. But very clean, if it's an assassination. Most people think that Maximilian just caught some strange disease. *I* think Rodolfo's tired of waiting for the emperor's crown, and heaven help us if he gets it." Iris pulled the spectacles from her face and rubbed at her eyes. Her mouselike features were small and tired in the firelight.

"Petra," Iris continued, "if you learn how to transform your father back into a human, you won't only be helping him. You could help other Gristleki. You could help your country." She sighed. "That is why I'm helping you." She shoved her spectacles back on, glanced at Tomik and Petra's empty plates, and said, "Now, go. Go to bed, the three of you."

Petra had a sudden, dizzingly tempting vision of a feather bed and the privacy of her own room.

She and Tomik were making their way toward the door, with Astrophil perched on her head, when Iris said, "Also . . . I always liked you, Petra."

Petra turned.

Iris wasn't looking at her, but at her desk, and at the blank sheet of paper covering the written one. "You've got some feist in you, girl, and hunger. I was hungry once, too. For different things, but, oh, what of that?"

Petra considered this. "The prince is hungry, too."

Iris nodded, and was quiet.

"Iris," said Tomik, "what did you mean, when you called Petra the 'peasants' darling'?"

She grinned. "You noticed. Interesting, eh? It seems that Petra has become a bit of a legend. The poorer folk of Bohemia have been under Rodolfo's thumb for a long time, and they're angry. Powerless, but angry. Somehow people have caught wind of some of Petra's adventures, and have made a few up, too. She's become a hero. A regular little Robin Hood." Iris wagged a finger at Petra. "Don't let that go to your head. It only makes the prince hate you more."

Tomik was staring at Petra. She shifted, uncomfortable.

"Well, what are you still doing here?" Iris snapped. "Lollygaggers! I told you to get out. Now, shoo!"

After the door had shut behind them, Iris stood and crossed to the dying fire to stab at it with a poker, trying to rouse a bigger flame.

It shot several sparks, then crumpled into chunks of charred wood. The fire was out.

"Bother!" Iris snatched a candle off the mantel, lit it, and returned to sit at her table. She rattled her quill in the inkpot and uncovered her half-finished letter. She began to write, and the room was filled with the scratching of pen on parchment.

> *I trust you will approve of my decision to send Petra and Tomik to the Academy. I have been careful. I will order them not to contact their family members in Bohemia, for fear of discovery. I will give them the address of my nephew and niece, and specify that any communication with me be sent through them. As for your part, I suggest you look into the existence of the Vatra. It seems that Gypsies have more to them than meets the eye, and that Neel of the Lovari has rather moved up in the world. A king! Who would believe it?*
>
> *Petra's opinion of you*

Iris paused—

> *is uncertain. Frankly, I think she doesn't know what to make of you. One thing is clear: she does not trust you. Therefore, I thought it best to say nothing of our friendship.*
>
> *Or shall I call it what it is: a partnership based on mutual interests? Don't forget who stands next in line to the Bohemian throne.*
>
> *—Irenka Grisetta December, Sixth Countess of Krumlov*
> *P.S. You should have told me about the spider! I didn't even know he existed. How embarrassing!*

Iris dusted sand on the letter to dry the ink. Then she folded it, sealed it with a wax stamp, and addressed it to John Dee.

20

Tea

S TOP GIVING ME this stale old stuff." Neel shoved a sheaf of papers at Nadia.

She shoved it right back across the marble-topped table. "You haven't even read it."

"You bet I have. It's about coir. *Again.* You've been forcing me to read this muck for weeks. I hate to break your heart, dear Nadia, but I don't care about coir."

"You should."

"It's coconut hair. Why in the name of the four tribes should I care about *coconut hair?*"

"Because," she said through her teeth, "it's used to make rope. Rope is important."

"Oh, *right.*" Neel smacked the heel of his hand against his forehead. His eyes went wide, sarcastic, and his voice turned mockingly sweet. "How could I forget? Rope! Rope's got magic in it, right, magic that'll turn me into a king who gives everyone the glow, they're so happy I'm theirs."

"Being a king is not about being liked."

"Can't argue with you. After all, you're the expert on being unpopular."

"I give up!" Nadia threw her hands in the air. "I'm not teaching you anything, anymore. You have been an insufferable snarl ever since your *gadje* friends left. You are so *obvious*. It's obvious you wanted nothing more than to tear after them and win their hearts a thousand times over, and be the prankster, the adventurer, the wink-quick Lovari getting in and out of scrapes. You're not that person anymore, Neel." She stood and glared down at him. "You never will be again."

Neel opened his mouth, but nothing came out as Nadia stormed from the library.

It took several seconds for Neel to realize that for the first time, Nadia's sharp tongue had actually cut him.

"Teatime, Your Majesty." Karim, Neel's adviser in manners, cracked open the library door to see Neel scowling at papers scattered in front of him.

"Not for me. I'm playing hooky."

"You cannot miss *tea*. How many times need I tell you that teatime is absolutely crucial for Roma royalty?"

Neel couldn't tear his eyes from a chart listing coir profits from last year. "Why?"

"Why?" Karim was flustered.

"You've never told me why you're always nagging me to lounge around on a pile of perfumed pillows and drink tea—when I like coffee, Karim, *coffee*—and listen to a bunch of witless courtiers natter away about nothing, 'cause nothing is all they know, since all they do is hang around the Vatran court. Tell me *why* I have to go to tea."

Karim gave Neel a look that questioned his intelligence. "To find out what your people want, of course."

"What they want," Neel repeated slowly. He thought of the clear glass bead, and the fact that someone in this palace wanted him dead. He stood. "Fine. I'll go. But send a message to my ma first. Ask her to come, too."

NEEL SAT ON A LARGE CUSHION stuffed with sweet dried seagrass. He didn't sprawl across the pillows, although he would have liked to. He sat carefully, his folded legs neatly tucked beneath a low lemonwood table with inlaid patterns of mother-of-pearl. On the table rested a copper teapot warmed to the perfect temperature. He poured himself a cup and didn't even make a face as he took a cautious sip. He stared at the courtiers arranged around the pool in brightly dressed clusters of color, and gazed at the pool itself. It looked temptingly deep and cool. Neel became conscious of the heat of the tearoom. He glanced away from the pool and took another sip.

"Mingle," Karim had hissed in his ear before crossing the room to talk with Arun. Both Karim and Neel's chief adviser had thought it best to keep their distance from the king in public. "No one needs reminding that you are in dire need of better manners," Arun had said. "And it will not improve your image if your people think that I am leading you around by the nose."

Mingle. Neel supposed that was fine advice—and, after all, he was here, drinking this vile, flowery tea, in order to get to know the court better. But—Neel took another sip, and let his dislike of the drink steady his nerves—it might be interesting to sit here, wait, and see who'd creep over to talk to him.

He didn't have to wait long. Treb glanced up from where he was playing a game of Vices with his brother. Tarn leaned across the table with its board of two large circles, a pawn in each center, and muttered something to Treb, who grinned, snatched his brother's pawn, and strode alongside the pool toward Neel, his boots crushing a few silk cushions along the way.

"I think you're supposed to wear slippers to tea," Neel told Treb when the captain reached him.

"And I think you couldn't care less what I wear." Treb sat across from Neel, blocking his view of the pool.

Neel sighed.

"Don't mind if I smoke here, do you?" Without waiting for an answer, Treb rapped his pipe against the table to knock out the old ashes. He thumbed a wad of tobacco into the pipe bowl and lit it.

"What do you want, Treb?"

Treb puffed out a cloud of smoke. "Who says I want anything, coz?"

"What does your *brother* want, then? Other than to never speak with me again."

"Oh, now, you can't blame him for that." Treb poured himself a cup of tea. "You took away that pretty toy of a throne from him."

"I won't give it back."

Treb slid his teacup toward Neel. "Then give me some sugar."

Neel didn't move. Treb shrugged and helped himself. "Give the Maraki something to sweeten our loss," said the captain. "Give Tarn, our leader, a reason to support you. Because the Maraki can play nice, or"—Treb smiled—"we can get in your way."

"And *now*, seeing as you've made your point, you might as well say what you want."

"Nothing. A small smidgeon of a thing. A patch of coconut trees. There's a coconut plantation on the other side of the mountain, and its ten-year lease is up. The Maraki would like to be its new lease-holders."

"Huh." Carelessly, Neel said, "Who's got the lease now?"

"The Ursari. They won't miss it, Neel. The Ursari raise and train animals. What could they possibly want with a bunch of coconuts?

They've hung on to that plantation just to spite us Maraki. Pure, petty spite, that's all it is."

Neel watched Treb wait to see if the young king would ask why the plantation was so important to the Maraki. Neel let a lazy look settle over his face. "I'll think about it."

"A quick answer's the best kind."

"If this is just a small smidgeon of a thing, you won't mind if I take time to think."

Treb stood. "Think fast."

Not a second after the captain strode back to his game, the red-slippered feet of Shaida, the Ursari tribe leader, whispered across the floor to meet Neel. She sat, and got straight to the heart of things.

The Ursari wanted to keep their lease of the coconut plantation.

Neel took pains to be polite, and was relieved when the entrance of his mother gave him an excuse to send the Ursari leader away with the promise that he would consider her tribe's request.

Damara looked out of place in the tearoom, even more so than Neel, who had put on every elegant article of clothing Karim had handed him, and had even allowed his manners instructor to smudge kohl around his eyes for the occasion. Neel's mother, however, always refused Neel's every effort to give her finery.

Damara took the place at the table vacated by the Ursari leader. "Thank you for inviting me."

Neel shifted uncomfortably. He had decided long ago, during that fall from the palace wall, that his mother wasn't to blame for the past, and that she'd done the best that she could by him. Why was it, then, that he couldn't bring himself to say so?

"I've missed you," she said.

Neel had sent her packages of dresses and bangles, yet ducked away from every opportunity to see her. He had had his guards send her away. And all because he couldn't bear to wear his heart on his sleeve.

"Ma," he said. "Will you help me?"

"Of course." She smiled, and Neel's throat tightened to see the happiness on her face. "What do you need?"

"Some advice." With an eye on the courtiers, to make certain they kept a respectful distance from his table, Neel told Damara about the coconut plantation. "I know why the Maraki want it," he said.

She raised one brow.

"Coir," Neel said. "The hair of a coconut is stripped away to make coir, which gets spun into rope. The *best* rope for seafaring. I sailed with the Maraki long enough to know that salt rots away most rope—except the kind made from coir. A ship needs yards and yards of rope for its rigging. If the hull and masts are a boat's skeleton, rope is its muscle. I've been reading charts on coir profits—"

Damara raised both brows.

"—and its price has been going no way but up in Europe. Whoever runs that coconut plantation could make oodles of money in trade. Not the Maraki, of course. They'd keep it all for themselves. But another tribe could sell that coir anywhere that'll accept Roma goods. The thing is . . . the Ursari *haven't* been selling it for much. I've seen the records. It's as if they don't know they've got gold in their hands, or they don't care. The Ursari want to keep that plantation, sure as sure, but I don't get *why*. What do coconuts have to do with training elephants and horses and bears?"

"I don't know," Damara said, "but I think you'd better find out." She looked at him. "You don't need me to tell you that."

Invisible fingers plucked a gold bracelet from Neel's pocket and slipped it onto his mother's wrist.

"Neel—"

"You keep that. You can't stroll around the palace wearing dowdy dregs of clothes. Karim has a fit every time he sees you."

"Neel."

"After all, you're the king's ma," Neel said. "Aren't you?"

Damara brushed a lock of hair off his forehead. "Oh, Neel."

"You, too," he said. "I've missed you, too."

They sat there in silence. Neel let a wave of secure peace flow through him, and tried to ignore the chilling current of a thought:

Everybody in that room, man and woman alike, wore crystal beads on their clothes.

21

Sid

———◆———

NEEL DUCKED INTO one of the city's alleyways, a dark crevice
between two walls of mountain rock with houses built on top
of them, covering the narrow divide. It was a tunnel, really, that Neel
was walking down, with sunlight at the beginning and at the end,
and none in between. There was no one in this alley but Neel, and it
was the perfect shadowy place for him to grab a fistful of dry dirt
and rub it into his face.

And—Neel looked at his hands—he should work some of that
grit under his nails, too. His hands were entirely too clean.

He stripped off his fine clothes and shrugged on some plain,
slightly tattered ones he'd filched from a clothing line. He kicked
the beautifully tooled leather sandals from his feet, wrapped the clothes
he had been wearing around them, and climbed one-handed up a
rock wall to wedge the soft bundle into a cranny where one of the
house beams joined the rock. Then he jumped down onto the street,
dirt puffing up around his feet.

Neel scrunched his toes into the fine layer of sandy soil and
smiled. Barefoot in a city.

It had been a while.

His destination, however, was not the city. He followed its winding ways down to the harbor, and its ships. He avoided the docked

Pacolet and padded over the beach to a rocky strip by the shore where a clan of Maraki—not Treb's—were sloshing through tide pools. They were crab-hunting.

Neel peered at the morning sun. He had time. Plenty of time for what he had to do later. It wouldn't hurt to muck around in the seaweed for a bit with these sailors before moving on. The slime would dirty him up nicely. Neel walked up to a cluster of five sailors, offered his help, and waited for any keen glances that would tell him they knew who he was.

"Know anything about crab-chasing, lad?" a short man asked, not bothering to unbend from his crouched position over a tide pool.

"D'you sail by the North Star?" Neel countered. "Does a gull fly free?" He knew the slang of the sea.

"Maraki, are you? Sure, you can hunt with us. If you use our nets, though, half goes to our clan."

"Fair's fair," Neel said, and took a net. A spidery-looking crab scuttled out from under a rock, close to his toes, and Neel snatched at its hindquarters, right behind its claws.

"You're a quick one." A woman smiled at him, showing a gold tooth.

Neel grinned back. "My name's Sid," he said, and thrust the crab into his net. This would be fun. Plus, he could catch up on some Maraki gossip.

Which, he discovered, was all about the lease of the coconut plantation.

"We deserve it," a girl said as she snagged a crab and dropped it into her net. "Greedy Ursari."

"*Ignorant* Ursari," the short man corrected her. "They don't understand that the world's changing."

"Europe's crazy about the sea," another sailor agreed. "They're poking their noses into new corners of the world. Sailing, searching for new lands, new riches, new routes to Asia. They're building boats faster than you can gut a fish. Now's the time to sell good rope to the *gadje*."

Neel glanced up. It hadn't occurred to him that the Maraki would *sell* the rope. He had assumed they'd want it all for themselves.

"Can't agree with you there," the gold-toothed woman said, then swore when she missed a crab. "Good coir rope gives *us* the edge at sea. A lot of battles take place on the water. Why hand our advantage over to the *gadje*?"

"Battles." The man scoffed. "You make it sound like we're at war with them. Nonsense. We want nothing the *gadje* got, and they don't even know what we have. They don't even know the Vatra exists. So what's the harm in turning a nice profit?"

"One thing's clear," said the girl. "Whether the Maraki keep the rope for ourselves, or sell it, that plantation should be *ours*."

There was a general grumble of agreement.

"But the king—"

Everyone moaned.

"—the king needs to see things our way."

There were a few muttered insults, which amused Neel. He guessed his disguise was complete if the sailors felt so free with their words. And he guessed that he'd probably spit out a few nasties about a king, too—if he wasn't one. If he was his old self.

"What do *you* think, Sid?" a boy about his age asked Neel.

"Me?"

"You're awfully quiet."

Neel swiped at a crab and stared, aghast, when he missed. He never missed. "Oh. Um. Can't stand the fellow, of course."

The boy nodded enthusiastically.

"I mean," Neel continued, "who's he to take the throne from our leader? I didn't think we'd see a Lovari as ruler of the Vatra for years to come. A juggler. A music-maker. Hey, know why the Lovari are such good musicians?"

"Oh, I know that joke," said the girl. "Because when you blow into a Lovari's ear, all that empty space inside his skull makes a pretty sound."

They laughed, and Neel did, too.

"My sis works at the palace," Neel said, "and she says no one likes him, not even the stuck-up courtiers."

"Well, and why would they?" said a sailor. "Did you hear about that trick with the globes? He thinks he's so smart."

The gold-toothed woman flipped over a rock, but there was nothing underneath. "Seems like it'd be a good thing to have a smart leader," she said. "And he shared the power of the globes. That's something."

The short man shook his head. "He's too young."

"Yeah," said the boy. "He probably sucks his thumb to sleep at night."

The sailors snickered. After a moment, Neel did, too. They began offering jokes about the king, each sailor coming up with a more ludicrous insult. Neel joined in, and his words had a special zing to them. "He's no looker," Neel said, "no matter how many silk shirts you throw on him. You can dress up a squid, but that doesn't make him any nicer to dance with."

The sailors went into fits of giggles. As soon as they choked back their laughter, they all began talking over each other, fighting to say the wittiest, cruelest thing they could about King Indraneel.

Then the word came, cutting through the talk like a knife: "bastard."

The smile dropped from Neel's face. He scanned the five faces. "Who said that?"

No one answered.

"He's got a mother, you know. A real mother who raised him," Neel said. "And so what if his blood parents weren't married? Lots of parents aren't. *Mine* weren't. What does that make me, then, to you?"

"You're fine, lad," said the short man. "We didn't mean any harm to you."

"But see, that's the thing," said the girl. "The king is exactly like *you*, Sid." She pointed at Neel. "He's ordinary. Kings aren't supposed to be ordinary."

"Yes," said Neel. "What a terrible thing that would be, if the people who decide our lives were just like us." He turned out his net, letting the crab fall to the sand and scuttle free. Then he dropped the net at the sailors' feet and walked away.

NEEL WAS SWEATY and his heart was beating with a fierce feeling when he pushed his way into the jungle that began not too far from the shore. A canopy of trees blocked the high noon sun, but the air was still heavy and hot.

By the time he reached the rows of coconut trees, Neel looked exactly as he'd hoped: like a grubby street boy looking for work.

In the palm trees overhead, light-limbed young men and women were climbing up the scaly bark to hack with knives at the coconuts, which fell to a soft landing of palm fronds littered over the moist jungle soil. In a small clearing, several shirtless men sat in front of mounds of hard coconuts, ripping off the brown fibers to toss them into a pile. Then the coconuts were broken open, their milky juice poured into one barrel, and the white meat chopped and tossed into another. Hiding behind a tree, Neel watched them for a while, and noticed that the men seemed to ask questions of the oldest one among them, whose long black and silver hair was tied back. He must be in charge, Neel decided, and approached him.

"Need a hand?" Neel asked. "I'm a good worker."

The man paused, but the others barely glanced up as they continued to break open coconuts. "Maybe." He peered at Neel. "Let's have a look at you." When he stood, he towered over Neel, and sized him up. "Hmm. We could use you in the trees. Can you climb?"

Neel laughed.

"I'll take that as a yes." The man rubbed his sun-lined cheek. He held Neel's eyes, then said carefully, "What kind of pay are you looking for?"

"Whatever I can get."

"Seeing as it's your first day on the job, I've got little to offer. You can have flatbread, mustard seed chicken, and as much coconut milk as you can drink during your break, and as much milk as you can carry home at the end of the day. Fair?"

"Sure."

The man handed him a knife. "I'm Shandor of the Ursari. You come see me when you're done."

"I'm Sid. Of the . . ." Neel paused, uncertain which tribe he should name. He didn't think this man would be easily lied to.

"Don't care what tribe you're from. Just do your job."

Neel shrugged and climbed the nearest tree.

It was peaceful high up, following the bend of the palm tree trunk into so much green. Green, green everywhere. Occasionally a parrot squawked its bright way out of a tree, but otherwise it was mostly quiet work, filled only by the rasp of Neel's knife as he cut the coconuts, and the thud as they fell to the earth.

It was tiring work, too, and when Neel took his break he could barely muster the energy to ask the other Roma his seemingly innocent questions about how they liked working on the plantation. Answers were short, and no one mentioned the lease. Neel drank the sweet, thin coconut milk and swallowed his disappointment. There was no gossip for him here. Just hard work.

"Break's over," Shandor told him. "Back to the trees. Unless you feel like quitting?"

Neel scowled. He walked away and climbed another tree.

When he saw the sun bury itself somewhere in the thick green wilderness, Neel returned to the forest floor and admitted to himself that the day had been a waste. And—he remembered the crab-hunting Maraki—a disheartening waste, at that. He wasn't even sure he'd be able to drag himself back to the city. Looking around at the plantation workers, who were collecting their pay (money, for some, milk for others), Neel figured they felt much the same way.

He stumbled past Shandor, who hefted a barrel full of coconut meat. "Sid," the man called.

Neel turned.

"Do you like horses?"

Neel's eyes lit up.

"Come along with me," said Shandor.

It was a long walk down a path that cut through the jungle and finally opened onto a stretch of beach Neel had never seen before. The sand here was sugary white, and Neel was sure that if Tomik were here he'd faint with happiness to see sand so perfect for making glass.

Neel snorted, forgetting for a moment that Shandor was just ahead of him.

"You don't like her?" Shandor said.

Neel looked up, confused, then shifted to see what the man was looking at, off in the distance, and which his broad body had blocked.

A sleek black horse. Standing, with trim legs, in front of a set of stables. Almost as if she knew Neel's heart begged for it, she broke into a gallop, spurring herself across the beach with such swift speed that Neel couldn't breathe.

"Ohhhh," he said.

Shandor smiled then, his first smile for Neel. "There's more where she came from," he said, and led Neel to the stables.

Such horses. They couldn't be real. They had to be prayers, Neel decided. They had to be what real horses prayed they could become.

"They're half-breeds," Shandor said. "Half Arabian, half wild Vatran." He seemed to expect some kind of response.

"Uh-huh." Neel nodded vaguely. He smoothed a hand down the gleaming brown nose of a horse leaning over its stable door.

"Why don't you help me with this barrel, Sid. That is, if you can tear yourself away."

With a backward, longing glance at the rows of horses, Neel helped the man lug the barrel into a room with horse tack on the walls and several people tipping barrels of coconut meat into a trough, where it was crushed with mallets and mixed with oats. "It's called copra." Shandor nodded at the mash in the trough. He hefted the barrel, and Neel reached inside to sweep the white hunks of coconut into the trough. "It's what gives the horses their shiny coats and strong bones." Shandor set the barrel down onto the floor and looked at him.

The realization struck Neel. Of course. *This* was why the Ursari wanted so badly to cling to the plantation. *This* was why they kept their reasons under wraps. The coconut meat was an Ursari trade secret, just like card tricks and sleights of hand were Lovari trade secrets.

Shandor turned and walked out the stable doors, leaving Neel standing there, perfectly still, as he listened to the thunk of mallets against the trough.

Why would Shandor share a trade secret with Neel—a perfect stranger from who knows what tribe? Why had this man singled him out?

Neel followed the man outside and found him waiting. He was

leaning against the wooden stable wall as he watched the black horse gallop through a sunset that blanketed the beach with an orange, hazy glow.

"Why are you showing me all of this?" Neel asked the man.

"I decided it wasn't a good idea to keep secrets from my king."

Neel didn't know what to say.

"I've been doing this"—Shandor waved a hand that seemed to include the stables, the horses, and even the jungle they could no longer see—"for ten years. In that time, you're the only ruler to take an interest."

"How did you know?" Neel found the words difficult to say. "How did you know who I am?"

Shandor looked him full in the face. "No one has eyes like yours."

Neel studied Shandor as he looked away again to watch the horse. There was a soft expression on the man's hard face. It was, Neel realized, pride. Shandor was looking at the black mare with pride. What would it take, Neel wondered, to make this man look at him like that? Neel was surprised by how much he wished he knew the answer.

22

A Vatran Ball

NEEL GUESSED that it was bound to happen sooner or later. A palace dance.

There had been one already, to celebrate his coronation—and a stuffy bore that was, what with him having to stand still the entire time, accepting congratulations from people who almost choked on their fake, smiley words.

What really got under his skin was that, usually, he loved to dance. He loved beautifully cut silk shirts, and jewels, and music. The coronation ball should have delighted Neel, but instead it made him feel like someone had sprinkled his favorite foods with a bitter spice. The thought of yet another court ball made him resentful—and resentful of his own resentment.

He tried to distract himself by talking with Petra, but she was busy. Iris was preparing her and Tomik for the Academy exam and lecturing them about the etiquette of polite Bohemian society. *She's trying to iron out my country accent*, Petra grumbled one afternoon in February. *And make me take smaller steps. This is stupid.*

Now you know how I feel, Neel said. He was in the library, trying to work on his reading skills without Nadia's help. It hadn't been going well.

You *don't have hair dyed the color of straw.*

Neel tried to imagine Petra with blond hair, and couldn't. He picked up a quill from a desk and held it as if ready to sketch her features. Then his fingers shifted, and he twirled the pen. *Really?*

Oh, yes. And Iris darkened my eyes and Tomik's hair. She refuses to change his eye color, though. She said that to tamper with such a gorgeous shade of blue would be a sin.

Neel dropped the pen back into the inkwell. *There's a ball tomorrow night,* he blurted out.

Another one? Petra said. *I suppose that's Karim's doing.*

No, Gita's. His adviser on international politics had insisted, and Arun had supported her. Neel couldn't fight both of them. *She says that these functions are all about making tribe leaders and clan leaders feel important and connected to each other and the Vatra. Everyone wants to be cozy. Plus, now that each tribe has a set of globes, lots of Roma will be able to attend that couldn't have before, and that'll "make my gift shine more brightly," she says. Guess she thinks it'll make 'em happy, and make me look good.*

That makes sense.

Neel shrugged. *Roses and sunshine, Pet. It's a nice idea, but it won't sell. Especially if Arun has his way. He wants me to use the dance as an occasion to pull the Maraki and Ursari leaders aside and tell 'em who's getting the coconut plantation. They're chomping at the bit for an answer, and Arun says I can't afford to look wishy-washy. I need to decide.* He told her about his day of chasing crabs and cutting down coconuts.

So both tribes have good reasons for wanting the lease, said Petra.

Yep.

That's tough.

Yep.

What will you do?

I don't know . . . Gita says to pick the Maraki, since they're the tribe that likes me least. Arun says that's exactly why I should choose the Ursari, so I don't look like a suck-up. What makes everything trickier is that this is a military decision, too.

Because better rope makes for better ships? Petra said. *Maybe you should choose the Maraki, then.*

Horses are also important in war.

There was a pause. *But the Roma are not at war.*

True. Neel struggled for a way to describe how he had felt when Shandor showed him the stables, then gave up. *I want to show you something.*

Petra went so silent that Neel might have thought she'd gone, except he seemed to sense her confusion. *I can't see anything,* she finally said. *I'm awake. I explained this to you. I wouldn't ever see what you see, even if we were dreaming while we spoke.*

Neel felt a surge of frustration. *By "show you something," I meant I want to look at something, and describe it. If that's all right by you.*

Her answer was quick. *Of course.*

Neel took a key from his pocket and unlocked the desk drawer. It was filled with a few little things—uncracked nuts, a cheap silver ring, a wooden whistle—and lots of fruit. The open drawer looked like a painting, with colored spheres of red, purple, and orange framed by the wooden rectangle of the drawer. Some of the fruit was old and shriveled. Neel described what he saw. *I stole it all. I can have almost anything I want, but I stole this. I don't even eat the fruit, or play the whistle. I just keep it here. I don't know why.* His eyes automatically sought a window, as if looking through one would help him see the answer, but his gaze met a blank wall. The library was the only room in the palace with no windows, to protect the books from sunlight and heat. The room was cool and dark and candlelit. *I don't know why I do it.*

Gently, Petra said, *You steal to remind yourself of who you are.*

Neel nodded, then remembered she couldn't see him do it. *Let's talk again tonight. You can come to me while I sleep, can't you? I can't reach you like that. I don't have the gift.* He didn't say that he had been going to bed early so that he would fall asleep before she'd expect it. *It'd be nice to see you.*

The stitch that linked their minds seemed to vibrate with tension. *I don't think that's a good idea,* Petra said.

Why?

Because it's confusing. It's strange to hear things that are real and see things that aren't.

You and me can handle strange. Things got pretty strange when we busted out of Salamander Castle, or when you summoned that air spirit.

This is different. There was a short silence. *Iris is calling for me,* Petra said. Then she was gone.

Neel stared at the open drawer of fruit. He thought about how Petra refused to use her gift in this one way that had become important to him. He knew that Petra, so sure of herself sometimes, could shrink away from her strengths, especially when it came to magic. If she had decided not to speak to him through dreams, well, wasn't that like her? Yet he couldn't shake a cold certainty.

She did not want to see him. She did not want him to see her.

Neel scooped up a pomegranate, then dropped it back in the drawer. He wasn't hungry. Why was he hoarding fruit he would never eat? Why did people cling to what they couldn't use, or long for what they didn't need, or shun what they had? Neel thought about the Maraki, the Ursari, and the coconut plantation. He thought about the ball.

Neel shut the drawer. He had come to a decision.

He was going to enjoy this party.

• • •

WHEN THE ROMA threw a ball, they did it right. And this time, un-like the coronation dance, the planning was largely placed in the hands of the Lovari tribe.

"But the king is not Lovari. He is one of us," Arun told Gita.

"They look on him as one of their own," Gita said. "He can use all the support he can get."

"But the seating arrangements for dinner!" Karim wailed. "It will be chaos if the Lovari are in charge!"

Neel, who had been half listening until this argument arose, immediately sided with Gita. The Lovari knew how to have fun, and fun was what he wanted.

The Lovari tribe leader was thrilled. Jasmine threw her people into a whirlwind of preparations, and they were eager to please the king. They had noticed the sullen, caged look he'd worn through-out the coronation ball. They did not want to see it on *their* night. They hired the best acrobats to entertain during the dinner. They consulted Neel's mother to make certain his favorite dishes would be served. With a wince and a shrug of the shoulders, they invited the *Pacolet* crew and sent them to the best Kalderash tailors in the Vatra. Those Maraki might be a little savage, but they were the king's special friends. Or at least they used to be.

The ball was a crush of color. The dresses were simply cut—the island was too hot for ruffles and flounces—but the embroidery alone proved that hours of needlework had been devoted to this night. No one wore the same shade, and the people crowding into the ball-room seemed like an almost liquid rainbow that shifted and trickled and poured.

The guests were lucky. As if on command, a high wind kicked up. It blew through the large windows and entrances to balconies that were designed for quiet, dark conversations. The wind eased the Va-tran heat and made the guests even livelier than usual. They would have been curious, anyway, to see what this night would bring. But the cool wind made their curiosity wide-eyed and awake.

They were not disappointed. When the king arrived, they fell silent.

Neel wore a long, loose, and sleeved tunic cut from cloth of gold. The effect was startling. It gave his eyes an unearthly color. It somehow drew attention away from the scars on his face—the rough marks left from a disease that had nearly killed him as a small child, and the short line made by the knife of a Spanish boy Neel had picked a fight with years ago. Despite the careful simplicity of his white pants and leather sandals, Neel's appearance seemed extravagant, even for a king. Maybe it was the sapphire that flashed on his ear, or the smirk he gave the crowd. Perhaps it was the scoot perched on his shoulder. Whatever it was, Neel did not look quite so young as everyone knew he was. He looked like an idea, an idea of what a new kind of king could be, and ideas have no age.

A fiddle was tuned, a piper blew an experimental trill of notes, and the crowd began to chatter and find partners for the first dance. Neel saw Karim trying to catch his eye. The adviser nodded meaningfully, no doubt referring to their earlier conversation about whom Neel should choose for his first dance. "Someone important," Karim had begged. "A tribe leader's daughter, perhaps?"

Poor Karim. He was about to be disappointed.

Neel scanned the crowd. He approached Nadia and said, "Hey."

Her eyes coolly measured him, then paused to stare at the scoot. "I see you've made at least one friend in the Vatra."

"Want to dance?"

"Not with that." She pointed at the fuzzy animal, which chittered angrily.

Neel gently removed it from his shoulder. "Scoot along," he told it, and it jumped from his hands to climb the walls to the ceiling, where copper plates nailed to the rafters caught the torchlight and glowed like small suns.

"Come on," Neel said as the musicians played the opening notes of a Lovari tune. He grabbed Nadia's hand and tugged her into the dance.

For a few uncomfortable minutes, neither of them said anything. Then Nadia commented, "You really can dance. You'd almost be the perfect partner. Too bad you're so short."

"Oh, I don't know," he said smoothly. "It gives you a good view of everyone else."

"I already see things pretty clearly."

"What do you mean?"

"I mean: I don't think you're dancing with me for the pleasure of my company."

Neel floundered for something to say. "There's no one here I'd rather dance with."

Nadia snorted. "Only because *she* isn't here." Neel started to speak, but Nadia cut him off. "What do you want, Neel?"

"Help me again. With reading."

"And why would I do that?"

"I want to be better. I want to be better at *this*." He waved a hand at the ballroom.

She looked at him just before he spun her in a circle. "Maybe I will," she said.

"Maybe?"

"What did you decide to do about the lease?"

He led her left, and back, and right, and didn't answer.

"Rumor has it you're going to tell Tarn and Shaida tonight," Nadia persisted.

"So this is the lay of the land. You won't help me unless I help the Maraki." The smile was back on Neel's face, but this time it looked cold.

"That's not how I meant it. I just want to know."

"You'll know soon enough," he said. "When the rest of the Vatra knows it, and not before." The dance ended and he released her. With the briefest of nods, he turned away.

She snagged his wrist. "I truly didn't mean it like that." Her voice, for the first time Neel could remember, was soft. "I will help you, whatever you decide. Even though you're an annoying, short-tempered student."

He relaxed. "Thanks, Nadia. I promise I'll be patient from now on."

"No, you won't. But it's nice of you to lie."

Neel acknowledged this with a half smile before walking away. He glanced at the table where the tribe leaders sat and squared his shoulders. He might as well get this over with.

After a quick whisper in Gita's ear, Neel stepped out onto a balcony and waited. It wasn't long before Tarn and Shaida joined him.

"Cousin." Tarn made the word sound like a threat. "What have you decided?"

"The lease will go to the Maraki."

Tarn smiled as Shaida tried to school the disappointment from her face.

"With conditions," Neel added.

"Conditions?" Tarn said.

"The Ursari already have a good operation going on that plantation. What do a bunch of sailors know about farming coconuts? You'd spend a year figuring out how to run everything. You'll employ whoever's working there now, and pay them their current wage."

"Fine," Tarn said impatiently.

"And—"

"And?"

"—you can only sell ten percent of the coir."

Tarn's eyes went dangerous.

"And you can't sell it in Europe," Neel continued. "Too likely it'd end up in the hands of the Hapsburg Empire, who isn't exactly our friend. Sell it to Asia if you like, or the Ottoman Empire. The rest, you keep and use."

"Are there any more *conditions* of yours?" Tarn said through gritted teeth.

"Matter of fact, yes. You'll give the coconut meat to the Ursari."

The corner of Shaida's mouth twitched.

"How do you expect us to turn a profit?" Tarn demanded.

"Oh, all right. You'll sell it to them at fifty percent of the market rate." Neel had calculated that the cost of that, per year, was about how much the Ursari would save when the Maraki were paying the plantation workers. The Ursari would break even.

"Happy?" Neel asked Tarn.

"Tickled," he snarled.

"The Maraki will like this deal. Especially if you explain it to them in a way that makes you look good. You're going to rig your ships with the best rope in the world, aren't you? You snagged this plantation out of Ursari hands, didn't you? You'll give the Ursari a cheap rate for coconut meat to ease their hurt, 'cause you're that kind of fine, upstanding man."

Tarn's eyes measured Neel slowly, warily, as if he had never seen this person before and had no idea what to make of him.

"That's the deal," Neel said. "Take it or leave it. I'm sure the Ursari won't mind renewing their lease, if you don't like the terms of this one."

Tarn scowled at the moon. He nodded, then went back inside the ballroom.

"Hungry?" Neel asked Shaida.

"Yes." She no longer hid her smile. They went inside.

The musicians had set their instruments aside and almost everyone was already seated—though, Neel noted, Tarn and Treb were still standing in a corner, conferring darkly. On a raised platform stood the king's table, with places for each tribe leader and (at Neel's insistence) his mother. She was seated next to Jasmine of the Lovari, and as Neel and Shaida took their places alongside them, Neel's stomach rumbled to see the food piled on his plate. There were fried lotus roots in a red-brown paste of tamarind, chili pepper, and ginger. He spied roasted eggplant mashed with garlic and rosemary, served on flatbread, and chickpeas dressed with lemon and cilantro. A large bowl rested on the table in front of him, filled with mango juice and mint.

Neel had reached for a handful of chickpeas when the scoot jumped from the ceiling onto his shoulder. It clambered down his arm and began munching on the chickpeas as if Neel's hand was a trough.

A slightly horrified silence echoed through the room, but Neel laughed. He kept laughing until the scoot stiffened with a high-pitched whine. It began to convulse, and flopped off Neel's arm into the bowl of juice, where it thrashed and suddenly went still. It floated on its back, its small mouth stretched open.

The chickpeas fell from Neel's hand as he realized what everyone in the room was realizing.

His food had been poisoned.

23

The Spy

THERE WAS A LOT of screaming after that.

Neel felt his mother grip his arm. He heard Jasmine and Shaida shouting in his ear as his advisers bore down on him from across the room. He stared as people shoved back their plates, but he knew they needn't worry. That poison had been for him alone.

He stepped back from the table. He ducked away from Arun, Gita, and Karim. He went to his rooms and stayed there, and didn't understand why, even though he was supposed to be king, he didn't have the power to make his guards keep everyone out. People pressed their way through the door.

"Are you all right? You didn't eat anything, did you?" Karim pressed a hand to Neel's forehead, as if the poison would have produced only a mild fever in him, instead of immediately striking him down as it had the scoot.

Neel jerked away.

"He's going to die right before our eyes!" someone cried.

"And he's so young!"

"The poor boy. Why, he's barely older than a child."

"Who could have done this?"

Arun and Gita pushed through the crowd. "Who had access to the king's food?" Arun demanded.

There was a brief silence as everyone turned toward Shaida, Jasmine, and Damara.

"Absurd," said Shaida. "Do you really think one of us would have poisoned the king's food in full view of everyone? Do you think his own mother would be capable of such a thing?"

"We must get to the bottom of this," someone said.

"Something must be done!"

"Too right," said Treb. "And one thing's sure as a dropped anchor: you've got to be tough on this, Neel. You've got to suss this person out, and punish like a king should punish, or you'll be looking over your shoulder in fear for the rest of your life. I'd like to catch the person myself. Someone daring to come after *my* family? Why, no one has more reason than the Maraki to snuff out my brat of a cousin, and even we—"

"Those aren't smart words, brother," Tarn said quietly.

People stared at Treb and Tarn. Neel heard snatches of whispers.

"What if his own family . . . ?"

"Or his mother . . . ?"

"Could it have been her?"

"Get out," Neel said. "All of you."

Everyone looked at each other.

"Get out!" he screamed.

There was a flurry of concern among the crowd, and some mild outrage, but Neel kept shouting until Treb glared at the guards and helped them muscle everyone out of the room.

Everyone except Damara.

When the door had shut behind the last courtier and Neel heard the rising and falling of the guards' voices in the corridor as they ordered people to clear this wing of the palace, Neel turned to his mother and buried himself in her arms.

Softly, she said, "This isn't the first time, is it?"

"Should I give it up?" Neel asked. "Should I give the throne to the Maraki?"

"Is that really what you want to do?"

Neel pulled away. *I don't know,* moaned a voice inside him, but then Neel realized that it was a weak liar. He knew.

Damara read the answer in his eyes. "Treb's right. A king has to react strongly to something like this. If you don't, you'll be seen as vulnerable. The Roma can't have a vulnerable ruler. And I can't bear the thought of someone trying to hurt my son again."

Neel sighed, and nodded. "I'm glad you're here, Ma."

"So am I."

"I wish Sadie was here, too. I asked her to come. I sent a royal summons. She should be here by now. Why isn't she?"

"Why are you still here?" Joel, the older of the two Riven brothers, pushed aside his mug of ale and frowned at Sadie. "Prague isn't safe for you. It hasn't been for a long time. Your own king *ordered* you—"

"The king, apparently, is my little brother," Sadie said dryly. "He can't tell me what to do."

Joel made an impatient noise, but Sadie merely gave him a steady look, and he became mesmerized, as he often was, by her beauty. In the light of the tallow candles that lit this noisy tavern, Sadie's pale skin glowed like a pearl. He glanced around them and dropped his voice to a whisper. "If these people knew what you are . . ."

"*What* I am? I am not a thing."

"I didn't say you were. But to be half Roma at a time like this . . ."

"No one would know, to look at me." In a bitter voice, she said, "I wish they could."

"You would be imprisoned. Worse. There are no Roma left in Bohemia, save you. The rest are gone, or dead, or jailed, or warped into monsters. Just go home, Sadie. Stop meeting with me."

"Don't say that. Don't ever say that. I'm risking everything to meet with you. The least you can do is hear what I have to say and send a message to the Vatra."

Joel pressed a hand to his eyes. "Tell me, then."

Sadie whispered, "A pack of Gristleki went missing in the No-vohrad Mountains. I heard the captain of the guard say so. It's the first time anything like this has happened. The prince doesn't know what to make of it."

"Is it possible that the Gray Men regained some of their human-ity? Maybe they remembered what they really are, and ran away."

Sadie bit her lip. "I don't think that's possible. The prince had a special prison built to house the Gray Men in the forest behind the castle. I've been there. There are rows and rows of cages, each barely big enough to hold a monster. They snarled behind the bars. Bashed their faces against the cages, scrabbling to get at me . . . they would have eaten me alive, Joel. There was nothing human about them."

"Maybe a group of Bohemian rebels killed the missing Gristleki. I hear the rebellion is gaining force. There are a lot of people in this country who'd like to toss the prince from his throne."

"Yes. Or maybe the prince is losing control of the Gray Men."

They went silent at this idea. The only thing worse than Prince Rodolfo having an army of monsters was the thought of them run-ning wild and hungry, under no one's command.

"I have to get back to the castle," Sadie said. "The prince is hav-ing a meeting with the captain of the guard tonight. I want to hear what they have to say."

"I'll give your information to my brother," Joel said. "Vincent will see that it gets to the Vatra. Also . . . there's something I should tell you."

"Yes?"

"Vincent received some news from your country. By now, your

brother's friends should have entered Bohemia. Tomik Stakan and Petra Kronos."

"Petra Kronos." The anger was back in Sadie's eyes. "Don't ever say her name to me again. If she hadn't tempted Neel into stealing from the Cabinet of Wonders, Prince Rodolfo wouldn't have turned his hatred toward the Roma. She's the cause of all of this."

SADIE'S BREATH sounded harsh and loud in her ears. She curled tighter inside the trunk, squeezing her arms around her chest. It felt like her heart would burst out of her body, it was beating so wildly. She heard the captain's guards checking obvious hiding places in the captain's suite of rooms. They probed the inside of the wardrobe with daggers. They swept a sword under the bed. They wouldn't, however, open a trunk they thought housed the captain's very personal possessions—his money, his weapons, his collection of silver codpieces. They wouldn't guess that Sadie had used her chambermaid's keys to enter this room earlier and quietly unpack the trunk. They wouldn't open it. The captain wouldn't remember something important he'd placed inside, something he needed right away.

Or so Sadie hoped.

The captain and his guards joked about which body part they'd cut off first if they found someone hiding in the captain's suite. Sweat trickled down Sadie's cheek and into her mouth, and an eerie silence filled her ears. For a moment, she thought her fear had deafened her. But then the captain said, "Your Highness," in a reverent voice. Sadie pressed her ear to the trunk's keyhole.

There was the sound of a door shutting and someone settling into a chair. Prince Rodolfo said nothing.

"The missing Gristleki have been found," said the captain. "Fiala Broshek examined the bodies, and says they were killed about a month ago. All four of the corpses had been stabbed in the neck or decapitated. It's as if someone—or someones—knew exactly where the Gray Men are vulnerable. Or they figured it out very quickly."

Sadie suddenly wondered if there was enough air in the trunk. The prince's silence seemed to be a rope tightening around her neck. She couldn't breathe. Would she suffocate in here?

"We've seen this before," the captain added. "More than a year ago."

The prince finally spoke, and Sadie wished he hadn't. He said, "Petra Kronos."

"I assume the Gray Men stumbled upon her when returning over the mountains from Austria. They must have been ravenous after what they did to your brother. Whoever they would have come across afterward, they would have attacked. But it's possible she somehow knew they were there, and was seeking them out. Of course, there's no proof that it was the Kronos girl."

"I hope it was her," said the prince. "That means she is in my country, close to me. I want her. I want her to suffer, and I want to see it."

"If she's here, it's only a matter of time before she's found. Everyone in Bohemia knows she's an outlaw. They've seen the sketches of her we've posted in town squares. They know the bounty on her head. If she dared set foot in your country, she'd be yours. My only worry is the rebels—"

"I do not wish to hear about the rebels. My Gray Men will destroy them the moment *you*, Captain, do your job and discover their identities and whereabouts. In any event, the rebels will shortly no longer matter. When the empire is mine, when its military might is mine, no one will dare question me."

"Well, in fact, that's one of the reasons I wanted to speak with you tonight." Sadie heard the captain stir. He crossed the room, his footsteps growing louder. He leaned against the chest, and it groaned under his weight. Sadie held her breath. "Can I make a suggestion?"

"You may."

"Despite the loss of the four Gristleki, their mission was a success. Your brother Maximilian is dead. I think it's time to turn our attention to your other brother, Frederic. If you'll permit me to send another pack of Gristleki into Hungary, in a few days you'll have condolences from every monarch in the world."

Sadie imagined the prince's smile. "If only they knew."

"No one will be able to prove you killed your brothers. And, technically, you didn't. The Gray Men did. All they had to do was slip into Maximilian's room early one night and scratch a finger on his skin. It must have been hard for them to scrape the skin and not feast on his blood. But they did it. They can do the same to Frederic. It's an excellent idea."

"Of course. It was mine."

"It's amazing, the way their poison works. Imagine how Maximilian slept on, letting the poison spread untreated through his blood for hours. And you know what? He was lucky." The captain pushed himself off the trunk's lid, and Sadie let out a slow breath. "After all, doesn't everyone want to die in their sleep?"

They laughed.

"I am sure my brother Frederic does," said the prince.

There was the sound of glass chiming against glass, and liquid being poured.

"To the heir of the empire," the captain said.

"Yes," said the prince. "To me."

The glasses clinked.

24

The Academy

—▸◆◂—

I'VE HEARD that the Academy beds are draped in velvet," said Tomik, "and that, in the winter, every student is given a metal box full of coals to place under the covers at the foot of the bed. The bed stays warm all night."

"Uh-huh." Petra stared out the carriage window.

"And the Academy food is as good as anything served at court. Roasted pheasant served with quinces. Suckling pigs. Slabs of cinnamon cake. Foamy ginger milk. And imported chocolate. You said you liked Iris's hot chocolate, didn't you?"

"Great."

Tomik looked at Petra, frustrated, and then at the spider on her shoulder. Astrophil was also watching the wintry countryside go by. "And the library. The library is excellent."

"Eh?" Astrophil perked up.

"So many books."

"Books?" Astrophil's green eyes glowed. "You know, I have not read a good book in ages. Do you think they have a copy of Ambroise Paré's book on medicine? When you hit your head in the woods, Tomik, it occurred to me that I would make an excellent doctor. I could even be a surgeon. Think of how many delicate procedures I could do with my fine, elegant legs. If I can weave a web, I can certainly stitch a wound. It is only a matter of research. And practice." Astrophil talked on, and the squeaky noise of his chatter let Petra sink deeper into her silent thoughts.

"Petra," Tomik said.

She shifted, uncomfortable in the fancy traveling dress Iris's maid had put on her. It pinched. Petra now had a trunk packed with pretty dresses, and vials of dye she and Tomik had to use daily.

"Petra."

Tomik's voice was starting to feel like the dress, laying pressure on her in places where she used to feel free. "What?"

"Are you worried that you won't pass the exam when we get there?"

"No."

Tomik waited for her to say something more, and when she didn't, he made an exasperated noise. "Aren't you even the littlest bit interested in the Academy?"

She kept her eyes on the road, which was snaking up a hill just outside Prague. The driver had told them they would arrive in less than half an hour. She turned to face Tomik. "No," she said. "And neither are you."

He stared.

"If you wanted to roll around in wealth and gorge yourself on imported food, you would have done that in the Vatra," Petra said. "You're excited because you think you'll learn something in the Academy. You won't."

"You . . . you think I'm not good enough?"

"You're *too* good. Tomik, what makes you think you need someone to teach you how to use your magic? Look at all you've done."

And look at everything you *have done, Petra,* Astrophil said. He jumped to Petra's hand, which rested palm up on her knee. She considered him, a treasure in her hand. "Maybe . . ." she said. "Maybe the things you learn best are the ones you teach yourself."

"How philosophical." Tomik's tone was sharp.

She looked at him, startled. She seemed to smell something bitter in the air.

"Why are you so distant?" he said. "You shut me out. You have, ever since the forest. You go away somewhere in your head and I've no idea what you're thinking, or feeling. Maybe you and Astro are having grand, long, silent conversations about the worth of education. I don't know. But if you want to exclude me I wish you would tell me *why.*"

It is true, Astrophil said. *You have been distant. I have noticed, too.*

That smell was growing worse. Petra recognized it, but couldn't remember what it was. She focused on her friends, and hesitated. She had never wanted to tell them about her link to Neel. She knew Astrophil and Tomik wouldn't like it. But something else held her back now, and she realized it was that her conversations with Neel had come to feel too special, too private for her to share the fact of them.

Petra felt suddenly weary. "None of this matters," she said, and realized she was talking to herself as well as to her friends. "Tomik, there are things I can't do. There are things I can't feel." She saw that he knew what she meant. She looked away from the hurt bleeding across his face. Gently, she said, "I know you're excited about the Academy. But for me it will never be anything more than a place. It's the place where I'm going to find out how to save my father. That's all. That's everything."

The carriage jerked and the horses squealed as the driver hauled on the reins. Something green streaked past Petra's window.

Tomik tore his gaze away from Petra's face. He flung open the door. "What is going on?"

Petra pushed her way out of the carriage and glanced behind to see what had run past them.

It was a girl in green Academy robes. She was screaming.

Tomik gasped, and Petra wheeled around to stare up the hill. That smell had been smoke. Hundreds of people were running toward them, tumbling down the slope, racing to put as much distance as they could between them and the smoldering heap of ruins that used to be the Academy.

25

An Address

PETRA AND TOMIK chased the girl and dragged her to a stop.
They tried to break through her hysteria.

"The rebels!" she gasped. "They set fire to the school! They'll
kill us all!"

"What are you talking about?" Petra demanded.

The girl shrank away. "You. You're one of them. Peasants! Why
don't you crawl back to the dirt you came from!" Just as Petra realized
that she hadn't bothered to hide the accent that marked her class, the
girl tore away from them and ran up the slope to the knot of students
and teachers staring at what used to be the school.

A sudden thought filled Petra with fear. "Come on," she shouted
to Tomik. With Astrophil buried deeply into her hair, Petra ran after
the girl.

When they reached the top of the hill, Petra shoved past weep-
ing students to find a professor whose robes were dyed a deep shade
of emerald. He was counting the students around him and didn't
notice Petra until she tugged at his sleeve. "Sir?" Petra tried to imi-
tate the stiff, sweet pitch of a high-class accent. "Where is Professor
Fiala Broshek?"

His look of worry deepened. "Missing."

The answer stabbed into her. Petra looked at the Academy and realized that her plans were in ruins, too. She reeled as if the ground had vanished beneath her.

"What happened here?" Tomik asked the professor.

A crease appeared between his brows. "Who are you?"

"Students, sir. At least, we hoped to be students," Tomik said humbly, in the perfect voice of a well-mannered young gentleman. Petra dimly realized that he was better at hiding himself than she was, and she should have let him do the talking to begin with. Well, that didn't matter now. Nothing mattered, if Fiala Broshek was dead.

"We are here to take the entrance exam," Tomik told the professor.

The man laid a hand on his shoulder. "I am sorry. It looks as if there will be no school for you to attend. After lunch, all students and professors returned to the classrooms, as usual. But today there was a note scrawled on the walls inside every room: 'Leave the Academy now, or pay with your lives.' As soon as we'd led the students out of the building, there was an explosion. I'm sure when we rake the ashes, we will discover that gunpowder was the cause, probably several kegs of it. Mercifully, every student is safe. Scared, yet safe. But Professor Broshek is missing. Perhaps we haven't noticed her yet, in the chaos." He shook his head and sighed heavily. "I am trying to fool myself. We have taken careful count of everyone here. There's only one place she can be." His eyes strayed to the rubble.

Petra had heard enough. She walked away. She registered the fact that one of the students was staring at her strangely, but she didn't care if she had been recognized. She didn't care if the boy decided to howl for everyone to seize her, or that, in the end, he didn't say anything. Petra kept walking until she reached the carriage. She got inside, slammed the door, and curled her knees to her chest.

The driver began pestering her through the open panel between the carriage and his seat. "What happened? How did the Academy burn down? Are there any dead?" Petra yanked the wooden panel shut, latched it, and ignored his knocking.

She ignored Astrophil, who was jumping up and down on her foot. She ignored Tomik, who wrenched open the door. "You don't know Fiala Broshek is dead," he said as he climbed inside. "There's no body. She's missing, Petra. *Missing.* Maybe she just walked away from the fire. We can find her."

Petra glanced at him then, and the expression on his face unleashed a fury inside her. He had no right to look so distraught. "Don't pretend you're upset. If you are, it's only because your precious Academy is gone."

"No." Tomik ran a hand through his dyed black hair. "No, I—"

"Tomik is correct," Astrophil said sternly. "All is not lost." He stood on his hind legs and rested two other legs on his thorax like a human might place impatient hands on his hips. "Is no one thinking of the possibility that Fiala Broshek started the fire, and she had reasons she wished to hide, and that *that* is why she is nowhere to be found?"

Petra blinked at him. The shreds of her thoughts began to knit together again. "I want to believe you," she whispered. "I need some kind of hope, even if it's a stupid hope."

"It's not stupid," Tomik said eagerly. "We just need to figure out how to find her. Maybe we should question the students and teachers. They might know something."

"No," said Astrophil. "A boy looked at Petra as if he recognized her. We have already attracted enough attention."

The three of them fell silent, and Petra seemed to hear Astrophil's gears whir faster as he pondered their next step. He glanced up and noticed them watching him, waiting. He sagged. "I do not know what to do," he said.

For one wild moment, Petra considered choosing between her two magics, as the Metis had taught her. But even if the Choice worked, Petra didn't see how it would help her now. The Choice wasn't just dangerous and costly. It was also useless. Petra shoved all thoughts of it from her mind.

Frustrated, she grabbed fistfuls of her gorgeous, awful, violet skirts. Something crinkled inside them.

A sudden light shone in Petra's eyes. She plunged her hand into a pocket and pulled out a scrap of paper. "There!" she said. "We can go there." She held the paper out to her friends.

Astrophil took it with four legs and held it stretched out in front of him. "Lucas and Zora December, 8 Molodova Street, Prague. Oh, an excellent idea, Petra!"

"But Iris gave us her niece and nephew's address so that we could send letters through them to her," said Tomik, "not interrogate them about Fiala Broshek."

"Ah, but Lucas and Zora December rank very highly in Bohemian aristocratic society," said Astrophil. "If they are in Prague, they must attend court regularly. Perhaps they will know something."

"But would they tell us?" said Tomik. "They don't even know who we are—and if they *did*, that might give them even more reason not to help us, even to turn us in."

"Iris would not have given us their address if she did not trust them," said Astrophil.

Tomik bit his lip. "It's a big risk."

"Not as big a risk as doing nothing," said Petra.

26

Suspects

THE MORNING AFTER THE POISONING, Neel made his way to the kitchen. He had snuck down there many times before to steal one thing or another. He knew the way well.

The head cook was a Lovari, and she trembled to see him enter. The king was younger than most Roma rulers, which would have made some people fear him less. But the cook's experience told her that youth could be unpredictable, and savage in its vengeance.

"Please, Your Majesty," she said, "it wasn't me. I didn't touch your food." She began to babble. "I mean, of course I *touched* it. Don't think I'd leave the preparation of the king's food to underlings! I cooked your meal with these very hands. But I didn't poison it. I tasted it myself." A sudden thought made her clap a hand to her mouth. "Not that I was *eating* your food! I was just tasting it from time to time to make sure it had enough salt and spice." Her eyes widened. "Not that your food was germy! I am a clean woman. Never a sick day in my life. And I cleaned the spoon each time before I dipped it in for a taste."

Neel winced. "I don't believe this."

"All right," the woman said miserably, "that was a lie, about the spoon. I didn't wash it each time. But it started out clean, I swear."

"No, I mean I don't believe you think I came down here to

accuse you of trying to kill me. Why would you? You're Lovari. The Lovari are about the only Roma happy to see me on the throne."

"Well . . . not all of them. Some of them think you're a turncoat. You know, because your blood's Kalderash." She gasped, then added, "Not that *I* think you're a traitor to your tribe!"

Neel fought a smile. "Course not. Even if you did, even if you wanted me trundling off to the cemetery in a one-way wagon, I don't think you'd try to kill me in a way so easily traced back to you— unless you wanted to be caught, or were kind of dumb."

"To tell the truth"—the cook lowered her voice—"I never was very smart."

"You're honest," Neel corrected. "Maybe you're playacting, but my guess is you're just calling things as you see 'em, and a killer wouldn't go out of her way to give me more reasons to say she's guilty."

"You're right!" said the cook. "You see? I couldn't have done it."

Neel smiled. "That's what I thought. Now, tell me the path the food took from here to the ballroom."

The cook swore with professional pride that she had brought the king's dishes to the ballroom herself, on the most fancy silver platter in the palace. "When I set it on the table, you were dancing with a girl. Karim was watching you. The other tribe leaders were at the table, and your ma, too."

Neel nodded. "Anyone else hovering around?"

"Your advisers, of course. Arun and Gita—and then Karim threaded his way through the crowd, looking disgusted and like he was bursting to tell them something."

So Karim hadn't liked him dancing with Nadia. No surprise there, but it wasn't Neel's greatest concern. "Thanks," Neel told the cook, and would have left, but she begged that he stay until she had roasted some sugared almonds for him. Then she said he was too skinny to fill himself up on treats, and he had better sit until she'd fried some fish with her special saffron sauce. Neel let her stuff him with food until his stomach was heavy, and listened to her complain about the Roma rulers she'd seen come and go in her time. "And I'm old. Guess how old. I'll tell you: I'm fifty and sixteen, which is a nicer, younger-sounding way of saying I'm sixty-six, don't you think? I've cooked for many a king and queen, and it's always the same. Every ruler pushes for his own tribe. If it's an Ursari on the throne, you can bet the Vatra will be teeming with animals, and horse manure up to your eyes. If it's a Kalderash, we learn that the palace needs new wings and a star-gazing tower or some such, because the Kalderash like to build things. I suppose it can't be helped. It's the way we rotate who rules. If you've spent twelve years watching three other tribes heap up goodies for themselves, when it comes your turn you got to do the same." She piled more food on Neel's plate, and asked, "So what are *you* going to do for your people?"

Neel swallowed a mouthful of fish and mumbled something. He didn't want to think about her question. He could only think of one thing, and that was the six names of the people who had had an opportunity to poison his food: Tarn, Jasmine, Shaida, Arun, Gita, and Karim.

And his mother, too. But he refused to consider that.

NIGHT HAD FALLEN, and Neel was holed up in his sitting room, reading a book he had taken from the library. It was hard work moving from each printed word to the next, but every time he turned a page he was surprised by how the sound of it—that quiet rasp and rustle of paper—pleased him. He was reading a book of Lovari tales. He had been sure he'd know them all, but there was one he didn't: the story of how the butterfly came to be. He paused and smoothed a finger over the last line on the last page. He touched the dot that marked the end of the sentence. A period. That's what Nadia had called it. "That's how you know when to stop," she'd said. "To take a breath and think, or stop reading altogether."

A shivery feeling stole over him, and Neel eagerly shut the book. Petra's voice rang in his head like a bell. *The plans have changed,* she said.

There was a taut quality to her words. She sounded determined, but shaken, and if Neel didn't know any better he'd say she was close to tears.

He had hoped to ease his buried fear of another attempt to kill him by discussing it with Petra. Now he set thoughts of that aside. He asked, *What's wrong?*

She told him about the destruction of the Academy. *We're in Prague now. It's dusk, and the carriage is going over Karlov Bridge. Once we get to the Decembers' house, I don't know what will happen.*

The sound of Petra's voice, so close, made her seem far away. *I remember that bridge,* Neel said. *We walked on it once.* He pulled the Romany coin she'd given him from his pocket and tilted it until it caught the candlelight. He wished he had something to give her. *That was the day we met. And you know what I thought of you?*

The question seemed to surprise her. It made her pause, anyway, and when she spoke there was a thin thread of humor in her words. *I'm afraid to ask.*

That you were smart, and sweet-hearted. Neel felt nervous for some reason. He lightened his tone. *Course, I didn't know you so well then.*

Your opinion of me has changed, I gather.

Neel imagined the look she would be giving him, were she here. There would be an arch slant to her eyes. She wouldn't smile, but she'd be ready to. And he would say something funny, like he always did.

Yet he didn't this time. *Maybe I see you differently. Yes, I do. You've always shown me a warm heart and a quick mind. But I didn't realize, that day on the bridge, what kind of friend I'd made.* He held the closed book with both hands and considered how to comfort

Petra, because he felt that comfort was what she needed. It occurred
to him that the truth might be the best thing he could give her.
*How could I know then what I do now? That you've got a light inside
you that's true and clear. Like the North Star. Even when there's a
storm, that star's shining under all those dangerous clouds. What
I'm saying is this: I think you feel a little lost now, but you'll find
your way.*

I hope so.

I know so.

There was a short silence that tasted of distraction, and Petra's
attention seemed pulled somewhere else. Abruptly, she said, *We're
here.*

Wait.

Yes?

*Petra . . . my sis is still in Prague. I sent for her, but she hasn't
come and there's no sign she's skipped town. I . . .* Neel fiddled with
the frayed bookmark. *I'm worried. If you can, stop by the Riven brothers' silk stall near Staro Square. They'll know how to reach her. Tell her
to come home. Will you? Please.*

Her answer was soft. *I will, Neel. I promise.*

Then she was gone.

Neel's mind echoed with her absence. He thought of all the
things he hadn't said, and the things he should have said better. He
groaned.

"Your Majesty?" Gita was standing in front of him. Neel had no
idea how long she had been there, watching him stare into space.
He hadn't even heard her enter. "Someone has arrived in the Vatra.
A *gadje.*"

"What?" There were few outsiders in the world who knew of the
Vatra's existence, and only two knew how to get there: Petra and
Tomik.

"He wants to see you. He says his name is John Dee."

27

The Queen's Offer

———◆———

"Ow GOOD OF YOU to see me immediately," John Dee said when he stepped into the Vatran throne room. Neel sat calmly as Dee approached, though his fingers were sweaty as they gripped the golden scepter. Dee lifted his foxy face and pinned Neel with a sharp brown gaze. Then Dee's eyes ranged around the room and acknowledged the many guards with a small smile. "I'm flattered to see how wary you are, Your Majesty, of one unarmed man. And yet you have chosen to meet me without your advisers, or other tribe leaders. Intriguing." Dee sat in the chair at the foot of Neel's throne.

"How did you get here?" Neel asked.

"Ah. I wondered whether 'how' or 'why' would be your first question."

"Answer it. You're on my turf, Dee, and I can toss you into prison for the rest of your creepy life."

Dee leaned back in his chair. "You have met my daughters."

"Madinia and Margaret. Nosy, noisy things. What have they got to do with . . . ?" The significance of Dee's suggestion registered with Neel as he remembered the girls' magical powers. "No. They can't have made a Loophole to *here*. Madinia can only open a Loophole to a place she's already been to, and if she's been to the Vatra—if someone brought *your* daughter *here*—that someone's going to pay."

"My daughters once visited India with me. They are well-traveled girls. It was little trouble to pass through a Loophole to the Manvadar palace in the western region of India, and to then travel to the Vatra by more ordinary means. As you see"—Dee spread his hands—"here I am. Now, King Indraneel, there is no need to try to wipe the anger from your face, or even to feel any. I hope you will see my presence here as a good thing for your people. As for the existence and location of the Vatra, that has been known to me for longer than you have been alive. If you truly want to 'make someone pay' for revealing it to me, I wish you good luck in punishing an air spirit."

"Ariel." Neel had met the creature before, when it had nearly killed him.

"Before I released Ariel from my service, it gave me many useful secrets. Ariel is made of air, after all, and little can be hidden from the wind." Dee rested a palm against his bearded cheek as he studied Neel. "That *you* would take the Romany throne, however, was something I couldn't have known, or guessed. But it is a nice surprise."

Neel's mind stretched for Petra's, but she wasn't there. She could give him no advice for how to deal with the man who had once been her captor. Neel looked back at Dee, who tapped his long-nailed fingers against the side of his face as if listening to music no one else could hear. "Why are you here?" Neel asked.

"Delightful. Now we have come to the *why* of things, which I always enjoy much more than the *how*. I have come to make an offer on behalf of my queen."

Neel blinked. Why would Queen Elizabeth of England have any interest in the Vatra, or *him*? "What is she offering?"

"Me."

"You?"

"Queen Elizabeth offers me as the English ambassador to the Romany kingdom. You are welcome to choose an ambassador from your people to send to England, in return."

There was a murmur from the startled guards.

"We don't have ambassadors," Neel said flatly. "We don't take 'em, we don't make 'em, we don't send 'em."

"Yes, because the Roma have long thought that keeping the Vatra secret would protect its people. And has it? Has hiding protected the Roma from Prince Rodolfo?"

Neel's heart spoke the answer, yet everything he knew about John Dee made him not want to be on the man's side. "Say we were a country. A real one—at least in the way you *gadje* think things are real. What kind of power could we have in the world? We're no empire. We're just a small island."

"So is England," said Dee. "Don't underestimate the assets of the Roma. You have a deep knowledge of different cultures at a time when international relations are becoming very important. You have access to markets all over the world, and produce goods many people want to buy. You could be a significant military power. If I'm not mistaken, the Roma possess the Terrestrial and Celestial Globes. They would give you the ability to transport troops in an instant, surprise an enemy, and retreat with few losses. Your people are generally well trained in fighting. They've had reason to be. They are not liked in Europe."

"But apparently Queen Elizabeth likes *me*."

"She likes being first," said Dee. "If England establishes diplomatic ties with you, other countries will follow." He opened his hands. "King Indraneel, don't you want to demand respect for your people? Why keep up the guise that the Roma are homeless travelers with no government to protect them?"

The guards were openly muttering now. Neel shot them a dirty look. They shut their mouths.

Dee leaned forward in his chair. "Can I persuade you to dismiss your guards, Your Majesty? I assure you that you do not need them—and if you did, they would be of little use."

Neel quirked a black brow. Then he laughed. "Go on, get out of here," he told the guards, and when they'd left he said to Dee, "I'm not defenseless myself, you know." His ghostly fingers could strangle a man.

"I do know. After all, you have survived two attempts on your life."

"What do you know about that? You just got here."

"Did I?" said Dee. "Or did I linger in the city for a while after my ship docked, learning what I could about this country's new king?"

Neel sighed. By now, the entire Vatra knew about the poisoning, and since his mother had urged him to tell his advisers and guards about being shoved off the palace wall, Neel guessed that that was public knowledge, too.

Dee tucked his hands inside the sleeves of his long robe. Neel couldn't understand why the Englishman wasn't sweating rivers, wearing such heavy fabric in this heat. Dee's face was cool and dry. Neel felt a twinge of jealousy. He wished he could be so untouched by everything around him.

"May I ask, Your Majesty," Dee said, "how you will investigate these attacks?"

"What business is it of yours?"

"My queen would like for you to stay alive. If you die, the throne goes to Tarn of the Maraki. He is not an open-minded man. He wouldn't even consider accepting an English ambassador, as you are doing."

"I'm *not* considering—" Neel broke off when he realized that, yes, he was.

Dee said, "I would like to offer you my help."

"Petra doesn't have a high opinion of your help." Neel was surprised to see a wince of something—frustration? irritation? regret?—cross Dee's face. But Dee merely said, "You have a high opinion of *her*. Ask her, then, whether you can trust me."

Neel was uneasy. "She's not here."

"Ask her when you next speak with her."

Neel didn't like this. Dee talked as if he could see the mental link between him and Petra branded on his face.

"I simply want to offer some advice," Dee said. "I've investigated many murders. Several of them were politically motivated." He smiled. "I am an expert."

"Fine, know-it-all. What's your advice? And let me tell you I'll take it or leave it, as I please."

"Very well. Let's start by assuming that only one person has tried to kill you, instead of several."

Neel's brain spun. He imagined the three other tribe leaders shoving him off the palace wall, or his three advisers pouring poison on his food. He hadn't even thought that there could be more than one would-be assassin.

"We could be wrong," said Dee. "But we'll start simply, with one attacker, until evidence suggests otherwise. Now, how would you discover his or her identity?"

"I guess by figuring out who most wants me dead." *Tarn*, Neel thought. It was clear.

Dee tsked. "You want the motive. You want the *why*. I understand. The *why* is enticing. But in this case, the *how* is just as important. Consider the two attacks. Describe them, with just one word. First, you are pushed to your doom on a moonless night."

"Impulsive." The word had popped out of Neel's mouth. "Don't you think? The fellow—lady—whatever—saw an opportunity and took it. Me staring out into space, talking to a scoot"—Neel's heart constricted as he thought of the poor animal—"my back turned. The attacker was impulsive."

"Good. Now, the second attempt. Your food is poisoned during a ball. A killer would have to be careful not to be seen."

"Planned," Neel said. "That one was planned."

"Yes, and for full effect. The poisoner hoped to see you die, dramatically, in front of the entire court. What does that tell you?"

Neel understood what Dee was driving at. "That whoever it is won't stop. That if he—she—wanted me dead to begin with, that wanting's growing fiercer."

"Yes."

Neel's gaze swept around the room, at the blue wall, the red one, the yellow, and the green.

Now, he thought, *how can I use this to my advantage?*

28

The House on Molodova Street

PETRA STOOD IN FRONT of the carved wooden door illuminated by a green-burning brassica lamp set in a stone wall. The horses stamped impatiently as the carriage waited and Tomik glanced up and down the street with an awed look. He had never before been to Mala Strana, the most luxurious part of Prague, and Petra supposed that he was impressed by the many-storied houses with their marble trimmings of birds and dragons and flowers. Probably he was wondering how the glass windows managed to be free of frost on this cold night.

Petra knocked at the door. A servant opened it, and Petra hoped that the light of the brassica lamp showed the woman nothing too strange. Just a pair of young, wealthy travelers.

"We would like to see Lucas and Zora December," said Petra. This time her high-class accent was perfect. "We're friends of their aunt."

They were invited into a hallway lined with tapestries and asked to wait.

What artistry! said Astrophil after the servant had left. *Those tapestries must have been sewn two centuries ago. Do you see how that dragonfly almost blends into the trees? You have to have a careful eye to notice it. And there is a frog, too, hidden in the grass. Why, it is like a seek-and-find game!*

Astrophil, please. I'm too nervous to talk about tapestries.

Astrophil burrowed deeper in Petra's hair as a girl came down the hall. She looked about fifteen years old, Petra guessed, and was marked by a quiet confidence. Petra recognized younger versions of Iris's tiny hands and feet, and the narrow chin that seemed to make this girl's eyes bigger. They were clear, intelligent eyes, and there was a smile on the small flower of her mouth.

"I'm Zora December," she said, "and I know exactly who you are. I have told the servants to unpack your bags from the carriage. The driver will be sent home to Aunt Iris. You will no longer need him. You will stay here until I say you can go." She turned and began to walk away.

"What's that supposed to mean?" Tomik hissed at Petra. "Are we under arrest?"

"Perhaps we are her guests," Astrophil whispered back, "and she is a rather bossy hostess."

"Come along," Zora called behind her. "The spider, too!"

Astrophil squeaked. His legs bit into Petra's earlobe.

Petra ran to catch up with Zora, and pulled the other girl's arm so that she swung around to face her. "We've come here for help," Petra said, "but no one's going to make us stay here. We need to know if we can trust you."

Tomik was right behind her. The three of them stood at the foot of a stone staircase. "The Academy—"

Zora tugged her arm out of Petra's grasp. "The hallway," she murmured, "is not the place to discuss this. A servant can pass by at any time, and I can't promise you that the whole of my household is loyal to my brother and me. I can't promise you anything. All I can say is that I want what my aunt Iris wants. If that's not good enough for you, you're welcome to leave. Otherwise, please follow me to my finest spare bedrooms. I'd lock you in the attic, but that would cause far too many tongues to wag. It's better if the servants think you are my dear friends." At that, the maid who had answered the door walked through it, carrying a trunk by one handle as a valet brought up the other end. "And you *are* so dear to me," Zora added in a loud voice. "It's been such a long time!" She kissed Petra's cheek, then Tomik's. "You must be glad to see me, too."

Tomik looked a little dazed. "Yes." Petra sighed. "I guess we are."

Zora led them to an upstairs room with dark walnut furniture and red hangings. A brassica lamp burned at a small table that was already set with three plates and a covered silver platter.

"Well," said Tomik after the servants had left, "if it's a prison, it's a nice one."

Zora smiled. "Petra, you'll sleep here. There's an adjoining room"— she pointed at a door near the fireplace—"for Tomik. Now, Astrophil, are you going to come out and say hello? It's not very polite to hide from your hostess, and I was led to believe that you are the very soul of politeness."

Astrophil crawled out from under Petra's hair and onto the top of her head. He executed a many-legged bow.

"Astrophil!" Petra, who could feel what he was doing, was a bit shocked that the spider was so forward.

"Zora does seem nice," he said in a small voice.

"I don't know about 'nice,'" said Zora, "but I like things to be as they should. Right now, very little in Bohemia is as it should be. I'm going to change that, and so are you, Petra, which makes us partners."

"Iris told you everything," said Petra.

"Actually, no. And she didn't tell me you'd turn up on my doorstep. She didn't tell me that your so-called disguises were this bad."

"But she dyed my hair," Tomik protested. "It has smelled like oil and licorice for a week now. It's got to do *something*."

Zora raised her eyes to the ceiling. "I love Aunt Iris. Since our parents died, she's the only family my brother and I have. But she is blinded by her obsessions with her work. She thinks color changes the world. Maybe it can, sometimes. You, Tomik, would probably escape notice if you weren't standing right next to Petra. There are leaflets with your faces all over the country—hers, especially, and when yours appears it's sketched next to hers. We'll be lucky if one of the servants doesn't notice who Petra is and decide to send us to Prince Rodolfo's dungeon."

"I might have been spotted by one of the Academy students," Petra said.

Zora grimaced. "Let's hope, then, that student couldn't guess where you were headed."

"It was chaos there," said Tomik. "The Academy's in ruins, and—"

"I know."

"It just happened. How can you possibly already know?" asked Astrophil. "What is your connection to Bohemia's school of magic?"

"None, really," said a new voice. They turned to see a fair-haired young man enter the room and shut the door behind him. He looked so much like Zora that it was immediately clear to Petra that this was Lucas, the older December. "None," he continued, "except for the fact that she and I are the leaders of the rebellion."

There was a pause, and someone would have said something eventually, if the silence hadn't been interrupted by a distant boom.

All eyes darted to the window. There was the sound of another explosion. On a dark hill above the city a green fire began to burn.

29

The Rebels

BEAUTIFUL!" said Lucas as he lifted a curtain to see the fire better.

"Lucas," his sister scolded. "Stop staring at the pretty inferno. Introduce yourself to our guests."

"Sorry." He gave them a sheepish grin. "But it's silly to do that now, isn't it? We all know who the other is. You're Petra and Tomik, and I'm Lucas. Er . . . Lucas December, duke of Moravia, I guess, if you want to be precise."

Petra didn't care about his title. "What is that?" She pointed at the green fire.

"Prague's biggest brassica warehouse," Lucas said.

"No." Astrophil was appalled. "It is not true. It cannot be true. A fire like that . . . the amount of oil it would take to cause it . . . oh! Barrels and barrels of delicious oil!" His gaze fixed upon Zora and Lucas. "You . . . you *caused* this. Do you care nothing for the tin spiders of the world?"

"I think you're the only one," Zora said with a smile.

"Did you set the Academy on fire?" asked Petra.

"Not personally," said Lucas, "but we planned it."

Petra stared. "How could you do that? People *died*."

"No." Lucas looked confused. "We were careful to prevent that.

We only wanted to destroy the building. Our agents set off an explosion in the cellar—but *after* everyone had escaped. In fact, two of the agents are Academy professors. They made sure everyone was safe."

"Everyone except Fiala Broshek."

"She fled the building. A rebel saw her."

"Are you sure?"

Lucas frowned at the excitement in Petra's voice. "It's nothing to be glad about. Believe me, Petra, there'd be no loss to the world if she'd stayed inside. She's one of the reasons we destroyed the Academy. Broshek was experimenting in the cellar laboratories. She's been using her power over human flesh to create new monsters. She had to be stopped." He sighed. "The truth is, she's probably carrying on her experiments someplace else. But at least her laboratory is gone, and so is the influence she had over Bohemia's magical youth."

"But so is the Academy," said Tomik. "The best school for magic in the whole Hapsburg Empire."

"Exactly," said Zora. "And who will inherit the empire? Emperor Karl still has a choice between two sons: Rodolfo and Frederic. We want him to choose Frederic. That's partly why we planned to destroy the Academy. That's also why Lucas blew up the brassica warehouse."

"That one I did myself," Lucas said with pride.

"Karl's old, but he's refused to name an heir because it gives him power over his children," Zora said. "His sons have always sought his favor. But now Prince Maximilian is dead, and Rodolfo is becoming a greater threat than ever. Do you know how many countries in Europe fear his army of Gray Men? Can you imagine what will happen if Rodolfo becomes the Hapsburg emperor, and takes possession of Austria, Hungary, and countless other territories? He could rule the world. We know what kind of ruler he would be. That can't happen."

A storm began to gather inside Petra.

"I know nothing of Prince Frederic," said Astrophil. "Is he really a better choice?"

"He has to be. Anybody would be better."

Petra squeezed her eyes shut.

"We have to make Emperor Karl see this," said Lucas. "So we attacked Prince Rodolfo where it would hurt the most. The loss of the Academy will be huge. Bohemia's biggest export is brassica oil, and that warehouse fire means Prince Rodolfo will have much less money to fund his army. It means that he's been weakened, and that his people hate him enough to make their own country bleed. Maybe now the emperor will understand that he has to name an heir, and that it has to be Frederic."

"Stop," said Petra. "Please stop talking about your plans and your politics and your efforts to change the world. I hate Rodolfo more than you can imagine, but don't you see that you can't control the fate of an entire empire? I wish you could. I wish for a lot of things. But right now I just want to find Fiala Broshek."

The room went still. Petra turned her back to everyone. She faced the window, trying to wrangle her emotions into something she could manage. Outside, the fire flared and cast an eerie green light over the city. Astrophil silently held on to her hair.

Tomik cleared his throat. Petra knew he was exchanging glances with Zora and Lucas. "I'm not sure how much Iris told you . . ." Tomik said hesitantly.

"Almost nothing," Lucas answered. "Just that she was helping you disguise yourselves, and that she had given you our address."

Petra watched the fire as Tomik explained why Petra needed Fiala Broshek so badly.

When Zora spoke, it was with sympathy. "We can find her, Petra. Lucas and I have court connections. We'll use them."

Petra looked over her shoulder at Zora.

"In fact, I have an idea," Zora continued. "We'll try it out tomorrow morning, at the Hall of Education. Tomik can help me."

Petra said, "I want to help."

"Sorry, but no. You're too recognizable. You can't leave this house."

At that, Petra wheeled around to face the Decembers. She couldn't believe that, yet again, she was trapped in a beautiful house by someone who claimed it was for her own safety. John Dee had done exactly the same thing.

"Petra," Lucas said, "it's for the best. You're too tired now to see things clearly. Sleep, and in the morning you'll realize that sometimes you have to sacrifice things to get what you want. Your personal freedom is a small price to pay for capturing Fiala Broshek."

With that, the Decembers left the room.

I think they are right, said Astrophil.

"Petra." Tomik rested a light hand on her shoulder. It felt soft and warm, and part of her wished she could accept this gesture and relax into it. Yet she knew this would be a mistake. He said, "Can we talk?"

There was so much to discuss, but Petra sensed what haunted his mind. *There are things I can't feel*, she had told him.

"Not now," she said.

"Not ever, you mean."

Astrophil glanced between the two of them. He tried very hard to seem invisible. Petra watched him shrink, gathering in his shiny legs.

Petra hated her mind-magic. She hated what it showed her sometimes, and how, even when it lined up perfectly with what her heart would have guessed anyway, she couldn't rely on it. She couldn't be sure that the Decembers were good people who wanted to protect her. She couldn't believe the tenderness that sometimes seeped through Neel's silent words to her.

And she couldn't know, for certain, that Tomik was now struggling to swallow his disappointment and say that everything would somehow still be all right.

"I'm tired," she said.

Tomik's hand slipped away. Just before he passed through the door to the bedroom next to hers, he murmured, "Sorry, Petra, about tomorrow morning. I know you don't like having to stay put."

Petra had nothing to say to that, because she had no intention of staying put.

30

The Horseshoe

———◆◆◆———

THE DECEMBERS trusted Petra—or at least they trusted her sense of self-preservation.

She and Tomik breakfasted with them, watching Lucas fuss with his doublet and rub fingertips against the sides of his face. "I must not smile, I must not smile," he muttered to himself. He was going to Salamander Castle. A messenger had come in the night from Prince Rodolfo, who was calling together the most powerful aristocrats in the country to discuss yesterday's attacks.

He left, and Zora and Tomik followed soon after that. "I'm going to squirrel the whereabouts of Fiala Broshek out of the secretary of education," Zora said cheerfully. "Just you wait." Then she and Tomik were gone.

Petra stood from the table. There was a determined glint in her eyes.

Astrophil jumped from a chair to her shoulder. He sighed. He wished, as he had wished many times and would do so again, that he was big enough to hold Petra. He wished he could hold her back from danger.

She plucked Astrophil from her shoulder and set him on the polished, dark surface of the table.

"Petra." His voice was small. "I am going with you."

She shook her head. "Not this time, Astro."

Petra opened the unlocked door of the dining room. She walked freely through the many-roomed house and passed through the front door to the street. She remembered how John Dee had posted guards outside her bedroom in London, and how cautious he had been to prevent any attempt she might make to flee. She thought of the Decembers' unlocked doors, and of the fact that Dee had, at least, understood her.

She walked through the morning bustle of Prague's streets. The air was glassy and cold, but there were signs that the city was inching toward spring. It was early March. The Vltava River was no longer frozen solid, though a thin lace of ice still clung to its banks. Petra crossed the river to Staro Square, where she tried not to look at the tall, magnificent clock her father had built. She turned down a street lined with shops and hugged the edges of the crowd until she found it: the Riven brothers' silk stall.

"Master Riven?" She approached the man standing behind piles of jewel-colored fabric.

He nodded. "That's me. Joel Riven. Who are you?"

Petra untied the leather string of her necklace, and set it on a square of blue silk so that the man could see the Romany words scratched on the tiny horseshoe dangling from its string. *This is Petali Kronos*, the words read. *Be kind to her, for she is bound by blood to Indraneel of the Lovari.*

Petra said, "I want to talk with Sadie."

"Be confident," Zora whispered in Tomik's ear as he looked across the street at the doors to the Hall of Education. The entrance was flanked by statues of giants. They looked as if they were holding the weight of the building on their stooped shoulders. Tomik imagined them coming to life and swatting him down with their huge, stone hands.

"You can even be a little arrogant," Zora added. "All aristocrats are."

But he was not an aristocrat. He was ordinary. A fifteen-year-old boy from the countryside. "Don't I need a title?" he asked Zora. "Shouldn't I say I'm Sir Something from Somewhere Important?"

"No. You'd be caught in a lie. Don't worry, Tomik. You're dressed like a rich and powerful person." Her eyes studied him. "You look the part. And you're with me. Say as little as possible and let the secretary assume the rest. Whatever you do, don't say what your magical ability is. Be mysterious about it. I don't *think* that someone will guess who you are, but one thing everyone knows about Tomik Stakan is that he's got a magical gift for glass."

Zora led him inside. She smiled at the guards, who seemed to recognize her, and wove her way down halls lit by candles stuffed into lamps designed to burn brassica oil. It looked as if Prague was already feeling the pinch of the oil shortage. Tomik didn't mind. The Decembers, who had known what was coming, had set aside barrels of oil. Astrophil would have plenty to drink. Anyway, there was something cozy about candlelight. It flickered merrily, and shone on Zora's blond hair.

A boy in a gray-blue uniform opened the door to the secretary's office. Tomik's heartbeat fumbled and raced. He would be caught. Of course he would. He would be punished for having always tried so hard to be better.

"Lady Zora." An old man rose from a velvet chair to greet them. He took one of Zora's gloved hands and pressed it with both of his. "On any other day, the sight of you would bring a smile to my face. Alas, I have no smile to give you today, nor even very much time."

"The Academy." Zora shook her head sadly.

"I'm heartbroken, dear. And overwhelmed with meetings. Parents across the country—even across the empire—are demanding to know what will become of their children's studies. We're trying to locate a suitable building to hold classes, but it will never be the same." He bit his lip. "Did you ever ride in one of the Academy hot-air balloons? I used to love that."

"No, sir. I never attended the school. You forget I have no magical talent."

"Nor I, but being the secretary of education has its benefits. Now, I hate to rush our conversation, but I have a meeting in"—he pulled a red enameled watch from his pocket and peered at its face— "ten minutes. What brings you here today, my lady? And who"—he finally focused on Tomik—"is this?"

The breath died in Tomik's throat.

"*He* is why I needed to see you." Zora beamed at him. "Stefan"— she laid a hand on Tomik's arm—"is a great talent. He could do so much for Bohemia, but with the Academy gone . . . you were right when you said that things will never be the same. Classes can be held in another building, of course, but that will take so long to organize."

The secretary nodded and sighed.

"Meanwhile, his education will suffer," Zora said. "Unless . . . well, I have an idea. You see, Stefan hoped to work with one Academy professor in particular: Fiala Broshek."

The secretary looked suddenly wary.

"Would it be possible to arrange an apprenticeship with her?" Zora continued. "I'd ask her myself, but no one knows where she is."

The secretary's eyes roved from Zora to Tomik, then back again. "How exactly do you know each other?"

Zora's hand slipped to link arms with Tomik. She nestled close to him and smiled. Tomik blushed.

"Oh." The secretary's gaze softened somewhat.

"You see, I want the very best for him," Zora said. "Professor Broshek is the best."

"The best of a certain kind," the secretary said slowly. "An apprenticeship might be possible—Professor Broshek *is* enthusiastic about gathering the most promising magical talents under her wing—"

"So she is safe and well," said Zora. "What a relief! There were rumors that she was missing."

"She and the prince had an arrangement, should something ever happen to the Academy. For her own safety, she had to return immediately to Prague. Once the rebels began to destroy public property—little things, at first, like bridges—Prince Rodolfo feared that the Academy could become a target. Professor Broshek's research then—and now—is a sensitive, secret matter. Which brings me back to your silent gentleman." The secretary's gaze focused again on Tomik. "If I ask Professor Broshek to take on an apprentice, I need to know what he can do. What, young man, is your magic skill?"

Zora's eyes flashed an anxious message at Tomik. It was easy to read: *Be careful.*

Tomik thought quickly. Neel had once taught him the trick to telling a good lie. "Tell the truth," Neel had said. "But skew it. Twist it."

"Heat," Tomik said finally.

The secretary frowned. "I'm not so sure that *heat* would be useful to Professor Broshek."

"Yes, it would." The next words flew out of Tomik's mouth: "I can prove it."

Zora struggled to keep her smile, but Tomik saw the dismay on her face, and her fear. There was no way that he could prove an ability he didn't have.

But he could heat and mold glass, sometimes, with the touch of his hand. If he was determined enough. It hurt his head and made him see double, but he could do it. He had done so last year, when he had made a glass knife from loose sand.

Zora's eyes were still on him. Tomik cursed his brazen words. Of course he could heat something in front of the secretary's eyes—but only glass, or something that could be made *into* glass. A secretary of education had to be an intelligent man. It wouldn't take him long to figure out Tomik's identity.

"Prove it, then," said the secretary, "or I'm going to wonder why you won't, and why you two are asking questions about Professor Broshek. Well, Stefan? Let's see if you have something the professor wants. And let's see it now. I am out of time."

Tomik had a flash of inspiration. "May I have your watch?"

The secretary's brows shot up. "My watch?"

"I'll give it back."

With a curious glance, the secretary handed his pocket watch to Tomik, who tightened his fingers around it. He felt its enamel-coated surface. He remembered how people don't think too hard about the objects they use. When the secretary looked at his watch, did he think about the red, opaque enamel that framed its face? Did he consider its shiny ceramic surface, and think about what enamel was made from, what it really was? Or, to him, was it just a pretty part of a watch? Enamel, after all, doesn't *look* like glass. It's not clear. It looks like floor tile.

But Tomik's hand knew what it was. His fingers began to burn. He felt like someone had thrust a torch down his throat and the flames were burning in his brain.

The watch turned into a hot coal in his hand. The enamel melted. The red fluid dripped through Tomik's fingers and exposed the metal gears underneath. Tomik squeezed his fist. He couldn't melt the metal, but he could crush the delicate gears for good measure with the ordinary strength of his fingers. He did just that.

He handed the molten mess back to the secretary, who yelped and dropped it. The old man shook his hand to ease the burn. "You ruined it!"

"I said I'd give it back," Tomik replied. "I didn't mention what condition it'd be in."

The secretary stared at the lump on the floor. It was unrecognizable.

"If I destroyed that so easily"—Tomik let a dangerous note creep into his voice—"imagine what else I can do. I want to serve Prince Rodolfo, and learn how to destroy what he wants destroyed. Well? Am I good enough for him? Am I good enough for Fiala Broshek?"

"Yes," the secretary said shakily. "I will pass along a recommendation."

"I'd prefer to speak with her myself. If you tell me the location of her new laboratory—"

"No. The prince would have my head. I can only say that she's nearby, in Prague, and that I'll arrange for you to see her."

Tomik opened his mouth to argue, but Zora's arm tightened around his.

"We'll have to be satisfied with that," she said.

SADIE'S BLACK EYES widened at the sight of Petra standing next to Joel Riven. She pushed her chair back against the tavern wall. She set her lovely mouth and said to Joel, "I can't believe you brought her here."

"She had this." Joel passed the horseshoe necklace to Sadie. "It's the token of a king. I had to bring her." Sadie stared at the Romany writing.

When Joel had left, Petra dragged a chair to sit next to Sadie, who stayed silent, head bowed, looking at the horseshoe on her palm. Then Sadie lifted her face, and Petra saw the young woman who had been her friend, and had whispered with her through the dark of the Salamander Castle dormitory. Sadie carefully placed the necklace in

Petra's outstretched hand. "My brother must like you very much," she said.

Petra tied the string around her neck and tucked the horseshoe inside her dress, where it warmed against her skin.

"It says you're bound by blood to him," Sadie said. "You took a blood oath with a Roma?"

Petra hesitated. It seemed to her that Sadie's thoughts were hovering, uncertain where to land, and that a single word from Petra would cause them all to fly away. She lifted her palm so that Sadie could see the faint scar that matched Neel's.

Sadie sighed. "Why are you in Prague, Petra?"

Petra told her everything except what might have been most important to Sadie. She said nothing about the little stitch she had sewn between her and Neel. Petra meant to tell her, but her mouth closed before the words could come out. She realized that she loved this secret, and sheltered it from everyone. Maybe this was because it wasn't her secret alone. It was Neel's, too. It occurred to her that a secret isn't simply a secret. It's a promise. Petra cherished hers.

"You know that I'm a spy," Sadie said flatly. "I guess you need my help. You've come to me for information."

"No."

Sadie blinked. "Then why are you here?"

"To tell you to go home. Neel—"

"Joel Riven already gave me the message. You don't have to repeat it."

"Yes, I do. Joel Riven doesn't know what I know. He can't tell you what Neel told me: that after a boy in Spain cut his face, you cried. He can't say that Neel has always tried to match his heart to yours, because he thinks yours is kinder and greater than his own. Joel Riven can't say that I think Neel is wrong." Petra took a breath. She held it, and steadied herself against the tears that threatened to well in her eyes. Her next words were very hard to say. "I thought about asking you for information. I considered asking you to find out where Fiala Broshek is. But I don't want to. I don't want to put you in danger." Petra's voice dropped. "I've lost my family. I don't want Neel to lose you. I don't want him to feel the way I feel."

Sadie's face softened. "You care for him."

"Yes."

"And you truly think I should leave Prague now?"

"Yes."

"When thousands of Roma are imprisoned, or changed into monsters? Is this what you would do? Would you leave? Would Neel?"

Petra was silent.

Sadie said, "For the longest time, I blamed you for what has happened to my people here. But now . . . well, I know Neel. He's willful. And he was getting himself into trouble long before he met you. Maybe it was insane to steal from the prince, but our clan did need the money, and Neel wanted so badly to help us. You didn't make him do anything. And I suppose . . . I suppose I'm willful, too. I want to help my people, too. So, no, Petra, I'm not leaving."

Petra started to protest.

"Isn't it strange?" Sadie laughed. "Neel and I aren't related by blood at all, and yet we're so alike."

"I don't think blood matters much."

Sadie rested a hand on Petra's, the one with the scar. "There's something your rebel friends should know. There's no point blowing up things to convince Emperor Karl to name Frederic as his heir. Gray Men have already been sent into Hungary to kill Frederic just like they killed Rodolfo's other brother. Prince Rodolfo will become heir to the empire. It's only a matter of time."

Even though it was only yesterday that Petra had thought that she couldn't let herself care about this very matter, her heart leaped with fear at Sadie's words.

"I'm spying for the Roma," Sadie continued, "not for you. But if I hear something about Fiala Broshek, I will let you know."

It took a great deal of strength for Petra to shake her head. "I'll find out what I need to know another way. Go home, Sadie."

Sadie spoke as if she hadn't heard. "I'm not doing this because you asked me to, but because I *want* to. You have to be careful, Petra. The prince suspects you're in the country."

Petra nodded. She wasn't surprised.

Sadie stood to leave, and Petra tried one last time, "Sadie, please—"

Sadie cocked her head, and for a flash of a second she truly did look like Neel. "I'll go home if you come with me."

Petra shut her mouth.

Sadie smiled. "Goodbye, Petra."

31

The Assassin

———◆———

NEEL REMEMBERED SOMETHING Petra had once told him: that the earth spins around the sun, not the other way around. It seemed like a screwy idea. It was the opposite of what everyone believed. But Neel's thoughts turned around that clear crystal bead he had found the night he'd been pushed off the palace wall, and he began to wonder if thinking the opposite of what made sense could, in the end, *make* sense.

If someone wants your heart on a dagger, what should you do?

Why, protect yourself.

And if you think that person's drinking down one cup of rage after another, hating you more every day, what should you do?

Find the source of the anger and stop it. Stop needling this person. Stop digging your own grave.

Neel, though, wasn't sure he agreed with what made sense. In fact, as he propped an elbow on his bedroom windowsill and mused at the moon, his chin cradled on a fist, he rather thought that he should be doing the opposite. And why not? Why not make himself as vulnerable as could be?

How best to spark a third attempt to kill him?

Neel shifted, and his sleeve grazed over something on the windowsill that made a faint, gritty noise. Dust. The wind had blown some of that red-brown dust through the window. Though Neel couldn't quite see it in the moonlight, he was sure he'd just smeared a good bit of dust on his shirt. There'd be a stain, and it'd be devilishly hard to get out. Karim wasn't going to like that. He'd practically wept when he saw the tunic Neel had been wearing the night he was tossed off the palace wall. The shirt had been shredded, and stained across the chest with reddish dirt from when Neel had pulled himself over the wall and had lain flat on the terrace.

A sudden idea made Neel stand up very straight. He fetched a candle from his nightstand and touched a match to the wick. He traced a finger through the fine layer of dust on the sill and looked at it. He thought of the crystal bead. He thought of the dust. And Neel knew he had been following the wrong clue.

He hoisted himself onto the sill and climbed out his window.

ONE BY ONE, Neel climbed through the open windows of rooms all over the palace. He crept past the sleeping forms of Tarn, Shaida, Jasmine, Arun, Gita, and Karim, and even after he had found what he was looking for, he riffled through the wardrobes in each room to make certain.

He now knew who had tried to kill him.

When Neel slipped back through his own window, his blood pulsed with an almost joyous feeling. At first he thought it was satisfaction with his own sneaky self. But then Neel remembered how he'd felt when he'd found the pair of crystal-beaded slippers, whose soles were stained with red-brown dust. He'd felt relieved.

He had been right not to search the room of one other person who could have poisoned his food. He hadn't even realized, until then, that the whispers of the court had planted a tiny black mustard seed of doubt in him. But he had been right. It could never have been his mother.

It was *him*. Neel should have known it was him.

Neel had noiselessly set the slippers in the exact place he'd found them and returned to his room.

As he lay in his bed and used invisible fingers to play absently with the white mosquito net, Neel pondered his next step. He was a king. He knew the criminal. Neel could name him, and jail him, and no one could question his decision. That was his right.

But dusty slippers are a pretty flimsy piece of proof. Reddish dust always blew somewhere in the Vatra, a few times a month. It wasn't rare to have red-soled shoes, and though the combination of that with crystal beads proved something to Neel, he imagined how his courtiers would see things. They'd see a young king they didn't trust accusing someone they did, based on the evidence of some dirty shoes.

Neel's mind spun back to the idea he'd had earlier that night: to provoke another attack. Now he knew how.

NEEL SUMMONED THE TRIBE LEADERS and his advisers to the throne room. He'd refused to let Karim choose his clothes. Neel had dressed in shades of yellow, the Lovari color, and laughed at Karim when the man sputtered, then pleaded, then looked gloomy.

"So"—Neel slouched in his throne, and threw one leg over the side—"I've been thinking. It's time I made my mark."

"What do you mean?" Gita asked warily.

Neel pulled the Jewel of the Kalderash from his ear and began to juggle it from one hand to the other. Gita gasped. Karim covered his eyes. Tarn raised a suspicious brow, and Jasmine looked amused. Shaida and Arun did not.

"Well," Neel continued, "I've only got a year and a half left to be king. Next time I get a turn to run things, I'll be almost twenty-nine years old. So I've got to bake my bread while the fire's hot. Every time a ruler takes the Romany throne, there's a chance to change decisions other kings and queens have made. Some things, though, can't be changed. Those things are a king's legacy. It's time I gave the Roma something to remember me by."

"You gave us the globes," said Shaida.

"Yeah," Neel drawled. The sapphire glittered in the air as it fell to his open palm. "It was a nice start. But I want to build something."

The Kalderash in the room—Arun, Gita, and Karim—perked up.

"A wonderful idea." Karim sounded relieved. "Your tribe will be pleased. A new building will put money in Kalderash pockets. What did you have in mind?"

"A theater for the Lovari."

Someone gasped. His advisers' faces went blank, then flashed anger. Jasmine grinned. Tarn shot his cousin an irritated look. "You don't stop stirring trouble, do you?"

"Nope. Which brings me to my topic: John Dee." The sapphire traced a blue arc from one hand to the other.

Now everyone in the room looked worried. "That problem needs to be contained," said Arun. "The *gadje* can never leave this island, or the whole world will learn of the Vatra's existence and location."

"You should consider having him executed," said Gita.

"Nah," said Neel. "We're going to accept him as the English ambassador, and send a Roma to England in his place."

There was a silence.

"Neel," Tarn said quietly. "If you open the doors to the world, no one will be able to close them."

"I know. That's my legacy." Neel caught the sapphire again. This time, he held it.

"Your mother never would have wanted this," Arun hissed.

"You mean Queen Iona? You're right. She would have hated the idea. But the dead can't hate, or love, or speak. She's gone. You've got me. And this is my decision."

Arun's hands clenched at his sides. "You selfish, stupid brat." The man's fists jerked open, and snatched a set of daggers that had been hidden in his clothes. He launched himself at Neel and smashed the king off his throne.

Neel flung out his hands. He snatched a knife by its blade, wrenching it away with ghost fingers that no edge could cut. He leaped to his feet. Arun swiped at Neel's neck with his other knife, but Neel danced back, nimble on his toes as he'd always been, as any Lovari should be. Then Neel stepped close. He ducked Arun's blade, gripped the man's wrist with invisible fingers, and twisted Arun's arm.

The man howled. His knife fell. He barreled into Neel, knocking him to the floor yet again, and wrapped his hands around Neel's throat. "You have betrayed the Kalderash!" Arun screamed. "You have betrayed my queen. Iona was wise, she was just. She was beautiful, and I loved her."

Neel choked against the band of pain crushing his throat. He scrambled his fingers out from under Arun's chest and slammed an invisible fist into his adviser's face. Arun slumped to the floor. He didn't move.

"Is he breathing?" Neel croaked. He struggled to his feet and looked at the stunned faces around him. "Is he *breathing*?" Neel had never killed someone.

Tarn's boots thudded toward the fallen body. Tarn knelt and checked Arun's pulse. "Yes," he said. "But not for long. When he wakes up, I want my chance at the man who made me look like my cousin's murderer."

"You already had your chance," Neel said. "You could have helped me out a minute ago."

Tarn wrinkled his nose at the idea. "Why? It was more fun to watch. In fact, I've decided that the next year or so is going to be entertaining, if nothing else. When you're sixteen, it'll be my turn to boot you off the throne. Until then, I'm going to relax and enjoy the show."

"Someone call the guards." Neel was suddenly weary. "Imprison Arun."

A glitter caught his eye. Grateful for the distraction, Neel limped across the room to pick the Jewel of the Kalderash off the floor.

"I can't believe it," Gita said. "Arun has always seemed so calm."

Yes, thought Neel. Except when Neel had found him in his room, the night he'd fallen down the cliff. Or when Neel had first met the adviser, and sullied the palace drinking water with his own filthy body. Or when Neel had announced the destruction of the globes.

"I have never seen him so angry," Gita said.

"Well, I wanted to make him angry," said Neel.

Understanding dawned on her face. "So this whole meeting was a charade? You suspected him and wanted him to lash out at you?"

Neel rubbed his head. He'd banged it against the throne. "It worked a little too well. But you had to see for yourselves what he was capable of doing. I couldn't accuse him without real proof, and I guess . . . I wanted to seem just."

"So you didn't really mean what you said about building a theater and establishing diplomatic relations with England."

"I sure did," said Neel. He looked around the room, and at Arun's unconscious body on the floor. "Look, politics is a dirty, tricky game. I know that. But how can the Roma win if we don't play?" Neel saw a number of expressions on the faces around him: reluctance, curiosity, fear. This would be hard. Yet all new things are.

"Now," he said, "why don't we decide who we'll pick to be *our* ambassador?"

"I let Gita choose," Neel told Dee later, in the sitting room of his royal suite. "She knew better than me who will make the Roma feel most comfortable about this."

"Fine, fine," said Dee.

"She picked a popular Ursari. He's smooth. Gets along with everybody. I chose his assistant, Nadia. They've already set sail for England."

"Nadia of the Maraki? She has a reputation for being rude. Ambassadors are supposed to be diplomatic."

Neel remembered Nadia making him study charts on the price of coir. It'd be tough to practice reading on his own, but he'd manage, and he knew he had made the right decision. "They're also supposed to get what they want."

Dee seemed as if he might protest, then smiled and said, "I'm glad everything has resolved so nicely."

"Yep. My problems are solved."

"Are they?"

Neel looked at him.

"Your Majesty," said Dee, "let's talk about Bohemia."

32

Feathers

"WHAT *ABOUT* BOHEMIA?" said Neel.

"Prince Rodolfo is poised to become the Hapsburg emperor. Thousands of Roma have suffered at his hand. Surely this doesn't please you."

"Well, what can I do about it?" Neel pressed a wet cloth against his bruised temple and wished for ice. "I've got my hands full." He was tired. Even though he was supposed to have come out on top this day, Neel felt a sneaking sense of powerlessness. He flung the cloth to the floor. "Do you think I haven't considered doing something? I'd send a small mission into Prague to try to spring the Roma from Rodolfo's prison, but that's impossible. Suicide, for anyone crazy enough to do it. Setting aside how downright hard it'd be to break people out of Salamander Castle's prison, there's the eensy teensy problem of *this*." Neel pressed a hand to the dark skin above the low collar of his shirt. "Any Roma who turn up in Prague can't hide what they are. They can't pretend to be guards or get friendly with the locals to scoop up information. All they can do is get caught themselves."

"There is another option."

"Oh, yeah?"

Dee trailed a hand down his beard. "Prince Rodolfo could die."

"A nice, warm, fuzzy idea. But how?"

"You could ask someone with motivation to do it. Someone who is in Prague, right now. Someone who could be incredibly gifted in the art of killing, if she wished."

Neel stared. He didn't stop to wonder how Dee knew where Petra was. He felt a mounting outrage. "I can't ask her that."

"Can't or won't? Because you *could*. You could touch the line of that mental link that ties you to her, and ask."

"How do you know about that?"

"I didn't. I only suspected. Now, however, I *do* know."

Neel's lip curled. "How did you suspect it, then?"

"I studied you from afar, before I announced my presence in your country."

"And what did you see?"

"Call it a faraway look in your eyes. Call it the smile that sometimes plays on your lips, for no reason."

"Get out," Neel muttered.

Dee bowed his head and left.

PETRA DIDN'T LEAVE the house on Molodova Street again for some time. She didn't tell its residents about her meeting with Sadie. She had prepared herself to confess it that evening, at dinner, when Zora proudly described how Tomik had melted the secretary of education's watch, but then Lucas had come home from court with the news that Prince Frederic was dead. Petra realized that this information was, really, the only thing Sadie had said that she would have been obligated to share. The rest was hers alone—and Neel's.

He rustled his way into her mind like windblown leaves, and Petra seemed to catch a flavor of feelings so mixed together she couldn't tell what they were. *I found him,* he said, and told her about Arun.

Petra let her forehead rest against the chilled window of her bedroom and exhaled. She saw the white fog form around her face and thought to herself, *So that is what relief looks like.* To Neel she said, *There's something I need to tell you.*

Wait, that's not all, Pet. John Dee is here. He's the English ambassador to the Vatra now. I've been meaning to tell you, but . . . well, I knew you wouldn't like it. And I can see why. He's a piece of work. Always looking for the slyest way forward, not caring who or what gets risked along the way. Sneaky, untrustworthy devil.

Petra thought about it, and as much as she didn't relish discussing John Dee, she liked it more than what she'd have to do: admit to Neel that she had failed in convincing Sadie to leave Prague. *You can trust him in one way.*

Oh?

As long as what you want matches what he wants, he will do his best to help you. And—she forced herself to admit it—*his best is pretty good.* She paused, then said, *Neel, I'm sorry.* She told as much as she could of her conversation with Sadie without betraying her own fragile feelings for him.

Can you . . . Neel's voice sounded strained. *Can you talk to her again? Make her see?*

I can try, but I'm worried about meeting with her too often. Zora says it'd be easy to recognize me, and if Sadie's caught with me, then . . .

Yeah. Neel was grim. *It'd be bad.* He fell silent, then said abruptly, *Look, Petali, you're just after Fiala Broshek, right? You wouldn't try to . . . I don't know, do something else?*

Petra was confused. *What "else"? All I want is for that woman to heal my father. That's it.*

You wouldn't try to do something even more dangerous, like going after Prince Rodolfo. 'Cause that'd be a surefire way to die. He's got an army of monsters around him, he's a step away from being emperor, and—

Go after? What do you mean, go after him?

You know . . . try to kill him.

Petra remembered chopping off the head of a Gray Man. She saw black blood jetting onto her skin. She swallowed. *No, Neel. I wouldn't do that.*

TOMIK SET UP a glassblowing room in the Decembers' attic. "I have to do something," he told Zora. "I hate waiting for a note from Fiala Broshek that might never come."

Zora leaned against a table and played with a pair of tongs. "You're not the only one. Rodolfo's the heir to the empire now. Nothing can change that, and ever since Bohemia went into mourning for Prince Frederic's death, Lucas and I have been wondering how to give the rebellion some purpose. We want to find Broshek's new laboratory."

"No one wants that more than Petra."

"Yes." Zora set the tongs on the table. "It's hard to look in her face every morning. It must be especially hard for you."

Tomik glanced at her.

"Because you're sweethearts." Zora was awkward.

"We're not." Tomik turned. He fanned a brassica fire into brighter flames.

"No? You mean, you were together, before? Or maybe some-day . . . ?"

"No. Not ever, I think." Tomik held a piece of glass in a brass bowl over the flames until the shard puddled into a clear pool. He thought about how glass can be shaped into almost anything. But its essence can be transformed only up to a certain point. Glass can become enamel, but it could never become metal. It could never become stone. "I guess things weren't what I thought they were."

Zora looked at him. She started to speak, stopped, and then said, "What will you do with that?" She nodded at the bowl of molten glass.

"I'm not sure yet."

Abruptly, she said, "What color was your hair, before my aunt meddled with it?"

"Blond. About your color."

"Hmm." Zora's long fingers stretched, lifted a lock of his black hair, and let it fall. "I suppose the color wouldn't change things, one way or the other. You are what you are."

Tomik felt the tingle on his cheek from where her fingers had brushed it. "And what's that?"

She smiled and would have replied, but they heard footfalls on the attic steps. A servant entered the room. "Oh, there you are, Lady Zora. I have been looking everywhere for you. This just arrived from the secretary of education."

Zora snatched the note and opened it so that she and Tomik could read it together.

I regret to say that Fiala Broshek has no intention of taking on any apprentices at this time. This is for reasons of security.

Your young gentleman should not be discouraged, but should keep up his studies. Who knows? He might be able to work with Professor Broshek someday, perhaps next year.

Zora folded the message.

"A year?" said Tomik. "We can't wait that long."

LATE THAT NIGHT there was a knock on the Decembers' door. A maid yawned and grumpily padded down the hall with a candle. She opened the door.

A dark-haired girl wearing a Salamander Castle uniform stood there, gripping a small square of paper in her hand. The maid rubbed her eyes, then looked again. The girl standing before her was a rare beauty. She had sweetly wide black eyes in a heart-shaped face.

And she had no business being here at this time of night.

"Please." The girl's voice was low, musical . . . and anxious. She held out the piece of paper. "Will you give this to Petra? It's important." Then she spun on her heel and walked quickly into the darkness.

The maid, who had been told that the Decembers' guests were named Stefan and Jana, stared at the folded note. Petra? There was no Petra here. How strange.

She yawned again, then slouched up the staircase to drop the note on the heaped-up pile of papers scattered across Lucas December's desk. He'd know what to do with it—once he got around to reading it. He had been so distracted lately. Well, she was going back to bed. In the morning, she would tell the duke about the young woman's visit and make sure he opened the note.

Except she forgot.

SADIE HURRIED THROUGH the foggy night to the castle. The weather was strange, like it always is when it transforms from one season to another. Soon it would be spring. What would Sadie's world look like, once spring was here?

The fog made everything look doubtful. Even though Sadie knew the way from Mala Strana to the castle very well, the steep, narrow streets seemed different. She almost missed a turn. She shook her head, angry with herself. She couldn't afford to lose her concentration tonight. The prince would be meeting with the captain of the guard.

Maybe Petra was right. Maybe Sadie should go home. The Roma needed information, yes, but what could any of them do now? Rodolfo would inherit the empire. He would own half of Europe. He would be unstoppable.

He already is, whispered a tiny voice within her.

At least she had helped Petra. That was something. Written in that note was the location of Fiala Broshek's new laboratory.

Sadie reached the castle gate. The guards, who knew her, waved her inside.

She would go home, Sadie decided. After tonight. There was never any fog in the Vatra. The sun was strong and brilliant. She would see her mother, and together they would tease Neel in his finery. She tried to imagine him sitting on a throne, and couldn't. All she could think about, for some reason, was the time she had taught him how to play cards. It had been years ago, when he was five.

Sadie took the stairs to the northwest wing of the castle and used her chambermaid keys to open the door marked by a snarling boar's head beaten into brass. She entered the captain of the guard's suite of rooms and shifted the contents of his trunk to a nearby unoccupied room. Later, after the captain had fallen asleep, she would replace them, just as she had done every other time.

She worked quickly and quietly, hoping that no one would chance down this hall—and that if they did, they'd see nothing odd about a chambermaid moving things from one room to another.

Sadie was lucky. No one strolled down the hall that night.

She checked a small clock resting on the captain's desk. It was nearly time. She crawled inside the trunk and shut the lid.

In the dark, she remembered the trundle of her family's wagon and the iron lamp swinging overhead as the horses pulled them south. Neel was supposed to be sleeping, but he had begged Sadie to teach him how to play cards. She had looked at him. He had been sick from the pox, and his face was thin and scarred. She agreed. They played for feathers.

Sadie heard the door to the captain's room open. Guards clanked into the room, and Sadie heard the usual ringing of sword hilts against chain mail as they searched. Again, Sadie was lucky. They didn't open the trunk.

Sadie remembered how, as she and Neel slapped the cards down on the wagon floor, a gleeful, cunning expression grew around his eyes. Sadie didn't understand why. After all, he was losing. She kept raking in goose feathers, and even had to lend him some so they could continue playing. She watched him carefully, and finally caught his hand stacking the deck.

He had been cheating. He had been cheating so that she would win.

Sadie heard the heavier steps of the captain. Then door hinges sighed, and Sadie could tell from the nervous silence that the prince was entering the room. The captain told his guards to leave.

"Good news, Your Highness," said the captain. "We have a lead on the whereabouts of Petra Kronos."

"Ah." The sound was long and satisfied.

Sadie's heartbeat quickened.

"It's a report from an Academy student. I think we would have gotten the information sooner, but there was such chaos after the Academy burned down—" The captain broke off, and Sadie wondered if it was because the prince had shot him a furious glance. The loss of the Academy had been a big blow. "Well. The student said he saw a girl who looked like the sketches, but had blond hair. She spoke with a professor, then got into a carriage with a young man about her age."

"A Gypsy?" said the prince.

"No, he was Bohemian."

"Tomik Stakan, then."

"Yes, and the carriage took the road to Prague. There's more. The carriage clearly belonged to a wealthy family. The student couldn't quite see the coat of arms on the door, but he could tell that there *was* one. That means that Kronos and Stakan are under the protection of an aristocratic family—located in Prague."

The prince let out a low hiss.

"Remember," the captain said nervously. "This is good news."

"Good news that one of Bohemia's highest born has betrayed me?"

"They will be discovered."

Petra has to leave Prague. Sadie's thought was wild. She wiped the sweat from her face. *She has to leave now.*

"I know you will be busy tomorrow," said the captain, "but rest assured that my best spies will be planted throughout the city, with an eye especially on Prague's finest houses."

"Yes, tomorrow." The prince's voice had changed. It sounded lazy and content. "I hope my valet and seamstresses are well prepared. It would not do for me to wear the same mourning clothes every time a family member of mine dies."

"They will need to sew a new set of emperor's robes as well, of course."

"So the Gray Men have returned from my father's palace."

"Yes. Tomorrow morning the world will wake to the news that Emperor Karl has died," said the captain, "and that you are the new Hapsburg emperor."

Sadie gasped. Then she bit her lip as if she could eat the sound she had just made. She pressed her hands to her mouth, and her chest heaved with short, sharp breaths.

They had not heard her. No, they couldn't have.

There was a scrape of chairs, and the sound of feet approaching.

They had.

The lid of the trunk was thrown open. The sudden light blinded Sadie as she was seized by her hair and dragged upright.

Sadie no longer tried to stop the tiny, fearful cries that escaped her mouth. She blinked, and now she could see clearly. She saw the prince—his young, pale face, his shiny brown hair, his full mouth. She saw that he held a knife in his hand.

Her mind flung back to years ago, and she remembered holding a fistful of goose feathers her brother had let her win.

The prince smiled at Sadie. The memory of those feathers scattered and blew away.

"You have a beautiful throat," he told her.

Then he cut it.

33

The Center of Staro Square

Petra stared blank-eyed at the dawn. She had not slept all night, nor had even spoken a word since Tomik had shown her the letter from the secretary of education. She pressed a palm against the window and drew her hand away. Her palm print faded almost instantly. *So that's what failure looks like,* she thought.

"Petra." Astrophil tugged on the sleeve of her nightgown. "It is time for breakfast. Come. I will bet you all eight of my legs that the Decembers will serve imported oranges."

Petra did not look at him.

"You like oranges," said Astrophil.

She made an impatient noise, which only encouraged the spider. At least she was responding. "I admit that Zora's plan looks like a dead end," he said, "but we will simply have to put our heads together. We will figure out a new way to find Fiala Broshek."

That made her turn toward him. Her eyes were dull. "How?"

Astrophil's legs fiddled and wavered. "I do not know," he admitted.

Petra nodded and drew her gaze back to the window.

"It is not like you to do nothing," Astrophil said desperately. "At least have breakfast." He wrapped his legs around her wrist. "Please. For me."

Petra sighed and reached for one of the lovely, uncomfortable dresses Iris had given her.

Voices were murmuring and trailing from the dining room even before Petra reached the open door. The others were awake.

"So that's it," she heard Lucas say. "It's over."

Petra entered the room. "What is?"

With a careful glance at the maid serving tea, Zora said, "Emperor Karl is dead. Rodolfo leaves today on a week's journey for Austria, where he will be crowned the new Hapsburg emperor."

Petra sank into a chair. Her fingers twisted around the fringe of the tablecloth as if holding on to that would somehow give her strength. "No."

Tomik's serious eyes met hers from across the table. "It's true."

Zora, who had clearly decided that no one at the table was doing a good enough job of playacting for the servants, said, "And it's high time we had Prince Rodolfo as emperor. He will energize Europe, and bring glory to Bohemia."

"Yes." Lucas did not look up from his plate. He poked at a poached egg until it bled yellow. "What am I going to do? I'll have nothing but free time on my hands, now that . . ."

Petra mentally finished the rest of his sentence: *now that the rebellion is over.* And it surely was, because however many people were secret members of the rebellion, they would never be enough to challenge a man who controlled the armies of half of Europe.

Lucas caught his sister's sharp glance, then watched the maid as she set the teapot on the table. He seemed to inspect the teapot's curlicues and narrow spout. In a forced way, he said, "I mean, I'll have nothing to do, now that Prince Rodolfo will have no need of my advice. He will have his father's old counselors to help him."

"Catch up on your correspondence," Zora said cheerfully. "Go over your accounts. Your papers are a mess, Lucas."

"So?" He balled up his napkin. "Let them be. Let everything go to the devil." He stood and stalked from the room.

Petra watched him go. Everyone left in the dining room seemed to be hovering. Every single one of them, Petra realized, felt that there was nothing to be done.

Well, there was one thing she could do. Maybe, at least, she could try once more to convince Sadie to leave Prague.

Petra returned to her room and changed into the plainest dress in her wardrobe. She did not want to draw attention to herself.

"Stay here," she told Astrophil. "If I'm recognized and caught, I don't want you to be with me."

"And I do not want you to go!" he cried. "You said it yourself: you could be caught."

She gave him a small smile. "Don't worry. I won't get caught."

"Then you can take me with you," he pleaded, but she was already gone.

Petra left the house on Molodova Street and crossed the river into Staro Square. As she wove around the stalls set up in the oldest part of the city, Petra noticed that people were muttering in hushed voices. Her ears strained to tell if they were talking about her. Had someone identified her?

She didn't think so. She couldn't hear what they were talking about, but no one looked at her. They must be discussing Rodolfo's ascension to the Hapsburg throne, she decided.

At first, Petra didn't think twice about Joel Riven's red-rimmed eyes. She assumed he had a cold, or was bothered by the raw morning wind.

She slipped close to him and leaned over piles of fabric layered in shades of crimson and pink. "Master Riven," she said, "could you arrange for me to see Sadie?"

He looked at her with glassy eyes. "She's dead."

"What?" The word stole the breath from Petra's lungs.

"Her body was dumped in the center of Staro Square. Her"—Riven closed his eyes—"her throat had been slashed. The knife lay next to her, and its hilt was embossed with a lion and a salamander. She was wearing a castle uniform. I saw her. We all saw the body, all the shopkeepers and merchant sellers who turn up here before the sun rises. We were meant to see it. That knife wasn't left there by accident. It was a message. A reminder that the prince—that Emperor Rodolfo is a man to be feared."

Petra stumbled back from the stall. She searched the man's face for some hint that he was lying, that he was wrong, that Sadie could not be dead.

A tear spilled down his cheek.

Petra ran. She wove through the morning crowd, her feet wobbling on the cobblestone streets, her vision blurry. She ignored everyone and everything around her. She hurtled across the bridge into Mala Strana—and it was there that she caught the eye of one of Prince Rodolfo's spies.

He slipped behind her, and was following her from not so far away when a carriage drawn by a set of matched gray horses passed between them and blocked his view. He swore. The carriage rattled past in a matter of seconds, but seconds was all it had taken for Petra Kronos to disappear.

He studied the street. It was a dead end. She must have gone into one of the houses.

He glanced at the prettily stenciled sign nailed to a stone wall. Molodova Street. Well, there were only so many houses on this street. They would have to be searched, one by one—and quietly, so that the Kronos girl wouldn't notice, and flee, before they got to hers.

But they would find her eventually. Perhaps even this very night.

34

A Golden Keyhole

ETRA WAITED UNTIL NIGHTFALL.
It was hard, every hour, to think about what she had learned. She carried a cruel thing inside her. It was as if she had swallowed a knife, and each time she tried to speak, the knowledge of Sadie's death cut her deep inside. She locked herself in her room, and everyone assumed it was the secretary of education's note that upset her, or the news about Rodolfo. Everyone left her alone.

Except Astrophil. "Please tell me what is wrong." He perched at the foot of her bed and studied her as she pulled the down blanket up to her chin.

She opened her mouth, then bit back the words. "I can't," she said. "There's someone else who needs to hear it first."

A confused look lit Astrophil's green eyes.

"I'll tell you later," Petra said. "I'm so tired. Astrophil? Will you sleep next to me?"

"What a silly question," the spider said. "I always do."

He crawled onto the pillow next to hers, and Petra blew out the candle. The darkness was dense, almost heavy, and Petra saw the same blackness whether she closed her eyes or opened them.

She heard someone walking down the hall. It was Lucas, muttering to himself. Petra could tell he was carrying a candle, because the empty keyhole to her room began to glow around the edges. During the few moments it took for him to pass her door, the keyhole became a golden jewel beaming into the darkness of Petra's room. Then it faded and went black, and Petra could no longer hear Lucas's footfalls.

But the flare of the golden keyhole was branded onto Petra's mind. She grasped its memory as her breaths slowed and deepened. She thought about that lovely, fleeting shape of light as she fell asleep, and reached through her dreams for Neel.

NEEL DREAMED A PALM TREE. He watched its thin green fronds stab at the blue sky, pull back, and lunge again, like the tree was fighting with the wind. Neel was surprised that anything could fight with so little noise. There was only a whisper and a flutter and a *shh* as the palm fronds struggled.

Then the wind stopped. The tree froze, its green leaves etched sharply against the sky.

"Neel," said a voice.

Petra was standing under the tree. Her bare feet were buried in pink sand, and behind her were motionless green waves that looked as if they had been carved from glass.

Neel knew that the real Petra had blond hair now. She had told him so. Her hair shouldn't have been a straight, glossy sheet of dark brown, her eyes shouldn't have been bright silver. Iris had dyed those, too. He knew this. But he had heard an unusual clarity in her voice when she'd said his name, and the worry on her face was too real for a dream.

"Thank you." Neel paused, startled at the words that had tumbled from his mouth. He stammered, "I mean, I know you didn't want to do this. Talk through dreams. But I . . . I have missed you. And everything's just like you described. I see a beach, and I bet that if we wait long enough the stars will come out."

She crossed the sand and took his hands into her own. She rested her fingers over the skin and ghost of his, and he felt a surge of something like happiness, yet richer. "Petra—"

"Neel," she said, "Sadie is dead."

The wind came back, the waves swelled again and crashed against the shore, and everything sounded too loud to Neel. There was a roaring in his ears. "That's not true."

"I'm sorry." Her voice was thick, and broke on the last word. She began to tell Neel about Joel Riven, and how he had seen his sister, and that Sadie had been wearing her chambermaid's uniform . . .

"Well, Riven was wrong." Neel lashed out. Who was that foul Joel Riven, to spread such lies?

"He seemed very sure."

Neel searched Petra's face. Fear iced his blood as he realized that she, too, seemed very sure. Petra believed this.

"No." He yanked his hands away. "This is a dream. You told me not to trust what I see in dreams. That look on your face is make-believe, something my mind cooked up to punish me. And I should be punished. I should have dragged Sadie out of Prague by now— somehow, some way. That's exactly what I'm going to do when I wake up. I'm going to travel there. I'll use the globes. I'll kidnap her, if I have to. I'll—"

"Neel," said Petra, "you can trust what I say. I'm sorry."

The green waves seemed to rush into Neel's ears and fill his eyes. He felt Petra's arms slip around him. Then the sea poured out of Neel's mouth, and it no longer sounded like waves, but like a harsh sobbing. Neel pressed his face against Petra's hair and wept.

"PETRA! PETRA!" Someone was hammering at the door.

Petra struggled out of the blankets. She blinked, dizzy with the realization that she was no longer sleeping. She was no longer with Neel. She was in Prague, in the Decembers' house.

Astrophil's green eyes opened. "Is that Lucas?"

"Wake up!" Lucas shouted. "It's important!"

Petra pulled a robe over her nightgown, stumbled through the dark, and threw open the door.

Lucas was clutching a candle with one hand and a scrap of paper with the other. "Read this." He thrust the paper at her. Astrophil, who had jumped to Petra's shoulder, read it along with her.

> *Fiala Broshek's laboratory is on Lady's Lace Pier, on the northern bank of the Vltava River, here in Prague. From the outside, it looks like a silk factory.*
> *Good luck.*
>
> Sadie

"I couldn't sleep," Lucas said excitedly, "so I decided to take Zora's advice and go through my papers. And look! It was lying on my desk, half-covered by letters from my annoying cousin in—"

He was interrupted by a muffled banging. It took Petra a moment to realize that the sound was coming from the heavy front door, several floors below. She and Lucas stared at each other, wondering who it could be at this time of night. There was a series of creaks and shuffles as a maid traveled through the house, and then a groan of hinges as the front door opened.

Petra heard thumps, a metallic ringing sound, and deep voices. *Armed men*, she realized. She looked at Lucas and Astrophil, and saw their eyes widen with the same thought.

A voice boomed from far below, echoing its way up the stairs: "We have permission to search this house for Petra Kronos."

35

The King's Decree

ASTROPHIL SQUEAKED, then clapped four legs over his mouth.
Lucas had gone pale. "We can leave by the windows in the
bathing room on this floor. Wake Tomik. I'm going to get Zora. You
wait for me here. Understand? Right here."

He ran down the hall as noiselessly as he could.

Petra ducked back into her bedroom and flung open the door
that joined Tomik's room to hers. "Get up!" she hissed as she threw
clothes at him. She felt almost sick with the push and pull of emotions. How had she gone so quickly from sorrow to hope to terror?
When Tomik touched a match to a candle, she was sure that he
could see every thought crawling across her face.

"What's going on?" he said fuzzily.

"You are getting up!" Astrophil jumped onto Tomik's bed and
pinched his wrist.

"Ow!"

"You are getting up *quietly!*"

As Tomik tugged clothes on under the blankets and she jammed
her feet into a pair of shoes and belted on her invisible sword, Petra
explained Sadie's note and the noises coming from downstairs. "We've
got to leave now."

"I've got to get something first." He raced for the door.

"No," Petra whispered after him, but he was already gone.

Moments later, Lucas and Zora appeared at the door. "Come on," Lucas said, "let's go!"

"Where's Tomik?" Zora asked.

"I don't know," Petra moaned.

The muffled voices and heavy footfalls grew closer.

"They are on the floor below us." Astrophil wrung his legs. "Oh, where *is* he?"

"Here." Tomik was in the hallway, panting. He had a bag slung over his shoulders. "I'm here."

"Follow me," said Lucas. He led them down the hall, and they filed into the bathing room. It was so cramped that they had to squeeze around the tub for everyone to fit. Lucas bolted the door just as they heard the sounds of men reaching the landing of their floor.

"It'd be easier if you come out right now!" one of them called. "A clever little maid has already told us what's been going on in this house. We know you're here, Petra Kronos. You, your friend Tomik, and the Decembers are coming with us."

A silence fell. The friends stared at one another.

"We'll do it the hard way." Then the man shouted, "Search this floor," and the thumping of boots and breaking down of doors told Petra that they were coming closer.

Lucas unlatched a large window.

"Do you really think this is possible?" Zora whispered at him.

"Do we have a choice?" he whispered back.

"How, exactly, are we supposed to get out of here?" Petra stuck her head out the window. "Oh."

"Oh, no," said Astrophil. "You are mad, Lucas December!"

Petra looked at the long gap between the window and the roof of the nearest house. "Don't worry, Astro. I'm sure you can jump that."

"Of course I can! I am worried about the rest of you!"

"I'll prove it can be done." Lucas gripped the top frame of the window and scrambled his feet onto the sill. He leaned back, then flung himself into the night. He slammed onto the nearby roof. He straightened, and noiselessly waved his hand for the others to follow him.

They flinched when they heard a banging on the door behind them. Shoulders beat against the door. The men would break it down soon.

"You'll be right behind me?" Zora asked breathlessly.

"Yes. Now go!" Tomik no longer bothered to lower his voice.

Zora leaped across the gap. She fell short of the roof, but snagged her hands on a gutter. Tomik and Petra watched as Lucas pulled her up.

The door to the bathing room splintered. Tomik started to take the bag off his shoulders.

"What are you doing?" Petra jerked the bag's straps back in place. "Please, just go. They want me most."

"You're not going to surrender."

"Of course I won't. When we're so close to getting *her*?" Petra didn't need to say Fiala Broshek's name. "But I want you to jump first."

Tomik's laugh was a little wild. "I guess I always do what you want," he said, and jumped.

He landed perfectly.

"Now, Petra," said Astrophil. "Let me tell you a little something about leaping across long distances. After all, I know a great deal on the topic, and—"

Petra jumped.

Her feet slapped down on the nearby roof. Her toes ran forward with the momentum from her leap, then tripped over the hem of her nightgown. She fell against the hard ceramic roof tiles, and the hilt of her sword rammed into her side. "Stupid nightgown," she muttered as Zora helped her up.

"It's not ideal for running across rooftops," agreed Zora, who had had the sense to put on a pair of her brother's trousers.

"This is why I do not wear clothes," said Astrophil.

Petra laughed. As the sound flew from her throat, Lucas pointed at the prince's men swarming around the bathing room window. "At least you're not wearing armor, Petra. There's no way they can jump after us with all that weight on them. We could stay here the whole night, if we wanted." He began to crow, shouting his words so that the soldiers would hear him. "We could watch the sun rise, and take breakfast and tea—with sugar! We could—"

A man hurtled through the air and slammed onto the roof.

"Or we could run," said Lucas.

They tore across the red tiles.

The soldier slipped after them, cursing, as they crossed from one house to another, jumping across gaps that were sometimes narrow, sometimes as wide as a creek. They were fleet and nimble and far faster than the lumbering guard, but he doggedly trailed behind them. Finally, they reached the end of the houses.

"The drainpipe," said Lucas, pointing. "Hold on to it with both hands, and put your feet on the rivets that bolt it to the wall. There are rivets all the way down, like steps on a ladder."

Zora went down first. "I get the feeling you've done this before, Lucas," she shouted up at him in a voice that was annoyed, amused, and ever so slightly frantic.

"Maybe." Lucas pulled Tomik to the edge and almost pushed him down the pipe. The soldier was closing the gap between him and them. "Just for fun, you know. To see if I could. Now, Petra: your turn."

"Got you!" The soldier snatched Petra's wrist and hauled her to him.

Petra heard Lucas shout her name and felt Astrophil pinch her ear. Her mind ground to a halt and stopped. She looked at the man's

meaty face grinning at her over his metal breastplate. Then Astrophil shouted, "Petra, do you remember how you saved my life?"

Her brain roared to life again. Yes, she remembered. She remembered zapping the spider's metal body with magical energy, and had
a good idea what something like that would do to a human encased
in metal.

She placed her palm flat against the man's steel breastplate. She
sucked in her breath, and pulsed power through her fingers and into
the shiny armor.

The man's hand on her wrist jittered, then locked, then jerked
open. His eyes rolled up into his head, and he keeled over with a
groan.

As soon as the man had flopped down onto the roof tiles, Petra
could see the rest of the soldiers, not very far away, running along
the roofs.

She and Lucas scrambled down the pipe. When Petra's toes
touched the ground, everyone broke into a run, ducking down
alleyways so that the guards' view of them was blocked by tall
buildings.

"To the river!" Petra shouted, and they skidded down streets so
steep they could have been slides.

When they burst onto the banks of the Vltava, and were sure
they were no longer being followed, their pace slowed. They picked
their way along the wharf, past piers and late-night rowboats with
hanging lanterns.

". . . and then she zapped him!" Lucas chuckled as he told the
others how he and Petra had escaped the soldier. "Just like that!
He fell down flat."

Tomik dragged at Petra's elbow so that she'd trail behind the
Decembers. "I didn't know you could do something like that," he
said.

"I didn't either," she confessed.

"That must have taken a lot of power. You keep getting stronger."

"I hope so." She thought of Fiala Broshek's laboratory. "I hope it will be enough."

Tomik looked at her, and Petra realized that something had changed in the chase across the rooftops. There was still a stiffness between them, one that had been there since the carriage ride to the Academy. Yet it no longer felt painful. Their friendship felt like a muscle that had been pulled or stretched past its limits. But Petra thought it would get better.

"It'll be enough," Tomik said.

"There it is!" Zora called. She pointed at a dark, looming silk factory.

"Petra," said Tomik, "I want to show you something." He shrugged off his bag and opened it. Inside were balls of fabric. Tomik lifted one out and unwrapped the rough cloth.

He held a Marvel. A large one, about the size of a fist. Inside glowed something that looked like fire.

"I made a lot of different kinds over the past week," said Tomik. "And trust me—these are *very* special."

NEEL SHUT THE DOOR to his mother's room behind him. He stood in the hallway, listening to the dulled sounds of her sobs. He put a hand to his face, then let it fall away. Neel stiffened his shoulders and walked down the hall.

He hadn't gone very far before John Dee turned down a corridor and joined him.

"Your Majesty," Dee said, "I am very sorry for your loss."

Neel didn't look at him. He pulled a golden coin from his pocket and rubbed a thumb over the bird of prey stamped on its surface. He considered the sign of his ancestor, Danior. "I've been thinking," Neel said, studying the coin and his hands and the ghostly fingers no one could see.

"Yes?"

"There is one other option for how to deal with Rodolfo."

THE SPACE BEFORE THE PALACE entrance was flooded with people, for Neel had ordered that the entire city be present to hear his announcement.

Neel held the golden scepter carefully. He had dressed in what Karim had chosen for him: deep blue, embroidered with silver. He did not fiddle with the sapphire on his ear. He had only raised his hand to block Karim when the man produced a stub of kohl to rub around his eyes. "No," Neel had said.

"But, Your Majesty, you look—"

He knew. He had seen a mirror. He looked awful. His eyes were grieving and stained with shadows. "The Vatra needs to see me for what I am," he had said.

Now he stood as tall as he could, and addressed the throngs of people. "I know what you think of me," he said. "But I want to say what I think of you. You are gifted and beautiful and brave and clever—and you are doomed. The Roma are doomed if we keep thinking that we are four tribes, and that we all need to fight for our own little corner of a four-pieced people. Am I really supposed to fight only for the Kalderash? I'm Lovari at heart. And I've sailed long enough with the Maraki to tie every sailor's knot. Sure, my ancestor was Danior of the Kalderash, but who was he, before he founded the Vatra? He was an Ursari. So I guess that means I'm Ursari, too, and if you doubt that I'll outride you all.

"My point is that we need to start thinking like one people. My sister gave her life for the Roma. Not for the Lovari or for me or for any one of you, but for *our* safety. It's time for us to step forward and show the world that we are a force to be reckoned with. We will storm down on Europe. We will fill its people with wonder and fear."

Neel took a deep breath. "The Roma are going to war."

36

Lady's Lace Pier

LUCAS CRUNCHED toward Petra and Tomik over the small pebbles strewn across the mud of the river's bank. "Why are you two dithering? Don't tell me you've got cold feet."

Zora came close, peered into Tomik's bag, and saw the glass ball flickering with flame. "What's that?"

"A bonfire." Tomik passed it to her. "Smash it when you need to. And here—Petra knows this one—water." Zora held a sphere in each hand as Tomik explained that the contents inside each Marvel would magnify when smashed. "It used to be a hundred times whatever was inside, but now . . . well, it's a lot more."

"How *much* more?" Lucas eyed his two Marvels. One sphere was filled with a gray mist, and the other held a curled-up snake that bared its fangs.

Tomik shrugged as if to say it was anybody's guess. "They haven't been tested."

Lucas stared at the snake, which reared its head and knocked its fangs against the glass.

"Only one for me," Petra said. "I need a hand free, for fencing."

Tomik unwrapped a Marvel and dropped it in her outstretched palm. It was filled with murky brown fluid and several clear, jelly-like beads. "Pond slime," he said, "with a touch of frog spawn."

"Frog spawn? I get *frog spawn?*"

Tomik grabbed a Marvel for himself and dropped the empty bag to the riverbank. He ignored Petra's comment, saying to the others, "I wish I'd been able to make more, but there wasn't enough time. These six will have to do."

Astrophil recoiled when he saw what Tomik held in his hand. "Tomik Stakan," Astrophil said in a shocked voice. "You trapped a *spider* inside a Marvel?"

"Its venom paralyzes people," Tomik said defensively. "It'll be great! And it'll get set free eventually. Come on, Astro. Don't be like that. I . . . well . . ." Tomik tried a lie. "I had the idea because of you. You can be scary, you know."

"Me?" Astrophil pointed a leg at his thorax.

"You're very fearsome," Petra said.

"Oh, well, yes." Astrophil's voice was proud. "No one had better mess with us spiders!"

Petra bit back a smile. "All right." She turned her gaze toward the factory at the end of the pier. "Let's figure out how we're going to break in."

"It looks like there are no guards set up outside," said Lucas, "which makes sense. Fiala Broshek wouldn't want anyone to guess that this is anything other than a factory. Once we're inside, though, we'll face serious opposition. Broshek's discoveries are very important to Rodolfo—he told me so himself—so she'll be well protected. We can expect her latest breeds of monsters. I don't know what they are, but I know they exist."

"How will we get inside?" said Zora.

Lucas scratched his head, then shrugged. "How about the front door?"

The group crept down the wooden planks of the pier toward the windowless factory. The river sparkled darkly under a slip of a moon. Petra peered, and thought she could see a long, metal object below the surface. It was almost the size of a small house—if a house happened to be skinny and oblong, with a funny-looking bulge at one end. "Do you see that?" she asked the others.

"See what?" said Zora, and Petra supposed that her gift for metal—or perhaps even her mind-magic—had shown her this. Well, the object in the water was intriguing, but she had a laboratory to storm. First things first.

They reached the double doors and quietly tried to open them.

"Locked," said Petra with disappointment, though she hadn't expected anything different.

"We could use a Marvel." Tomik pointed at Zora's fireball.

"Too noisy," said Petra. "Let's at least *try* not to be noticed." She frowned at the lock. She stuffed the frog spawn Marvel into her robe's one pocket and thought, frustrated, that she'd barely managed to bring anything useful with her. "I could pick the lock if I had a knife, or a pin, or"—her eyes flicked to Astrophil. "Astro, do you think you could help?"

"Help? Certainly. Shall I break down the door?"

Petra watched him flex his tiny legs. "How about I give you a short lesson in how to pick locks, courtesy of Neel?"

Following Petra's instructions, Astrophil squeezed several of his legs into the keyhole and began tinkering with the lock. He hummed under his breath as he felt for the little springs that would set the tumblers free. He jabbed, and pressed, and there was a satisfying *thunk* as the lock opened. The door creaked, and everyone slipped inside.

Zora lifted her fireball. It cast an orange light, and they could see the echoing, almost empty space of the factory. It held nothing but trays of worms that spun, weaving faint threads that would be gathered and made into silk. "It looks like an ordinary silk factory," Zora whispered. "Maybe Sadie was wrong."

Petra shook her head. "Let's keep looking."

They tiptoed around the edges of the cavernous room, searching for a doorway, but the walls were smooth. Once, Petra felt a crinkle on the back of her neck and was positive—absolutely sure—that they were being followed. But when she looked behind them she saw nothing, and when she listened she couldn't hear the faintest sound. She focused again on finding a door. "This can't be *all*," said Petra. "We're missing something."

"Let's say we are," said Lucas. "How much time do you think it'll take before someone realizes we've broken in?"

"No time," said a strange voice.

They spun around.

Dozens of soldiers grinned at them. Their swords were drawn.

And they had no feet.

37

The Tank

———◆———

PETRA STARED AT where the soldiers' legs tapered off into shiny blobs that looked like giant slugs. This was how they had been able to move so silently. But where had they come *from*? Had they slipped in through the front door? Or—Petra scanned the room again—was there an entrance to another part of the factory, one she couldn't see?

The slug-soldiers hung back, sneering, clearly relishing the fear they had struck in the young friends' eyes.

Petra's gaze darted to the trays of silkworms. She felt a flash of impatience at her mind-magic, which seemed to be trying to tell her something. *How are* worms *supposed to help me?* she told that part of her she liked least, the part Dee had called her "intuition."

If there was an answer, she couldn't hear it, because Tomik threw his Marvel at the soldiers. It smashed, and spiders teemed over the soldiers in a black cloud. The soldiers yelled with pain and surprise, slapping their tails against the spiders, crushing them into black smears. Some of them toppled over from the venom of the spider bites, but three soldiers had been far enough from the blast that they had only gotten a few bites. Apparently, that wasn't enough.

With a chorus of snarls, the three slug-soldiers attacked.

A sword stabbed at Petra. She parried it and thrust back. The soldier skimmed away from Petra's swiping blade and zipped across the floor on its tail. With greasy ease, it swung back to join the other two soldiers in a knot around Petra, and she could hear Tomik shouting, "No! Don't throw anything! You'll hurt her." Astrophil, who had scrambled to the top of her head, cried, "Behind you!"

Petra whirled around. A sword nicked her arm, and the sharp pain sent a splinter of inspiration into her brain. She swung down her rapier and sheared off a slug-soldier's tail. He fell to the floor, gushing blood from the ankles while his tail flopped alongside him.

Petra turned on the remaining two soldiers. One of them tried to slither away, but she stomped on his tail and chopped it off. The third soldier crumpled to the floor, too, amid a slick of blood and the meaty wriggling of tails.

"Ugh," said Zora. She looked ill.

Petra backed away from the bloody mess until her shoulder brushed against Tomik's. She glanced at her wound and was relieved to see it was a shallow cut.

"Where did those monsters come from?" Tomik said.

Petra was about to tell him she had been wondering the same thing, when a tray of silkworms slid aside. A large tentacle as thick as a tree trunk groped its way out of the square hole beneath. Another tray slid aside, and another tentacle crept out. Then another, and another.

Zora screamed and flung her fireball.

The rows of silkworms erupted into flames. There was a rubbery screeching as the tentacles curled and thrashed and beat against the trays, where thousands of silkworms shriveled in the fire. Flames licked the factory ceiling.

"Zora!" Astrophil shrilled. "Finding Fiala Broshek's laboratory will do us no good if we are burned to a crisp! Throw your other Marvel!"

Zora threw. The glass sphere smashed, and water gushed over the flames. The fire went out in a cloud of smoke. Water cloaked the floor of the factory, spreading to the walls and past the friends' knees. Then there was a sucking sound, and the water swirled in a circle. Petra and her friends grabbed each other to keep their balance. The water poured past the limp tentacles, down the holes where the silkworm trays had been, and disappeared.

"It's underneath," Petra breathed. "The laboratory is underneath the pier. It's probably built underwater." She walked toward the rows of charred, wet silkworm trays.

"Petra," Zora protested. "That thing—that octopus, or whatever it is—"

But the burned tentacles were still. Zora gathered her courage and followed Petra.

The friends worked to pull away the trays, and looked down into a brassica-lit chamber. A spiral staircase that once led below had collapsed in the flames. "How are we going to get down?" asked Zora.

"That way." Lucas pointed at the massive, tentacled thing whose dead body squatted on the floor below, and whose limbs were stretched up to the main floor of the factory. "We'll climb down on that."

"I know all sisters say this to their brothers," Zora told him, "but you, Lucas, are disgusting."

Disgusting or not, the tentacles were their only choice. They climbed down, slipping over the thing's body until they touched the wet floor below.

"I won't!" They heard a woman's voice. It was faint, and echoed down a corridor to meet them.

It was Fiala Broshek.

The voice shouted again. "I shouldn't *have* to get into the Tank! *You* should be able to take care of the invaders! I created you, didn't I? Go show me what you're made of!"

Something began to race down the hall toward them.

The friends looked at each other.

"It cannot be too bad," said Astrophil. "I hear only one set of feet, and they belong to a person—er, *being*—who does not sound particularly large. We can handle this."

The creature burst into view.

"Uh-oh," said Tomik.

It was shaped like a man—almost. Ten muscled arms waved from its torso. Its skin was dotted with countless mouths that gnashed their pointed teeth.

Petra faced the monster. All of its mouths smiled at her. The ten hands reached toward a belt around its waist and drew forth ten daggers.

Steadying her courage, Petra rushed to meet it—and tripped over the hem of her nightgown.

She fell, landing on her side. The Marvel in her pocket burst, and she was engulfed in ooze.

Petra surged to her feet, spitting out frog spawn. She slipped, then caught her balance again and wiped mud out of her eyes. Slime covered the corridor. Her friends had been standing still at the time of the blast and had kept their balance, grimacing as the goo lapped their ankles. Petra could see Astrophil, who had fallen from her head, picking his way through frog spawn toward the safety of a clean wall.

The creature was on its back, floundering in the slime.

Petra stalked—as best as one can stalk through slime—toward the monster. With a single movement, it propped all ten arms against the floor and pushed itself upright. Petra let her anger burn, and funneled its energy into her magic. "I"—she chopped off an arm— "should not"—she chopped off another—"have to fight"—and another—"in a *nightgown!*"

Blood spurted from the creature's torso as three arms fell to the floor, but the many mouths just laughed. One arm dropped a dagger and pulled a flask from its belt. It brought the flask to one of the mouths on its face and drank.

Three new arms sprouted out of its chest.

"Petra, get back!" Lucas shouted.

Petra, who saw the Marvel in his hand, slipped and skidded out of the way.

Lucas threw. The Marvel with the snake coiled inside smashed at the creature's feet. It was a perfect throw. Snakes writhed up the monster's body.

But the mouths grinned. They opened wide and chomped down on the snakes. There was a slurping sound, and the snakes were sucked into the mouths as if they had been noodles.

"Mmm," the mouths said. "Yummy."

Petra closed her eyes. She usually built walls around her mind-magic, but now she let it trickle in, gush, and fill her. She looked at the creature, and seemed to see each twitching move those ten arms would make. She thought she knew what to do.

She found her balance. She ran, skating along the slime as if it were ice. She ducked under the swinging arms and snatched the flask from the creature's belt.

It howled and tried to swipe the flask back. She chopped off an arm. It fell, and no arm grew back in its place. Petra stuffed the flask into her wet pocket.

The monster drove several daggers toward her. Petra twisted aside and tried to stab its neck. An arm blocked her. When her rapier point sank into the arm's skin, Petra tugged, and that arm thumped to the floor.

The mouths were screaming now, their voices high and low, shrill and booming. The chaos of sound distracted Petra. An arm swatted her to the ground and her body skidded. The slime wheeled her away from the monster, taking her out of danger for a moment—but only a moment.

The monster was steady on its feet. It strode toward her as she struggled to stand. A dagger stabbed toward her stomach, and another toward her eye. Petra rolled in the slime, and in one breathless instant she saw a clear path through all the wild arms. The space between the arms was almost like a tunnel, and Petra thrust her rapier through it to pierce the monster's throat. She drove her blade home.

The mouths roared and howled, and Petra thought she would go deaf from the sound. Then the screams died, and silence filled the corridor.

Lucas helped Petra to her feet. "Fiala Broshek?" He nodded toward the end of the corridor.

"Fiala Broshek," Petra agreed. She snatched one of the creature's fallen daggers, and the friends slipped as quickly as they could over the slime, down the hall.

The corridor dead-ended, and there was a gorgeous, angel-faced woman struggling to open a small metal door in the wall. It vaguely reminded Petra of doors she had seen on the *Pacolet*.

Fiala Broshek froze, and glanced over her shoulder at Petra, whose sword was visible with blood. "Stay back! You'd better stay back, or I'll . . ."

Yet Petra suddenly knew, as surely as she knew her own name, that Fiala Broshek's threats were empty. Fear had made the woman's hands clumsy with a door she must open every day. She was defenseless. She had no weapons. Her weapons had been her monsters.

Petra sheathed her rapier. She gripped her dagger with one hand, and with the other she snatched the gray, misty Marvel from Lucas. She hoped it would do what she thought. She smashed it on the ground. Smoke curled from the shards and spread through the room.

Her friends were shouting at her, but Petra didn't listen. She rushed through the fog, dagger in hand. It felt like she was swimming. She couldn't see. But, even blind, she could sense Fiala Broshek. She could tell that the woman had frozen, then fumbled again with the door, trying to open something she couldn't see.

Petra slipped up behind Fiala and held the dagger to her throat.

"You changed my father into a Gray Man." Petra's voice was harsh. "I want you to change him back. Do it, or I will kill you. I will."

"I would rather die!"

The mist began to clear. With her free hand, Petra pulled the slime-covered flask from her pocket and shoved it in front of Fiala's face. "If you don't cure my father," Petra said, "I will pour this down your throat."

There was a silence. Petra saw her friends' faces, and wondered if their horror reflected what they saw in Fiala's eyes.

"You are so *pretty*." Petra pressed her knife until she felt the edge just barely part the skin. "How would you look with ten arms, and hundreds of mouths? How does this stuff work, anyway? Does one sip grow one arm? If you drink the whole bottle, what happens then?"

Fiala croaked, "Let's talk."

Petra's arm sagged in relief, and her bare wrist touched the metal door. With a sharp gasp, Petra brought the dagger back to Fiala's throat before the woman could wriggle free. That brief brush of skin against metal had told Petra something. She remembered the strange metal object she'd seen below the water by the pier. She remembered how frantically Fiala had tried to open the door, as if what lay beyond it was desperately important.

"*That* is the Tank!" Petra told her friends. "We've seen nothing that *looks* like a laboratory, have we? With brass bowls and brassica fires and alembics and weird ingredients. It must be here, behind this door."

"Clever, clever," Fiala spat.

Tomik stepped forward and, after careful consideration of the mechanism, opened the door. They saw a metal chamber lit by a green glow. Petra pushed Fiala inside, keeping the knife steady. Her friends filed in behind her.

The chamber was lined by tables littered with metal instruments, glass tubes, and the splayed bodies of cut-open animals. A single pink rose graced a beaker, and Petra wondered if it had been a gift or was destined for a potion. Two small doors on either end of the room seemed to lead to other chambers, and odd-looking buttons studded the walls. A glass porthole was dark with the water of the Vltava River.

Tomik slammed the small door shut and spun a knob that locked it. He looked at Fiala. "We need some rope."

"Rip the hem of my nightgown." Petra told Zora. "*Please.*"

After Zora had ripped away enough strips of fabric for Tomik to bind Fiala's hands and feet and strap her to a chair, Petra relaxed the arm that held the dagger. "Now," she said to Fiala, "it's time to talk."

"Hey," said Lucas, "what do you think *these* do?" He was looking at the buttons on the wall, and his finger hovered over a red one.

"Don't touch that button!" Fiala shouted.

But Lucas already had.

38

Underwater

———◆———

THE METAL WALLS shuddered and groaned as the chamber filled with a pumping sound. The room seemed to slide and veer. Petra had no clue where the Tank was going, but it was definitely moving.

"You're going to kill us all," Fiala told Lucas matter-of-factly.

"What did that button do?" Petra demanded.

"You unmoored the Tank."

"What do you mean?"

"To 'moor' means to anchor a ship or fasten it to a pier," said Astrophil. "So I assume that this thing is a boat, and that we have become, well . . . unanchored and unfastened. I believe we have left Lady's Lace Pier."

The Tank *chug chug chugged*, and picked up speed.

"Where, exactly, are we going?" asked Tomik.

Fiala shrugged as best as she was able with her arms bound by slime-covered strips of Petra's nightgown. "Somewhere through the river. We're underwater, in case you seed-brains haven't figured that out. We're going to crash into something—a pier, or maybe Kampa Island." Her voice smoothed into honey. "I think you should untie me." The Tank vibrated and hummed. "I know how to sail this ship."

"Bad idea," said Petra.

"You're the one willing to die," Zora told Fiala. "You said so. You're only afraid of being turned into a monster. You wouldn't think twice about steering us into an island. You'd blow us up."

"Maybe," Fiala said, "or maybe I was just being dramatic. Or maybe I was buying time until I had the opportunity to crack open your skulls and see what's inside. I may be many things, Petra Kronos, but I am far from stupid. Why should I believe your threat to kill me? If you truly want your doddering father back, you *cannot* kill me. Unbind me, and I will steer us to safety."

"You'd steer us right to Rodolfo," said Petra.

The Tank made a grinding noise, like it was dragging itself across the bottom of the riverbed.

"I think," Fiala said sweetly, "that you have no choice."

"Yes, we do," said Petra. "We can figure out how to sail it ourselves."

Fiala giggled.

"Maybe we should push another button and see what happens," said Zora.

Tears of laughter streamed down Fiala's ivory face. The grinding noise of the Tank worsened, and the floor began to shake.

Astrophil said, "Zora, I am not sure that is the best idea—"

But Zora had already pushed a purple button close to her. The ceiling sprayed water.

Petra sprang across the room and slapped her hand against the wall, pressing the button again. The water stopped. Fiala kept laughing. "Zora, Lucas, you watch her," said Petra. She pointed at the two doors on either side of the long chamber. "The rest of us are going to see where these lead."

Petra and Astrophil took one end, and Tomik another. "It's a bedchamber," shouted Tomik from his end of the Tank. Petra, with Astrophil peering anxiously from her shoulder, opened her door. "Tomik, come here!"

It was a small, round room barely large enough for two people. Two chairs covered with slipcases of pink ostrich feathers faced a table of dials and a big wheel. Beyond that was a curved glass panel that took up almost the entire room. The window was black, just as the portal had been in the laboratory.

Tomik shouldered through the narrow doorway, and he and Petra each took a pink seat.

"I don't care how thick the metal hull of this ship is," said Tomik. "If we keep dragging along the riverbed, the rocks will tear it apart. One of these dials has to make the Tank rise."

"Please," said Astrophil, "can we forgo the trial and error process that has thus far brought us close to a watery grave?"

"Your fear is making you hard to understand," Petra muttered.

"Stop pushing buttons when you have no idea what they do," said Astrophil. "And I am *not* afraid."

Petra set her dagger on the metal table and pressed the heel of her hand against her eyes. A sickening headache was starting to build, and Petra became aware of how much magical energy she'd already spent that day. She had poured almost every physical resource she had into her magic, and felt as if she hadn't slept or eaten in a long time.

The scraping sound of the Tank turned into a screech.

Petra gritted her teeth. She would ask the metal a few questions. Dee had taught her how to do this, long ago, and she could do it now. She ran a palm over the metal table with its knobs and buttons, and begged, *Which way is up?*

Her fingers seized a dial and twisted it.

The Tank rocketed upward. They were rising so fast and straight that Petra felt like her brain had slammed against the roof of her skull. She and Tomik held tight to the pink ostrich chairs, and Astrophil gripped her ear. The black water outside the window in front of them dropped away. Thin, clear water now sheeted down over the window, and Petra could see city lights flickering through it. The water slowed and ribboned, and there was Karlov Bridge, shining with green brassica lamps. Its statues looked as if they were peering down at the river, at this strange metal ship that cruised below.

"Someone might see us," said Tomik. "By now Rodolfo—or his captain of the guard—might know about the attack on the factory, and if the Tank is spotted on the river's surface . . ."

Petra dialed the knob back—slowly, this time. The ship sank underwater, and the window went black again.

"This ship is obviously designed to stay hidden underwater," said Astrophil, "and one could not possibly sail it through the dark. There must be lights of some kind."

Petra's fingers fluttered over the dials, asking, *What is your history? What were you designed to do?* She pushed a button. Funnels of light shot into the dark water, and she could see something through the murk. Something gray and large, like a building with huge arches cut into it. "Is that . . . ?"

"The bridge!" shouted Tomik. "It's the foundations of Karlov Bridge!"

They were about to crash right into it.

Tomik had no gift for metal, but he hadn't sailed with the Maraki for nothing. He knew a captain's wheel when he saw it. He grabbed the wheel in the center of the table and spun. The Tank hummed, and veered, and skimmed through one of the arches.

The Tank now swam through the open river. Trout darted in and out of the ship's light.

Petra slumped against her feathered seat, sick with exhaustion. "Tomik," she said, "you know the basics of this thing. Do you think you can take over?"

"If I can do one thing well, it's sail."

She rested a hand on his shoulder. "You can do a lot of things well," she said, and headed back to the laboratory.

The Decembers had been dutiful in their role as Fiala's guards. Zora had the many-armed monster's flask at the ready, and Lucas was standing next to her, holding a white, blue-eyed cat.

"Please don't hurt her," Fiala pleaded with him.

"Why is there a *cat* in an underwater, movable ship of a laboratory?" asked Petra.

The cat meowed.

"I found it in the bedroom," said Lucas. "You wouldn't *believe* what it looks like in there. Everything is a shade of pink, even the chamberpot."

Petra turned to Fiala. "Is this cat one of your experiments?"

"No. Amoretta was a gift from Rodolfo," said Fiala. "He loves me. I'm going to be the Hapsburg empress."

Lucas's mouth crinkled in amusement. "Never in your rotten life. I know Rodolfo. He's not going to share his new power—and if he did, it wouldn't be with you. You don't come from an aristocratic family. If Rodolfo married anybody, it'd be someone like my sister."

Zora made a face.

"Don't worry," Lucas told her. "I think that our recent exploits have killed any romantic notions he might have had toward you." He pretended to wipe away a tear. "Alas, there will be no wedding in Krumlov Castle."

"I *am* going to be the empress!" Fiala strained against her slimy bonds. Her hands twisted and balled into fists. "Just you wait! Rodolfo has already set off for Austria in a grand procession, with all the Bohemian forces and his army of Gray Men. When he is crowned emperor in less than a week's time, he will look for me to be by his side. You'll see!"

"His army of Gray Men," Petra repeated. "All of them?"

"Of course. Can you imagine how terrified the Austrian court of his dead father will be? They will fall over themselves to serve his every wish."

Through the shadows of Petra's weariness, an idea sparked into a small flame. "The Vltava River starts from near the Austrian border," she said. "It flows north to here, to Prague."

Zora turned to Petra with a sudden smile. "And the river passes through Krumlov before it reaches here."

"Fiala," said Petra, "you're going to come up with a cure for my father or I'll turn you into a monster *and* toss your cat overboard. Lucas, Zora, we're going to visit your aunt."

39

The Roma General

PETRA STUMBLED TO THE HUGE, frilly pink bed and fell into a sleep so thick and black that she never noticed when Lucas, Zora, and Tomik came to share the bed with her, or when they left. She didn't hear the constant chugging of the Tank. She didn't hear Tomik instructing Lucas and Zora how to steer it. She didn't feel the white cat, Amoretta, kneading her back and biting her hair. She slept for two days, and dreamed of nothing.

When she woke, Amoretta was purring next to her and Astrophil was sleeping in a nest made by the cat's front paws. Petra slipped from the bed and entered the laboratory, where Lucas was supervising Fiala as she burned a foul-smelling dust in a beaker. Fiala's waist and legs were still bound to the chair, and Lucas watched her hands carefully. Zora, Petra assumed, was with Tomik, steering the ship.

"Is the cure ready?" Petra asked.

Fiala tossed her long, pale hair. "You're not very bright."

"And *you* are this close to having Amoretta made into a fur hat."

Lucas chuckled. Petra glared at the cat twining about her ankles, though she in fact had a growing affection for Amoretta, and could never make good on her threats.

"If I gave you a vial of sewer water," said Fiala, "and told you it would turn Master Kronos back into your doting daddy, you would

never know I'd tricked you until you poured it down his throat—
and I'd like to see *that*." Fiala giggled. "Imagine! Trying to make a
Gristleki drink something that isn't steaming hot blood!"

"That"—Petra strove to keep her voice even—"is why we won't
release you until he's cured."

"He'll try to kill you, you know. I've seen it happen. Gristleki don't
care whose blood they drink. They love only two things: to serve their
master and their hunger."

"That's not your concern. Make the cure."

"And make it into a gas," said Tomik, who had stepped from the
cockpit into the laboratory.

"Well, aren't you picky!" said Fiala. In a cloying tone, she added,
"Would you like me to make it cherry-flavored while I'm at it?"

Tomik ignored her. "A gas will be easier to give to Master Kronos,"
he told Petra.

"Let's make one thing clear," said Fiala, "I'll do my best to reverse
one of my finest creations ever. But I'll make a cure for one Gray
Man only. I'm sure Rodolfo will forgive me for this, since the last
thing he would want is for me—or Amoretta—to suffer at your
hands."

Petra and Lucas exchanged a skeptical look.

"But I will *not* give you a recipe," Fiala continued. "I'm no fool.
I'm sure Your Grace"—she batted her eyes with sarcastic flirtation at
Lucas—"would *love* to turn Rodolfo's Gristleki army into hundreds
of useless humans. You'd love to weaken him. After all, you're next
in line to the Bohemian throne."

Petra and Tomik stared at Lucas. He looked away.

"It is true." Astrophil's legs clicked against the metal floor as he
crawled into the room. "This is not news, Petra. I have told you before. Lucas, as the duke of Moravia, is the highest born aristocrat in
Bohemia after Rodolfo. If the new emperor dies without children,
Lucas will inherit our country."

Petra said to Lucas, "So this is why you helped us. This is why you started the rebellion. You wanted to seize power for yourself."

Lucas shifted uncomfortably. The smile that always seemed to hover on his lips was gone. "I know the line of succession to the Bohemian throne. I can't help but know it. But it's not why I do the things I do."

Fiala glanced between the friends, gleeful at the sudden tension in the room.

"What's going on in there?" Zora called from the cockpit.

"Just steer the Tank," Petra called back.

"We should arrive in Krumlov the day after tomorrow," Tomik said, looking grateful for a change in topic. "We found a tube like a spyglass that pokes up through the water to give a view of the surface. Judging from what we've seen, we're getting close."

"Hurry," Petra told Fiala.

"You might command things, but that doesn't mean they'll happen," the woman said. "Who do you think changed the Gristleki into the glorious beasts they are? Me. And I never made them to be changed back. There is not a single drop of human blood left in a Gray Man's body. None. Your father has Shadowdrake blood pumping through his veins, and if you think I can so easily clap my hands and make him a man again, you're even dumber than I thought.

"I'll try. I confess I'm curious to see whether my genius will succeed, and sparkle in the night of other people's stupidity. But it makes me very happy to tell you that there may be no cure. What you want, little girl, is probably impossible."

"Neel." Treb strode through the ballroom toward the king. "We need to talk."

"Not you, Treb," said Neel. He rubbed his eyes and gazed around the ballroom, which was the only space in the palace big enough to hold the tribe leaders, their clan leaders, and anybody who might have resources to contribute to the war effort. Maps of Europe were spread across the floor, and tables were blanketed with papers that listed the amounts of everything from weapons to horses to tents. The noise was incredible. "I don't have the energy to convince you that this war is necessary."

"I loved Sadie, too, coz. But—"

Neel flinched. His voice came out broken: "This isn't just about her."

"Will you let me finish? I know it's not. You'd be surprised at how many people know it. Sure, Queen Iona wanted to keep our noses out of European affairs, and sure, my brother would have done the same. Even he sees things differently now, though, and it's not because your sis died. It's because of what her death means."

Neel, to whom Sadie's death was a whirling, keening storm of meaninglessness, looked at the captain. Treb's face was earnest, and filled with an expression Neel had never seen before.

"Somewhere inside me is my best self," said Treb, "and I betray it every day. I lash out at people I like. I . . . well, I won't even list the ways in which I let my worst self win. But Sadie . . . she was the best version of all of us. Everyone who knew her knew that, and a lot of people knew her. I think the Roma see that we need to protect the very best in us. If that comes with a cost, we'll pay it."

"You're saying that the Roma support this war?"

"They support you."

Neel's throat was dry. He looked at his open hand as if it held what Treb was offering, the respect of his people, and felt like he had bought it with earth from his sister's grave.

"You'll help me," Neel stated.

"I've always loved a battle. I'm a warring type. Knocking heads, whipping people in line, charging the enemy. As I said"—Treb grinned—"I'm good at bringing out the worst in me."

"Did you come over here to ask if you could be my general?"

"No. But if you're offering . . ."

"I am. You're it. Now, was there something else?"

Treb's face lit up, and Neel realized that he rarely saw his cousin happy. Then the usual dark cloud of a scowl settled in, and Treb said, "We're hopelessly outnumbered."

Neel sighed. "I know. Everyone who doesn't live underground has heard that Rodolfo will be crowned emperor in Austria. The coronation is in three days. The Roma will have a force of maybe ten thousand. The Hapsburg army will be ten times that."

"He doesn't have control of it yet. We have a few days before that happens. What's Rodolfo doing right now? Why, he's traipsing across the countryside, heading to Austria. And I'll bet you a figure-eight knot that he's traveling with a pack of spoiled courtiers and drunken soldiers who've shined up their armor to hide how little muscle they have. It's a political trip, after all. Rodolfo doesn't need an army. If we were to intercept him . . ."

"Yes," said Neel, and felt a flicker of something. He couldn't be sure, but he thought it was hope. "If we kill him, the Hapsburg Empire will fall apart. There will be no heir. Each of its territories will be taken over by local royalty. Bohemia would be snapped up by . . ." Neel spun, found a table, and dashed back to Treb with a sheaf of papers in his hand. He shuffled through the notes until he found what he wanted. Slowly, he read out loud, "Some fellow named Lucas, duke of"—he peered—"Moravia." He widened his eyes at the sudden recognition that Petra was staying in the home of someone so high up in the Bohemian aristocracy. Well, that was good. That'd mean he'd be better able to to keep her safe. And she *was* safe. She had to be. Though . . . he had to admit he didn't know this for sure. He had hesitated to try to reach her, ever since his dream of the beach. Ever since seeing his tears darken her hair, he had felt . . . how had he felt?

"The problem isn't Bohemia," said Treb. "It's Rodolfo, and the people who follow him. And you know what? I think the Roma can handle a traveling party of courtiers."

"You're right." Neel focused on what Treb had told him. "It could work. It'd be a sight easier than taking on the Hapsburg army—or even the whole Bohemian army. The Bohemians would outnumber us three to one, plus there are the Gray Men . . ." Neel trailed off as he realized something that his excitement had blotted out. "It's impossible. We can't get to where Rodolfo is in less than three days. Even with the globes. The nearest Loophole to Bohemia is the one Petra took, and we can't haul an army—with horses and wagons— down freezing mountains. Even if we did, we still wouldn't have enough time to reach Rodolfo before he enters Austria."

"There's that Loophole from Portugal to the countryside near Prague. You know, the one Tomik stepped through, more than a year ago."

Neel shook his head. "Dee's pesky daughter sewed that one up. She—" Neel's eyes went wide. He shouted so that the whole room could hear him: "Somebody go and get John Dee!"

40

A Treaty

———◆◆◆———

Y OU SAID THAT your daughters can open a Loophole to western
India," said Neel. He and Dee were in the royal sitting room,
though Neel was absolutely incapable of sitting. He paced the floor.

"I did, didn't I?" Dee reached for a small ivory statue of an elephant that decorated the end table next to his chair. "This is lovely."

"It's yours. So, Madinia and Margaret could get from England to
India pretty quickly, right?"

"Very quickly," Dee said in a bored tone. "Especially since they
are in India."

Neel stopped pacing.

"Yes." Dee smiled. "They like India. I saw no reason to send them
home after they brought me there. They are amusing themselves in
the Manvadar court right now." Dee cradled the ivory elephant in his
hand and traced one finger down its arching nose. "I suppose that if,
say, you wanted them to visit *you*, a fleet ship and a few horses could
make the trip there and back in a little more than a day." Dee
glanced up from the elephant. "Would you care to see them, Your
Majesty?"

Neel choked on a fizzing mix of astonishment and eagerness.
"Yes. Yes, I would. You see—"

"You'd like them to open a Loophole to Bohemia."

"Can they? Would they? I—"

"I imagine that you'd prefer a location near the Austrian border, ideally along the route Rodolfo would take to be crowned emperor. Would Krumlov Castle do? Iris December is an old friend and has hosted my family before. Madinia will know the way there."

Neel sagged into the chair across from Dee. The relief started in his stomach, traveled up his throat, and flowed out in laughter. "That's perfect. Thanks, Dee. I don't care what Petra says about you, you're all right. You like that elephant? I'll give you a case of 'em. I'll—"

"My ambition ranks a little higher than ivory elephants." Dee pulled a sheet of parchment from a deep, hidden pocket in his robes.

Neel took it. "What is this?"

"A treaty between your country and mine. After your rousing speech yesterday, I took the liberty of preparing this. It's quite simple. You are about to embark on a war, and would like my daughters' help—which is to say, *England's* help. England has no love of Rodolfo, and no interest in seeing him on the Hapsburg throne. In fact, we would not be sad to see the Hapsburg Empire crumble. That would allow, well, *other* countries to become more powerful after its downfall. You and my queen are in a position of mutual interest. Therefore, Madinia and Margaret would be glad to help you—as glad, I'm sure, as *you* will be to help England." Dee pointed to the bottom of the beautifully written page. "Sign here."

Neel narrowed his eyes. He began to read the treaty—but not before he noticed a twitch of surprise on Dee's face. "You thought I still couldn't read," Neel said. "You assumed I'd sign it right away, because I'm desperate. You assumed I wouldn't show it first to an adviser who *could* read, because I'm too proud."

"I assume nothing," said Dee, yet his words sounded hollow.

"It's fine. You act in the best interests of your country. I'll do the same for mine." Neel took the paper to a nearby desk. He took his time reading it, because it was still difficult for him to string each word into a sentence—and it wouldn't do any harm to let Dee worry.

When Neel reached the end of the page, he unscrewed an ink-pot and dipped in a quill. He scratched out a few sentences, then scribbled changes in the margins. "If this is all right by you"—Neel brought the treaty back to Dee—"I'll sign it."

Dee's face changed as he read the treaty. "You have altered the most important clause. My queen would like her own set of globes."

"Pity. I don't have any to spare. I'm sure you understand my position. But if Queen Elizabeth ever wants to *borrow* a set, I'll send someone who'll use them for her, and lead your people where they want to go—so long as the queen's plans don't conflict with the Roma's. I've written all that down in the margins."

"Yes," said Dee, "in very poor penmanship."

"Look, I'll tell you what. I'll throw in a little something extra. See, the Vatra makes great coir rope. Normally we wouldn't sell to Europe, but we can make an exception for you, and give you a good deal. England's an island. Ruling the sea around you is as important to the English as it is to us. You must want good ships. With our coir rope, you can have the best. What do you say, Dee?"

TOMIK TOUCHED THE PINK ROSE in its beaker. Fiala looked up from her work to shoot him an evil glare, but said nothing when he plucked a petal and put it in his pocket. He could hear Petra and Astrophil talking in the bedroom. Their muffled voices rose and fell in a duet, with the spider's voice piping in a tinny whistle, and Petra's low like a flute. An impatient flute. She was searching for something to wear that wasn't a shredded nightgown stiff with dried slime. It was their fourth day in the Tank. Petra had discovered a privy that funneled away waste with a push of a button, and a glass closet in the bed-chamber that sprayed water, so they'd managed to stay more or less clean. But for the longest time, Petra couldn't bring herself to do what Zora had done—wear Fiala's clothes. Tomik could imagine Astrophil's glee as Petra tried things on. The spider loved to see Petra dressed her best.

The friends had fallen into a steady pattern on the underwater ship. They knew now how to steer it well—as the Decembers were doing at the very moment—and had figured out many of its secrets, like a panel that opened to reveal dried food, a faucet that poured river water for drinking, and a button that shot metal spears out of the Tank's bow. Soon they would have to figure out how to stop the ship and dock it, because they would arrive in Krumlov later that day.

Fiala cleared her throat, deliberately rude. Tomik glanced at her. "Give me that," Fiala said. She leaned against the fabric that bound her to the chair and pointed.

He gripped the flask that had made the many-mouthed creature grow more arms. It was the chief weapon they had against Fiala. He shook his head. "Say how much you want, and I'll pour it in a glass."

She huffed with impatience. "A drop."

When Tomik had given it to her, Fiala poured it into the potion that filled the brass bowl in front of her. She set fire to the oily liquid, which erupted into flame.

"Hey!" Tomik hauled Fiala, chair and all, away from the work-table. "What do you think you're doing?" He reached for water to douse the fire.

"Shut up! Don't do that!" Fiala slapped at him. "It's part of the process. Let me handle it."

Zora stepped from the cockpit, took in the situation, and put her finger on the purple button that had sprayed water from the ceiling on their first day aboard the Tank. "Handle it, then," she told Fiala coolly. "I'll put it out if you don't."

Fiala looked over her shoulder at Tomik. "Push me to the table, you fool." The flames climbed higher.

Tomik shoved the chair. Fiala clapped another brass bowl over the fire, lifted it, and held an open vial over the bitter smoke. She stoppered it with a cork. "There." She set the smoke-filled vial on the worktable. "One Gristleki cure, forced out of me by a bunch of rude infants with no respect for me or my cat."

Petra entered the laboratory with Astrophil on her shoulder. She had managed to find what was perhaps the only non-pink dress in Fiala's wardrobe. It was pearly white, with simple, elegant lines. Tomik noticed how it brought out the brightness of Petra's light eyes, and the richness of her dark hair. She had begun to look more like herself as Iris's dyes, which required daily application, had faded away. As Petra stood there, her eyes resting on the vial as if beholding a miracle, Tomik realized that, not so long ago, his pulse would have raced to see her like this. Yet now his heart was as steady as the Tank's constant thrum.

"You did it?" Petra said to Fiala. "You made the cure?"

"Well, how am *I* supposed to know?" Fiala said. "Do you *see* a Gray Man here, for me to test it on? Maybe it will work." She shrugged. "Maybe not. I added a touch of Regeneration—my very own invention—which *might* cause the human organs inside a Gray Man's body to produce blood. Or it might make your father grow a few arms. Oh!" Her eyes widened. "What a beautiful idea! A Gristleki with ten arms! Fiala Broshek, your ingenuity astonishes me. Now, little girl," she said to Petra, "bring me my cat. I would like a cuddle."

But Petra was no longer paying attention to the woman. In fact, she appeared to be paying attention to nothing at all. She gazed into space, her head slightly tilted as if straining to catch a whisper.

"Petra?" Now Tomik's heart *was* racing—with urgency, as he thought back to their mountain trek and how she had somehow known, through her mind-magic, that the Gristleki would attack. What danger lurked in the Vltava waters?

A smile glowed across Petra's face. "Neel is there—he's in Krumlov Castle. With . . ." She frowned, and seemed to continue to listen to something no one else could hear. "*John Dee.* And . . . Madinia and Margaret?"

"What?" said Tomik. "Why would *Neel* be in Krumlov? And how do you—?"

Petra raised her hand. "There's more." Her smile grew wider. "Neel has an army."

41

Plan of Attack

W HEN I SAID you were welcome to visit me any time," Iris had
told Dee earlier that day, "I didn't say you could bring *ten
thousand people* with you. And their horses! Do you have any idea
how much manure they will spread all over my grounds?"

"It will be good for the soil," Dee said smoothly.

"You're lucky the ground is still hard. It's spring, you know. If
that army had arrived a few weeks later, it'd be floundering in mud.
Oh, and another thing—my castle is off-limits to anyone carrying
a weapon. I won't have it, you hear? They'll sleep outside."

"We'd prefer to sleep in tents anyway," said Neel.

"Ah-hah." She peered at him. "I remember you. You've grown up
some. King Neel, is it?"

"Indraneel, technically."

"Well, I don't care who you are, you're still a whippersnapper to
me, got that? I'm not taking orders from you."

"I wouldn't give them."

"Stop being so agreeable! What's wrong with you?"

"He's not very much fun," Madinia confessed. She was the more
freckled of the Dee girls. "He's a real bore. I don't remember him
being this serious, do you, Meggie?"

"Madinia." Margaret's voice was low. "How can you expect him to be otherwise? He—" She stopped, but the entrance hall of Krumlov Castle seemed to echo with her unspoken words.

Neel glanced away. It seemed that, every day, he could remember Sadie's face less clearly. It was unfair that even her memory was being stolen from him. It helped, sometimes, to stare at his mother's face. They looked so much alike. But Damara had chosen to stay in the Vatra. "Don't do this," she had told him. Her large black eyes had accused Neel of cruelty, and wept at the thought of losing both children. "Don't go," she'd begged, yet he had.

Neel became aware that, in the silence of Margaret's unfinished sentence, all eyes had turned toward him. Iris's pursed mouth had gentled. "Come," she said, "search my house for anything you need. Krumlov Castle is at your disposal."

It was late afternoon when Neel burst from his tent and raced through the weak light. He searched the rows of peaked tents stretched like small mountain chains over the hills surrounding Krumlov Castle.

He found Treb swearing at a soldier. "I'm a sailor, and I can shoe a horse better than that!" Treb yelled.

"Treb." Neel caught his shoulder. "We need to gather the tribe leaders, and the leaders of the divisions. We have to talk. Petra is arriving today—tonight—with Tomik and—"

"Petra? Why should I care about one Bohemian girl? I've got a would-be emperor to kill. Anyway . . ." He frowned. "How does she even know we're here? And if she *is* coming, how would you know that?"

"She told me."

"She . . . *oh.*" Treb's face screwed in distaste. "A mind-link, eh? With a *gadje.*"

"Treb, the mind-link is the least of our concerns. She said—"

"Hey, it's your mind, lad. I think what you've done is as weird as a three-legged fish, but who knows? Maybe it'll come in handy during this little enterprise of ours." He waved a hand proudly over the view of hills dotted by tents.

"Treb, listen to me. It's not a little enterprise. Everything's bigger than we thought—a lot bigger. Rodolfo isn't strolling through the countryside with frilly courtiers. He has soldiers with him—the entire Bohemian army."

NEEL WENT DOWN to the river to meet Petra. The metal ship surfaced with a growl of turning gears. A hatch in the top of the long-bodied part of the ship flung open, and a girl Neel didn't recognize—Zora, he told himself, remembering what Petra had said—crawled awkwardly over the ship's slick hull. She slid, and jumped in the shallow water. Then Tomik hauled himself out, and a ribbon of gladness to see his friend threaded through Neel, then twisted with a darker feeling he didn't want to examine too closely.

Tomik was reaching below to tug at something. He dragged out a woman that could only be Fiala Broshek. Bound at the arms, she screamed at Tomik until she managed to wrench herself away from him—and fall into the water.

Then came a lanky young man carrying a cat under his arm. With his free hand, Lucas December helped Tomik pull the thrashing woman onto the riverbank.

Petra came last, her shoulder sparkling with Astrophil, lit by the setting sun. She ran along the hull in bare feet, and leaped from the bow onto the riverbank. Neel saw her walking toward him, her dress fluttering in the wind like a white flame. When she stood before him and smiled, an emotion struggled through him, and even though he had wanted to see her for months, he looked away.

He shook her hand. Then Tomik's, then their friends'.

He led the way to the castle.

• • •

THE FRIENDS SAT around the dining table. They were joined by Iris, Dee, the Roma tribe leaders, Neel's advisers, Treb, and the commanders of each army division.

"Scouts have returned with reports of Rodolfo's army," said Treb. "It's not good. Rodolfo moves in the center of about five hundred Gray Men. Getting to him through those vicious beasts would be nigh impossible, even if the rest of his army didn't exist. And it does. It's moving in a line of about six to ten soldiers wide, like any army on a good road. In the front's half the cavalry—"

"That means soldiers on horseback," Astrophil said helpfully.

"Followed by Gray Men surrounding Rodolfo," Treb continued. "Behind them's some infantry—"

"Soldiers on foot," said Astrophil, who squeaked when Treb gave him a murderous glare.

"Then come wagons with supplies, followed by more infantry, then more wagons, with the other half of the cavalry bringing up the rear. The army's well organized. There are about thirty thousand of 'em, all told."

"Thirty thousand," said Tarn. "*Thirty thousand.*"

"We already knew the size of his army," said Neel. "We just didn't think Rodolfo would take it with him."

"We are outnumbered three to one."

"Yes, Tarn," Neel said wearily. "I can do the math."

"But *why*?" Shaida pressed a hand to her eyes. "Why did Rodolfo have to take his army with him? He's going to his coronation. It's a political party. Why such a show of force?"

Iris said, "Rodolfo likes to impress."

"We have advantages," said Neel. "Rodolfo doesn't know a battle's coming his way. Surprise is on our side. Every Roma can fight well hand to hand, and our horses are the best."

"They've never been trained in battle," said Tarn.

"They'll do what their masters tell them," said Shandor, whom Neel had appointed as head of the cavalry.

"The truth is," said John Dee, "*none* of you has been trained in battle. The Roma might know how to fight hand to hand, but they have never fought a war."

A silence fell. Petra had been rubbing her finger along the wooden grain of the table, frowning as others spoke. Now she raised her eyes to meet Dee's. "Then we need to play to our strengths," she said. "We need to be clever. Most of all, we need to eliminate the Gristleki."

"Petra," said Dee. "I have fought these creatures—"

"So have I."

"Then you know how difficult it will be for anyone else without our gifts to prevail against them."

"We're not going to fight them. We're going to eliminate them. We're going to change them back into humans. We have a cure."

"For one man only," said Dee. "One man whom you are still putting above everything and everyone else. I know you'd like to transform Master Kronos back into the person you knew. But one dose—one changed man—will not help the Roma army."

"It will," Petra insisted, "if Tomik puts that dose into a Marvel."

"Petra, what an excellent idea!" said Astrophil. "Why, it is almost worthy of me. It is true: if Tomik were to make a Marvel that would multiply the cure by approximately five hundred, and smash it in the center of the Gristleki battalion, the gas would transform them all."

"*If* the gas works," said Dee. "And *if* it works quickly enough. If it takes a day for a Gristleki to turn human, that will not help Neel's forces."

"You, sir"—Astrophil shook a leg at him—"are a killjoy."

Tomik had ignored Dee's cautions. He was studying Petra seriously. "It's a good idea, but the cure's a gas. The wind would have to be right—that is, there must be *no* wind, or the cure will blow away. The section of the army with the Gray Men would have to be passing through a valley—someplace where the wind isn't strong."

Treb unfolded a map of the area. "There are plenty of valleys around here. But even if we do what Petra says, that still won't make the rest of Rodolfo's army disappear."

Astrophil piped up, "I have read several books on warfare—"

Those who didn't know the spider well stared at him.

"—and it is common knowledge that when one army is vastly outnumbered by another, there is only one intelligent thing to do."

"Run?" said Tarn.

"Cut the larger army in half."

"Yes!" Treb slapped his hand on the table. "You're fighting with *me*, spider!"

Astrophil gave him a shy smile.

"Say the army passes over a bridge where the water below is too deep for men to ford," said Treb. "Let half the force pass, then blow that bridge up. The army will be split by the river."

Lucas raised his hand. "I can blow up bridges."

"And I know a way to distract the soldiers on the bridge while he does it," said Zora.

Neel pulled the map in front of him. His finger traced the road from Prague, and paused where it forked right before the Vltava curled around Krumlov. One section of the road branched east, across the Zim Bridge into a series of steep hills. The other section of the road traveled south along the river, where it widened and crossed the Dalo Bridge into fairly flat land. "We can hide in these hills." Neel pointed to the bumpy marks on the map near the Zim Bridge. "If Rodolfo's army makes for the Zim, and we blow it up when they're halfway over it, we'll have a fighting chance. Rodolfo and the Gristleki will be on our side of the river, and the hills should block the wind enough for Petra's plan to work. Even if it doesn't, we'll be better matched, numbers-wise—our ten thousand to their fifteen—until the other half of their army makes it across the Dalo Bridge to join up with the rest. We beat one half of the army, then the other. Fifteen thousand and then fifteen thousand, not thirty all at once. We could do it. We'd have surprise on our side, and height."

"It is always easier to attack from above," Astrophil agreed.

"And maybe we won't have to face the Gray Men," said Neel. "With a little luck, it should work."

"With a lot of luck," said Dee. "There is no reason why Rodolfo should take the Zim Bridge when he can take the Dalo Bridge toward Austria. For a man moving an entire army, the flatter land on the other side of the Dalo will be more appealing. And that bridge is wider, which means more soldiers can cross it quickly. What will you do if he takes the Dalo?"

Neel rubbed his forehead. "Blow up that bridge, I guess. Shift our forces south. Still cut the army in half. We'd be on even ground, so we'd lose the advantage of height. We'd have to fight them out in the open."

Tomik said, "And if there's wind by the Dalo Bridge—"

"It's spring," said Iris. "There will be wind. I know my lands."

"—then we'd have to fight the Gray Men, too."

"Then you will lose," said Dee. "The Gristleki will overpower your forces even before Rodolfo's ordinary soldiers get their chance— and if they do, they will wipe you out."

"Rodolfo has to take the Zim Bridge," said Petra.

Neel's shoulders slumped. "We have to hope."

42

Sacrifice

———◆———

ASTROPHIL WATCHED PETRA pull the bed curtains shut around them. She rested her head on the pillow and lay silent and awake in the dim green light of his eyes.

"Are you using your mind-link to speak with Neel now?" he asked.

"What?" She focused on him. "No. I was thinking. I haven't talked with Neel—not that way—since yesterday."

If that was true, then they were barely speaking. After Petra had set foot on the Krumlov riverbank, she and Neel had exchanged very few words that could be heard. An hour ago, when everyone was filing out of Iris's dining room, Petra had wished Neel good night and stood so stiffly that Astrophil, who was curled in the crook of her neck, could feel the hesitation in the set of her shoulders. "I'll walk with you to your room," she had offered.

"I'm sleeping outside, in my tent," Neel said, then added, "Iris's orders," though Astrophil highly doubted that Iris would make a king sleep on the ground, whatever rules she might have about his soldiers.

"Anyway, it's nice to see the stars," said Neel. He flipped his hand in a wave and left the castle. Astrophil did not feel the tension in Petra's shoulders lessen.

"I wish you had told me," the spider said to her now, in the dark. "I wish you had told me about Neel."

There was a silence. "What about him?" she asked, and it was such a strange question (was it not clear that he had meant their mind-link? Had they not been discussing just that?) that a slow understanding seeped into Astrophil's mind. There was more for Petra to say about Neel than the mind-link they shared. Astrophil interpreted that tension in Petra's shoulders very differently now.

"I meant your mind-link," he said gently.

"I didn't think you'd approve." The answer was automatic, as if she'd been practicing it. She paused, then said, "That's not really true. I just . . . I wanted to keep it a secret. Do you ever keep secrets from me?"

Of course he did. He hid his worry for her. He hid the quiet terror that snaked through him every day, when he wondered if his gears would turn forever, and someday he would be alive, and Petra would not. "Yes," he said.

"I'm sorry," she whispered.

"It is all right." He crawled onto the pillow next to hers. "Friends do not have to tell each other everything. I respect your secrets." He thought of one other thing Petra had told them yesterday: the death of Sadie, who had been kind to him. He curled up, suddenly sad— for Sadie, and for all his brave friends in Krumlov, whose tomorrow would bring such horror. Yet the keenest edge of his sadness was for Petra. "Go to sleep," he told her. "I will see you in the morning."

"I love you, Astrophil."

"I love you, too."

WHEN ASTROPHIL WAS ASLEEP, Petra pushed her way through the bed curtains and wandered the dark castle, the stone floor icy against her bare feet. She knew that downstairs, in Iris's laboratory, Tomik was probably still awake, making Marvels, but she didn't head in that direction. When she saw firelight flickering from Iris's sitting room, Petra drew close.

The door was slightly ajar, and a murmur drifted through it. "I am worried," said John Dee.

Iris's voice answered, "But if Rodolfo takes the northern bridge—the Zim Bridge—"

"He won't. There is no reason why he would. This has become a hopeless enterprise."

A silence followed these words. Petra pushed the door, and it creaked open.

Iris and Dee looked up from where they sat by the fire. "Petra," said Dee. He was startled, and uncharacteristically hesitant.

"Can't sleep?" said Iris.

"May I sit with you?" said Petra.

Dee stood and brought a third chair closer to the fire.

"I didn't know you were friends," Petra said when they were settled before the crackling flames.

"Friends?" Iris shot Dee a sly smile. "I believe what we have is a partnership based on mutual interests." She drew out the words in a way that sounded teasing, like she was repeating something she found absurd.

Dee shifted uncomfortably in his chair. "Did I really say that, all those years ago?"

"It sounds like something you'd say."

"I suppose you'll never let me forget it." To Petra, Dee said, "Let's call what we have . . . a mutual respect."

Iris snorted.

"Very well," said Dee. "Friendship."

He looked awkward, and for the first time, Petra felt a touch of pity for him. It occurred to her that Dee had very few friends. She pulled a cushion onto her lap, ran a hand over its emerald velvet, and changed the subject. "Why is color so important to you?" she asked Iris.

"Why, because it's my gift," Iris said, but then seemed to recognize that this answer was too easy. "Well . . . I like that there are so many shades. You think you know a color, and then it darkens or lightens or blends with another, and becomes something new. Sometimes I feel like an explorer of undiscovered countries." She gave a self-conscious laugh. "Also . . . color means something to people— and not always the same thing. It's fascinating to think about how, for example, white means purity to Europeans, whereas to the Chinese it means death."

Her last word seemed to echo in the room. Iris shut her mouth. Then she grinned, as if the brightness of her smile could somehow chase away what she had said, and what seemed to wait for them when the sun rose.

"I'd better get some sleep." Iris rose from her chair. "I need to rest up the Roma army's greatest weapon."

John Dee gave her a disapproving look. He appeared ready to say something, then pressed his lips into a line.

"What do you mean?" asked Petra.

"*Me*, of course," said Iris. "Didn't you see that ruined tower of mine? I did that when I was about your age. Some fool of a boy broke my heart and made me cry acid tears. Now, what was his name? I can't even remember! Well, no matter." She raised her hand and made a fist. "I will rot the ground beneath Rodolfo's feet!" She grinned again, and her small, frail frame disappeared behind the door.

Petra played with the green pillow. Dee watched her with a mildly surprised expression, and it took Petra a moment to realize that it wasn't because she was fidgety, but because she was *there*, remaining in this room with no other company but him. "Dee," she said, then stopped.

"Yes?"

"Could mind-magic . . . could it make someone do something he doesn't want to do?"

"You are full of questions tonight."

"Can it?"

"No, Petra. There is no magic that can force someone's will."

"But could mind-magic lead someone to make a choice he wouldn't otherwise? Could it make him believe something that isn't true?"

"It's not impossible. It's a matter of making a lie very convincing. If I had mind-magic, I might be able to sense what would make a lie particularly believable to you. This would require a great deal of power, and subtlety. It would not be easy." He studied her, and said abruptly, "Petra, I will not be here for the battle. I will return to England with my daughters in the morning."

She shouldn't have been surprised, yet she was.

"Please understand." He didn't look at her, but seemed to address the fire. "I can't let anything happen to them, any more than your father would allow anything to happen to you, were it in his power." He paused. "You should come with us."

She gave him a look that said everything she had to say about that idea.

Dee nodded and sighed.

"I have one last question," said Petra. "Why did you give me that letter in London? I've been thinking about what it said, and I don't understand why you wanted to tell me that Rodolfo has no magic talent."

His answer was simple. "Because I wanted you to know that you are stronger than he is."

Petra stood and set the pillow on the chair. "I won't see you tomorrow, so I'll say goodbye now."

"Goodbye, Petra," he said softly.

She left the room.

When she returned to her bedchamber, she watched Astrophil sleep for a moment, then let the bed curtain fall. She left her invisible rapier where it was, hanging from the back of a chair. She pulled on shoes. She slipped into the white dress. It would make her more visible in the darkness. And, after all, white is the color of sacrifice.

SHE WALKED MANY MILES in the dark, holding a brassica lantern that she had lit only once she was too far from Krumlov Castle and the Roma army to be seen by anyone she cared about. By the time she reached the sea of Rodolfo's tents, the hem of her dress was ragged and dirty, and the sky was the eerie gray that comes before dawn.

Petra approached the nearest soldier, who stared as if he had seen a ghost.

"I'm Petra Kronos," she said. "I'm here to surrender myself to Emperor Rodolfo."

43

The Truth

———✦———

NEEL JOLTED AWAKE. He had rolled from his low pallet to the hard earth, and lay there, breathing in the smell of dirt. Terror racked his heart until he thought it would shatter inside him.

He'd had a nightmare.

Neel had dreamed of Petra. She had stood against the night sky, lit by brilliant stars. She had spoken quickly, and her first few words told him that this was no mere dream. The pleasure this gave him shifted into confusion. Then came shocked disbelief. He listened, and his emotions decayed rapidly.

"You're insane," he shouted. "He will kill you! You can't do this!"

"It's already done," Petra said. "I'm being led to Rodolfo's tent now. I will make him take the Zim Bridge." She tried to explain how, but Neel grabbed her shoulders hard and shook her. "Don't, Petra. Get away from there."

"This is the best plan for everybody."

"Everybody but you!" *And me*, he wanted to say, because he could not lose her, and he knew that he surely would. "Even if you trick Rodolfo into taking that bridge, what do you think he's going to do with you?"

"Just make sure everything goes according to plan."

Neel was desperate. "I will hate you forever if you do this."

But she was gone, and he was awake.

THE SOLDIERS MARCHED her quickly, and she stumbled many times. If their hands hadn't been cinched around her arms, she would have fallen.

The army was so massive that it took some time before Petra was brought before the enormous, elegant tent, its flag flying Rodolfo's coat of arms. She looked at the flag's lion and salamander, and thought of the four-colored flag that flew from Neel's tent.

Rodolfo's flag snapped in the wind. The sound of it drove something into Petra's brain: this would be a windy morning, just as Iris had predicted. Petra strengthened her resolve. The Gristleki cure *had* to be released in the valley on the other side of the Zim Bridge, where the hills blocked the wind. It was the only way.

The guards shoved her through the tent's entrance. Word must have been sent ahead to Rodolfo. He was waiting for her. He was immaculately dressed, and his fingers thrummed against the arm of his fur-covered chair, even though the rest of him was perfectly still. Petra could tell it was an effort for him to remain that way.

The sight of him frightened her, so she looked away. She studied the rich hangings inside the tent, the table covered with maps and papers, and the bed heaped with furs.

"Petra Kronos." Rodolfo smiled, and now there was no help for it. She had to look at him. She did. She fought down her fear, and made her Choice.

It worked like the Metis had said it would. She could feel her sensitivity to every metallic object in the room fade away into nothing. Her magic for metal drained from her. If Petra survived this, she would fumble with a sword and dagger, just like any other fourteen-year-old girl with only a year or so of training. She would never be able to speak silently with Astrophil again.

But Petra's other magic swelled within her. She glanced at a paper on Rodolfo's desk, and even though she was too far away to read the writing, she knew that it was his coronation speech. She knew every word. More than that—she knew every word he had almost written, and then decided against. All the different shapes the speech could have taken appeared to her, and hovered in layers of possibility.

She sensed the soldiers flanking her, and knew what they had had for dinner, and how many hours they had slept. She turned to Rodolfo, and saw conflicting futures. She saw him crowned emperor, and slowly capturing every free European country until he owned the whole continent, and more. She saw him dead, a sword buried in his chest. She saw him place a crown on her head. The different futures confused her, but one thing was certain. When Petra looked at Rodolfo, she knew exactly what he planned to do to her.

She was dizzy. Her own power bewildered her. She would soon be sick.

Rodolfo was entranced by the emotions that flared across her face. "I understand that you came here willingly, Petra. How very curious. Why on earth would you do that?"

Petra remembered that she was supposed to lie in a way that he would believe, but her ideas now seemed childish. If she told Rodolfo that Fiala Broshek was held captive on the other side of the Zim Bridge, he wouldn't try to rescue her. If she said that the Terrestrial and Celestial Globes were hidden in that valley, he would laugh in disbelief. Petra saw Rodolfo's thoughts shifting and wavering, and she realized that she had no perfect lie to tell. She could predict his reaction to each one. She looked into the future, and saw her failure.

Rodolfo softly approached her, and Petra was glad again that the guards held her. If not, she would have collapsed to the ground.

"Have I frightened the very breath out of you?" Rodolfo was pleased by this thought. "I prefer you quiet. Yet not *quite* so quiet. I would like an answer. Why are you here?"

Petra opened her mouth to speak, and instead of sensing one string of words ready to rise from her throat, she felt several. All the things she might say filled her and knotted together. She choked on them.

"You do not wish to say?" Rodolfo's voice was sweet. "No matter. I will make you answer me." He turned, and walked to a locked chest in a corner of his tent. "I inherited something very interesting upon the death of my father. It just came into my possession. I had often wondered how he had kept his power for so many years, and over so many territories." Rodolfo opened the chest and lifted out a wooden band shaped like a plain crown.

Petra looked at it and knew what it could do. She wanted to weep.

"I am lucky," Rodolfo continued, "that he never thought to use it on his own son. And what, you may ask, is this? What have I inherited?"

Petra said nothing.

"It is the Truth." Rodolfo moved toward her. "It will tell me what you are thinking. You do not need to say a single word, Petra. Your thoughts will write themselves across this crown. I confess that I am eager to see them. Now"—he smiled—"this will not hurt." He set the crown on her head.

Tears flowed down her cheeks, because Petra didn't need to see the band to know that she was betraying her friends, and herself. The words scrawled silently across the wood: *A Roma army is waiting for you across the river.*

Rodolfo's pale face went white.

They are outnumbered by you, three to one.

His eyes brightened.

They are hiding in the hills beyond the Zim Bridge.

Something about Rodolfo seemed to shift, and Petra realized with dread that she had done what she had come to do. But not this way.

Rodolfo would now cross the Zim Bridge. He would massacre her friends. He would destroy the entire army.

She could feel the band sucking at her mind, pulling out the information that hovered closest to its surface, because it was the most important at this moment. A dim idea occurred to her, and Petra strained to keep it buried. She needed to listen to this idea while keeping it thrust below into the depths of her mind.

Petra suddenly understood. She had to keep one grain of a secret from the wooden crown. Rodolfo could not know that the bridge would be blown up. He could not know the plan to cut his army in half and transform the Gristleki. This was the key information. Without it, Rodolfo might still lose this battle.

Petra reached for the thought she had had just a moment ago. She floated it to the surface of her mind: *You will destroy them.*

Petra held on to her secret. She held on to it by ignoring it, and pretending it was unimportant. She lied to herself. She brought all of her power to bear upon this lie, and forced herself to believe it. *There is nothing else,* the band told Rodolfo, *that you need to know.*

Rodolfo lifted the crown from her head. It was smoking. "This is a delicate object," he said, "and must be used sparingly. Yet, as you yourself say, I have what I need to know." He said to the soldiers, "Tell the general to set a march for the Zim Bridge. We have a task to accomplish, one that will mark my coronation with glory."

Petra slumped. Her thoughts were wild. Visions of the future beat against her, and contradicted themselves. She saw her father whole and human; she saw him as a Gray Man, scraping ribbons of blood across Tomik's skin. She saw Neel dead; she saw him alive. She saw Astrophil crushed under a soldier's boot.

There was too much knowledge. It overwhelmed her.

Her vision whitened, and Petra knew she would faint. She gathered her strength for one last effort. *They are taking the Zim Bridge,* she thought to Neel, *and they know you are waiting. Keep to the plan.*

She collapsed.

WHEN SHE WOKE UP, she was in a wheeled cage dragged by horses. Gristleki teemed around the cart, their bodies slithering.

Petra wasn't dead, but she felt that way. Her mind and body were numb, and it was as if something had been stolen from her while she slept.

Her magic was gone.

44

The Spyglass

———◆———

S HE DID *WHAT*?" Tomik shouted at Neel. "Why didn't you stop her?" Astrophil clung to his shoulder. Several legs covered his face, and his small body was trembling.

John Dee and Iris waited for Neel's response. He looked down at the stones in the courtyard of Krumlov Castle as an orange layer of light crept over him. The sun was rising. "How was I supposed to stop her?" Neel said dully. "She didn't tell me until it was too late."

"Did she say anything else?" asked Dee.

"That it worked. Rodolfo's taking the Zim. And he knows we're here."

"This is good news." Dee put a firm hand on Neel's shoulder. "You've lost some element of surprise, but your army is in a much better position to win." In a softer voice, he added, "There was nothing you could do to help Petra." Neel looked up. "I know how stubborn she is," Dee continued. "She made her decision, and it can't be changed. There will be no daring rescue of her, Your Majesty. Not unless you win this battle."

Neel's eyes held his. "You knew she would do this."

Dee faltered. "I . . . am not surprised she did."

Neel turned to Tomik, who was still seething. "Do you have the Marvel?"

Tomik pulled the smoky sphere from his pocket.

"Then tell Zora to get into the Tank and steer it toward the Zim Bridge. You and Lucas get into position. Treb's already moved the Roma into the hills. I'm going to join them now." He nodded at his black mare, which stamped outside the castle gates, and at the chestnut horse beside her. "Ready, Iris?"

"Just make sure I'm off that horse when I get good and angry and acidic," she said. "I'd rather not kill it. It's a nice color."

"Astro?" Neel said hesitantly. No one had really discussed what role the spider would play in the battle. "Maybe you should stay here, in the castle."

The legs dropped away from Astrophil's face. He had stopped shaking, and his green tears were wiped away. "Treb said I was fighting with him," said the spider. "So that means that I should go with you and Iris into the hills."

"All right," said Neel, and was heartened to know that a piece of Petra would stay with him. He lifted his palm. Astrophil jumped onto it, and the cold prickle of his legs against Neel's skin felt almost like hope. Neel tried not to think of the silence that had filled his mind since Petra's last message.

"Here." Tomik shoved a bag at him. He looked calmer, but the stony quality of his face told Neel that he was not forgiven. Neel understood. He couldn't forgive himself. "What's this?" he asked.

"More Marvels. As many as I could make in one night, and as deadly as I could make them."

"Thanks, Tom. I'll spread them out among the army. Now, Dee." Neel turned to him. "You—"

"There is no role for me in this battle," said Dee. "I am leaving now with Madinia and Margaret, through a Loophole."

Neel shrugged. He shouldn't have expected anything different. Dee was too canny to risk himself, or anything he cared about. Neel had known this all along.

"Good luck," said Dee, and walked back into the castle to tell his daughters it was time to leave.

A FEW HOURS LATER, when the rising sun had split the sky into bands of color, Treb peered through the spyglass Tomik had modified long ago. He swore.

"What?" Astrophil bounced on his shoulder. "What is it? Let me see."

Neel, who had seen if not heard his general's unhappiness over the noise of thousands of horses and soldiers, sidled his black mare near. He snatched the long tube out of Treb's hands. He looked through it, and almost wished Tomik hadn't been able to magnify the lens's power so well. Neel didn't like what he saw marching along the road on the other side of the river, heading to the Zim Bridge. "Rodolfo has changed the order of his army," he said grimly.

"He's bulked up the head of the line," Treb explained to Astrophil. "Yesterday, Rodolfo and his Gray Men were sitting pretty behind a bit of the cavalry, right up front. Now he and his monsters are farther back, better protected behind a thicker wall of horses and infantry. This means we've got to bite off more of his army to give Tomik and his Marvel a chance."

"Oh." Astrophil sagged.

"Don't you worry, spider. As long as that Marvel works, and Lucas blows up that bridge, we'll be all right."

Neel hadn't spent much time around royalty, and didn't know what a king should do in a situation like this. He decided calling his general a liar wasn't it. He collapsed the spyglass so that each segmented tube slid inside another. He jammed the thing into Treb's hands and rode off to tell Shandor to get his horses in line, and to take Tomik with him.

45

A Proposal

PETRA GRIPPED THE BARS of her cage and scanned the gray waves of monsters surging around her. She couldn't find her father. She didn't even know for certain that he was here. The Gristleki looked alike, loping on all fours as they poured down the road toward the Zim Bridge. Their scaly skulls were identical in the rising sun. She was too far away to see their eyes.

She shifted her gaze to the front of the army. The first line of horses had just crossed the bridge. She reached for the little stitch that linked her mind to Neel's, but it was gone. It had burned up like straw in a fire. She remembered his last words to her, his promise to hate her. Again, Petra felt hollow.

The sea of Gristleki parted with a screech. Rodolfo, who had been riding ahead of Petra's cage, guided his horse toward her. The Gristleki fell back from the horse, but howled longingly at it. The stallion threw its head nervously. Rodolfo yanked on the bit and pulled his horse alongside the cage.

"I have been thinking," he told Petra in a merry tone.

She closed her eyes. She thought she knew what he would say, though not because her magic had returned. She would never gain that back. But she remembered what she had seen in the tent. She remembered his plans for her. Perhaps, though, he had changed his mind.

He hadn't. "You should marry me," he said.

It still shocked her. "I can't marry you. I'm only fourteen."

"Which means that you are of age. You are an adult. In the Hapsburg Empire, you have the legal right to marry."

"You're too old." The words blurted out of her mouth before she could remind herself that people in cages have no luxury to be rude.

"Twenty years old is a fine age for a husband. What is six years between us? They only mean that I am wiser, with more experience, and can better guide you in life."

"I don't understand," Petra said. She decided that people in cages have a very dim future, and should be honest while they can. "Why would you want to marry me? You hate me."

"Yes, but the people *love* you." He leaned on his horse, looking up at her. "And if they think you love me, then they will love me, too. It will be like a fairy tale. In fairy tales, a prince always marries some unworthy peasant girl. Of course, in the stories, the girl is beautiful. But I am willing to overlook your shortcomings. Who knows? Maybe you will look better in a few years."

Petra kept her eyes trained on the front of the army. The cavalry had passed over the bridge.

"It *does* happen," the prince said encouragingly. When he received no response, he said, "Your choice is simple. Either you will marry me, or you will be executed at my coronation. As a traitor to the crown, you can expect a painful death. Well? What is your answer?"

She looked down at him. "No."

"Death, then," he said cheerfully, and rode away.

Zora steered the Tank under the river until its lights caught the pillars of the Zim Bridge. She pressed a button that brought it to a halt. It hovered below the water's surface, humming quietly. She pulled a tube out of the wall and pressed a button that would send the other half of the tube out of the Tank's hull, snake it through the water, and pop it through the surface. Zora peered through her end of the tube. She studied what was marching over the bridge and cursed. Treb would have been impressed to hear that an aristocratic lady knew as many swear words in her language as he did in his.

She sat back in the pink chair and considered what she had seen. Rodolfo had changed the order of his army. This would make things more difficult for the Roma forces, but what should Zora do about it? When should she give Lucas the signal he needed to blow up the bridge?

Zora had a good mind for strategy. She wouldn't have done well in the thick of a battle, seeing blood and bodies all around her, but there are different kinds of strengths. Some people might have panicked alone in a ship underwater, cut off from any communication with their friends. Zora, however, calmly listened to the engine's heartbeat, and realized that pure numbers weren't so important. It made sense to cut an army in half, but Rodolfo's was no ordinary army. The Gray Men surrounding him were worth several soldiers, and given the fact that Rodolfo had moved more of his army in front of him, maybe a blown-up bridge shouldn't split the army *exactly* in half. Lucas should do it right after Rodolfo and the Gray Men had crossed to the other side. That would give the Roma slightly more than half of Rodolfo's total forces to deal with at first, which wouldn't make things easy. But the most important thing was to eliminate the threat of the Gristleki, every last one.

She peered through the tube again, and turned it so that the view focused on Lucas. He was a small figure dressed in brown to match the dirt, huddling under the end of the bridge on the Roma's side of the river. He was waiting for her signal.

Zora turned the tube's view back to Rodolfo's army, and squinted when she saw a cage being dragged across the bridge, surrounded on all sides by a rippling gray flood of monsters. She looked harder and gasped. Petra was in that cage. Relief and worry warred within Zora. Iris had told her what Petra had done, and now Petra was clearly in a desperate situation. Yet she was alive.

Zora wished she could tell her friends what she had seen. But, well, she *couldn't*. She could only do what she was there to do. She focused, and when Petra and Rodolfo and his monsters had crossed the bridge, Zora brought the Tank to the surface.

PETRA EXHALED when she saw Rodolfo cross the bridge into the valley. Gray Men flowed after him, and the horses hauled her cart off the stone bridge and onto the dirt road. Bare brown hills rose steeply on either side of her. There were few trees, and they stood naked, waiting for spring to truly show itself.

Petra was in the valley. There was no wind. *Soon*, she told herself. Lucas would blow up the bridge soon. She kept herself perfectly still. She could not look behind her. She could not alert Rodolfo or anyone else to what was about to happen.

But then she heard it: shouts of surprise from the foot soldiers following the last lines of Gristleki that traveled behind her. Petra decided it wouldn't seem strange if she turned to look now, so she did. Archers ranged along the bridge, shooting arrows into the water below.

"What is going on?" shouted Rodolfo, who swung his horse around and passed Petra's cage, heading back toward the bridge. "Why are you firing without my command?" The Gray Men turned their heads and followed their master, flowing toward the Zim Bridge.

"No," Petra whispered. Her father might be among those lines of Gristleki ready to creep back onto the bridge they had just crossed. He could not step onto that bridge. In minutes, it would be gone in an explosion of gunpowder and flame. She stared at the slithering Gristleki. What could she do to make them stop?

Petra ran her hands over the cage, searching for something, anything that could help her. She found a rough edge of metal. She looked at it, then at the Gristleki. She set her bare arm against the edge and began to saw at her skin.

As ARROWS *thunked* harmlessly against the hull of the Tank, Zora saw Lucas dart from his hiding place. He crawled along the dirt under the foot of the bridge to the barrel of gunpowder he had wedged there during the night. She saw small sacks of gunpowder stretching in a line along the arc of the bridge, below the sight of the soldiers—unless they happened to peer down at the bridge, and not at the Tank below.

Zora fired one of the Tank's metal spears. It soared up through the air and over the bridge to bury itself in a man.

A small flame burst below Lucas's swift hands. He turned, ran, and jumped into the water below. Soldiers trained their arrows on him and fired as he swam toward the Tank.

The fuse Lucas had lit sputtered and seemed to go out. Then it flared again, and burned its way toward the gunpowder.

BLOOD STREAMED from Petra's arm and dripped to the ground below. A Gray Man crawling toward the bridge whipped his head around toward Petra. Then another did the same, and another.

With an inhuman howl, the entire pack of Gristleki launched itself at Petra's cage.

They battered it, shaking it, snaking bony arms through the bars. Petra recoiled to the center of the cage, gripping her bleeding arm. Her breath shuddered, and she couldn't help a cry of fear when a Gray Man, frustrated by the smell of blood it couldn't reach, leaped on the neck of one of the horses pulling her cage. The Gray Man rubbed its scaled skin against the horse, which squealed and reared, slamming into the other horse. The cage tilted, and threatened to topple to the ground.

"Stop!" Rodolfo's horse was surging through the monsters, pushing to reach Petra's cage. Rodolfo pulled out a whip and brought it down on a Gray Man's back. "You can eat her in front of the Hapsburg court, not *now*! Has everyone gone completely mad?"

There was a crackling sound, and the bridge exploded behind him.

46

The Battle Begins

ASTROPHIL FLINCHED AT THE SOUND of the explosion in the valley below, then clung harder to Treb's shoulder.

"Now," Neel told Treb, and wheeled his black horse to take the center of the front line, alongside Iris.

"But," Treb said in a low voice only Astrophil could hear, "he's supposed to say something to our soldiers. Something to rouse their ire. Neel's supposed to make a speech."

"It seems that he does not want to," said Astrophil. "Perhaps you should do it. You are the general."

"Neel . . . he's good with words. But me . . ."

"You do not have to sound noble," said Astrophil. "Be fierce. Be mean. You can do that."

"Yes," said Treb. "That I can." He turned his horse to face the Roma cavalry and the foot soldiers behind them, and began to speak.

Astrophil didn't listen. He was too nervous. He glanced at the two sides of the valley—at theirs, the southern side, which was steep but not too treacherous for the Roma horses, and at the northern side, where Tomik, Shandor, and a small portion of the cavalry waited in hiding. The northern side of the valley looked impossible for any horse. It was perilously steep and stony, and the hope was that Rodolfo's forces would assume an attack was coming from the south, and would direct their attention there.

It was difficult to say which portion of the Roma army had the harder task, Neel's or Tomik's. Tomik's force was small, and would have to come down a tricky slope that could break their horses' legs. Once they reached the valley, they would make hard for the Gray Men, and try not to be taken down along the way.

Neel's force would bear the brunt of the battle. It would divert the attention of Rodolfo's army and clear a path for Tomik and his Marvel. Astrophil had read enough on warfare to know that the logic of this plan was sound, but he had also read enough to know that both parts of the Roma army could expect heavy losses.

Treb shouted something incoherent, and Astrophil startled. "Oh, yes," said the spider. "A battle cry." He sucked in his breath and screamed as loud as he could.

Treb winced. "Not in my ear, Astro."

The cavalry charged down the slope.

FROM THE OTHER SIDE of the valley, Tomik watched the rest of the Roma army spill toward Rodolfo's forces.

"Just wait," said Shandor, keeping his horse still alongside Tomik's.

Tomik touched the Marvel where it bulged inside his breast pocket, then wiped sweaty hands against his legs. "I told you. I told Neel. I can't ride. Somebody else should throw the Marvel, somebody who could actually make it down this slope. I should be with Neel, or Zora, or Lucas."

"Would this 'somebody' of yours have a magical gift for glass, too, so that his aim might be better than anybody else's?" asked Shandor. "Would this 'somebody' be able to touch the Marvel's glass and spin it into the air with a special sort of energy that will fling it farther than anyone else could manage? Because I haven't met that 'somebody,' unless he is you."

Tomik bit his lip. "All right," he said softly.

"These are my horses. They're good horses, and they're trained to follow each other. The hardest thing about going down this slope will be picking out the right path. You follow me, and you'll be fine."

ZORA THREW OPEN the Tank's hatch, grabbed her brother's arms, and hauled him inside. He slumped against her, and it took her a frantic moment to realize that his blood was streaming down her. "Lucas!" He had an arrow sticking out of his shoulder, and another in his thigh.

She lowered him gently to the metal floor, slammed the hatch shut, and punched her fist against a button. The Tank slipped below the river's surface. She kneeled by her brother's side.

"It's not so bad," Lucas said weakly. His blond hair was dark with river water and plastered against his face. "These aren't the kinds of wounds you die from."

"Unless you bleed to death!"

"Very comforting, Zora. You are a terrible nurse."

That made her laugh a little—until Lucas told her what she would have to do. "Get one of those dresses and tear it up. You'll have to pull out the arrows and bind me."

Zora went pale, but fetched a dress and shredded it. She gritted her teeth and tugged the arrow from Lucas's shoulder.

He screamed.

"Lucas! Are you all right?"

He screwed his eyes shut and gasped. "I know all brothers say this to their sisters," he finally said in a halting voice, "but you are a pain."

They both laughed, slightly hysterical, and the second arrow came out more easily.

When Lucas's wounds were bound as tightly as possible, he said, "Tell me what's going on out there."

Zora looked through the tube. She saw the Roma cavalry narrowing the gap between them and Rodolfo's forces. There was her aunt, and Neel, and Treb in the front line. Zora swung the tube back toward Rodolfo's army, and saw a man who could only be the general, sitting on his horse, shouting commands at his soldiers. Then the general went still, staring at the front line of the Roma cavalry. Zora stared as well, and realized how utterly recognizable Iris was—an old, pale woman streaming white hair, standing out like a flag against the dark Roma army. Zora realized, too, what a public figure her aunt was, and how everybody knew her—and to stay away from her, because of her acid skin that could melt stone floors.

"Oh, no," Zora said.

"JUST GET ME CLOSE ENOUGH," Iris shouted. The reins in her hands and the saddle beneath her were smoking. "I'll get down off this horse and show Rodolfo who's in charge! I'll rain acid destruction down on him! I'll—"

Rodolfo's general notched an arrow, and shot it straight through Iris's heart.

TREB YANKED ON THE REINS, hauling his horse out of the way as Iris's careened. Her body slumped, toppled to the ground, and was lost in a maze of stampeding horses.

"Iris!" Astrophil shouted. He tugged on Treb's earlobe. "We must help her!"

"She's gone," said the general. Gripping the reins with one hand, he pulled out a curved sword with his other. The front line of the Roma army was about to crash into Rodolfo's.

"No, Treb, listen to me—" Astrophil stopped when he heard the man suck in his breath. Astrophil followed Treb's gaze to the wagons behind Rodolfo's infantry. They were being unpacked. In fact, several of them had already been unloaded, and it was only now that Astrophil could see what had been inside.

"Cannons," Treb whispered. One was aimed directly at him. "Jump, Astro! Jump now!"

The cannon boomed, and a black ball sped toward them. Astrophil froze. Then the ball slammed into Treb's horse and Astrophil was flung into the air. He spiraled, tumbling, his legs waving in every direction. He shot silvery webs randomly, hoping one of them would cling to something solid. They didn't. He wheeled, and fell to the ground.

Astrophil jumped to his feet. "Treb!" he shouted, but then saw the ruins of the man and his horse. Astrophil ducked away from a blur of galloping hooves, and tumbled. He shot a web to a horse's saddle, and was climbing up its side when the Roma army finally clashed with Rodolfo's. The force of Astrophil's horse ramming into another one sent him flying again to the ground.

He stood and looked around, then up.

A soldier's boot came crushing down on him.

47

The Marvel

NEEL TORE HIS EYES from Iris's falling body just in time to see the cannonball sailing through the sky. "Veer left!" he shouted at the cavalry and spurred his horse out of the cannonball's path.

Treb and his horse exploded. Something silvery shot through the air like a tiny comet.

Neel's heart clenched. "Astro," he whispered. He galloped toward where he thought Astrophil had fallen, and plunged into the thick of Rodolfo's army. A sword slashed at him. Neel's ghost fingers shot out, wrapped around the blade, jerked it out of the man's hands, and threw it down. Though Neel wasn't an expert swordsman, he was good at cheating. With one ghostly hand around the man's neck, holding him still on his bucking horse, Neel used his other hand to stab his sword into the man's side. The soldier fell to the ground.

"Astrophil!" he shouted, then spotted the spider climbing up a horse's flank. Astrophil fell again. Neel was chopping a path through Rodolfo's army to reach the spider when another cannonball sailed overhead and slammed into the Roma infantry.

Neel wheeled his horse and snared the arm of the nearest Roma. It was Shaida. "Here." He took a fireball Marvel from his pocket and shoved it at her. "Destroy those cannons. Tell anyone who's got a

Marvel to use them, and use them now. Aim for the wagons. Aim for the cannons."

"What are *you* going to do?" she yelled, but he rode ahead, scanning the ground for a bright bit of tin.

A fireball Marvel arced through the air and hit the wagons. The explosion shook the ground, and several horses fell. The black mare scrambled under Neel, but found her feet. Neel steadied her, and in the glare of the fire he saw something shiny and crumpled lying on the ground near a fallen soldier wearing Rodolfo's livery. Neel sheathed his sword to free both hands. His ghost fingers unfurled in front of him, and with one hand he batted aside a charging foot soldier, then shoved back an enemy's horse as it stomped toward where Astrophil lay. Neel's other ghostly hand swept down then, scooped up the spider, and brought him close.

More Marvels flew into the air. The segment of Rodolfo's army that had been infantry, wagons, and cannons turned into a blazing hole.

Even though this was the most dangerous time to look down at the palm of his hand, Neel did. Astrophil was twitching. One of his legs was crushed, and two were simply gone. He bled brassica oil.

"Astro!" Neel shouted. "Astro, please answer me!"

Faintly, the spider said, "I appear to be missing a few legs."

"You'll be all right," Neel told him, because he refused to believe anything else.

"Good!" Shandor said, watching the battle below.

"Good?" said Tomik. "How can that be good?" He couldn't see any details from so far away and didn't know enough about war to judge what was taking place before him. He saw a bewildering, disastrous mess.

"Didn't you notice what your Marvels did? The Roma are eating up the front lines, and Rodolfo's artillery has been destroyed. We're in as good shape as we'll ever be. Time to go."

Tomik closed his eyes. "Straight for the Gray Men?"

"That's right. Rodolfo's army has turned to face Neel's, so we can come at the Gray Men from the side. Ready?"

No, Tomik thought. "Yes," he said.

The force of about a thousand horses started down the steep slope.

"Stay right behind me," Shandor said, and Tomik did just that, his stomach plunging every time his horse slipped. Behind him, he heard a yell of fear, and a horse came tumbling down. Its legs buckled beneath it, and the rider spun over its shoulders. The woman's neck broke.

"Right behind me," Shandor said again.

Tomik followed.

His nerves were frayed and his legs were shaking by the time the horses reached more even ground. *I'll be no good when it really matters,* Tomik thought. He could barely see straight through his fear. But Shandor kicked his horse into a gallop, and Tomik's horse followed. The cavalry was streaming around him now, heading straight for the knot of gray. The Roma drew closer, and Tomik had just enough time to spot a cage and narrow his eyes at it when a monster lifted its head and stared at the Roma cavalry. It opened its mouth in a toothless grin. It broke from the pack and ran toward them.

"Shandor!" Tomik shouted, but the creature had already leaped through the air to wrap its arms around the Roma. Shandor kept his seat, but the Gray Man clawed at his face, ripping away skin.

"Now, Tom!" the man yelled. "Do it now!"

Tomik pulled the smoky Marvel with the Gristleki cure from his pocket. He cocked his arm back and prepared to throw.

"Losing? We are not *losing,*" Petra heard Rodolfo shout at his general. "Where is the rest of my army?"

"They went south, to cross the Dalo Bridge. They'll be here to reinforce us, but it will take time—"

"Time?" Rodolfo slapped the soldier with his metal glove. The man reeled, his face distorted. His jaw had been broken. Several Gristleki glanced at Rodolfo as he listened to the general groan. The monsters' hollow faces were eager.

"Isss he oursss?" one of the monsters asked. "Can we have him? Pleassse?"

"Oh, fine," said Rodolfo, and a cluster of Gristleki fell on the man and dragged him down.

Petra saw yet another fireball Marvel sail through the air and smash into the infantry. The earth shook with the explosion.

"You!" Rodolfo had turned his horse toward Petra's cage. "I wouldn't be here if it wasn't for you. This was supposed to be easy!" He took a key from his pocket and unlocked the cage. Then he climbed off his horse and through the cage door to grab Petra by the neck. He dragged her out and threw her to the ground.

"Isss she oursss?" a Gray Man asked.

Rodolfo jumped back on his horse and grinned. "Ye—" he started to say, when an invisible force grabbed the reins of his horse and hauled him away from Petra. She looked up from the dirt. Beyond the twisting bodies of the Gristleki surrounding her, she could see Neel, a hand stretched out in front of him, his ghostly fingers dragging Rodolfo and his horse toward him.

A Gray Man hissed, "I think that was a yesss. Did our massster not sssay yesss?"

"Yesss," the Gristleki answered, and closed around Petra.

She could see nothing now but gray skin and leering faces. Her heart shuddering, Petra searched for the silver eyes of her father. Then a thought struck her, and she squeezed her eyes shut. She didn't want to see him, not like this. She didn't want her last memory to be this.

She heard a howl—not of pleasure, but pain. Her eyes flew open, and saw a sword slicing through the neck of a Gray Man. The head rolled onto the earth, spitting black blood. The headless body crumpled, and in the space it left stood John Dee.

He sliced the throat of another Gristleki, reached into the circle of monsters to grab Petra's arm, and dragged her to him. "Come with me," he said. "There's a Loophole right behind me. Come!"

But Petra had frozen, astonished that he was here, that he would do this, and that she wanted, suddenly, to embrace him.

A Gristleki leaped at them, and Dee raised his sword.

"No!" she shouted. "Don't kill them! One of them could be my father! They're *people!*"

"Not at the moment." He chopped off the monster's head. Dee started to say something else when Petra snagged his sword arm and pointed. There, beyond the Gray Men, and far to the right of Rodolfo's horse as it was dragged over the ground toward Neel, was Tomik.

The Marvel in his hand caught the light of the sun. Tomik drew back his hand and threw.

48

Monsters

THE MARVEL SMASHED on the ground exactly in the center of Rodolfo's Gristleki army. Thick, bitter smoke flowed from the shards. A nearby Gray Man gagged, and soon the air was filled with the sound of retching as the monsters bent double. They coughed, choked, and vomited black blood. It gushed from their mouths, pouring onto the ground. The Gray Men sagged and fell. They lay still.

Petra started to cry. Fiala's cure had not worked, it had not worked at all, and the woman had probably never intended it to work. The Gray Men were dead.

"Petra, stop," Dee said roughly. "This isn't like you."

Maybe he was right. Maybe it wasn't like her to weep, but who was she, without a family? Who would she be, without her father? She could not stop the tears. Dee kept speaking to her, but she didn't listen. She heard Rodolfo shouting somewhere in the background, telling the Roma not to touch him. She heard Tomik pushing his way toward her side, and he was telling her not to cry, too. Then Neel was standing in front of her, and she could see his dark face and strange yellowy eyes through her tears. He didn't tell her that she shouldn't weep. He simply held out his hand, and opened it.

Astrophil lay crumpled and still on his palm. Petra looked at Neel, remembered him saying he would hate her forever, and wondered if this was his revenge. "How dare you?" she whispered. "How can you show me this? How can you show me that I have nothing left?"

"Petra," squeaked the spider.

She gasped.

"I find it very insulting that you are so quick to assume I am dead," Astrophil continued. "Have you no faith in my survival skills? I am only a little damaged."

"Astrophil!" She started to take him from Neel, then stopped, worried she would hurt him further.

"Everyone is trying to tell you to calm down. Why, if Iris were here"—the spider's voice hitched, then continued—"she would tell you to stop your hysterics. Take a deep breath and look around you. Just look."

Petra did. Somewhere up ahead, the battle was still raging, but in a muted way, and in the spot where the Gristleki army had stood there was a soft quiet, like the kind that comes when you wait for the stars to appear. Petra forced her gaze to fall on the gray bodies around her, and her eyes widened. A change was creeping over their dead skin. The scales were fading. Color flushed along the limp limbs. Chests rose, then fell, then rose again. Finally, someone stood.

The people who had once been monsters shakily pushed themselves off the ground and looked around them.

"Petra," said Dee, and pointed.

It was her father. He was gaunt and hairless. His silver eyes were large in his thin face. Yet he smiled at her.

She ran, and threw herself into his arms. She pressed her face against his chest, and didn't see what the others saw.

They saw the skeletal, changed people look at each other, and remember everything that had been done to them, and everything that they had done. Then they turned toward Rodolfo, who had been taken from his horse by the Roma cavalry. They moved toward him, their feet slow but determined as they picked their way across the battlefield.

Rodolfo had never shown an ounce of fear toward the Gristleki when they were monsters. Now, though, he stumbled back from their human forms. His eyes widened at the sight of their faces. He retreated. He scrambled over a smashed wagon. He fled across the ravaged ground until he tripped over the body of his general, and fell on the dead man's sword.

49

A Gift

AFTER THE BATTLE, Master Kronos repaired Astrophil. He offered to replace the spider's two missing legs, but Astrophil declined. "I am proud of my war wounds," he said, and did not mind that he limped.

Even with only six legs, he proved himself very skilled at sewing up wounds, and in the days that followed the Battle of Zim Bridge, he received a lot of practice. There were not, however, as many dead and wounded as had been feared, particularly since Rodolfo's reinforcements, once they had crossed the Dalo Bridge and rode to the rest of the army's rescue, had decided there was little point in fighting. Rodolfo was dead, as was their general, and a bloodied blond man soaked with river water had joined the Roma to face the reinforcements. Many Bohemians recognized him as Lucas December, the duke of Moravia. Enough of them realized that if Rodolfo was dead, they had a new ruler. The reinforcements laid down their weapons.

As agile as Astrophil's legs were, there were things he couldn't mend. Nothing could replace the skin torn from Shandor's face, although Dee applied leeches to suck the Gristleki poison from his wounds and saved his life. Yet Treb could not be brought back from the dead, nor Iris.

No one wore black to her funeral. Zora, who had inherited Krumlov Castle, hung banners of bright fabric from its windows, and if her poppy-colored dress brought out the red of her eyes, it did not matter. There were many people with red eyes in the crowd gathered in the Krumlov cemetery. The stone that marked Iris's grave sparkled in the light.

"I know you wanted the Bohemian crown for me," Lucas whispered to the gravestone when the rest of the people had begun filing out of the cemetery. "But I don't think that was such a good idea." He thought of everything he would have to do. Fiala Broshek would be put on trial. He would have to work to replace the things he himself had destroyed—the Academy, bridges, and a good deal of brassica oil. Most important, he would have to gain the trust of people who had lived under Rodolfo's rule. Lucas didn't think it could be done.

"Iris had faith in you," someone behind him said. It was John Dee. He had quite a talent for sneaking up on people.

"She was crazy. Look what she did," Lucas added in an angry voice. "Riding into battle at her age. I shouldn't have let her. I should've—" he broke off, and pressed the heel of his hand against a fresh flow of tears. "I am going to make a mess of everything."

"Let's look on the bright side," said Dee. "After Rodolfo, you cannot possibly do worse."

Lucas looked at him. He couldn't quite tell, but he thought Dee was trying to be funny. If so, it was a bad, dark joke. Lucas laughed anyway, because if he didn't he would have kept crying, and sometimes you have to accept what people give you, even if the gift comes badly wrapped. Dee was trying to cheer him up. Lucas let him.

John Dee would depart soon for England with his daughters, once the Roma army had left for the Vatra and Margaret had closed the Loophole behind them. His stay in London would be a brief holiday. He was, after all, the English ambassador to the Vatra, and he had every intention of returning to that country and fulfilling his duties

Petra was among the last to leave the cemetery, and when she did she fell in step with John Dee. They took a path that led away from where the Roma army's tents still spread over the land, and toward hills where the battle hadn't taken place. A light green was creeping over the earth.

Petra had gotten into the habit of taking walks—usually with her father, but sometimes with John Dee, which surprised many people, including herself. On the day of Iris's funeral, Petra was silent as they wandered to a narrow bend in the river. She was trying to understand the source of her surprise. It wasn't so much due to the fact that she enjoyed spending time with John Dee. She remembered their conversation the night before the battle, and how a knowing look had sharpened his eyes when she had questioned him about mind-magic. He had known what she would do. He might not have known the details, but he had understood that she would go to Rodolfo, and might never come back. Yet he had not tried to stop her.

Some people might have interpreted this as a lack of feeling on his part, but Petra remembered how Dee had risked his life to save hers and knew this couldn't be it. It must be something else. As Petra tried to identify it, she understood what was odd about her walks with him. What possible interest could he have in her, now that her magic was gone? Petra's surprise lay not in the fact that she walked with him, but that *he* walked with *her*.

She told him so. "I'm not useful to you anymore, you know."

"Useful?"

Petra looked at the muddy swirl of the river. "I keep thinking about the letter you gave me saying that Rodolfo had no magic, and about how this meant I was stronger than him. But I'm not anymore. I'm ordinary, just like he was."

"Petra, you're still one of the strongest people I have ever met. That hasn't changed."

"Everything has changed."

Dee slipped his hands into his deep pockets.

"I would like to know why you're here, talking with me," said Petra.

He frowned, and seemed to consider his words carefully. "Despite what Iris would say"—Dee glanced at Petra, and kept speaking as if he hadn't seen the pain flash across her face—"I still think that my definition of friendship is a good one."

Petra's brow furrowed. "You mean that friendship is a partnership based on mutual interest?"

"No," he said. "Mutual respect."

She looked at him. He smiled, then added lightly, "Don't worry, Petra. I'm sure I'll always be able to find a use for you."

When Petra returned to her room in Krumlov Castle, she found Astrophil reading a book on the identification of different diseases. His missing legs didn't seem to make him race any less quickly down the page.

"Astrophil," she said.

He looked up from his reading and slid down the crease in the center of the open book to be closer to her.

"Does it bother you that my magic is gone?" she asked.

"Does it bother you that my legs are?"

"No, of course not. I mean, *yes*. I worry that your missing legs bother *you*. But . . ." She grew frustrated with her inability to explain. "We won't ever be able to talk the way we used to, Astro. We won't be able to talk secretly. We won't talk silently."

"Well, then," he said, "we will have to whisper."

A FEW DAYS LATER, Petra looked out her window, toying with a wooden practice sword. She had asked Shandor to make it. He had been glad to see her when she'd walked into the castle ballroom, which was now filled with beds for injured soldiers. When she had told him what she wanted, he smiled with the good half of his face and started to say yes. Then he paused. The half smile still lingered, but had grown thoughtful. It looked like he was hiding something. But he often looked this way now. The mass of scars had turned the left side of his face into a hideous, immovable mask. When one half of him couldn't show an emotion, and the other half wouldn't, Shandor was a daunting man to face. "I can't make you a wooden sword," he said. "It'd be against the rules."

"Rules? What rules?"

"All weapons in the Roma army are distributed or approved by the general. We don't have one right now."

Petra bit her lip, remembering Treb's grin when he announced her Coming of Age, so many months ago on the deck of his ship.

"That means," Shandor said slowly, "that you should ask the king."

"I'm asking for a wooden sword. It's for learning swordplay. It's not a weapon."

"Hit someone with it hard enough, and you'll see that's not true."

"Fine," said Petra. "I'll make one myself."

He stopped her before she could whirl away from the side of his bed. "I'll break a rule for you," he said, though Petra suspected that no such rule existed in the first place. Then she reminded herself that different cultures had different rules, and so did people, and sometimes they were hard to know until they'd been broken. *I will hate you forever if you do this*, Neel had told Petra, and if his attitude toward her since the end of the battle was anything to go by, he had meant it.

Petra sighed, and laid the wooden sword lengthwise along the windowsill. She turned away from the view, which showed thousands of tents still surrounding the castle. She told herself she was turning away from the sword she had just set down.

Petra was pathetic at fencing. She hadn't realized until recently how much of her former skill had relied on magic. She had found

Nicolas, the Maraki who had trained her on board the *Pacolet*, and asked him for a lesson. He had come through the battle without a scratch on him, and was fidgeting for something to do. "Sure, I'll teach you," he said. "Better than sitting around doing nothing. What're we waiting for, anyway? Lucas has already commanded the release of Roma prisoners in Prague, and we can heal our wounded just as well in the Vatra. It's time we Roma went home."

During their lesson, Petra stumbled and had trouble holding the wooden sword straight. Nicolas, who had loved her deadly grace, couldn't quite hide his shock. It would be a long time before she used her father's invisible rapier again.

It had taken courage for her to wield that sword, yet it took more to ask her father a simple question. "How do you feel?" she had said when he was allowed to leave the infirmary. He leaned on her arm as they walked to his new room in the castle.

He didn't answer at first. "Heavy," he said.

Petra remembered how Sadie had taught her how to hide small objects by sewing them into her skirts. She felt again the weight of those secret things, and thought of the griefs her father would carry, and she would carry. She tightened her arm around him, and he kissed the top of her head. "Thank you," he said.

Now she stood alone in her bedroom, her back turned to the window with its view of tents. Astrophil had twinkled down the hall to talk with her father, and though she was reluctant to share the hours when her father felt well enough to see people, she understood when Astrophil asked to see Master Kronos by himself.

Petra turned around the room, unsettled—and unsure what, if anything, might settle her. She started toward the open bedroom door, and yelped when something scratched her ankle.

It was Amoretta. The white cat purred, giving Petra a very innocent look.

Whatever fate awaited Fiala Broshek, who was imprisoned in Krumlov Castle's dungeon, Zora had decided that the cat was guilty of nothing worse than a bad habit of bringing dead birds indoors. Amoretta became the castle pet. She had a special fondness for Petra, and one of her favorite games was to claw the girl until Petra chased her. She did this now.

Petra ran after Amoretta, happy that some things don't change. She could still outrace almost anyone and anything.

If, that is, she knew where it had gone. Petra slowed her pace when it was clear that the cat hadn't gone upstairs after she'd disappeared around a corner. Petra moved stealthily, her eyes searching for a white paw. She tiptoed down the third-floor hallway, then paused when she realized exactly where she was. She stood outside Iris's sitting room. Her heart tightened when she recalled her last conversation with the woman, and how Iris had said that making new colors made her feel like an explorer of undiscovered countries. Petra wondered what color the land of the dead was. She hoped it was beautiful.

Like during that night, voices floated from Iris's sitting room. "I made this for you," she heard Tomik say.

"For me?" It was Zora. "It's beautiful."

"Break it."

"What? I can't break your gift."

"The gift is in the breaking. Go on, Zora. It's just like any other Marvel."

Too curious to stop herself, Petra peered through the slightly open door. Zora and Tomik were standing close together, Zora cradling a glass sphere in the palm of her hand. Petra was too far away to see what was inside the Marvel. "Well," Zora said reluctantly. "If you're sure . . ."

"I am."

Zora dropped the Marvel. It shattered on the stone floor, and a plume of rose petals drifted into the air, swirling around Zora and

Tomik like a pink blizzard. Zora laughed, trailing her fingers through the flowery swirl.

Petra caught her breath. She ducked out of sight—but not before Tomik glanced up and saw her there. She pulled away and rushed down the hall.

That night, Petra knocked on Tomik's door. He opened it. "Can we talk?" she asked.

"Finally." He beckoned her inside with a smile. "Petra comes to talk to *me*. Have I gone to sleep and woken up in some upside-down, backward world where Petra Kronos tries to find out what *I'm* thinking?"

She hesitated.

"I'm teasing you," he said.

"Right. Um. So . . . Zora?"

Tomik gave her a shy, blissful look. "Zora."

"Oh. Good. I didn't know . . . but I'm glad."

It was Tomik's turn to look tentative. "You're not . . . jealous, are you?"

Her answer was honest. "No."

He gave her a relieved grin. "I didn't think you would be." He shrugged slightly and said, "I'm not exactly sure where things are going with Zora. I mean, they're going well. But I have to visit my family and face my father's wrath. He's not going to be thrilled about me going missing for more than a year. And then Zora and I . . . will see." Tomik looked at his hands and said awkwardly, "We're very different. After all, she's got a castle."

"That doesn't mean that *you* are different, as people."

"Maybe. I guess we'll find out." He smiled, and Petra could see how much joy he took in the prospect of this discovery. It occurred to her that this joy was a kind of courage, and that if certain feelings need to be protected as a lamp protects a flame, others need the wind to let them burn, and breathe to life.

"You know," Tomik said, "I'm not the only person you ought to talk to."

"What do you mean?"

Tomik's smile grew sly. "I don't think the entire Roma army is still here, waiting to go home, because Neel wants to talk with *me*."

50

The Jewel

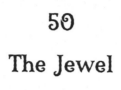

Petra *had* talked to Neel, right after the battle, when everyone had returned to the castle. She had thanked him for saving Astrophil's life.

"It was nothing." Neel had spoken as if it had *meant* nothing.

His indifference hurt. Petra wanted to tell him that the Neel she knew wouldn't shrink something so important into nothing. She wanted to say even more. Her throat felt full with words she had guarded for so long. She wished she could have her mind-magic back—just once, only for a minute—so that she could predict what Neel's face would look like when she spoke.

His eyes darted past her to Master Kronos, who was asking a repaired Astrophil to test each remaining leg. Petra followed Neel's gaze. When she saw what he did, she couldn't keep the happiness from her face.

Neel's expression closed, and everything Petra had wanted to say tasted suddenly bitter. How could she ask Neel for anything, when his family was broken and hers was now whole? How could she ask him to give her any part of his heart, when he had lost so much?

She stayed silent. He went cold, and went away. She had not seen him since.

The morning after she visited Tomik's room, Petra set out toward the tent-covered hills. The sight of them made her feel outnumbered and small, so she kept her eyes trained on the four-colored flag of the king. Soldiers gave her keen glances and got out of her way. She didn't stop until she reached Neel's tent, where she paused with the awkward realization of the obvious: that there was no door, only a closed flap cut into the cloth. She couldn't very well knock. She supposed she should call out. She should let Neel hear her voice, and decide whether she could enter. But she was afraid of being turned away. She lifted the fabric door and stepped inside.

Neel was sitting on his bed, which was little more than a pallet and a blanket. He looked up from the book in his hands. The expression on his face stopped her breath.

He dropped the book and scrambled to his feet.

"Sorry," Petra mumbled. "I shouldn't have—but—"

"It's all right—"

"I wanted to talk to you," they said, and heard their voices mingling together. They laughed.

"I thought you were angry with me," said Petra.

Neel stuffed his hands in his pockets. "Nah."

"I seem to remember someone saying he would hate me forever."

Neel grew serious. "Truth, then?"

"Truth."

"I was angry. I was furious. I thought my anger would eat me whole. It was just . . ." Neel ran a rough hand through his black hair. "After Sadie, it would have been too much. It would have been too much to lose you, too." He gave her a hard look. "I need to know something. I've been wanting to know for a while. Why didn't you want to talk to me through dreams? Why didn't you want to see me?"

"Truth?"

"Truth."

"I wanted to see you too much," said Petra.

The corner of Neel's mouth lifted. A soft silence fell.

He almost spoke, then paused and glanced at the sloping walls of his tent with an air of slight confusion. Petra wondered if he, too, expected to see green waves and pink sand. He touched the sapphire on his ear—not anxiously, as he once had, but thoughtfully. "Let's go for a walk," he said. "You like to do that, don't you? I've seen you."

"Yes."

When they stepped out of the tent, Petra noticed that there were many more soldiers gathered around it than there had been before. They all seemed to have a very important task to do, one that needed to be done within view of the king's tent. Petra heard their voices fade. She caught their sidelong looks. She smiled and slipped her hand into Neel's. His tightened around hers. They drew close, their shoulders and arms brushing. They walked like that away from the encampment, sheltering each other from the raw spring wind.

He led her to a new place, a hill high enough to see very far. They saw the tents, the castle, the curled ribbon of the river, and the scar in the earth where the battle had been.

"What will you do now?" Neel asked.

"I'm not sure. It's strange *not* to have anything to do. I feel like the rest of my life is waiting for me, and I have no idea what it will look like. Does that sound silly?"

"It sounds about right."

"My father and I will go south with Astro to see our cousins. After that . . . I'll let my father decide." Her voice lowered. "He's not well. I think he will be, someday, but being a Gray Man . . . it's left him sick at heart. So I'll go where he goes." She looked at Neel to see if he understood.

"Yeah. I need to have a long talk with my ma, too." Neel rubbed at his forehead. "I have to tell her I'm sorry."

"What for?"

"Oh"—he gave her a mischievous look—"for gambling my life when she begged me not to."

"I'm sorry," said Petra.

"No need to be. Everything turned out all right, didn't it?"

"I guess so. Maybe 'sorry' is the wrong word. But I'm not sure what the right one is."

"We'll figure it out," he said. He peered, and pointed at a butterfly. It was too early in the season for butterflies, but there it was, a scrap of yellow carried by the wind. Neel watched it fly, then said, "Hey, maybe after you visit southern Bohemia, your da would like to rest up someplace really warm. Someplace tropical."

"Like someplace off the coast of India?"

He looked at her.

"I'd like that," said Petra. "I'll ask him."

"It'd be all right if he doesn't want to. I've only got about a year left of this king business, and then I'm free . . . at least until I'm practically thirty." His eyes widened, and they both laughed at how old and far away that sounded. "But a year is just a year," he said. "And I've got the globes, which means . . ." He trailed off, hesitant.

"We'd never be too far away, wherever we are," said Petra. "That's good, because otherwise I would miss you."

"You would?"

"I miss you even now," she said, thinking of the mind-link they had once shared. "I miss this." She let go of his hand to touch the air, and couldn't swallow her sadness that she'd never again feel the fluid ghosts that flowed from Neel's fingers. She felt only the wind. "It's hard to be ordinary."

"You? Never." Neel seemed to brush his hair out of his face, but Petra realized that this had been a sleight of hand when his palm opened and revealed the Jewel of the Kalderash. "Here."

"What?"

"Take it."

"I can't take that."

"Borrow it, then."

"Neel." She closed his fingers around the sapphire. "That's not something you can give away."

He sighed. "Maybe not."

"Anyway, I don't have anything like that to give you in return. A treasure."

"Not true," he said. "Not true."

She smiled, though she didn't quite believe him, and said, "Will you tell me a story?"

He lifted his brows.

"I always like your stories. You tell them well. Give one to me, and I will give something to you."

He let out a breath. "A fellow can't refuse an offer like that, can he? Hmm. Well." He glanced away from her, and his gaze lighted again on the butterfly, which had dwindled into a dancing yellow mote. "Why don't I tell you the story of how the butterfly came to be? It's a Lovari tale."

"Those are the best kind."

"Once upon a time there was a little shell that lived in the deep sea," Neel said. "A plain shell, one that opened and closed itself like a mouth. This shell had a secret. It loved to sing. And it tried to share its song, but its music was lost on the waves. So it went to the sea witch and revealed its hidden heart's desire. 'Why, you foolish thing,' said the witch. 'Everyone knows that music is for the air, not the sea. You need to go above the waves to be heard.'

"The shell sank into the sand. 'But I can't,' it said.

"'You leave that to me,' said the witch. 'I'll change you into an air creature. For a price.'

"'Anything.'

"The witch smiled, and cast her spell. The little shell rose through the waves, floating through the black until the water became blue, then green. The shell skimmed along the sea foam, and unfolded into the air. The two halves of its shell became transparent wings, and stretched, and caught the wind. The shell wondered what it had become, but decided it didn't matter, because its tiny, colorless, frail body was full of joy. It would sing. It would sing and be heard. It opened its mouth . . . but nothing came out."

"Neel?"

"Shh. The witch had her price, you see, and had taken the little shell's voice."

"Neel, I thought this was going to be a happy story."

"But there are songs that don't need to be heard," Neel continued his tale. "The shell's hopes and longings were so strong that they seeped through its papery wings. Its song became color and pattern. Since then, the butterfly has flown silent. But it always wears its heart on its wings."

Golden eyes smiled into silver ones. Petra kissed Neel, and as the wind streamed over them she understood the truth of something she had already known. It glittered like a jewel.

Before her lay the rest of her life.

Acknowledgments

I WOULD LIKE TO THANK—

Francesco and Roberta Franco, for graciously hosting me, and giving me a beautiful place to inspire the Vatra.

David Levithan, also for being a wonderful host while I worked on this book.

Rohini and Mrinal Pande, for advice on India.

Jenny and Mordicai Knode, for discussing a plot twist with me.

David Frankland, for yet another amazing book cover.

Thomas Philippon, for helping me plan out the battle, and always lending a willing ear.

Everyone at FSG, including Simon Boughton, Jay Colvin, Liz Kerins, and especially my editor, Janine O'Malley.

Meredith Kaffel, Joan Rosen, and Charlotte Sheedy, for taking excellent care of me.

My readers, with much gratitude: Betsy Bird, Donna Freitas, Daphne Grab, Jill Santopolo, and Eliot Schrefer.

Gerald and Nicole Fortini, Christiane and Jean-Claude Philippon, Marilyn and Robert Rutkoski, and especially Shaida Khan, for watching over Eliot while I wrote.

And Eliot Philippon, for being such a good boy.